Zombie Fighter

Pistol, carbine and Precision Rifle

Warm Ups, Drills and Qual To Survive the coming apocalypse

NAME: _____ UNIT: _____

www.GUNFIGHTERSERIES.com ©

Weapon Conditions

- Condition 4: No mag inserted. Slide forward on empty chamber. Hammer forward (if applicable). Weapon on safe (if applicable).

- Condition 3: Loaded mag inserted. Slide forward on empty chamber. Hammer forward (if applicable). Weapon on safe (if applicable).

- Condition 2: Loaded mag inserted. Slide forward with round in chamber. Hammer forward (if applicable). Weapon on safe (if applicable).

- Condition 1: Loaded mag inserted. Slide forward with round in chamber. Hammer cocked (if applicable). Weapon on safe (if applicable).

Always know the condition of your weapon!

Safety

- Treat every weapon as if it were loaded.
- Never point your weapon at anything you do not intend to shoot/destroy.
- Know your target and it's background.
- Keep your finger off the trigger until you intend to fire.
- Keep your weapon on safe until you are ready to fire.
- Always wear eye and ear protection, and proper protective clothing.
- Never shoot faster than you can effectively keep rounds on target.
- Be extremely cautious with back splatter and ricochets when shooting steel.

Warning

Perform these drills at your own risk. Only perform these drill in a safe manner which do not violate your range rules. Consult range staff for rules and regulations regarding drawing from a holster, rapid fire and multiple target engagements.

GUNFIGHTER is not responsible for any injury or death that may occur due to the use of this book. We recommend never shooting alone and under supervision of trained safety officers.

Table of Contents:

Admin and Logistics.

Carbine & Pistol Diagnostics

Pistol Drills.
1. In the Face!!!
2. Serum 391
3. My Safe Space
4. Merle Dixon
5. Out Of Touch
6. Z Rule #2
7. Hearts and Minds
8. Death Metal
9. Dueces
10. Baba Yaga
11. Stephan and the Fat man
12. You Have To Fight For Your Right
13. Victor Actual
14. Dead Sprint
15. UDRL

Carbine Drills.
1. I'm Good
2. I'm Solid
3. Nose Job
4. 10K
5. Lefty, Righty, Lay-O
6. Leprechaun
7. Segen
8. Boom Stick
9. Feed
10. Throes
11. Swarm
12. Dead Prezidents
13. Meat Grinder
14. Cardio
15. Z Formation

Transition Drills.
1. Trans
2. Finish Him!!!
3. Creepy Crawlers
4. Get Off The X
5. Serpentine

Precision Rifle Drills.
Precision Rifle Diagnostics
1. Cold Body
2. Fundamentally Awesome
3. Tyrant Virus
4. Boundaries
5. Sit, Kneel, Stand
6. That Was Close
7. Run Away!!!
8. Clear The Way
9. Zniper
10. Head Hunter
11. PRZ Skillz 1

Z Standard 1

Custom Drill

Notes

The Threats:

⊕ **Undead Zombies** are slow, but only head shots will put them down.

⊕ **Infect Humans** are fast, but you can slow them down with body shots. Head shots to put them down permanently.

⊕ **Mutants**, charge at you with thick scabby armor. Multi shots to the chest and head while sidestepping to survive a mutant's charging attack.

www.GUNFIGHTERSERIES.com ©

How to use this book:

This book offers a carefully crafted catalog of training drills and is designed to log and track training progression as well as shot pattern placement analysis. **All targets may be downloaded for free** of our www.GunfighterSereis.com website and printed at home for free with the exception of cardboard IPSC and steel head steel /circle targets which may be purchased at numerous online retailers.

For best results, conduct and record every drill at least once starting at the beginning. The more data you collect the better your results will be.

Most drills offer defensive time and scoring goals to achieve. Competitive shooters may set different goals. Everyone's goal should be to improve their recorded personal best.

For proper weapons handling and marksmanship coaching, seek out well respected firearms instructors and courses.

Train safe. Train hard. Train to win.

Afterwards:

Upon mastering all the drills in this book, continue to increase your skills by utilizing the entire Gunfighter training log book series.

Be sure to follow Gunfighter on social media and pick up a copy of **ZNIPER** - *A Sniper's Journey Through The Apocalypse.*

Gunfighter Skill Books 2019 © - Gunfighter, LLC - All Rights Reserved

ISBN: 9781073531837

Pistol Round Count Log

Pistol Make & Model: SN#:

Date	Ammo	Lot #	Fired	Total

Notes:

This Page	
Previous Logs	
TOTAL	

Pistol Maintenance Log

Date	Weapon	Full Cleaning	Damage Inspection
		Y / N	Y / N
		Y / N	Y / N
		Y / N	Y / N
		Y / N	Y / N
		Y / N	Y / N
		Y / N	Y / N
		Y / N	Y / N
		Y / N	Y / N
		Y / N	Y / N
		Y / N	Y / N
		Y / N	Y / N
		Y / N	Y / N
		Y / N	Y / N
		Y / N	Y / N

Notes:

Z Fighter ©

Carbine Round Count Log

Rifle Make & Model: _____ SN#: _____

Date	Ammo	Lot #	Fired	Total

Notes:

This Page	
Previous Logs	
TOTAL	

Carbine Maintenance Log

Date	Weapon	Full Cleaning	Damage Inspection
		Y / N	Y / N
		Y / N	Y / N
		Y / N	Y / N
		Y / N	Y / N
		Y / N	Y / N
		Y / N	Y / N
		Y / N	Y / N
		Y / N	Y / N
		Y / N	Y / N
		Y / N	Y / N
		Y / N	Y / N
		Y / N	Y / N
		Y / N	Y / N
		Y / N	Y / N

Notes:

Rifle Round Count Log

Rifle Make & Model: SN#:

Date	Ammo	Lot #	Fired	Total

Notes:			This Page	
			Previous Logs	
			TOTAL	

Rifle Maintenance Log

Date	Weapon	Full Cleaning	Damage Inspection
		Y / N	Y / N
		Y / N	Y / N
		Y / N	Y / N
		Y / N	Y / N
		Y / N	Y / N
		Y / N	Y / N
		Y / N	Y / N
		Y / N	Y / N
		Y / N	Y / N
		Y / N	Y / N
		Y / N	Y / N
		Y / N	Y / N
		Y / N	Y / N
		Y / N	Y / N

Notes:

ZF-3 Carbine & Pistol Diagnostics Instructions

Purpose: Test different carbine and pistol skills to determine which Z Fighter Gunfighter drills to work on.

Distance: 7-5 Yards   **Target:** ZF-3

Par Time: 30 Seconds.

Extra Equipment: Shot timer, 1 carbine magazine, 2 pistol magazines, 1 pistol magazine pouch.

Load Out: 1 Carbine magazine with 10 rounds. 1 Pistol magazine with 4 rounds, 1 Pistol magazine with 6 rounds.

Starting Position and Condition: Standing - Carbine in low ready with pistol holstered. Condition 1 both weapons.

Description: Starting at 7 yard line. At the timer beep:

- With carbine, aim and fire 1 round into the rectangular block (A1), then immediately

- Rapid fire 6 rounds into the diamond target (B6), then immediately

- Shoot 1 round in each of the remaining head targets (C1,D1,E1) starting with largest and finishing with the smallest.

- Your carbine will go dry, take 2 steps forward (5 yards) while carefully transitioning to your pistol, then immediately

- With pistol, shoot one round into the rectangular block (A1), then immediately

- Rapid fire 6 rounds into the diamond target (B6), with a reload, then immediately

- Shoot 1 round in each of the remaining head targets (C1,D1,E1) starting with largest and finishing with the smallest.

Record your name, date and the time it took you to complete the course of fire. If you don't hit the goals on a given skill, practice on the listed drills for that goal.

Goals and Performance Diagnostics

If all rounds are not in, determine if rapid fire marksmanship or slow fire marksmanship is needed.	1st Shot Goal: Hit within or touching rectangle under 2 seconds. If not, practice:	Ave Split Time of Shots 2-7 Goal: Hit within or touching diamond with shot to shot intervals at 0.5 seconds or less. If not, practice:	Shots 8-10 Goal: Big, medium, and small Z heads: hit within or touching the boxes. If not, practice:
IN THE FACE!!!	NOSE JOB	THROES	I'M GOOD
SERUM 391	10K	THREE'S A CROWD	I'M SOLID
I'M GOOD	FLASH UP (FUNDAMENTAL CARBINE)	DEAD PREZIDENTS	GET OFF MY KOOL-AID
I'M SOLID	SOLID SHOT (FUNDAMENTAL CARBINE)	SLEDGE HAMMER (FUNDAMENTAL CARBINE)	5 FOR 10 (FUNDAMENTAL CARBINE)
	Transition to pistol.		
Shot 11 Goal: Hit within or touching rectangle under 3.5 second split time. If not, practice:	Ave Split Time of Shots 12-17 Goal: Hit within or touching diamond with shot to shot intervals at 0.5 seconds or less. If not, practice:	Reload Split Time of Shot 14-15 Goal: Reload while shooting in the diamond: 2.75 seconds par time between shots. If not, practice:	Shots 18-20 Goal: Big, medium, and small Z heads: hit within or touching the boxes. If not, practice:
IN THE FACE	DEATH METAL	Z RULE #2	IN THE FACE!!!
TRANS	DUECES	HEARTS AND MINDS	SERUM 391
FINISH HIM	CADENCE (FUNDAMENTAL PISTOL)	GET THAT PISTOL LOADED QUICKLY (FUNDAMENTAL PISTOL)	BABA YAGA
Overall Completion Time:		Goal: Under 30 second par time.	DEAD SPRINT

Z Fighter ©

www.GUNFIGHTERSERIES.com ©

Carbine and Pistol Performance Diagnostics

Date: B.Z.	Battle Ground:	Carbine:	Pistol:
Overall Completion Time:	1st Shot Time:	Ave Split Time of Shots 2-7:	Shots 8-10 In: Y / N
Shot 11 Time:	Ave Split Time of Shots 12-17:	Split Time of Shot 14-15:	Shots 18-20 In: Y / N
All Carbine Rounds in: Y / N	All Pistol Rounds in: Y / N	Notes:	

Date: B.Z.	Battle Ground:	Carbine:	Pistol:
Overall Completion Time:	1st Shot Time:	Ave Split Time of Shots 2-7:	Shots 8-10 In: Y / N
Shot 11 Time:	Ave Split Time of Shots 12-17:	Split Time of Shot 14-15:	Shots 18-20 In: Y / N
All Carbine Rounds in: Y / N	All Pistol Rounds in: Y / N	Notes:	

Date: B.Z.	Battle Ground:	Carbine:	Pistol:
Overall Completion Time:	1st Shot Time:	Ave Split Time of Shots 2-7:	Shots 8-10 In: Y / N
Shot 11 Time:	Ave Split Time of Shots 12-17:	Split Time of Shot 14-15:	Shots 18-20 In: Y / N
All Carbine Rounds in: Y / N	All Pistol Rounds in: Y / N	Notes:	

Date: B.Z.	Battle Ground:	Carbine:	Pistol:
Overall Completion Time:	1st Shot Time:	Ave Split Time of Shots 2-7:	Shots 8-10 In: Y / N
Shot 11 Time:	Ave Split Time of Shots 12-17:	Split Time of Shot 14-15:	Shots 18-20 In: Y / N
All Carbine Rounds in: Y / N	All Pistol Rounds in: Y / N	Notes:	

Carbine and Pistol Performance Diagnostics

Date:	B.Z.	Battle Ground:	Carbine:	Pistol:
Overall Completion Time:		1st Shot Time:	Ave Split Time of Shots 2-7:	Shots 8-10 In: Y / N
Shot 11 Time:		Ave Split Time of Shots 12-17:	Split Time of Shot 14-15:	Shots 18-20 In: Y / N
All Carbine Rounds in: Y / N		All Pistol Rounds in: Y / N	Notes:	

Date:	B.Z.	Battle Ground:	Carbine:	Pistol:
Overall Completion Time:		1st Shot Time:	Ave Split Time of Shots 2-7:	Shots 8-10 In: Y / N
Shot 11 Time:		Ave Split Time of Shots 12-17:	Split Time of Shot 14-15:	Shots 18-20 In: Y / N
All Carbine Rounds in: Y / N		All Pistol Rounds in: Y / N	Notes:	

Date:	B.Z.	Battle Ground:	Carbine:	Pistol:
Overall Completion Time:		1st Shot Time:	Ave Split Time of Shots 2-7:	Shots 8-10 In: Y / N
Shot 11 Time:		Ave Split Time of Shots 12-17:	Split Time of Shot 14-15:	Shots 18-20 In: Y / N
All Carbine Rounds in: Y / N		All Pistol Rounds in: Y / N	Notes:	

Date:	B.Z.	Battle Ground:	Carbine:	Pistol:
Overall Completion Time:		1st Shot Time:	Ave Split Time of Shots 2-7:	Shots 8-10 In: Y / N
Shot 11 Time:		Ave Split Time of Shots 12-17:	Split Time of Shot 14-15:	Shots 18-20 In: Y / N
All Carbine Rounds in: Y / N		All Pistol Rounds in: Y / N	Notes:	

Z Fighter ©

www.GUNFIGHTERSERIES.com ©

Carbine and Pistol Performance Diagnostics

Date: B.Z.	Battle Ground:	Carbine:	Pistol:
Overall Completion Time:	1st Shot Time:	Ave Split Time of Shots 2-7:	Shots 8-10 In: Y / N
Shot 11 Time:	Ave Split Time of Shots 12-17:	Split Time of Shot 14-15:	Shots 18-20 In: Y / N
All Carbine Rounds in: Y / N	All Pistol Rounds in: Y / N	Notes:	

Date: B.Z.	Battle Ground:	Carbine:	Pistol:
Overall Completion Time:	1st Shot Time:	Ave Split Time of Shots 2-7:	Shots 8-10 In: Y / N
Shot 11 Time:	Ave Split Time of Shots 12-17:	Split Time of Shot 14-15:	Shots 18-20 In: Y / N
All Carbine Rounds in: Y / N	All Pistol Rounds in: Y / N	Notes:	

Date: B.Z.	Battle Ground:	Carbine:	Pistol:
Overall Completion Time:	1st Shot Time:	Ave Split Time of Shots 2-7:	Shots 8-10 In: Y / N
Shot 11 Time:	Ave Split Time of Shots 12-17:	Split Time of Shot 14-15:	Shots 18-20 In: Y / N
All Carbine Rounds in: Y / N	All Pistol Rounds in: Y / N	Notes:	

Date: B.Z.	Battle Ground:	Carbine:	Pistol:
Overall Completion Time:	1st Shot Time:	Ave Split Time of Shots 2-7:	Shots 8-10 In: Y / N
Shot 11 Time:	Ave Split Time of Shots 12-17:	Split Time of Shot 14-15:	Shots 18-20 In: Y / N
All Carbine Rounds in: Y / N	All Pistol Rounds in: Y / N	Notes:	

Carbine and Pistol Performance Diagnostics

Date:	B.Z.	Battle Ground:	Carbine:	Pistol:
Overall Completion Time:		1st Shot Time:	Ave Split Time of Shots 2-7:	Shots 8-10 In: Y / N
Shot 11 Time:		Ave Split Time of Shots 12-17:	Split Time of Shot 14-15:	Shots 18-20 In: Y / N
All Carbine Rounds in: Y / N		All Pistol Rounds in: Y / N	Notes:	

Date:	B.Z.	Battle Ground:	Carbine:	Pistol:
Overall Completion Time:		1st Shot Time:	Ave Split Time of Shots 2-7:	Shots 8-10 In: Y / N
Shot 11 Time:		Ave Split Time of Shots 12-17:	Split Time of Shot 14-15:	Shots 18-20 In: Y / N
All Carbine Rounds in: Y / N		All Pistol Rounds in: Y / N	Notes:	

Date:	B.Z.	Battle Ground:	Carbine:	Pistol:
Overall Completion Time:		1st Shot Time:	Ave Split Time of Shots 2-7:	Shots 8-10 In: Y / N
Shot 11 Time:		Ave Split Time of Shots 12-17:	Split Time of Shot 14-15:	Shots 18-20 In: Y / N
All Carbine Rounds in: Y / N		All Pistol Rounds in: Y / N	Notes:	

Date:	B.Z.	Battle Ground:	Carbine:	Pistol:
Overall Completion Time:		1st Shot Time:	Ave Split Time of Shots 2-7:	Shots 8-10 In: Y / N
Shot 11 Time:		Ave Split Time of Shots 12-17:	Split Time of Shot 14-15:	Shots 18-20 In: Y / N
All Carbine Rounds in: Y / N		All Pistol Rounds in: Y / N	Notes:	

Z Fighter ©

PISTOL DRILL: IN THE FACE!!!

Purpose: Develop consistent marksmanship follow through.

Distance: 3, 5, or 7 Yards.

Target: 1 inch Z dot.

Rounds Fired Per Rep: 1 Round.

Total Rounds Fired: 5 Rounds.

Point Penalty: Live / Die.

Repetitions: 5 Reps.

Starting Position & Condition: Standing – Surrender / Interview. Weapon Condition 1.

Description: At your own personal go, draw your pistol and fire 5 rounds into the 1 inch Z dot target at 3 yards. Once you can consistently fire all 5 rounds into or touching the 1 inch Z dot target, shoot from 5 yards. Once you can make shots consistently at 5 yards, shoot from 7 yards. This drill has no time limit, so take your time and make good shots. You may holster your pistol between shots. Good hand placement during the draw and trigger control is essential to master this drill.

Goals: Meat Bag: All rounds in or touching the 1 inch Z dot from 3 yards.   Survivor: From 5 yards.   Z Fighter: From 7 Yards

Variations:

⊕ Infected Humans: Take 1-2 steps backwards before each shot.

⊕ Mutants: Take 1-2 steps left or right before each shot.

IN THE FACE!!!

Date:	B.Z.	Battle Ground:	Weapon:	Sights:	Undead / Infected / Mutant
Drill Time:		Distance: 3Y / 5Y / 7Y		# Out:	Live / Die

Date:	B.Z.	Battle Ground:	Weapon:	Sights:	Undead / Infected / Mutant
Drill Time:		Distance: 3Y / 5Y / 7Y		# Out:	Live / Die

Date:	B.Z.	Battle Ground:	Weapon:	Sights:	Undead / Infected / Mutant
Drill Time:		Distance: 3Y / 5Y / 7Y		# Out:	Live / Die

Date:	B.Z.	Battle Ground:	Weapon:	Sights:	Undead / Infected / Mutant
Drill Time:		Distance: 3Y / 5Y / 7Y		# Out:	Live / Die

Date:	B.Z.	Battle Ground:	Weapon:	Sights:	Undead / Infected / Mutant
Drill Time:		Distance: 3Y / 5Y / 7Y		# Out:	Live / Die

Z Fighter ©

Pistol Drills - 1

IN THE FACE!!!

Date: B.Z.	Battle Ground:	Weapon:	Sights:	Undead / Infected / Mutant
Drill Time:	Distance: 3Y / 5Y / 7Y		# Out:	Live / Die

Date: B.Z.	Battle Ground:	Weapon:	Sights:	Undead / Infected / Mutant
Drill Time:	Distance: 3Y / 5Y / 7Y		# Out:	Live / Die

Date: B.Z.	Battle Ground:	Weapon:	Sights:	Undead / Infected / Mutant
Drill Time:	Distance: 3Y / 5Y / 7Y		# Out:	Live / Die

Date: B.Z.	Battle Ground:	Weapon:	Sights:	Undead / Infected / Mutant
Drill Time:	Distance: 3Y / 5Y / 7Y		# Out:	Live / Die

Date: B.Z.	Battle Ground:	Weapon:	Sights:	Undead / Infected / Mutant
Drill Time:	Distance: 3Y / 5Y / 7Y		# Out:	Live / Die

IN THE FACE!!!

Date:	B.Z.	Battle Ground:	Weapon:	Sights:	Undead / Infected / Mutant
Drill Time:		Distance: 3Y / 5Y / 7Y		# Out:	Live / Die

Date:	B.Z.	Battle Ground:	Weapon:	Sights:	Undead / Infected / Mutant
Drill Time:		Distance: 3Y / 5Y / 7Y		# Out:	Live / Die

Date:	B.Z.	Battle Ground:	Weapon:	Sights:	Undead / Infected / Mutant
Drill Time:		Distance: 3Y / 5Y / 7Y		# Out:	Live / Die

Date:	B.Z.	Battle Ground:	Weapon:	Sights:	Undead / Infected / Mutant
Drill Time:		Distance: 3Y / 5Y / 7Y		# Out:	Live / Die

Date:	B.Z.	Battle Ground:	Weapon:	Sights:	Undead / Infected / Mutant
Drill Time:		Distance: 3Y / 5Y / 7Y		# Out:	Live / Die

Z Fighter ©

Pistol Drills - 1

IN THE FACE!!!

Date:	B.Z.	Battle Ground:	Weapon:	Sights:	Undead / Infected / Mutant
Drill Time:		Distance: 3Y / 5Y / 7Y		# Out:	Live / Die

Date:	B.Z.	Battle Ground:	Weapon:	Sights:	Undead / Infected / Mutant
Drill Time:		Distance: 3Y / 5Y / 7Y		# Out:	Live / Die

Date:	B.Z.	Battle Ground:	Weapon:	Sights:	Undead / Infected / Mutant
Drill Time:		Distance: 3Y / 5Y / 7Y		# Out:	Live / Die

Date:	B.Z.	Battle Ground:	Weapon:	Sights:	Undead / Infected / Mutant
Drill Time:		Distance: 3Y / 5Y / 7Y		# Out:	Live / Die

Date:	B.Z.	Battle Ground:	Weapon:	Sights:	Undead / Infected / Mutant
Drill Time:		Distance: 3Y / 5Y / 7Y		# Out:	Live / Die

IN THE FACE!!!

Date:	B.Z.	Battle Ground:	Weapon:	Sights:	Undead / Infected / Mutant
Drill Time:		Distance: 3Y / 5Y / 7Y		# Out:	Live / Die

Date:	B.Z.	Battle Ground:	Weapon:	Sights:	Undead / Infected / Mutant
Drill Time:		Distance: 3Y / 5Y / 7Y		# Out:	Live / Die

Date:	B.Z.	Battle Ground:	Weapon:	Sights:	Undead / Infected / Mutant
Drill Time:		Distance: 3Y / 5Y / 7Y		# Out:	Live / Die

Date:	B.Z.	Battle Ground:	Weapon:	Sights:	Undead / Infected / Mutant
Drill Time:		Distance: 3Y / 5Y / 7Y		# Out:	Live / Die

Date:	B.Z.	Battle Ground:	Weapon:	Sights:	Undead / Infected / Mutant
Drill Time:		Distance: 3Y / 5Y / 7Y		# Out:	Live / Die

Z Fighter ©

Pistol Drills - 1

PISTOL DRILL: **SERUM 391**

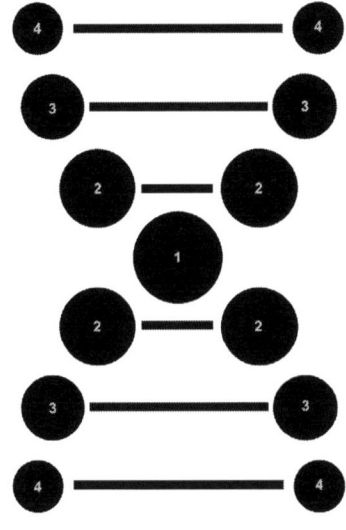

Purpose: Develop consistent marksmanship fundamentals while target transitioning.

Distance: 3 Yards. **Target:** Helix

Rounds Fired Per String: 4 Round. **Total Rounds Fired:** 16 Rounds.

Point Penalty: Per target score.

Repetitions: 1 Rep of 4 strings.

Starting Position & Condition: Standing – Surrender / Interview. Weapon Condition 1.

Description:

- At your own personal go, draw your pistol and fire 4 rounds into the #1 circle in the center of the target then holster.

- At your personal go, draw and fire 1 round into each of the #2 circles in a clockwise pattern.

- At your personal go, draw and fire 1 round into each of the #3 circles in a counterclockwise pattern.

- At your personal go, draw and fire 1 round into each of the #4 circles in a Z pattern.

Goals: Meat Bag: 18 Points.   Survivor: 30 Points.   Z Fighter: 40 Points

Variations:

- Infected Humans: Start at 3 yard for each string, but take 1-2 steps backwards before each shot.

- Mutants: Start at 5 yard for each string, but take 1-2 steps left or right before each shot.

SERUM 391

Date:	B.Z.	Battle Ground:	Pistol:	Undead / Infected / Mutant	Notes:
String 1 # Out:		String 2 # Out:	String 3 # Out:	String 4 # Out:	
String 1 Score:		String 2 Score:	String 3 Score:	String 4 Score:	**Total Score:**

Date:	B.Z.	Battle Ground:	Pistol:	Undead / Infected / Mutant	Notes:
String 1 # Out:		String 2 # Out:	String 3 # Out:	String 4 # Out:	
String 1 Score:		String 2 Score:	String 3 Score:	String 4 Score:	**Total Score:**

Date:	B.Z.	Battle Ground:	Pistol:	Undead / Infected / Mutant	Notes:
String 1 # Out:		String 2 # Out:	String 3 # Out:	String 4 # Out:	
String 1 Score:		String 2 Score:	String 3 Score:	String 4 Score:	**Total Score:**

Z Fighter ©

Pistol Drills - 2

SERUM 391

Date:	B.Z.	Battle Ground:	Pistol:	Undead / Infected / Mutant	Notes:
String 1 # Out:		String 2 # Out:	String 3 # Out:	String 4 # Out:	
String 1 Score:		String 2 Score:	String 3 Score:	String 4 Score:	**Total Score:**

Date:	B.Z.	Battle Ground:	Pistol:	Undead / Infected / Mutant	Notes:
String 1 # Out:		String 2 # Out:	String 3 # Out:	String 4 # Out:	
String 1 Score:		String 2 Score:	String 3 Score:	String 4 Score:	**Total Score:**

Date:	B.Z.	Battle Ground:	Pistol:	Undead / Infected / Mutant	Notes:
String 1 # Out:		String 2 # Out:	String 3 # Out:	String 4 # Out:	
String 1 Score:		String 2 Score:	String 3 Score:	String 4 Score:	**Total Score:**

SERUM 391

Date:	B.Z.	Battle Ground:	Pistol:	Undead / Infected / Mutant	Notes:
String 1 # Out:		String 2 # Out:	String 3 # Out:	String 4 # Out:	
String 1 Score:		String 2 Score:	String 3 Score:	String 4 Score:	**Total Score:**

Date:	B.Z.	Battle Ground:	Pistol:	Undead / Infected / Mutant	Notes:
String 1 # Out:		String 2 # Out:	String 3 # Out:	String 4 # Out:	
String 1 Score:		String 2 Score:	String 3 Score:	String 4 Score:	**Total Score:**

Date:	B.Z.	Battle Ground:	Pistol:	Undead / Infected / Mutant	Notes:
String 1 # Out:		String 2 # Out:	String 3 # Out:	String 4 # Out:	
String 1 Score:		String 2 Score:	String 3 Score:	String 4 Score:	**Total Score:**

Z Fighter ©

Pistol Drills - 2

SERUM 391

Date:	B.Z.	Battle Ground:	Pistol:	Undead / Infected / Mutant	Notes:
String 1 # Out:		String 2 # Out:	String 3 # Out:	String 4 # Out:	
String 1 Score:		String 2 Score:	String 3 Score:	String 4 Score:	**Total Score:**

Date:	B.Z.	Battle Ground:	Pistol:	Undead / Infected / Mutant	Notes:
String 1 # Out:		String 2 # Out:	String 3 # Out:	String 4 # Out:	
String 1 Score:		String 2 Score:	String 3 Score:	String 4 Score:	**Total Score:**

Date:	B.Z.	Battle Ground:	Pistol:	Undead / Infected / Mutant	Notes:
String 1 # Out:		String 2 # Out:	String 3 # Out:	String 4 # Out:	
String 1 Score:		String 2 Score:	String 3 Score:	String 4 Score:	**Total Score:**

SERUM 391

Date:	B.Z.	Battle Ground:	Pistol:	Undead / Infected / Mutant	Notes:
String 1 # Out:		String 2 # Out:	String 3 # Out:	String 4 # Out:	
String 1 Score:		String 2 Score:	String 3 Score:	String 4 Score:	**Total Score:**

Date:	B.Z.	Battle Ground:	Pistol:	Undead / Infected / Mutant	Notes:
String 1 # Out:		String 2 # Out:	String 3 # Out:	String 4 # Out:	
String 1 Score:		String 2 Score:	String 3 Score:	String 4 Score:	**Total Score:**

Date:	B.Z.	Battle Ground:	Pistol:	Undead / Infected / Mutant	Notes:
String 1 # Out:		String 2 # Out:	String 3 # Out:	String 4 # Out:	
String 1 Score:		String 2 Score:	String 3 Score:	String 4 Score:	**Total Score:**

Z Fighter ©

Pistol Drills - 2

PISTOL DRILL: MY SAFE SPACE

Purpose: Establishing your life saving pistol fighting comfort zone.

Distance: 3 Yards to ?

Target: ZIPSC (Undead) with hostage target (attach a picture of your loved one).

Total Rounds Fired: ? Rounds

Starting Position & Condition: Standing - Surrender / Interview. Condition 1 pistol.

Description: Stating at 3 yards, at your personal go, draw and fire 1 round into the head ocular Z box. Holster then walk to the target to inspect your shot placement. Return to the firing line and add 1 yard from you previous successful shot. Continue this drill until you miss the ocular Z box. Then continue this drill further until you miss the head entirely or hit the hostage. Record your max accurate life saving zombie killing distance.

Goals: Meat Bag: 7 Yards.   Survivor: 15 Yards.   Z Fighter: 25 Yards.

Variations:

⊕   Infected Humans: Add a 2 second par time restraint for each draw. Run, instead of walk, to check your target then back to the firing line.

⊕   Mutants: Start with your back facing the target at each yard line, with a 2.5 second par time.

MY SAFE SPACE

Date:	B.Z.	Battle Ground:	Pistol:	Undead / Infected Human / Mutant
Max Z Box Distance:			**Max Distance Inside Head:**	Hostage Hit: Y / N
Date:	B.Z.	Battle Ground:	Pistol:	Undead / Infected Human / Mutant
Max Z Box Distance:			**Max Distance Inside Head:**	Hostage Hit: Y / N
Date:	B.Z.	Battle Ground:	Pistol:	Undead / Infected Human / Mutant
Max Z Box Distance:			**Max Distance Inside Head:**	Hostage Hit: Y / N
Date:	B.Z.	Battle Ground:	Pistol:	Undead / Infected Human / Mutant
Max Z Box Distance:			**Max Distance Inside Head:**	Hostage Hit: Y / N
Date:	B.Z.	Battle Ground:	Pistol:	Undead / Infected Human / Mutant
Max Z Box Distance:			**Max Distance Inside Head:**	Hostage Hit: Y / N
Date:	B.Z.	Battle Ground:	Pistol:	Undead / Infected Human / Mutant
Max Z Box Distance:			**Max Distance Inside Head:**	Hostage Hit: Y / N
Date:	B.Z.	Battle Ground:	Pistol:	Undead / Infected Human / Mutant
Max Z Box Distance:			**Max Distance Inside Head:**	Hostage Hit: Y / N
Date:	B.Z.	Battle Ground:	Pistol:	Undead / Infected Human / Mutant
Max Z Box Distance:			**Max Distance Inside Head:**	Hostage Hit: Y / N
Date:	B.Z.	Battle Ground:	Pistol:	Undead / Infected Human / Mutant
Max Z Box Distance:			**Max Distance Inside Head:**	Hostage Hit: Y / N

Z Fighter ©

MY SAFE SPACE

Date:	B.Z.	Battle Ground:	Pistol:	Undead / Infected Human / Mutant
Max Z Box Distance:			**Max Distance Inside Head:**	Hostage Hit: Y / N
Date:	B.Z.	Battle Ground:	Pistol:	Undead / Infected Human / Mutant
Max Z Box Distance:			**Max Distance Inside Head:**	Hostage Hit: Y / N
Date:	B.Z.	Battle Ground:	Pistol:	Undead / Infected Human / Mutant
Max Z Box Distance:			**Max Distance Inside Head:**	Hostage Hit: Y / N
Date:	B.Z.	Battle Ground:	Pistol:	Undead / Infected Human / Mutant
Max Z Box Distance:			**Max Distance Inside Head:**	Hostage Hit: Y / N
Date:	B.Z.	Battle Ground:	Pistol:	Undead / Infected Human / Mutant
Max Z Box Distance:			**Max Distance Inside Head:**	Hostage Hit: Y / N
Date:	B.Z.	Battle Ground:	Pistol:	Undead / Infected Human / Mutant
Max Z Box Distance:			**Max Distance Inside Head:**	Hostage Hit: Y / N
Date:	B.Z.	Battle Ground:	Pistol:	Undead / Infected Human / Mutant
Max Z Box Distance:			**Max Distance Inside Head:**	Hostage Hit: Y / N
Date:	B.Z.	Battle Ground:	Pistol:	Undead / Infected Human / Mutant
Max Z Box Distance:			**Max Distance Inside Head:**	Hostage Hit: Y / N
Date:	B.Z.	Battle Ground:	Pistol:	Undead / Infected Human / Mutant
Max Z Box Distance:			**Max Distance Inside Head:**	Hostage Hit: Y / N

MY SAFE SPACE

Date:	B.Z.	Battle Ground:	Pistol:	Undead / Infected Human / Mutant
Max Z Box Distance:			**Max Distance Inside Head:**	Hostage Hit: Y / N
Date:	B.Z.	Battle Ground:	Pistol:	Undead / Infected Human / Mutant
Max Z Box Distance:			**Max Distance Inside Head:**	Hostage Hit: Y / N
Date:	B.Z.	Battle Ground:	Pistol:	Undead / Infected Human / Mutant
Max Z Box Distance:			**Max Distance Inside Head:**	Hostage Hit: Y / N
Date:	B.Z.	Battle Ground:	Pistol:	Undead / Infected Human / Mutant
Max Z Box Distance:			**Max Distance Inside Head:**	Hostage Hit: Y / N
Date:	B.Z.	Battle Ground:	Pistol:	Undead / Infected Human / Mutant
Max Z Box Distance:			**Max Distance Inside Head:**	Hostage Hit: Y / N
Date:	B.Z.	Battle Ground:	Pistol:	Undead / Infected Human / Mutant
Max Z Box Distance:			**Max Distance Inside Head:**	Hostage Hit: Y / N
Date:	B.Z.	Battle Ground:	Pistol:	Undead / Infected Human / Mutant
Max Z Box Distance:			**Max Distance Inside Head:**	Hostage Hit: Y / N
Date:	B.Z.	Battle Ground:	Pistol:	Undead / Infected Human / Mutant
Max Z Box Distance:			**Max Distance Inside Head:**	Hostage Hit: Y / N
Date:	B.Z.	Battle Ground:	Pistol:	Undead / Infected Human / Mutant
Max Z Box Distance:			**Max Distance Inside Head:**	Hostage Hit: Y / N

Z Fighter ©

MY SAFE SPACE

Date:	B.Z.	Battle Ground:	Pistol:	Undead / Infected Human / Mutant
Max Z Box Distance:			**Max Distance Inside Head:**	Hostage Hit: Y / N
Date:	B.Z.	Battle Ground:	Pistol:	Undead / Infected Human / Mutant
Max Z Box Distance:			**Max Distance Inside Head:**	Hostage Hit: Y / N
Date:	B.Z.	Battle Ground:	Pistol:	Undead / Infected Human / Mutant
Max Z Box Distance:			**Max Distance Inside Head:**	Hostage Hit: Y / N
Date:	B.Z.	Battle Ground:	Pistol:	Undead / Infected Human / Mutant
Max Z Box Distance:			**Max Distance Inside Head:**	Hostage Hit: Y / N
Date:	B.Z.	Battle Ground:	Pistol:	Undead / Infected Human / Mutant
Max Z Box Distance:			**Max Distance Inside Head:**	Hostage Hit: Y / N
Date:	B.Z.	Battle Ground:	Pistol:	Undead / Infected Human / Mutant
Max Z Box Distance:			**Max Distance Inside Head:**	Hostage Hit: Y / N
Date:	B.Z.	Battle Ground:	Pistol:	Undead / Infected Human / Mutant
Max Z Box Distance:			**Max Distance Inside Head:**	Hostage Hit: Y / N
Date:	B.Z.	Battle Ground:	Pistol:	Undead / Infected Human / Mutant
Max Z Box Distance:			**Max Distance Inside Head:**	Hostage Hit: Y / N
Date:	B.Z.	Battle Ground:	Pistol:	Undead / Infected Human / Mutant
Max Z Box Distance:			**Max Distance Inside Head:**	Hostage Hit: Y / N

MERLE DIXON

Date:	B.Z.	Pistol:					Sights:		Undead / Infected / Mutant	
Left Handed Colum Dots:		2"	1.75"	1.5"	1.25"	1"	Notes:			
2 Handed Column Dots		2"	1.75"	1.5"	1.25"	1"				
Right Handed Colum Dots:		2"	1.75"	1.5"	1.25"	1"	Number of Missed Dots:		Total Score:	

Date:	B.Z.	Pistol:					Sights:		Undead / Infected / Mutant	
Left Handed Colum Dots:		2"	1.75"	1.5"	1.25"	1"	Notes:			
2 Handed Column Dots		2"	1.75"	1.5"	1.25"	1"				
Right Handed Colum Dots:		2"	1.75"	1.5"	1.25"	1"	Number of Missed Dots:		Total Score:	

Date:	B.Z.	Pistol:					Sights:		Undead / Infected / Mutant	
Left Handed Colum Dots:		2"	1.75"	1.5"	1.25"	1"	Notes:			
2 Handed Column Dots		2"	1.75"	1.5"	1.25"	1"				
Right Handed Colum Dots:		2"	1.75"	1.5"	1.25"	1"	Number of Missed Dots:		Total Score:	

Date:	B.Z.	Pistol:					Sights:		Undead / Infected / Mutant	
Left Handed Colum Dots:		2"	1.75"	1.5"	1.25"	1"	Notes:			
2 Handed Column Dots		2"	1.75"	1.5"	1.25"	1"				
Right Handed Colum Dots:		2"	1.75"	1.5"	1.25"	1"	Number of Missed Dots:		Total Score:	

Z Fighter ©

www.GUNFIGHTERSERIES.com ©

MERLE DIXON

Date:	B.Z.	Pistol:					Sights:		Undead / Infected / Mutant
Left Handed Colum Dots:		2"	1.75"	1.5"	1.25"	1"	Notes:		
2 Handed Column Dots		2"	1.75"	1.5"	1.25"	1"			
Right Handed Colum Dots:		2"	1.75"	1.5"	1.25"	1"	**Number of Missed Dots:**	**Total Score:**	

Date:	B.Z.	Pistol:					Sights:		Undead / Infected / Mutant
Left Handed Colum Dots:		2"	1.75"	1.5"	1.25"	1"	Notes:		
2 Handed Column Dots		2"	1.75"	1.5"	1.25"	1"			
Right Handed Colum Dots:		2"	1.75"	1.5"	1.25"	1"	**Number of Missed Dots:**	**Total Score:**	

Date:	B.Z.	Pistol:					Sights:		Undead / Infected / Mutant
Left Handed Colum Dots:		2"	1.75"	1.5"	1.25"	1"	Notes:		
2 Handed Column Dots		2"	1.75"	1.5"	1.25"	1"			
Right Handed Colum Dots:		2"	1.75"	1.5"	1.25"	1"	**Number of Missed Dots:**	**Total Score:**	

Date:	B.Z.	Pistol:					Sights:		Undead / Infected / Mutant
Left Handed Colum Dots:		2"	1.75"	1.5"	1.25"	1"	Notes:		
2 Handed Column Dots		2"	1.75"	1.5"	1.25"	1"			
Right Handed Colum Dots:		2"	1.75"	1.5"	1.25"	1"	**Number of Missed Dots:**	**Total Score:**	

MERLE DIXON

Date:		B.Z.	Pistol:					Sights:			Undead / Infected / Mutant	
Left Handed Colum Dots:			2"	1.75"	1.5"	1.25"	1"	Notes:				
2 Handed Column Dots			2"	1.75"	1.5"	1.25"	1"					
Right Handed Colum Dots:			2"	1.75"	1.5"	1.25"	1"	**Number of Missed Dots:**			**Total Score:**	

Date:		B.Z.	Pistol:					Sights:			Undead / Infected / Mutant	
Left Handed Colum Dots:			2"	1.75"	1.5"	1.25"	1"	Notes:				
2 Handed Column Dots			2"	1.75"	1.5"	1.25"	1"					
Right Handed Colum Dots:			2"	1.75"	1.5"	1.25"	1"	**Number of Missed Dots:**			**Total Score:**	

Date:		B.Z.	Pistol:					Sights:			Undead / Infected / Mutant	
Left Handed Colum Dots:			2"	1.75"	1.5"	1.25"	1"	Notes:				
2 Handed Column Dots			2"	1.75"	1.5"	1.25"	1"					
Right Handed Colum Dots:			2"	1.75"	1.5"	1.25"	1"	**Number of Missed Dots:**			**Total Score:**	

Date:		B.Z.	Pistol:					Sights:			Undead / Infected / Mutant	
Left Handed Colum Dots:			2"	1.75"	1.5"	1.25"	1"	Notes:				
2 Handed Column Dots			2"	1.75"	1.5"	1.25"	1"					
Right Handed Colum Dots:			2"	1.75"	1.5"	1.25"	1"	**Number of Missed Dots:**			**Total Score:**	

Z Fighter ©

MERLE DIXON

Date:	B.Z.	Pistol:					Sights:	Undead / Infected / Mutant
Left Handed Colum Dots:		2"	1.75"	1.5"	1.25"	1"	Notes:	
2 Handed Column Dots		2"	1.75"	1.5"	1.25"	1"		
Right Handed Colum Dots:		2"	1.75"	1.5"	1.25"	1"	Number of Missed Dots:	Total Score:

Date:	B.Z.	Pistol:					Sights:	Undead / Infected / Mutant
Left Handed Colum Dots:		2"	1.75"	1.5"	1.25"	1"	Notes:	
2 Handed Column Dots		2"	1.75"	1.5"	1.25"	1"		
Right Handed Colum Dots:		2"	1.75"	1.5"	1.25"	1"	Number of Missed Dots:	Total Score:

Date:	B.Z.	Pistol:					Sights:	Undead / Infected / Mutant
Left Handed Colum Dots:		2"	1.75"	1.5"	1.25"	1"	Notes:	
2 Handed Column Dots		2"	1.75"	1.5"	1.25"	1"		
Right Handed Colum Dots:		2"	1.75"	1.5"	1.25"	1"	Number of Missed Dots:	Total Score:

Date:	B.Z.	Pistol:					Sights:	Undead / Infected / Mutant
Left Handed Colum Dots:		2"	1.75"	1.5"	1.25"	1"	Notes:	
2 Handed Column Dots		2"	1.75"	1.5"	1.25"	1"		
Right Handed Colum Dots:		2"	1.75"	1.5"	1.25"	1"	Number of Missed Dots:	Total Score:

MERLE DIXON

Date:	B.Z.	Pistol:					Sights:		Undead / Infected / Mutant	
Left Handed Colum Dots:		2"	1.75"	1.5"	1.25"	1"	Notes:			
2 Handed Column Dots		2"	1.75"	1.5"	1.25"	1"				
Right Handed Colum Dots:		2"	1.75"	1.5"	1.25"	1"	Number of Missed Dots:		Total Score:	

Date:	B.Z.	Pistol:					Sights:		Undead / Infected / Mutant	
Left Handed Colum Dots:		2"	1.75"	1.5"	1.25"	1"	Notes:			
2 Handed Column Dots		2"	1.75"	1.5"	1.25"	1"				
Right Handed Colum Dots:		2"	1.75"	1.5"	1.25"	1"	Number of Missed Dots:		Total Score:	

Date:	B.Z.	Pistol:					Sights:		Undead / Infected / Mutant	
Left Handed Colum Dots:		2"	1.75"	1.5"	1.25"	1"	Notes:			
2 Handed Column Dots		2"	1.75"	1.5"	1.25"	1"				
Right Handed Colum Dots:		2"	1.75"	1.5"	1.25"	1"	Number of Missed Dots:		Total Score:	

Date:	B.Z.	Pistol:					Sights:		Undead / Infected / Mutant	
Left Handed Colum Dots:		2"	1.75"	1.5"	1.25"	1"	Notes:			
2 Handed Column Dots		2"	1.75"	1.5"	1.25"	1"				
Right Handed Colum Dots:		2"	1.75"	1.5"	1.25"	1"	Number of Missed Dots:		Total Score:	

Z Fighter ©

PISTOL DRILL: OUT OF TOUCH

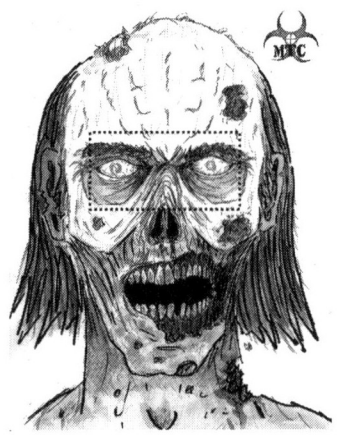

Purpose: Pistol accuracy with dominant hand only.

Distance: 3 Yards.

Target: MTC Z-1 (Undead).

Par Time: 2 Seconds.

Extra Equipment Needed: Shot timer. Melee weapon.

Rounds Fired Per Rep: 1 Round.

Total Rounds Fired: 5 Rounds.

Point Penalty: 1 Point per perfect rep.

Repetitions: 5 Reps.

Starting Position & Condition: Standing, with melee weapon pointing at target in support hand. Condition 1 pistol holstered.

Description: At the timer beep, lower your melee weapon to your side or to your chest, while simultaneously drawing you pistol from holster. Aim using dominant hand only and fire 1 round into the ocular Z box. Check for threats. Holster. Count number of shots inside ocular Z box, subtract number of shots over par to equal your final score.

Goals: Meat Bag: 3 Rounds in Z box.   Survivor: 4 Rounds in Z box.   Z Fighter: 5 Rounds in Z box

Variations:

⊕ Infected Humans: Engage from 5 yards with a par time of 1.75 seconds.

⊕ Mutants: Engage from 5 yards. Take 1 - 2 steps left or right while drawing.

OUT OF TOUCH

Date:	B.Z.	Battle Ground:	Undead / Infected / Mutant	Melee Weapon:
Pistol:		Sights:	Ammo:	Notes:
Shots inside Z Box:		Shots under par:	**Final Score:**	

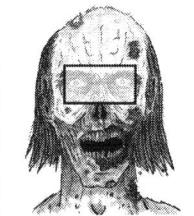

Date:	B.Z.	Battle Ground:	Undead / Infected / Mutant	Melee Weapon:
Pistol:		Sights:	Ammo:	Notes:
Shots inside Z Box:		Shots under par:	**Final Score:**	

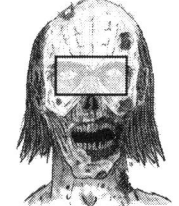

Date:	B.Z.	Battle Ground:	Undead / Infected / Mutant	Melee Weapon:
Pistol:		Sights:	Ammo:	Notes:
Shots inside Z Box:		Shots under par:	**Final Score:**	

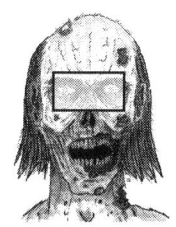

Date:	B.Z.	Battle Ground:	Undead / Infected / Mutant	Melee Weapon:
Pistol:		Sights:	Ammo:	Notes:
Shots inside Z Box:		Shots under par:	**Final Score:**	

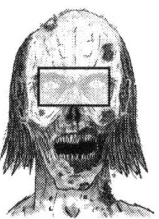

Z Fighter ©

OUT OF TOUCH

Date: B.Z.	Battle Ground:	Undead / Infected / Mutant	Melee Weapon:
Pistol:	Sights:	Ammo:	Notes:
Shots inside Z Box:	Shots under par:	**Final Score:**	

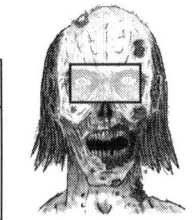

Date: B.Z.	Battle Ground:	Undead / Infected / Mutant	Melee Weapon:
Pistol:	Sights:	Ammo:	Notes:
Shots inside Z Box:	Shots under par:	**Final Score:**	

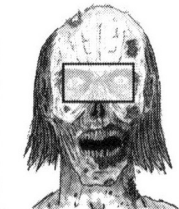

Date: B.Z.	Battle Ground:	Undead / Infected / Mutant	Melee Weapon:
Pistol:	Sights:	Ammo:	Notes:
Shots inside Z Box:	Shots under par:	**Final Score:**	

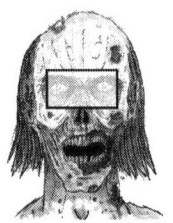

Date: B.Z.	Battle Ground:	Undead / Infected / Mutant	Melee Weapon:
Pistol:	Sights:	Ammo:	Notes:
Shots inside Z Box:	Shots under par:	**Final Score:**	

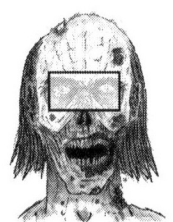

OUT OF TOUCH

Date:	B.Z.	Battle Ground:	Undead / Infected / Mutant	Melee Weapon:
Pistol:		Sights:	Ammo:	Notes:
Shots inside Z Box:		Shots under par:	**Final Score:**	

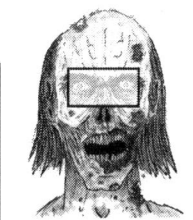

Date:	B.Z.	Battle Ground:	Undead / Infected / Mutant	Melee Weapon:
Pistol:		Sights:	Ammo:	Notes:
Shots inside Z Box:		Shots under par:	**Final Score:**	

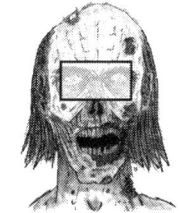

Date:	B.Z.	Battle Ground:	Undead / Infected / Mutant	Melee Weapon:
Pistol:		Sights:	Ammo:	Notes:
Shots inside Z Box:		Shots under par:	**Final Score:**	

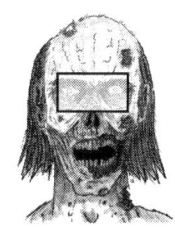

Date:	B.Z.	Battle Ground:	Undead / Infected / Mutant	Melee Weapon:
Pistol:		Sights:	Ammo:	Notes:
Shots inside Z Box:		Shots under par:	**Final Score:**	

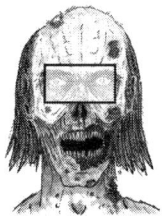

OUT OF TOUCH

Date:	B.Z.	Battle Ground:	Undead / Infected / Mutant	Melee Weapon:
Pistol:		Sights:	Ammo:	Notes:
Shots inside Z Box:		Shots under par:	**Final Score:**	

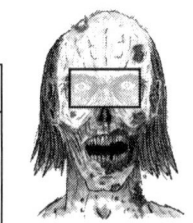

Date:	B.Z.	Battle Ground:	Undead / Infected / Mutant	Melee Weapon:
Pistol:		Sights:	Ammo:	Notes:
Shots inside Z Box:		Shots under par:	**Final Score:**	

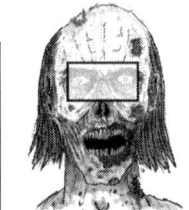

Date:	B.Z.	Battle Ground:	Undead / Infected / Mutant	Melee Weapon:
Pistol:		Sights:	Ammo:	Notes:
Shots inside Z Box:		Shots under par:	**Final Score:**	

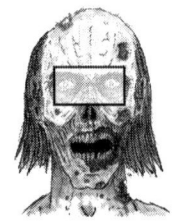

Date:	B.Z.	Battle Ground:	Undead / Infected / Mutant	Melee Weapon:
Pistol:		Sights:	Ammo:	Notes:
Shots inside Z Box:		Shots under par:	**Final Score:**	

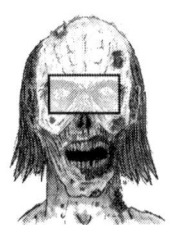

OUT OF TOUCH

Date:	B.Z.	Battle Ground:	Undead / Infected / Mutant	Melee Weapon:
Pistol:		Sights:	Ammo:	Notes:
Shots inside Z Box:		Shots under par:	**Final Score:**	

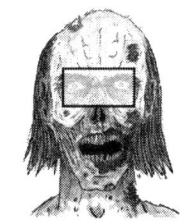

Date:	B.Z.	Battle Ground:	Undead / Infected / Mutant	Melee Weapon:
Pistol:		Sights:	Ammo:	Notes:
Shots inside Z Box:		Shots under par:	**Final Score:**	

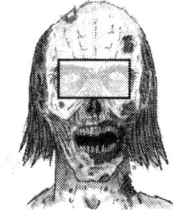

Date:	B.Z.	Battle Ground:	Undead / Infected / Mutant	Melee Weapon:
Pistol:		Sights:	Ammo:	Notes:
Shots inside Z Box:		Shots under par:	**Final Score:**	

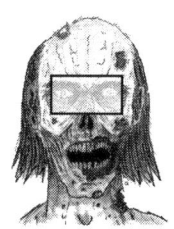

Date:	B.Z.	Battle Ground:	Undead / Infected / Mutant	Melee Weapon:
Pistol:		Sights:	Ammo:	Notes:
Shots inside Z Box:		Shots under par:	**Final Score:**	

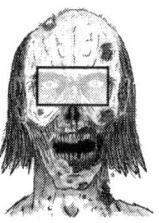

PISTOL DRILL: Z RULE #2

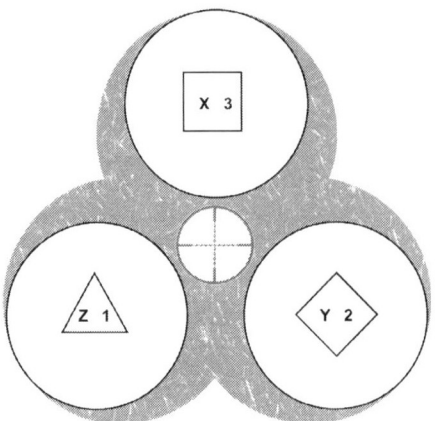

Purpose: To develop nervous system memory of draw stroke, hammer pair, and emergency reload.

Distance: 3 Yards.

Target: HAZARD (Undead).

Extra Equipment Needed: Shot timer, holster, 3 mags with 2 rounds each.

Round Fired Per Rep: 6 Rounds.

Total Rounds Fired: 18 Rounds.

Point Penalty: All rounds must hit inside the bio-circles under par to survive.

Repetitions: 3 Reps.

Starting Position & Condition: Standing - surrender / interview position. Condition 1 holstered.

Description:

Rep 1: At the beep of the timer, draw and fire a hammered pair into the circles in sequence of 1, 2, then 3. Reload as needed.

Rep 2: At the beep of the timer, draw and fire a hammered pair into the circles in sequence of X, Y, then Z. Reload as needed.

Rep 3: At the beep of the timer, draw and fire a hammered pair into the circles in sequence of Diamond, Square, then Triangle. Reload as needed.

Goals: Meat Bag: 3 Perfect reps with par time of 13 sec.   Survivor: 3 Perfect reps with par time of 11 sec.   Z Fighter: 3 Perfect reps with par time of 9.5 sec.

Variations:

⊕ Infected Humans: Same drill performed at 5 yards taking a step back while reloading.

⊕ Mutants: Same drill performed at 7 yards taking 1-2 steps left or right while reloading.

Z RULE #2

Date: B.Z.	Battle Ground:	Pistol:	Undead / Infected / Mutant
Rep 1 Reload 1:	Re 2 Reload Time 1:	Rep 3 Reload Time 1:	Notes:
Rep 1 Reload 2:	Re 2 Reload Time 2:	Rep 3 Reload Time 2:	
Live / Die	Live / Die	Live / Die	
Rep 1 Time:	Rep 2 Time:	Rep 3 Time:	**Average Rep Time:**

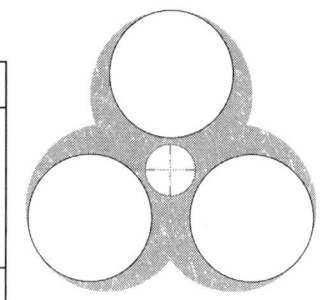

Date: B.Z.	Battle Ground:	Pistol:	Undead / Infected / Mutant
Rep 1 Reload 1:	Re 2 Reload Time 1:	Rep 3 Reload Time 1:	Notes:
Rep 1 Reload 2:	Re 2 Reload Time 2:	Rep 3 Reload Time 2:	
Live / Die	Live / Die	Live / Die	
Rep 1 Time:	Rep 2 Time:	Rep 3 Time:	**Average Rep Time:**

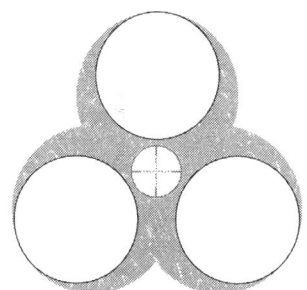

Date: B.Z.	Battle Ground:	Pistol:	Undead / Infected / Mutant
Rep 1 Reload 1:	Re 2 Reload Time 1:	Rep 3 Reload Time 1:	Notes:
Rep 1 Reload 2:	Re 2 Reload Time 2:	Rep 3 Reload Time 2:	
Live / Die	Live / Die	Live / Die	
Rep 1 Time:	Rep 2 Time:	Rep 3 Time:	**Average Rep Time:**

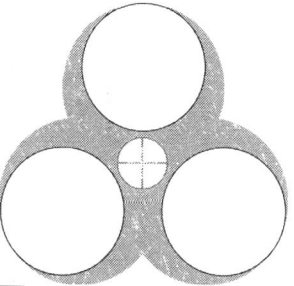

Z Fighter ©

Z RULE #2

Date:	B.Z.	Battle Ground:	Pistol:	Undead / Infected / Mutant
Rep 1 Reload 1:		Re 2 Reload Time 1:	Rep 3 Reload Time 1:	Notes:
Rep 1 Reload 2:		Re 2 Reload Time 2:	Rep 3 Reload Time 2:	
Live / Die		Live / Die	Live / Die	
Rep 1 Time:		Rep 2 Time:	Rep 3 Time:	**Average Rep Time:**

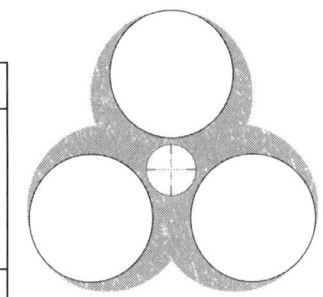

Date:	B.Z.	Battle Ground:	Pistol:	Undead / Infected / Mutant
Rep 1 Reload 1:		Re 2 Reload Time 1:	Rep 3 Reload Time 1:	Notes:
Rep 1 Reload 2:		Re 2 Reload Time 2:	Rep 3 Reload Time 2:	
Live / Die		Live / Die	Live / Die	
Rep 1 Time:		Rep 2 Time:	Rep 3 Time:	**Average Rep Time:**

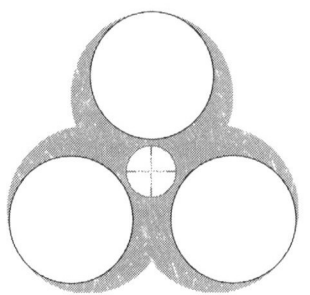

Date:	B.Z.	Battle Ground:	Pistol:	Undead / Infected / Mutant
Rep 1 Reload 1:		Re 2 Reload Time 1:	Rep 3 Reload Time 1:	Notes:
Rep 1 Reload 2:		Re 2 Reload Time 2:	Rep 3 Reload Time 2:	
Live / Die		Live / Die	Live / Die	
Rep 1 Time:		Rep 2 Time:	Rep 3 Time:	**Average Rep Time:**

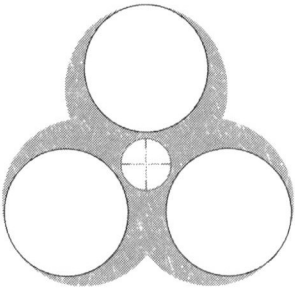

Z RULE #2

Date: B.Z.	Battle Ground:	Pistol:	Undead / Infected / Mutant
Rep 1 Reload 1:	Re 2 Reload Time 1:	Rep 3 Reload Time 1:	Notes:
Rep 1 Reload 2:	Re 2 Reload Time 2:	Rep 3 Reload Time 2:	
Live / Die	Live / Die	Live / Die	
Rep 1 Time:	Rep 2 Time:	Rep 3 Time:	**Average Rep Time:**

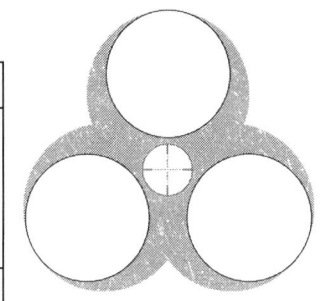

Date: B.Z.	Battle Ground:	Pistol:	Undead / Infected / Mutant
Rep 1 Reload 1:	Re 2 Reload Time 1:	Rep 3 Reload Time 1:	Notes:
Rep 1 Reload 2:	Re 2 Reload Time 2:	Rep 3 Reload Time 2:	
Live / Die	Live / Die	Live / Die	
Rep 1 Time:	Rep 2 Time:	Rep 3 Time:	**Average Rep Time:**

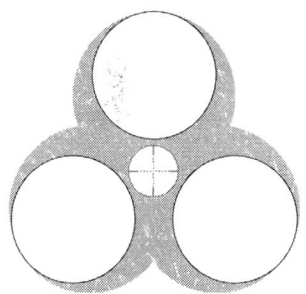

Date: B.Z.	Battle Ground:	Pistol:	Undead / Infected / Mutant
Rep 1 Reload 1:	Re 2 Reload Time 1:	Rep 3 Reload Time 1:	Notes:
Rep 1 Reload 2:	Re 2 Reload Time 2:	Rep 3 Reload Time 2:	
Live / Die	Live / Die	Livc / Dic	
Rep 1 Time:	Rep 2 Time:	Rep 3 Time:	**Average Rep Time:**

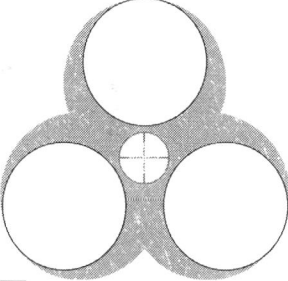

Z Fighter ©

Pistol Drills - 6

Z RULE #2

Date:	B.Z.	Battle Ground:	Pistol:	Undead / Infected / Mutant
Rep 1 Reload 1:		Re 2 Reload Time 1:	Rep 3 Reload Time 1:	Notes:
Rep 1 Reload 2:		Re 2 Reload Time 2:	Rep 3 Reload Time 2:	
Live / Die		Live / Die	Live / Die	
Rep 1 Time:		Rep 2 Time:	Rep 3 Time:	**Average Rep Time:**

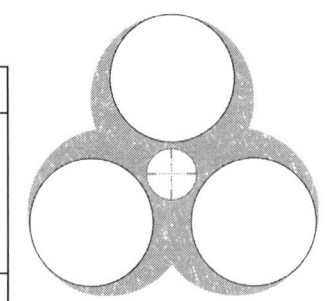

Date:	B.Z.	Battle Ground:	Pistol:	Undead / Infected / Mutant
Rep 1 Reload 1:		Re 2 Reload Time 1:	Rep 3 Reload Time 1:	Notes:
Rep 1 Reload 2:		Re 2 Reload Time 2:	Rep 3 Reload Time 2:	
Live / Die		Live / Die	Live / Die	
Rep 1 Time:		Rep 2 Time:	Rep 3 Time:	**Average Rep Time:**

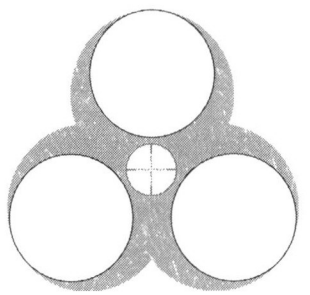

Date:	B.Z.	Battle Ground:	Pistol:	Undead / Infected / Mutant
Rep 1 Reload 1:		Re 2 Reload Time 1:	Rep 3 Reload Time 1:	Notes:
Rep 1 Reload 2:		Re 2 Reload Time 2:	Rep 3 Reload Time 2:	
Live / Die		Live / Die	Live / Die	
Rep 1 Time:		Rep 2 Time:	Rep 3 Time:	**Average Rep Time:**

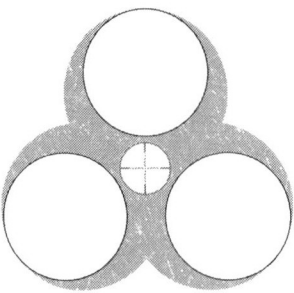

Z RULE #2

Date: B.Z.	Battle Ground:	Pistol:	Undead / Infected / Mutant
Rep 1 Reload 1:	Re 2 Reload Time 1:	Rep 3 Reload Time 1:	Notes:
Rep 1 Reload 2:	Re 2 Reload Time 2:	Rep 3 Reload Time 2:	
Live / Die	Live / Die	Live / Die	
Rep 1 Time:	Rep 2 Time:	Rep 3 Time:	**Average Rep Time:**

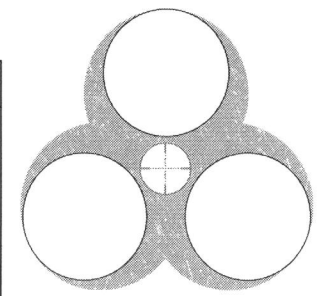

Date: B.Z.	Battle Ground:	Pistol:	Undead / Infected / Mutant
Rep 1 Reload 1:	Re 2 Reload Time 1:	Rep 3 Reload Time 1:	Notes:
Rep 1 Reload 2:	Re 2 Reload Time 2:	Rep 3 Reload Time 2:	
Live / Die	Live / Die	Live / Die	
Rep 1 Time:	Rep 2 Time:	Rep 3 Time:	**Average Rep Time:**

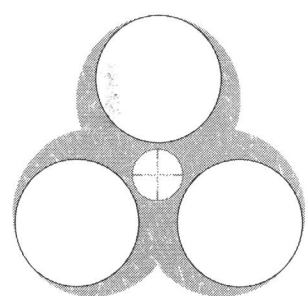

Date: B.Z.	Battle Ground:	Pistol:	Undead / Infected / Mutant
Rep 1 Reload 1:	Re 2 Reload Time 1:	Rep 3 Reload Time 1:	Notes:
Rep 1 Reload 2:	Re 2 Reload Time 2:	Rep 3 Reload Time 2:	
Live / Die	Live / Die	Live / Die	
Rep 1 Time:	Rep 2 Time:	Rep 3 Time:	**Average Rep Time:**

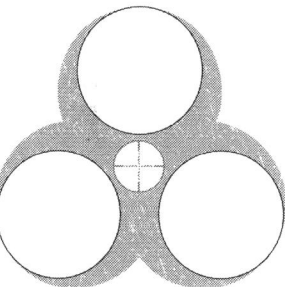

Z Fighter ©

Pistol Drills - 6

PISTOL DRILL: HEARTS AND MINDS

Purpose: To develop nervous system memory of draw stroke, hammer pair, emergency reload and failure to stop.

Distance: 3 Yards.

Target: ZIPSC (Undead).

Extra Equipment Needed: Shot timer, holster, 1 mag with 2 round, 1 mag with 1 round, magazine carrier.

Par time: 4.5 Seconds.

Round Fired Per Rep: 3 Rounds.

Total Rounds Fired: 15 Rounds.

Point Penalty: Live or Die.

Repetitions: 5 Reps.

Starting Position & Condition: Standing - surrender / interview position. Condition 1 holstered.

Description: At the beep of the timer, draw and fire a hammered pair into the body a box. Take one step back while performing an emergency reload. Aim and fire 1 round into the ocular Z box. Holster and repeat for a total of 5 reps. Must get all 3 shots in the A & Z box under par time to pass.

Goals: Meat Bag: Live with 3 perfect reps.   Survivor: Live with 4 perfect reps.   Z Fighter: Live with 5 perfect reps.

Variations:

⊕   Infected Humans: Same drill performed at 5 yards. Par Time: 4 Seconds.

⊕   Mutants: Same drill performed at 7 yards taking a sidestep while reloading. Par Time: 4.2 Seconds.

HEARTS AND MINDS

Date: B.Z.	Battle Ground:	Weapon:	Sights:	Undead / Infected / Mutant
Rep 1 Time:	Rep 2 Time:	Rep 3 Time:	Rep 4 Time:	Rep 5 Time:
Reload Time:	Reload Time:	Reload Time:	Reload Time:	Reload Time:
Live / Die	Live / Die	Live / Die	Live / Die	Live / Die
Ave Reload Time:	**Ave Total Rep Time:**		Notes:	

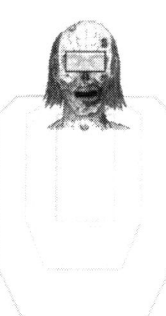

Date: B.Z.	Battle Ground:	Weapon:	Sights:	Undead / Infected / Mutant
Rep 1 Time:	Rep 2 Time:	Rep 3 Time:	Rep 4 Time:	Rep 5 Time:
Reload Time:	Reload Time:	Reload Time:	Reload Time:	Reload Time:
Live / Die	Live / Die	Live / Die	Live / Die	Live / Die
Ave Reload Time:	**Ave Total Rep Time:**		Notes:	

Date: B.Z.	Battle Ground:	Weapon:	Sights:	Undead / Infected / Mutant
Rep 1 Time:	Rep 2 Time:	Rep 3 Time:	Rep 4 Time:	Rep 5 Time:
Reload Time:	Reload Time:	Reload Time:	Reload Time:	Reload Time:
Live / Die	Live / Die	Live / Die	Live / Die	Live / Die
Ave Reload Time:	**Ave Total Rep Time:**		Notes:	

Z Fighter ©   Pistol Drills - 7

HEARTS AND MINDS

Date: B.Z.	Battle Ground:	Weapon:	Sights:	Undead / Infected / Mutant
Rep 1 Time:	Rep 2 Time:	Rep 3 Time:	Rep 4 Time:	Rep 5 Time:
Reload Time:	Reload Time:	Reload Time:	Reload Time:	Reload Time:
Live / Die	Live / Die	Live / Die	Live / Die	Live / Die
Ave Reload Time:	**Ave Total Rep Time:**		Notes:	

Date: B.Z.	Battle Ground:	Weapon:	Sights:	Undead / Infected / Mutant
Rep 1 Time:	Rep 2 Time:	Rep 3 Time:	Rep 4 Time:	Rep 5 Time:
Reload Time:	Reload Time:	Reload Time:	Reload Time:	Reload Time:
Live / Die	Live / Die	Live / Die	Live / Die	Live / Die
Ave Reload Time:	**Ave Total Rep Time:**		**Notes:**	

Date: B.Z.	Battle Ground:	Weapon:	Sights:	Undead / Infected / Mutant
Rep 1 Time:	Rep 2 Time:	Rep 3 Time:	Rep 4 Time:	Rep 5 Time:
Reload Time:	Reload Time:	Reload Time:	Reload Time:	Reload Time:
Live / Die	Live / Die	Live / Die	Live / Die	Live / Die
Ave Reload Time:	**Ave Total Rep Time:**		Notes:	

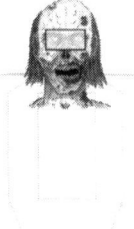

HEARTS AND MINDS

Date: B.Z.	Battle Ground:	Weapon:	Sights:	Undead / Infected / Mutant
Rep 1 Time:	Rep 2 Time:	Rep 3 Time:	Rep 4 Time:	Rep 5 Time:
Reload Time:	Reload Time:	Reload Time:	Reload Time:	Reload Time:
Live / Die	Live / Die	Live / Die	Live / Die	Live / Die
Ave Reload Time:		**Ave Total Rep Time:**		Notes:

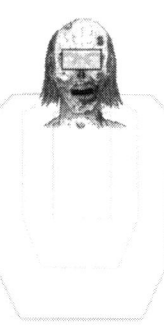

Date: B.Z.	Battle Ground:	Weapon:	Sights:	Undead / Infected / Mutant
Rep 1 Time:	Rep 2 Time:	Rep 3 Time:	Rep 4 Time:	Rep 5 Time:
Reload Time:	Reload Time:	Reload Time:	Reload Time:	Reload Time:
Live / Die	Live / Die	Live / Die	Live / Die	Live / Die
Ave Reload Time:		**Ave Total Rep Time:**		Notes:

Date: B.Z.	Battle Ground:	Weapon:	Sights:	Undead / Infected / Mutant
Rep 1 Time:	Rep 2 Time:	Rep 3 Time:	Rep 4 Time:	Rep 5 Time:
Reload Time:	Reload Time:	Reload Time:	Reload Time:	Reload Time:
Live / Die	Live / Die	Live / Die	Live / Die	Live / Die
Ave Reload Time:		**Ave Total Rep Time:**		Notes:

Z Fighter ©

Pistol Drills - 7

HEARTS AND MINDS

Date:	B.Z.	Battle Ground:	Weapon:	Sights:	Undead / Infected / Mutant
Rep 1 Time:		Rep 2 Time:	Rep 3 Time:	Rep 4 Time:	Rep 5 Time:
Reload Time:		Reload Time:	Reload Time:	Reload Time:	Reload Time:
Live / Die		Live / Die	Live / Die	Live / Die	Live / Die
Ave Reload Time:			**Ave Total Rep Time:**		Notes:

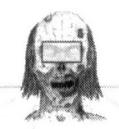

Date:	B.Z.	Battle Ground:	Weapon:	Sights:	Undead / Infected / Mutant
Rep 1 Time:		Rep 2 Time:	Rep 3 Time:	Rep 4 Time:	Rep 5 Time:
Reload Time:		Reload Time:	Reload Time:	Reload Time:	Reload Time:
Live / Die		Live / Die	Live / Die	Live / Die	Live / Die
Ave Reload Time:			**Ave Total Rep Time:**		Notes:

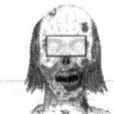

Date:	B.Z.	Battle Ground:	Weapon:	Sights:	Undead / Infected / Mutant
Rep 1 Time:		Rep 2 Time:	Rep 3 Time:	Rep 4 Time:	Rep 5 Time:
Reload Time:		Reload Time:	Reload Time:	Reload Time:	Reload Time:
Live / Die		Live / Die	Live / Die	Live / Die	Live / Die
Ave Reload Time:			**Ave Total Rep Time:**		Notes:

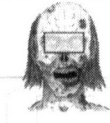

HEARTS AND MINDS

Date:	B.Z.	Battle Ground:	Weapon:	Sights:	Undead / Infected / Mutant
Rep 1 Time:		Rep 2 Time:	Rep 3 Time:	Rep 4 Time:	Rep 5 Time:
Reload Time:		Reload Time:	Reload Time:	Reload Time:	Reload Time:
Live / Die		Live / Die	Live / Die	Live / Die	Live / Die
Ave Reload Time:			**Ave Total Rep Time:**		Notes:

Date:	B.Z.	Battle Ground:	Weapon:	Sights:	Undead / Infected / Mutant
Rep 1 Time:		Rep 2 Time:	Rep 3 Time:	Rep 4 Time:	Rep 5 Time:
Reload Time:		Reload Time:	Reload Time:	Reload Time:	Reload Time:
Live / Die		Live / Die	Live / Die	Live / Die	Live / Die
Ave Reload Time:			**Ave Total Rep Time:**		Notes:

Date:	B.Z.	Battle Ground:	Weapon:	Sights:	Undead / Infected / Mutant
Rep 1 Time:		Rep 2 Time:	Rep 3 Time:	Rep 4 Time:	Rep 5 Time:
Reload Time:		Reload Time:	Reload Time:	Reload Time:	Reload Time:
Live / Die		Live / Die	Live / Die	Live / Die	Live / Die
Ave Reload Time:			**Ave Total Rep Time:**		Notes:

Z Fighter ©

Pistol Drills - 7

PISTOL DRILL: **DEATH METAL**

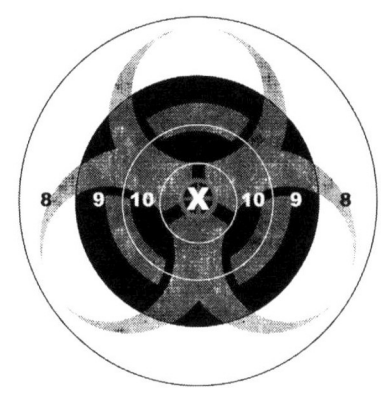

Purpose: Develop controlled fire recoil management.

Distance: 7 Yards.

Target: ZF-1

Par Time: Varies per repetition round count.

Extra Equipment Needed: Shot timer.

Total Rounds Fired: 14 Rounds.

Point Penalty: As per target score.

Repetitions: 1 Rep of 4 stages.

Starting Position & Condition: Standing – Pistol aimed at target. Weapon Condition 1.

Description: At the timer beep, fire the prescribed number of rounds into the GF-1 target within the listed stage par time. Record time. Repeat drill with 2, 3, 4 and 5 rounds fired. Having good sight alignment, sight picture, a solid stance and trigger control is essential to master this drill.

Stage 1 – 2 rounds in 2 seconds. Z Fighter par time: 1.5 seconds.

Stage 2 – 3 rounds in 2.75 seconds. Z Fighter par time: 2 seconds.

Stage 3 – 4 rounds in 3.5 seconds. Z Fighter par time: 2.5 seconds.

Stage 4 – 5 rounds in 4.25 seconds. Z Fighter par time: 3 seconds.

Goals: Meat Bag: 126 points with all rounds in or touching the black.   Survivor: 140 points.   Z Fighter: 140 points within listed Z Fighter par time.

Variations:

- Infected Humans: Start rep at 7 yards. Carefully taking 1-2 steps backwards while firing.

- Mutants: Start rep at 7 yards. Carefully taking 1-2 steps left or right while firing.

DEATH METAL

Date: B.Z.	Location:	Pistol:	Undead / Infected / Mutant	Notes:
Rep 1 Time:	Rep 2 Time:	Rep 3 Time:	Rep 4 Time:	
# Out of Black:	# of 9's:	# of 10's:	**Total Score:** X's	

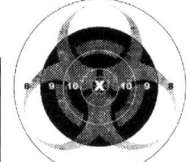

Date: B.Z.	Location:	Pistol:	Undead / Infected / Mutant	Notes:
Rep 1 Time:	Rep 2 Time:	Rep 3 Time:	Rep 4 Time:	
# Out of Black:	# of 9's:	# of 10's:	**Total Score:** X's	

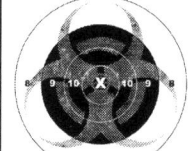

Date: B.Z.	Location:	Pistol:	Undead / Infected / Mutant	Notes:
Rep 1 Time:	Rep 2 Time:	Rep 3 Time:	Rep 4 Time:	
# Out of Black:	# of 9's:	# of 10's:	**Total Score:** X's	

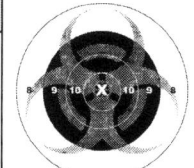

Date: B.Z.	Location:	Pistol:	Undead / Infected / Mutant	Notes:
Rep 1 Time:	Rep 2 Time:	Rep 3 Time:	Rep 4 Time:	
# Out of Black:	# of 9's:	# of 10's:	**Total Score:** X's	

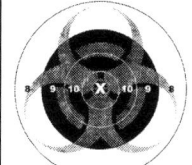

Date: B.Z.	Location:	Pistol:	Undead / Infected / Mutant	Notes:
Rep 1 Time:	Rep 2 Time:	Rep 3 Time:	Rep 4 Time:	
# Out of Black:	# of 9's:	# of 10's:	**Total Score:** X's	

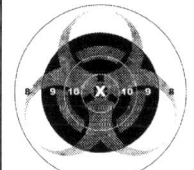

DEATH METAL

Date: B.Z.	Location:	Pistol:	Undead / Infected / Mutant	Notes:
Rep 1 Time:	Rep 2 Time:	Rep 3 Time:	Rep 4 Time:	
# Out of Black:	# of 9's:	# of 10's:	Total Score: X's	
Date: B.Z.	Location:	Pistol:	Undead / Infected / Mutant	Notes:
Rep 1 Time:	Rep 2 Time:	Rep 3 Time:	Rep 4 Time:	
# Out of Black:	# of 9's:	# of 10's:	Total Score: X's	
Date: B.Z.	Location:	Pistol:	Undead / Infected / Mutant	Notes:
Rep 1 Time:	Rep 2 Time:	Rep 3 Time:	Rep 4 Time:	
# Out of Black:	# of 9's:	# of 10's:	Total Score: X's	
Date: B.Z.	Location:	Pistol:	Undead / Infected / Mutant	Notes:
Rep 1 Time:	Rep 2 Time:	Rep 3 Time:	Rep 4 Time:	
# Out of Black:	# of 9's:	# of 10's:	Total Score: X's	
Date: B.Z.	Location:	Pistol:	Undead / Infected / Mutant	Notes:
Rep 1 Time:	Rep 2 Time:	Rep 3 Time:	Rep 4 Time:	
# Out of Black:	# of 9's:	# of 10's:	Total Score: X's	

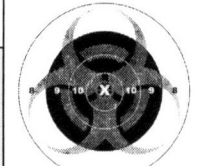
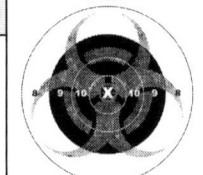
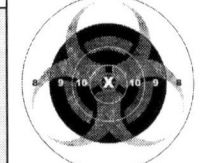
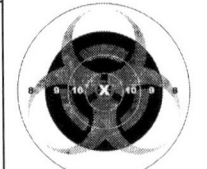

DEATH METAL

Date: B.Z.	Location:	Pistol:	Undead / Infected / Mutant	Notes:
Rep 1 Time:	Rep 2 Time:	Rep 3 Time:	Rep 4 Time:	
# Out of Black:	# of 9's:	# of 10's:	**Total Score:** X's	
Date: B.Z.	Location:	Pistol:	Undead / Infected / Mutant	Notes:
Rep 1 Time:	Rep 2 Time:	Rep 3 Time:	Rep 4 Time:	
# Out of Black:	# of 9's:	# of 10's:	**Total Score:** X's	
Date: B.Z.	Location:	Pistol:	Undead / Infected / Mutant	Notes:
Rep 1 Time:	Rep 2 Time:	Rep 3 Time:	Rep 4 Time:	
# Out of Black:	# of 9's:	# of 10's:	**Total Score:** X's	
Date: B.Z.	Location:	Pistol:	Undead / Infected / Mutant	Notes:
Rep 1 Time:	Rep 2 Time:	Rep 3 Time:	Rep 4 Time:	
# Out of Black:	# of 9's:	# of 10's:	**Total Score:** X's	
Date: B.Z.	Location:	Pistol:	Undead / Infected / Mutant	Notes:
Rep 1 Time:	Rep 2 Time:	Rep 3 Time:	Rep 4 Time:	
# Out of Black:	# of 9's:	# of 10's:	**Total Score:** X's	

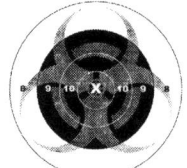
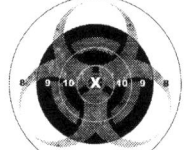
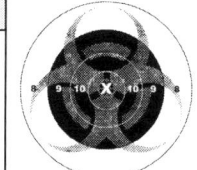
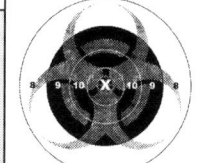
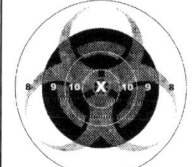

DEATH METAL

Date: B.Z.	Location:	Pistol:	Undead / Infected / Mutant	Notes:
Rep 1 Time:	Rep 2 Time:	Rep 3 Time:	Rep 4 Time:	
# Out of Black:	# of 9's:	# of 10's:	**Total Score:** X's	

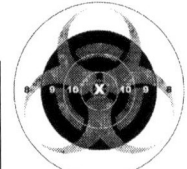

Date: B.Z.	Location:	Pistol:	Undead / Infected / Mutant	Notes:
Rep 1 Time:	Rep 2 Time:	Rep 3 Time:	Rep 4 Time:	
# Out of Black:	# of 9's:	# of 10's:	**Total Score:** X's	

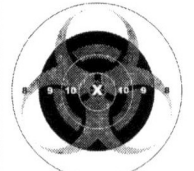

Date: B.Z.	Location:	Pistol:	Undead / Infected / Mutant	Notes:
Rep 1 Time:	Rep 2 Time:	Rep 3 Time:	Rep 4 Time:	
# Out of Black:	# of 9's:	# of 10's:	**Total Score:** X's	

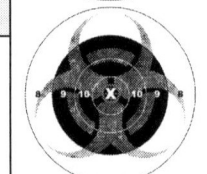

Date: B.Z.	Location:	Pistol:	Undead / Infected / Mutant	Notes:
Rep 1 Time:	Rep 2 Time:	Rep 3 Time:	Rep 4 Time:	
# Out of Black:	# of 9's:	# of 10's:	**Total Score:** X's	

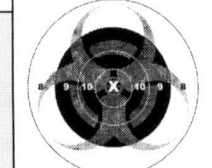

Date: B.Z.	Location:	Pistol:	Undead / Infected / Mutant	Notes:
Rep 1 Time:	Rep 2 Time:	Rep 3 Time:	Rep 4 Time:	
# Out of Black:	# of 9's:	# of 10's:	**Total Score:** X's	

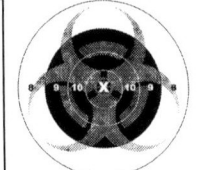

DEATH METAL

Date: B.Z.	Location:	Pistol:	Undead / Infected / Mutant	Notes:
Rep 1 Time:	Rep 2 Time:	Rep 3 Time:	Rep 4 Time:	
# Out of Black:	# of 9's:	# of 10's:	**Total Score:** X's	
Date: B.Z.	Location:	Pistol:	Undead / Infected / Mutant	Notes:
Rep 1 Time:	Rep 2 Time:	Rep 3 Time:	Rep 4 Time:	
# Out of Black:	# of 9's:	# of 10's:	**Total Score:** X's	
Date: B.Z.	Location:	Pistol:	Undead / Infected / Mutant	Notes:
Rep 1 Time:	Rep 2 Time:	Rep 3 Time:	Rep 4 Time:	
# Out of Black:	# of 9's:	# of 10's:	**Total Score:** X's	
Date: B.Z.	Location:	Pistol:	Undead / Infected / Mutant	Notes:
Rep 1 Time:	Rep 2 Time:	Rep 3 Time:	Rep 4 Time:	
# Out of Black:	# of 9's:	# of 10's:	**Total Score:** X's	
Date: B.Z.	Location:	Pistol:	Undead / Infected / Mutant	Notes:
Rep 1 Time:	Rep 2 Time:	Rep 3 Time:	Rep 4 Time:	
# Out of Black:	# of 9's:	# of 10's:	**Total Score:** X's	

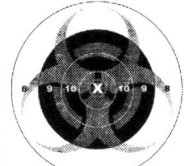
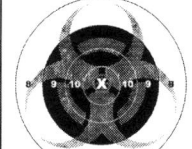
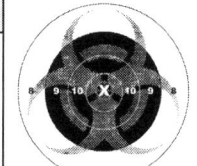
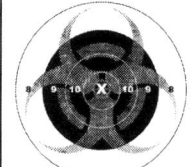
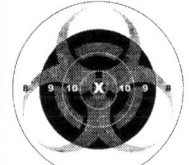

PISTOL DRILL: DUECES

Purpose: Pistol draw speed and quick shot cadence.

Distance: 3 & 5 Yards.

Target: ZIPSC X 2 targets. Position the targets 3 feet apart at 3 and 5 yards.

Extra Equipment Needed: Shot timer.

Rounds Fired Per Rep: 2-6 Rounds.

Total Rounds Fired: 6-18 Rounds.

Point Penalty: Live or Die.

Repetitions: 3 Reps.

Starting Position & Condition: Standing - Surrender / Interview. Condition 1.

Description: At the timer beep, draw and fire 1 round into the ocular Z box of each target starting with the 3 yard target then transition to the 5 yard target. Record time, score targets. All rounds must be inside or touching the ocular Z box. Average all of the repetitions for score time.

Hint: Beginners should focus more on accuracy than speed.

Goals: Meat Bag: 3.25 Seconds.   Survivor: 2.75 Seconds.   Z Fighter: 2.25 Seconds.

Variations:

⊕ Infected Humans: 2 shots to the body A Box and 1 to the ocular Z box of each target. (Add 1.25 seconds to goal par times.)

⊕ Mutants: 2 shots to the body A Box and 1 to the ocular Z box of each target with targets at 5 & 7 yards. (Add 1.5 seconds to goal par times.)

5 Yards

3 Feet

3 Yards

DUECES

Date: B.Z.	Battle Ground:	Weapon:	Undead / Infected / Mutant
Rep 1 Time:	**Rep 2 Time:**	**Rep 3 Time:**	Notes:
# Outside Box:	# Outside Box:	# Outside Box:	
Rep 1: Live / Die	Rep 2: Live / Die	Rep 3: Live / Die	**Ave Rep Time:**

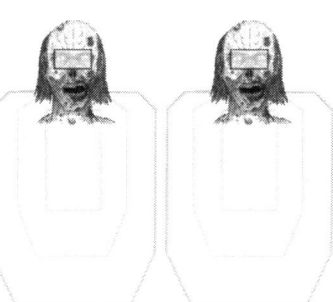

Date: B.Z.	Battle Ground:	Weapon:	Undead / Infected / Mutant
Rep 1 Time:	**Rep 2 Time:**	**Rep 3 Time:**	Notes:
# Outside Box:	# Outside Box:	# Outside Box:	
Rep 1: Live / Die	Rep 2: Live / Die	Rep 3: Live / Die	**Ave Rep Time:**

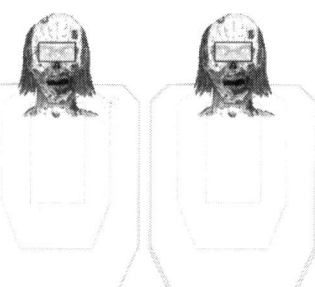

Date: B.Z.	Battle Ground:	Weapon:	Undead / Infected / Mutant
Rep 1 Time:	**Rep 2 Time:**	**Rep 3 Time:**	Notes:
# Outside Box:	# Outside Box:	# Outside Box:	
Rep 1: Live / Die	Rep 2: Live / Die	Rep 3: Live / Die	**Ave Rep Time:**

Z Fighter ©

DUECES

Date: B.Z.	Battle Ground:	Weapon:	Undead / Infected / Mutant
Rep 1 Time:	**Rep 2 Time:**	**Rep 3 Time:**	Notes:
# Outside Box:	# Outside Box:	# Outside Box:	
Rep 1: Live / Die	Rep 2: Live / Die	Rep 3: Live / Die	**Ave Rep Time:**

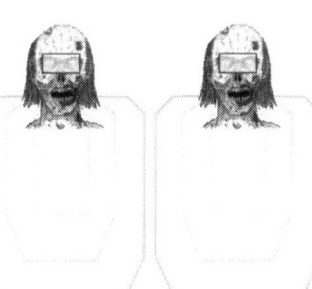

Date: B.Z.	Battle Ground:	Weapon:	Undead / Infected / Mutant
Rep 1 Time:	**Rep 2 Time:**	**Rep 3 Time:**	Notes:
# Outside Box:	# Outside Box:	# Outside Box:	
Rep 1: Live / Die	Rep 2: Live / Die	Rep 3: Live / Die	**Ave Rep Time:**

Date: B.Z.	Battle Ground:	Weapon:	Undead / Infected / Mutant
Rep 1 Time:	**Rep 2 Time:**	**Rep 3 Time:**	Notes:
# Outside Box:	# Outside Box:	# Outside Box:	
Rep 1: Live / Die	Rep 2: Live / Die	Rep 3: Live / Die	**Ave Rep Time:**

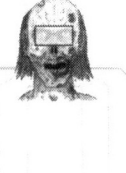

DUECES

Date: B.Z.	Battle Ground:	Weapon:	Undead / Infected / Mutant
Rep 1 Time:	**Rep 2 Time:**	**Rep 3 Time:**	Notes:
# Outside Box:	# Outside Box:	# Outside Box:	
Rep 1: Live / Die	Rep 2: Live / Die	Rep 3: Live / Die	**Ave Rep Time:**

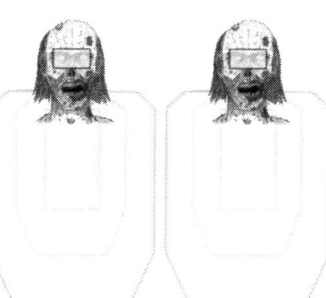

Date: B.Z.	Battle Ground:	Weapon:	Undead / Infected / Mutant
Rep 1 Time:	**Rep 2 Time:**	**Rep 3 Time:**	Notes:
# Outside Box:	# Outside Box:	# Outside Box:	
Rep 1: Live / Die	Rep 2: Live / Die	Rep 3: Live / Die	**Ave Rep Time:**

Date: B.Z.	Battle Ground:	Weapon:	Undead / Infected / Mutant
Rep 1 Time:	**Rep 2 Time:**	**Rep 3 Time:**	Notes:
# Outside Box:	# Outside Box:	# Outside Box:	
Rep 1: Live / Die	Rep 2: Live / Die	Rep 3: Live / Die	**Ave Rep Time:**

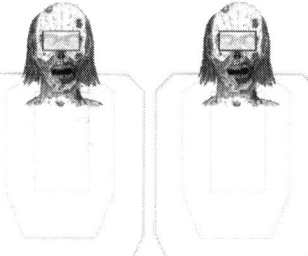

Z Fighter ©

DUECES

Date: B.Z.	Battle Ground:	Weapon:	Undead / Infected / Mutant
Rep 1 Time:	**Rep 2 Time:**	**Rep 3 Time:**	Notes:
# Outside Box:	# Outside Box:	# Outside Box:	
Rep 1: Live / Die	Rep 2: Live / Die	Rep 3: Live / Die	**Ave Rep Time:**

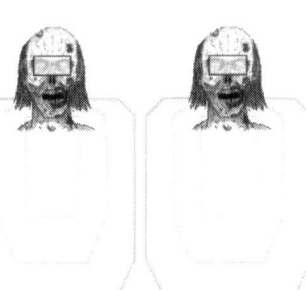

Date: B.Z.	Battle Ground:	Weapon:	Undead / Infected / Mutant
Rep 1 Time:	**Rep 2 Time:**	**Rep 3 Time:**	Notes:
# Outside Box:	# Outside Box:	# Outside Box:	
Rep 1: Live / Die	Rep 2: Live / Die	Rep 3: Live / Die	**Ave Rep Time:**

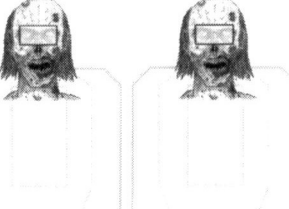

Date: B.Z.	Battle Ground:	Weapon:	Undead / Infected / Mutant
Rep 1 Time:	**Rep 2 Time:**	**Rep 3 Time:**	Notes:
# Outside Box:	# Outside Box:	# Outside Box:	
Rep 1: Live / Die	Rep 2: Live / Die	Rep 3: Live / Die	**Ave Rep Time:**

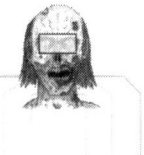 

DUECES

Date: B.Z.	Battle Ground:	Weapon:	Undead / Infected / Mutant
Rep 1 Time:	**Rep 2 Time:**	**Rep 3 Time:**	Notes:
# Outside Box:	# Outside Box:	# Outside Box:	
Rep 1: Live / Die	Rep 2: Live / Die	Rep 3: Live / Die	**Ave Rep Time:**

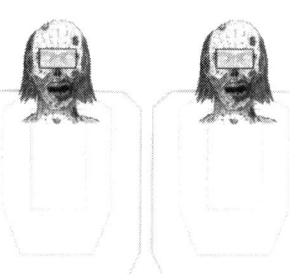

Date: B.Z.	Battle Ground:	Weapon:	Undead / Infected / Mutant
Rep 1 Time:	**Rep 2 Time:**	**Rep 3 Time:**	Notes:
# Outside Box:	# Outside Box:	# Outside Box:	
Rep 1: Live / Die	Rep 2: Live / Die	Rep 3: Live / Die	**Ave Rep Time:**

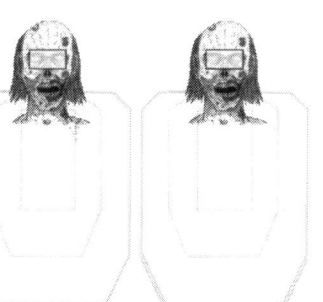

Date: B.Z.	Battle Ground:	Weapon:	Undead / Infected / Mutant
Rep 1 Time:	**Rep 2 Time:**	**Rep 3 Time:**	Notes:
# Outside Box:	# Outside Box:	# Outside Box:	
Rep 1: Live / Die	Rep 2: Live / Die	Rep 3: Live / Die	**Ave Rep Time:**

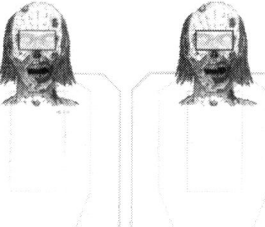

Z Fighter ©

PISTOL DRILL: BABA YAGA

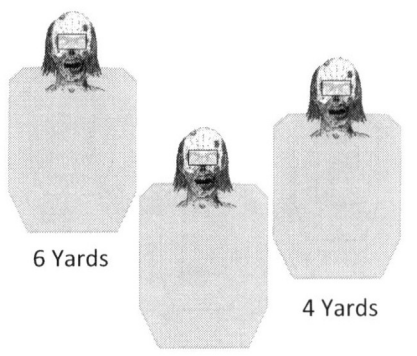

6 Yards
4 Yards
2 Yard

Purpose: Retracted / Compressed carry, close range body positioning shooting and shot cadence.

Target Distance: ZIPSC x3 targets. Position the targets at 2, 4, and 6 yards with little dispersion.

Extra Equipment Needed: Shot timer.

Rounds Fired Per Rep: 9 Rounds.   **Total Rounds Fired:** 27 Rounds.

Point Penalty: Time plus penalty.

Repetitions: 3 Reps.

Starting Position & Condition: Standing - Retracted / Compressed Carry . Condition 1.

Description: (The retracted carry position is when you have a 2 handed grip on the pistol, pulling your dominant arm back towards your armpit while your support arm is flat across your chest, pistol pointing forward.) At the timer beep, fire 2 rounds into the closest threat's body A box from the retracted carry, extending both arms forward into full presentation and fire 1 round into the ocular Z box. Transition to the 4 yard target firing 2 rounds into the body A box and 1 round into the ocular Z box. Transition to the 6 yard target firing 2 rounds into the body A box then 1 round into the ocular Z box. All rounds must be inside the A / Z box to live another day. For every hit outside the A or Z box, add 2 seconds to your time. For every miss outside the head or body, add 5 seconds to your time. Add the penalty tonto your recorded time for that repetition.

Goals: Meat Bag: 6 Seconds.   Survivor: 5 Seconds.   Z Fighter: 4.5 Seconds.

Variations:

⊕   Infected Humans: Same drill with targets at 3, 5 and 7 yards. Same goal times.

⊕   Mutants: Targets at 4, 6 and 8 yards firing 3 - 4 rounds into body A box and 1 round into ocular Z box.   Must reload at least once.

BABA YAGA

Date:	B.Z.	Battle Ground:	Weapon:	Sights
Rep 1 Time:		**Rep 2 Time:**	**Rep 3 Time:**	Notes:
Penalty:		Penalty:	Penalty:	
Rep 1 Time Score:		Rep 2 Time Score:	Rep 3 Time Score:	Undead / Infected / Mutant

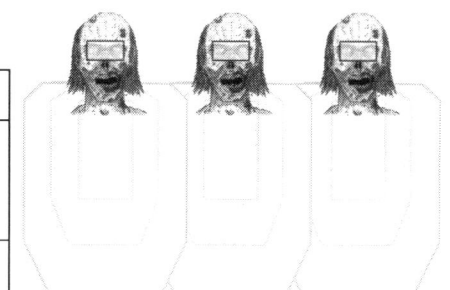

Date:	B.Z.	Battle Ground:	Weapon:	Sights
Rep 1 Time:		**Rep 2 Time:**	**Rep 3 Time:**	Notes:
Penalty:		Penalty:	Penalty:	
Rep 1 Time Score:		Rep 2 Time Score:	Rep 3 Time Score:	Undead / Infected / Mutant

Date:	B.Z.	Battle Ground:	Weapon:	Sights
Rep 1 Time:		**Rep 2 Time:**	**Rep 3 Time:**	Notes:
Penalty:		Penalty:	Penalty:	
Rep 1 Time Score:		Rep 2 Time Score:	Rep 3 Time Score:	Undead / Infected / Mutant

Z Fighter ©

BABA YAGA

Date:	B.Z.	Battle Ground:	Weapon:	Sights
Rep 1 Time:		Rep 2 Time:	Rep 3 Time:	Notes:
Penalty:		Penalty:	Penalty:	
Rep 1 Time Score:		Rep 2 Time Score:	Rep 3 Time Score:	Undead / Infected / Mutant

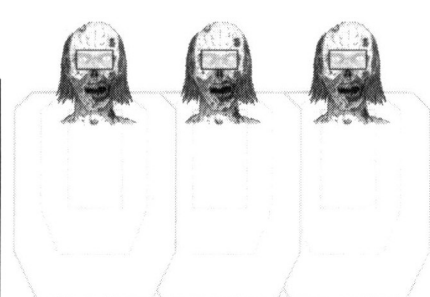

Date:	B.Z.	Battle Ground:	Weapon:	Sights
Rep 1 Time:		Rep 2 Time:	Rep 3 Time:	Notes:
Penalty:		Penalty:	Penalty:	
Rep 1 Time Score:		Rep 2 Time Score:	Rep 3 Time Score:	Undead / Infected / Mutant

Date:	B.Z.	Battle Ground:	Weapon:	Sights
Rep 1 Time:		Rep 2 Time:	Rep 3 Time:	Notes:
Penalty:		Penalty:	Penalty:	
Rep 1 Time Score:		Rep 2 Time Score:	Rep 3 Time Score:	Undead / Infected / Mutant

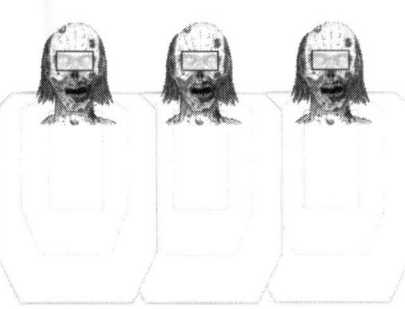

BABA YAGA

Date:	B.Z.	Battle Ground:	Weapon:	Sights
Rep 1 Time:		**Rep 2 Time:**	**Rep 3 Time:**	Notes:
Penalty:		Penalty:	Penalty:	
Rep 1 Time Score:		Rep 2 Time Score:	Rep 3 Time Score:	Undead / Infected / Mutant

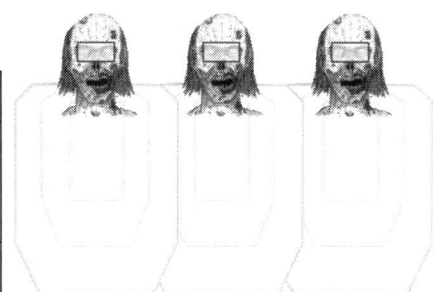

Date:	B.Z.	Battle Ground:	Weapon:	Sights
Rep 1 Time:		**Rep 2 Time:**	**Rep 3 Time:**	Notes:
Penalty:		Penalty:	Penalty:	
Rep 1 Time Score:		Rep 2 Time Score:	Rep 3 Time Score:	Undead / Infected / Mutant

Date:	B.Z.	Battle Ground:	Weapon:	Sights
Rep 1 Time:		**Rep 2 Time:**	**Rep 3 Time:**	Notes:
Penalty:		Penalty:	Penalty:	
Rep 1 Time Score:		Rep 2 Time Score:	Rep 3 Time Score:	Undead / Infected / Mutant

Z Fighter ©

Pistol Drills - 10

BABA YAGA

Date:	B.Z.	Battle Ground:	Weapon:	Sights	
Rep 1 Time:		**Rep 2 Time:**	**Rep 3 Time:**	Notes:	
Penalty:		Penalty:	Penalty:		
Rep 1 Time Score:		Rep 2 Time Score:	Rep 3 Time Score:	Undead / Infected / Mutant	

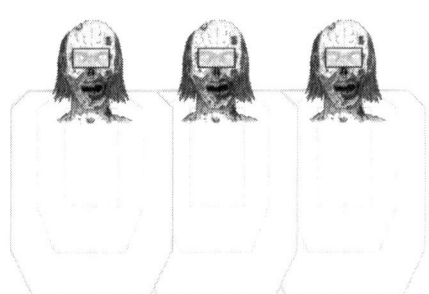

Date:	B.Z.	Battle Ground:	Weapon:	Sights	
Rep 1 Time:		**Rep 2 Time:**	**Rep 3 Time:**	Notes:	
Penalty:		Penalty:	Penalty:		
Rep 1 Time Score:		Rep 2 Time Score:	Rep 3 Time Score:	Undead / Infected / Mutant	

Date:	B.Z.	Battle Ground:	Weapon:	Sights	
Rep 1 Time:		**Rep 2 Time:**	**Rep 3 Time:**	Notes:	
Penalty:		Penalty:	Penalty:		
Rep 1 Time Score:		Rep 2 Time Score:	Rep 3 Time Score:	Undead / Infected / Mutant	

BABA YAGA

Date:	B.Z.	Battle Ground:	Weapon:	Sights
Rep 1 Time:		**Rep 2 Time:**	**Rep 3 Time:**	Notes:
Penalty:		Penalty:	Penalty:	
Rep 1 Time Score:		Rep 2 Time Score:	Rep 3 Time Score:	Undead / Infected / Mutant

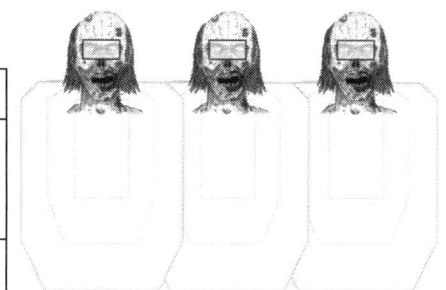

Date:	B.Z.	Battle Ground:	Weapon:	Sights
Rep 1 Time:		**Rep 2 Time:**	**Rep 3 Time:**	Notes:
Penalty:		Penalty:	Penalty:	
Rep 1 Time Score:		Rep 2 Time Score:	Rep 3 Time Score:	Undead / Infected / Mutant

Date:	B.Z.	Battle Ground:	Weapon:	Sights
Rep 1 Time:		**Rep 2 Time:**	**Rep 3 Time:**	Notes:
Penalty:		Penalty:	Penalty:	
Rep 1 Time Score:		Rep 2 Time Score:	Rep 3 Time Score:	Undead / Infected / Mutant

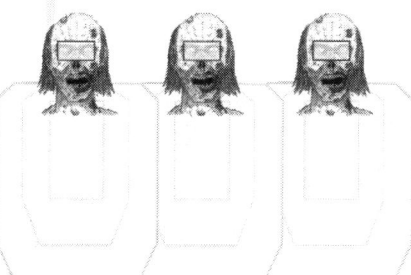

Z Fighter ©

Pistol Drills - 10

PISTOL DRILL: STEPHAN AND THE FAT MAN

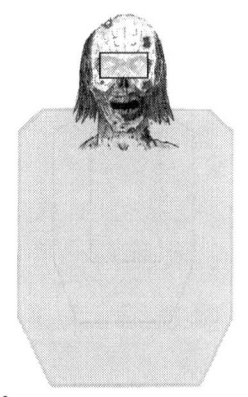

Purpose: Develop nervous system memory of getting off line after retention shooting.

Distance: Arms length from target. **Target:** ZIPSC

Extra Equipment Required: Shot timer.

Rounds Fired Per Rep: 5 Rounds. **Total Rounds Fired:** 20 Rounds. **Repetitions:** 4 Reps.

Point Penalty: As per target score. 3 Points on body or head. 5 Points in A zone body box and ocular Z box.

Starting Position & Condition: Standing – Surrender / Interview. Weapon Condition 1.

Description: At your own personal go, take your dominant firing hand/arm, bring your elbow straight back and clear your concealment garment (if you have one) with your firing hand and establish a good grip on the pistol. As you bring your firing hand to establish a good pistol grip, move your support hand to the side and just in front of your face with your palm facing to your dominant side, at the same time draw your pistol straight up just under your arm pit and rotate pistol towards target (5 point) A Zone body box. When you point your pistol at the target, lean the slide away from your body just enough so when fired from that position, it will not contact your clothing or chest causing a malfunction.

Fire 2 rounds from retention into the A Zone body box, <u>carefully</u> take 2 steps diagonally back to the left or right, taking up a two-handed grip, fire 2 more rounds in the (5 point) A Zone body box then 1 final round to the ocular Z box, while moving back. Record time for each rep and score. Perform drill moving in each direction twice, 2 right, 2 left. Make sure at no point, does your pistol point at any body part while performing drill. Start out slow and increase speed as you gain proficiency.

Goals: Meat Bag: To safely perform shooting from retention and getting off line smoothly and deliberately.   Survivor: 80 Points   Z Fighter: 100 Points

Variations:

⊕ Infected Humans: Continue to moving backwards diagonally while firing.

⊕ Mutants: Perform 5 push ups. Add a second ZIPSC target.

STEPHAN AND THE FAT MAN

Date:	B.Z.	Battle Ground:	Pistol	Undead / Infected / Mutant
Left 1 Time:		Right 1 Time:	Cover Garment: Y / N	Notes:
Left 2 Time:		Right 2 Time:	**Total Score:**	

Date:	B.Z.	Battle Ground:	Pistol	Undead / Infected / Mutant
Left 1 Time:		Right 1 Time:	Cover Garment: Y / N	Notes:
Left 2 Time:		Right 2 Time:	**Total Score:**	

Date:	B.Z.	Battle Ground:	Pistol	Undead / Infected / Mutant
Left 1 Time:		Right 1 Time:	Cover Garment: Y / N	Notes:
Left 2 Time:		Right 2 Time:	**Total Score:**	

Date:	B.Z.	Battle Ground:	Pistol	Undead / Infected / Mutant
Left 1 Time:		Right 1 Time:	Cover Garment: Y / N	Notes:
Left 2 Time:		Right 2 Time:	**Total Score:**	

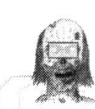

Date:	B.Z.	Battle Ground:	Pistol	Undead / Infected / Mutant
Left 1 Time:		Right 1 Time:	Cover Garment: Y / N	Notes:
Left 2 Time:		Right 2 Time:	**Total Score:**	

Z Fighter ©

STEPHAN AND THE FAT MAN

Date:	B.Z.	Battle Ground:	Pistol	Undead / Infected / Mutant
Left 1 Time:		Right 1 Time:	Cover Garment: Y / N	Notes:
Left 2 Time:		Right 2 Time:	**Total Score:**	

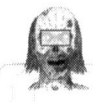

Date:	B.Z.	Battle Ground:	Pistol	Undead / Infected / Mutant
Left 1 Time:		Right 1 Time:	Cover Garment: Y / N	Notes:
Left 2 Time:		Right 2 Time:	**Total Score:**	

Date:	B.Z.	Battle Ground:	Pistol	Undead / Infected / Mutant
Left 1 Time:		Right 1 Time:	Cover Garment: Y / N	Notes:
Left 2 Time:		Right 2 Time:	**Total Score:**	

Date:	B.Z.	Battle Ground:	Pistol	Undead / Infected / Mutant
Left 1 Time:		Right 1 Time:	Cover Garment: Y / N	Notes:
Left 2 Time:		Right 2 Time:	**Total Score:**	

Date:	B.Z.	Battle Ground:	Pistol	Undead / Infected / Mutant
Left 1 Time:		Right 1 Time:	Cover Garment: Y / N	Notes:
Left 2 Time:		Right 2 Time:	**Total Score:**	

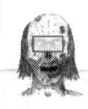

STEPHAN AND THE FAT MAN

Date:	B.Z.	Battle Ground:	Pistol	Undead / Infected / Mutant
Left 1 Time:		Right 1 Time:	Cover Garment: Y / N	Notes:
Left 2 Time:		Right 2 Time:	**Total Score:**	

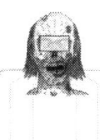

Date:	B.Z.	Battle Ground:	Pistol	Undead / Infected / Mutant
Left 1 Time:		Right 1 Time:	Cover Garment: Y / N	Notes:
Left 2 Time:		Right 2 Time:	**Total Score:**	

Date:	B.Z.	Battle Ground:	Pistol	Undead / Infected / Mutant
Left 1 Time:		Right 1 Time:	Cover Garment: Y / N	Notes:
Left 2 Time:		Right 2 Time:	**Total Score:**	

Date:	B.Z.	Battle Ground:	Pistol	Undead / Infected / Mutant
Left 1 Time:		Right 1 Time:	Cover Garment: Y / N	Notes:
Left 2 Time:		Right 2 Time:	**Total Score:**	

Date:	B.Z.	Battle Ground:	Pistol	Undead / Infected / Mutant
Left 1 Time:		Right 1 Time:	Cover Garment: Y / N	Notes:
Left 2 Time:		Right 2 Time:	**Total Score:**	

Z Fighter ©

Pistol Drills - 11

STEPHAN AND THE FAT MAN

Date:	B.Z.	Battle Ground:	Pistol	Undead / Infected / Mutant
Left 1 Time:		Right 1 Time:	Cover Garment: Y / N	Notes:
Left 2 Time:		Right 2 Time:	**Total Score:**	

Date:	B.Z.	Battle Ground:	Pistol	Undead / Infected / Mutant
Left 1 Time:		Right 1 Time:	Cover Garment: Y / N	Notes:
Left 2 Time:		Right 2 Time:	**Total Score:**	

Date:	B.Z.	Battle Ground:	Pistol	Undead / Infected / Mutant
Left 1 Time:		Right 1 Time:	Cover Garment: Y / N	Notes:
Left 2 Time:		Right 2 Time:	**Total Score:**	

Date:	B.Z.	Battle Ground:	Pistol	Undead / Infected / Mutant
Left 1 Time:		Right 1 Time:	Cover Garment: Y / N	Notes:
Left 2 Time:		Right 2 Time:	**Total Score:**	

Date:	B.Z.	Battle Ground:	Pistol	Undead / Infected / Mutant
Left 1 Time:		Right 1 Time:	Cover Garment: Y / N	Notes:
Left 2 Time:		Right 2 Time:	**Total Score:**	

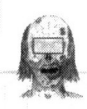

STEPHAN AND THE FAT MAN

Date:	B.Z.	Battle Ground:	Pistol	Undead / Infected / Mutant
Left 1 Time:		Right 1 Time:	Cover Garment: Y / N	Notes:
Left 2 Time:		Right 2 Time:	**Total Score:**	

Date:	B.Z.	Battle Ground:	Pistol	Undead / Infected / Mutant
Left 1 Time:		Right 1 Time:	Cover Garment: Y / N	Notes:
Left 2 Time:		Right 2 Time:	**Total Score:**	

Date:	B.Z.	Battle Ground:	Pistol	Undead / Infected / Mutant
Left 1 Time:		Right 1 Time:	Cover Garment: Y / N	Notes:
Left 2 Time:		Right 2 Time:	**Total Score:**	

Date:	B.Z.	Battle Ground:	Pistol	Undead / Infected / Mutant
Left 1 Time:		Right 1 Time:	Cover Garment: Y / N	Notes:
Left 2 Time:		Right 2 Time:	**Total Score:**	

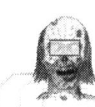

Date:	B.Z.	Battle Ground:	Pistol	Undead / Infected / Mutant
Left 1 Time:		Right 1 Time:	Cover Garment: Y / N	Notes:
Left 2 Time:		Right 2 Time:	**Total Score:**	

PISTOL DRILL: YOU HAVE TO FIGHT FOR YOUR RIGHT...

Purpose: Creating pistol fighting distance while engaging in hand to hand combat.

Distance: 0-3 Yards.

Target: ZIPSC (Undead).

Extra Equipment Needed: Shot timer.

Rounds Fired Per Rep: 1 Rounds

Total Rounds Fired: 4 Rounds.

Point Penalty: Live or Die

Repetitions: 4 Reps.

Starting Position & Condition: Standing, surrender / interview position within 1 arms reach of target. Condition 1 holstered pistol.

Description: At the timer beep, simulate a hand to hand combat fight by performing 3 push ups. *Push ups are on the clock, do them quickly** Upon completion stand then immediately push off from the target with your support hand. While carefully taking 2-3 steps backwards, simultaneously retracting your support hand towards your chest, draw your pistol into a 2 handed grip, aim then fire 1 round into the head ocular Z box. Rounds must impact inside A/Z box under goal par time to survive.

NOTE: Keep the stapler handy on this drill, you'll need to replace Z heads from muzzle blast.

Goals: Meat Bag: 10 Seconds.   Survivor: 6.5 Seconds.   Z Fighter: 5 Seconds.

Variations:

⊕ Infected Humans: Perform 4 push ups and take 3-4 steps backwards while firing 2 rounds into the A zone body box and 1 round into the ocular Z box. Add 1 second to goal par times.

⊕ Mutants: Perform 5 push ups and take 3 - 4 steps left or right while firing 2 - 5 rounds into the A zone body box and 1 round into the head Z box.

YOU HAVE TO FIGHT FOR YOUR RIGHT...

Date:		B.Z.	Battle Ground:			Pistol:		
Rep 1 Time:	Live	/ Die	Rep 1 Time:	Live	/ Die	Undead / Infect Human / Mutant	
Rep 2 Time:	Live	/ Die	Rep 2 Time:	Live	/ Die	Notes:		
Rep 3 Time:	Live	/ Die	Rep 3 Time:	Live	/ Die			
Rep 4 Time:	Live	/ Die	Rep 4 Time:	Live	/ Die	# Of Misses & Shots Over Par:		
Rep 5 Time:	Live	/ Die	Rep 5 Time:	Live	/ Die	**Total Score:**		

Date:		B.Z.	Battle Ground:			Pistol:		
Rep 1 Time:	Live	/ Die	Rep 1 Time:	Live	/ Die	Undead / Infect Human / Mutant	
Rep 2 Time:	Live	/ Die	Rep 2 Time:	Live	/ Die	Notes:		
Rep 3 Time:	Live	/ Die	Rep 3 Time:	Live	/ Die			
Rep 4 Time:	Live	/ Die	Rep 4 Time:	Live	/ Die	# Of Misses & Shots Over Par:		
Rep 5 Time:	Live	/ Die	Rep 5 Time:	Live	/ Die	**Total Score:**		

Date:		B.Z.	Battle Ground:			Pistol:		
Rep 1 Time:	Live	/ Die	Rep 1 Time:	Live	/ Die	Undead / Infect Human / Mutant	
Rep 2 Time:	Live	/ Die	Rep 2 Time:	Live	/ Die	Notes:		
Rep 3 Time:	Live	/ Die	Rep 3 Time:	Live	/ Die			
Rep 4 Time:	Live	/ Die	Rep 4 Time:	Live	/ Die	# Of Misses & Shots Over Par:		
Rep 5 Time:	Live	/ Die	Rep 5 Time:	Live	/ Die	**Total Score:**		

Z Fighter ©

YOU HAVE TO FIGHT FOR YOUR RIGHT...

Date:		B.Z.	Battle Ground:			Pistol:		
Rep 1 Time:	Live	/ Die	Rep 1 Time:	Live	/ Die	Undead	/ Infect Human	/ Mutant
Rep 2 Time:	Live	/ Die	Rep 2 Time:	Live	/ Die	Notes:		
Rep 3 Time:	Live	/ Die	Rep 3 Time:	Live	/ Die			
Rep 4 Time:	Live	/ Die	Rep 4 Time:	Live	/ Die	# Of Misses & Shots Over Par:		
Rep 5 Time:	Live	/ Die	Rep 5 Time:	Live	/ Die	**Total Score:**		

Date:		B.Z.	Battle Ground:			Pistol:		
Rep 1 Time:	Live	/ Die	Rep 1 Time:	Live	/ Die	Undead	/ Infect Human	/ Mutant
Rep 2 Time:	Live	/ Die	Rep 2 Time:	Live	/ Die	Notes:		
Rep 3 Time:	Live	/ Die	Rep 3 Time:	Live	/ Die			
Rep 4 Time:	Live	/ Die	Rep 4 Time:	Live	/ Die	# Of Misses & Shots Over Par:		
Rep 5 Time:	Live	/ Die	Rep 5 Time:	Live	/ Die	**Total Score:**		

Date:		B.Z.	Battle Ground:			Pistol:		
Rep 1 Time:	Live	/ Die	Rep 1 Time:	Live	/ Die	Undead	/ Infect Human	/ Mutant
Rep 2 Time:	Live	/ Die	Rep 2 Time:	Live	/ Die	Notes:		
Rep 3 Time:	Live	/ Die	Rep 3 Time:	Live	/ Die			
Rep 4 Time:	Live	/ Die	Rep 4 Time:	Live	/ Die	# Of Misses & Shots Over Par:		
Rep 5 Time:	Live	/ Die	Rep 5 Time:	Live	/ Die	**Total Score:**		

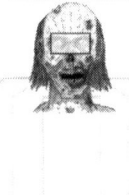

YOU HAVE TO FIGHT FOR YOUR RIGHT...

Date:		B.Z.	Battle Ground:			Pistol:		
Rep 1 Time:		Live / Die	Rep 1 Time:		Live / Die	Undead / Infect Human / Mutant		
Rep 2 Time:		Live / Die	Rep 2 Time:		Live / Die	Notes:		
Rep 3 Time:		Live / Die	Rep 3 Time:		Live / Die			
Rep 4 Time:		Live / Die	Rep 4 Time:		Live / Die	# Of Misses & Shots Over Par:		
Rep 5 Time:		Live / Die	Rep 5 Time:		Live / Die	**Total Score:**		

Date:		B.Z.	Battle Ground:			Pistol:		
Rep 1 Time:		Live / Die	Rep 1 Time:		Live / Die	Undead / Infect Human / Mutant		
Rep 2 Time:		Live / Die	Rep 2 Time:		Live / Die	Notes:		
Rep 3 Time:		Live / Die	Rep 3 Time:		Live / Die			
Rep 4 Time:		Live / Die	Rep 4 Time:		Live / Die	# Of Misses & Shots Over Par:		
Rep 5 Time:		Live / Die	Rep 5 Time:		Live / Die	**Total Score:**		

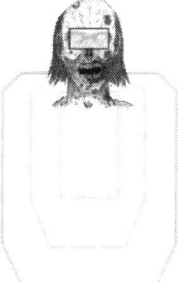

Date:		B.Z.	Battle Ground:			Pistol:		
Rep 1 Time:		Live / Die	Rep 1 Time:		Live / Die	Undead / Infect Human / Mutant		
Rep 2 Time:		Live / Die	Rep 2 Time:		Live / Die	Notes:		
Rep 3 Time:		Live / Die	Rep 3 Time:		Live / Die			
Rep 4 Time:		Live / Die	Rep 4 Time:		Live / Die	# Of Misses & Shots Over Par:		
Rep 5 Time:		Live / Die	Rep 5 Time:		Live / Die	**Total Score:**		

Z Fighter ©

Pistol Drills - 12

YOU HAVE TO FIGHT FOR YOUR RIGHT...

Date:		B.Z.	Battle Ground:			Pistol:		
Rep 1 Time:		Live / Die	Rep 1 Time:		Live / Die	Undead / Infect Human / Mutant		
Rep 2 Time:		Live / Die	Rep 2 Time:		Live / Die	Notes:		
Rep 3 Time:		Live / Die	Rep 3 Time:		Live / Die			
Rep 4 Time:		Live / Die	Rep 4 Time:		Live / Die	# Of Misses & Shots Over Par:		
Rep 5 Time:		Live / Die	Rep 5 Time:		Live / Die	**Total Score:**		

Date:		B.Z.	Battle Ground:			Pistol:		
Rep 1 Time:		Live / Die	Rep 1 Time:		Live / Die	Undead / Infect Human / Mutant		
Rep 2 Time:		Live / Die	Rep 2 Time:		Live / Die	Notes:		
Rep 3 Time:		Live / Die	Rep 3 Time:		Live / Die			
Rep 4 Time:		Live / Die	Rep 4 Time:		Live / Die	# Of Misses & Shots Over Par:		
Rep 5 Time:		Live / Die	Rep 5 Time:		Live / Die	**Total Score:**		

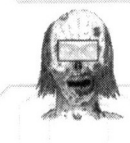

Date:		B.Z.	Battle Ground:			Pistol:		
Rep 1 Time:		Live / Die	Rep 1 Time:		Live / Die	Undead / Infect Human / Mutant		
Rep 2 Time:		Live / Die	Rep 2 Time:		Live / Die	Notes:		
Rep 3 Time:		Live / Die	Rep 3 Time:		Live / Die			
Rep 4 Time:		Live / Die	Rep 4 Time:		Live / Die	# Of Misses & Shots Over Par:		
Rep 5 Time:		Live / Die	Rep 5 Time:		Live / Die	**Total Score:**		

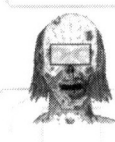

YOU HAVE TO FIGHT FOR YOUR RIGHT...

Date:		B.Z.	Battle Ground:			Pistol:		
Rep 1 Time:	Live	/ Die	Rep 1 Time:	Live	/ Die	Undead / Infect Human / Mutant		
Rep 2 Time:	Live	/ Die	Rep 2 Time:	Live	/ Die	Notes:		
Rep 3 Time:	Live	/ Die	Rep 3 Time:	Live	/ Die			
Rep 4 Time:	Live	/ Die	Rep 4 Time:	Live	/ Die	# Of Misses & Shots Over Par:		
Rep 5 Time:	Live	/ Die	Rep 5 Time:	Live	/ Die	**Total Score:**		

Date:		B.Z.	Battle Ground:			Pistol:		
Rep 1 Time:	Live	/ Die	Rep 1 Time:	Live	/ Die	Undead / Infect Human / Mutant		
Rep 2 Time:	Live	/ Die	Rep 2 Time:	Live	/ Die	Notes:		
Rep 3 Time:	Live	/ Die	Rep 3 Time:	Live	/ Die			
Rep 4 Time:	Live	/ Die	Rep 4 Time:	Live	/ Die	# Of Misses & Shots Over Par:		
Rep 5 Time:	Live	/ Die	Rep 5 Time:	Live	/ Die	**Total Score:**		

Date:		B.Z.	Battle Ground:			Pistol:		
Rep 1 Time:	Live	/ Die	Rep 1 Time:	Live	/ Die	Undead / Infect Human / Mutant		
Rep 2 Time:	Live	/ Die	Rep 2 Time:	Live	/ Die	Notes:		
Rep 3 Time:	Live	/ Die	Rep 3 Time:	Live	/ Die			
Rep 4 Time:	Live	/ Die	Rep 4 Time:	Live	/ Die	# Of Misses & Shots Over Par:		
Rep 5 Time:	Live	/ Die	Rep 5 Time:	Live	/ Die	**Total Score:**		

PISTOL DRILL: VICTOR ACTUAL

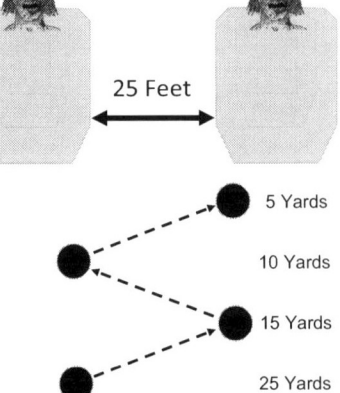

Purpose: Develop accuracy and speed from moving at a high rate of speed rom cover position to cover position.

Distance: 25, 15, 10, 5 Yards.   **Target:** ZIPSC X2 spaced 25 feet apart.

Par Time: Per goal standard.

Extra Equipment Needed: Shot timer, 2 magazines of 8 rounds each, position markers or optional barriers/barricades.

Rounds Fired Per Yard Marker: 4 Rounds.   **Total Rounds Fired:** 16 Rounds.

Point Penalty: Time plus 2 seconds for every hit in the 3 scoring zone, add plus 5 seconds for any misses off silhouette.

Starting Position & Condition: Standing – Hands to side or interview. Weapon Condition 1.

Description: Starting at the 25 yard maker/barricade, at the timer beep, draw and fire 2 rounds into the (5 point) A Zone body box of each target. While safely controlling your pistol, quickly move to the 15 yard marker/barricade, fire 2 rounds into the (5 point) A Zone body box of each target. Quickly move to the 10 yard marker/barricade, fire 2 rounds into the (5 point) A Zone body box of each target. Quickly move to the 5 yard marker/marker, fire 2 rounds into the (5 point) ocular Z box of each target. Re-load as needed. Record repetition time, score and penalties. For every hit in the 3 scoring zone, add 2 seconds to your time. For every hit in the 0 scoring zone, add 5 seconds to your time.

Follow the firearm safety rules, keep your pistol pointed in the direction of the target during movement or in a safe position.

Goals: 60 Seconds.   Expert: 50 Seconds.   Gunfighter: 40 Seconds.

Variations:

⊕ Infected Humans: 2 shots to the body A Box and 1 to the ocular Z box to each target at every yard line marker. 24 Rounds total.

⊕ Mutants: 4 shots to the body A Box and 1 to the ocular Z box to each target at every yard line marker. 40 Rounds total.

VICTOR ACTUAL

Date: :	B.Z.	Weapon:	Sights:	Holster:	Cover Garment: Y / N
Undead / Infected / Mutant			Notes:		
Time: Sec		# in A Zone:	# in 3 Zone:	# Outside Body:	**Total Score:** Sec

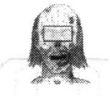

Date: :	B.Z.	Weapon:	Sights:	Holster:	Cover Garment: Y / N
Undead / Infected / Mutant			Notes:		
Time: Sec		# in A Zone:	# in 3 Zone:	# Outside Body:	**Total Score:** Sec

Date: :	B.Z.	Weapon:	Sights:	Holster:	Cover Garment: Y / N
Undead / Infected / Mutant			Notes:		
Time: Sec		# in A Zone:	# in 3 Zone:	# Outside Body:	**Total Score:** Sec

Date: :	B.Z.	Weapon:	Sights:	Holster:	Cover Garment: Y / N
Undead / Infected / Mutant			Notes:		
Time: Sec		# in A Zone:	# in 3 Zone:	# Outside Body:	**Total Score:** Sec

Z Fighter ©

Pistol Drills - 13

VICTOR ACTUAL

Date: :	B.Z.	Weapon:	Sights:	Holster:	Cover Garment: Y / N
Undead / Infected / Mutant			Notes:		
Time:	Sec	# in A Zone:	# in 3 Zone:	# Outside Body:	Total Score: Sec

 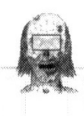

Date: :	B.Z.	Weapon:	Sights:	Holster:	Cover Garment: Y / N
Undead / Infected / Mutant			Notes:		
Time:	Sec	# in A Zone:	# in 3 Zone:	# Outside Body:	Total Score: Sec

Date: :	B.Z.	Weapon:	Sights:	Holster:	Cover Garment: Y / N
Undead / Infected / Mutant			Notes:		
Time:	Sec	# in A Zone:	# in 3 Zone:	# Outside Body:	Total Score: Sec

Date: :	B.Z.	Weapon:	Sights:	Holster:	Cover Garment: Y / N
Undead / Infected / Mutant			Notes:		
Time:	Sec	# in A Zone:	# in 3 Zone:	# Outside Body:	Total Score: Sec

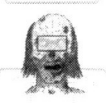 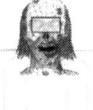

VICTOR ACTUAL

Date: :	B.Z.	Weapon:	Sights:	Holster:	Cover Garment: Y / N
Undead / Infected / Mutant			Notes:		
Time:	Sec	# in A Zone:	# in 3 Zone:	# Outside Body:	**Total Score:** Sec

Date: :	B.Z.	Weapon:	Sights:	Holster:	Cover Garment: Y / N
Undead / Infected / Mutant			Notes:		
Time:	Sec	# in A Zone:	# in 3 Zone:	# Outside Body:	**Total Score:** Sec

Date: :	B.Z.	Weapon:	Sights:	Holster:	Cover Garment: Y / N
Undead / Infected / Mutant			Notes:		
Time:	Sec	# in A Zone:	# in 3 Zone:	# Outside Body:	**Total Score:** Sec

Date: :	B.Z.	Weapon:	Sights:	Holster:	Cover Garment: Y / N
Undead / Infected / Mutant			Notes:		
Time:	Sec	# in A Zone:	# in 3 Zone:	# Outside Body:	**Total Score:** Sec

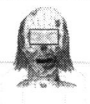 

Z Fighter ©

Pistol Drills - 13

VICTOR ACTUAL

Date: :	B.Z.	Weapon:	Sights:	Holster:	Cover Garment: Y / N
Undead / Infected / Mutant			Notes:		
Time:	Sec	# in A Zone:	# in 3 Zone:	# Outside Body:	Total Score: Sec

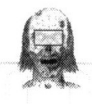 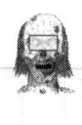

Date: :	B.Z.	Weapon:	Sights:	Holster:	Cover Garment: Y / N
Undead / Infected / Mutant			Notes:		
Time:	Sec	# in A Zone:	# in 3 Zone:	# Outside Body:	Total Score: Sec

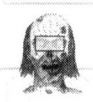

Date: :	B.Z.	Weapon:	Sights:	Holster:	Cover Garment: Y / N
Undead / Infected / Mutant			Notes:		
Time:	Sec	# in A Zone:	# in 3 Zone:	# Outside Body:	Total Score: Sec

Date: :	B.Z.	Weapon:	Sights:	Holster:	Cover Garment: Y / N
Undead / Infected / Mutant			Notes:		
Time:	Sec	# in A Zone:	# in 3 Zone:	# Outside Body:	Total Score: Sec

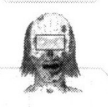 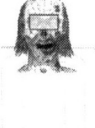

www.GUNFIGHTERSERIES.com ©

VICTOR ACTUAL

Date: :	B.Z.	Weapon:	Sights:	Holster:	Cover Garment: Y / N
Undead / Infected / Mutant			Notes:		
Time:	Sec	# in A Zone:	# in 3 Zone:	# Outside Body:	**Total Score:** Sec

Date: :	B.Z.	Weapon:	Sights:	Holster:	Cover Garment: Y / N
Undead / Infected / Mutant			Notes:		
Time:	Sec	# in A Zone:	# in 3 Zone:	# Outside Body:	**Total Score:** Sec

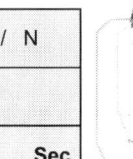

Date: :	B.Z.	Weapon:	Sights:	Holster:	Cover Garment: Y / N
Undead / Infected / Mutant			Notes:		
Time:	Sec	# in A Zone:	# in 3 Zone:	# Outside Body:	**Total Score:** Sec

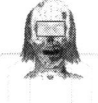

Date: :	B.Z.	Weapon:	Sights:	Holster:	Cover Garment: Y / N
Undead / Infected / Mutant			Notes:		
Time:	Sec	# in A Zone:	# in 3 Zone:	# Outside Body:	**Total Score:** Sec

Z Fighter ©

Pistol Drills - 13

PISTOL DRILL: DEAD SPRINT

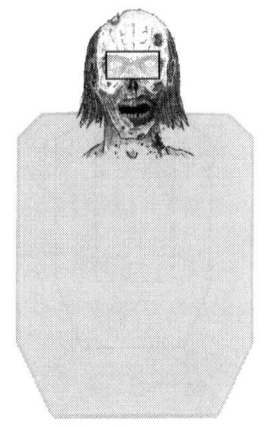

Purpose: Accuracy with stress.

Distance: 25, 20, 15, 10, and 5 Yards.

Target: ZIPSC

Extra Equipment Needed: Shot timer.

Rounds Fired Per Yard Line: 1 Round.

Total Rounds Fired: 5 Rounds.

Point Penalty: Time plus penalty.

Starting Position & Condition: Standing, Surrender / Interview position. Condition 1. Holstered.

Description: From the 25 yard line, at the timer beep, run to the target then back to the 25 yard line. Draw and fire 1 round into the ocular Z box. Holster your pistol, run to the target then back to the 20 yard line. Draw and fire 1 round into the ocular Z box. Holster your pistol, run to the target then back to the 15 yard line. Draw and fire 1 round into the ocular Z box. Holster your pistol, run to the target then back to the 10 yard line. Draw and fire 1 round into the ocular Z box. Holster your pistol, run to the target then back to the 5 yard line. Draw and fire 1 round into the ocular Z box. Reload as needed. Record last shot time plus penalties. Add 3 seconds for each round outside A / Z box. Add 5 seconds for each round outside body.

Goals: Meat Bag: 125 Seconds.   Survivor: 100 Seconds.   Z Fighter: 75 Seconds.

Variations:

⊕ Infected Humans: 2 Shots to the A zone body box and 1 round to the ocular Z box to each target at every yard line marker. 15 Rounds total.

⊕ Mutants: Same as Infected Humans, but in reverse order starting at the 5 yard line with 3 magazines of 5 rounds each.

DEAD SPRINT

Date:	B.Z.	Battle Ground:	Weapon:	Sights:	Undead / Infected / Mutant
Time:	Sec	# in A/Z Zone:	# in 3 Zone.	# Off Target:	Total Score: Sec

Date:	B.Z.	Battle Ground:	Weapon:	Sights:	Undead / Infected / Mutant
Time:	Sec	# in A/Z Zone:	# in 3 Zone.	# Off Target:	Total Score: Sec

Date:	B.Z.	Battle Ground:	Weapon:	Sights:	Undead / Infected / Mutant
Time:	Sec	# in A/Z Zone:	# in 3 Zone.	# Off Target:	Total Score: Sec

Date:	B.Z.	Battle Ground:	Weapon:	Sights:	Undead / Infected / Mutant
Time:	Sec	# in A/Z Zone:	# in 3 Zone.	# Off Target:	Total Score: Sec

Date:	B.Z.	Battle Ground:	Weapon:	Sights:	Undead / Infected / Mutant
Time:	Sec	# in A/Z Zone:	# in 3 Zone.	# Off Target:	Total Score: Sec

Z Fighter ©

Pistol Drills - 14

www.GUNFIGHTERSERIES.com ©

DEAD SPRINT

Date:	B.Z.	Battle Ground:	Weapon:	Sights:	Undead / Infected / Mutant
Time:	Sec	# in A/Z Zone:	# in 3 Zone.	# Off Target:	**Total Score:** **Sec**

Date:	B.Z.	Battle Ground:	Weapon:	Sights:	Undead / Infected / Mutant
Time:	Sec	# in A/Z Zone:	# in 3 Zone.	# Off Target:	**Total Score:** **Sec**

Date:	B.Z.	Battle Ground:	Weapon:	Sights:	Undead / Infected / Mutant
Time:	Sec	# in A/Z Zone:	# in 3 Zone.	# Off Target:	**Total Score:** **Sec**

Date:	B.Z.	Battle Ground:	Weapon:	Sights:	Undead / Infected / Mutant
Time:	Sec	# in A/Z Zone:	# in 3 Zone.	# Off Target:	**Total Score:** **Sec**

Date:	B.Z.	Battle Ground:	Weapon:	Sights:	Undead / Infected / Mutant
Time:	Sec	# in A/Z Zone:	# in 3 Zone.	# Off Target:	**Total Score:** **Sec**

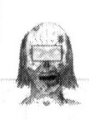

DEAD SPRINT

Date:	B.Z.	Battle Ground:	Weapon:	Sights:	Undead / Infected / Mutant
Time:	Sec	# in A/Z Zone:	# in 3 Zone.	# Off Target:	Total Score: Sec

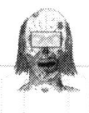

Date:	B.Z.	Battle Ground:	Weapon:	Sights:	Undead / Infected / Mutant
Time:	Sec	# in A/Z Zone:	# in 3 Zone.	# Off Target:	Total Score: Sec

Date:	B.Z.	Battle Ground:	Weapon:	Sights:	Undead / Infected / Mutant
Time:	Sec	# in A/Z Zone:	# in 3 Zone.	# Off Target:	Total Score: Sec

Date:	B.Z.	Battle Ground:	Weapon:	Sights:	Undead / Infected / Mutant
Time:	Sec	# in A/Z Zone:	# in 3 Zone.	# Off Target:	Total Score: Sec

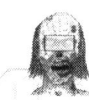

Date:	B.Z.	Battle Ground:	Weapon:	Sights:	Undead / Infected / Mutant
Time:	Sec	# in A/Z Zone:	# in 3 Zone.	# Off Target:	Total Score: Sec

Pistol Drills - 14

DEAD SPRINT

Date:	B.Z.	Battle Ground:	Weapon:	Sights:	Undead / Infected / Mutant
Time:	Sec	# in A/Z Zone:	# in 3 Zone.	# Off Target:	**Total Score:** **Sec**

Date:	B.Z.	Battle Ground:	Weapon:	Sights:	Undead / Infected / Mutant
Time:	Sec	# in A/Z Zone:	# in 3 Zone.	# Off Target:	**Total Score:** **Sec**

Date:	B.Z.	Battle Ground:	Weapon:	Sights:	Undead / Infected / Mutant
Time:	Sec	# in A/Z Zone:	# in 3 Zone.	# Off Target:	**Total Score:** **Sec**

Date:	B.Z.	Battle Ground:	Weapon:	Sights:	Undead / Infected / Mutant
Time:	Sec	# in A/Z Zone:	# in 3 Zone.	# Off Target:	**Total Score:** **Sec**

Date:	B.Z.	Battle Ground:	Weapon:	Sights:	Undead / Infected / Mutant
Time:	Sec	# in A/Z Zone:	# in 3 Zone.	# Off Target:	**Total Score:** **Sec**

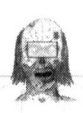

DEAD SPRINT

Date:	B.Z.	Battle Ground:	Weapon:	Sights:	Undead / Infected / Mutant	
Time:	Sec	# in A/Z Zone:	# in 3 Zone.	# Off Target:	**Total Score:**	**Sec**

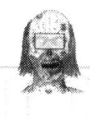

Date:	B.Z.	Battle Ground:	Weapon:	Sights:	Undead / Infected / Mutant	
Time:	Sec	# in A/Z Zone:	# in 3 Zone.	# Off Target:	**Total Score:**	**Sec**

Date:	B.Z.	Battle Ground:	Weapon:	Sights:	Undead / Infected / Mutant	
Time:	Sec	# in A/Z Zone:	# in 3 Zone.	# Off Target:	**Total Score:**	**Sec**

Date:	B.Z.	Battle Ground:	Weapon:	Sights:	Undead / Infected / Mutant	
Time:	Sec	# in A/Z Zone:	# in 3 Zone.	# Off Target:	**Total Score:**	**Sec**

Date:	B.Z.	Battle Ground:	Weapon:	Sights:	Undead / Infected / Mutant	
Time:	Sec	# in A/Z Zone:	# in 3 Zone.	# Off Target:	**Total Score:**	**Sec**

Z Fighter ©

Pistol Drills - 14

PISTOL DRILL:

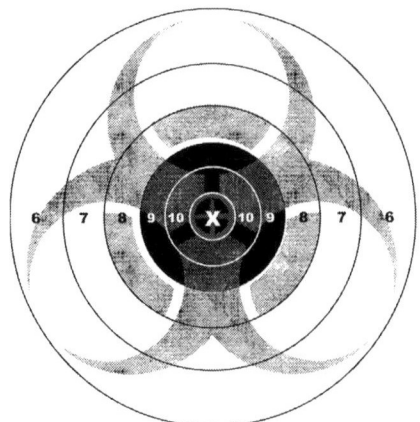

Purpose: Accuracy while moving.

Distance: 10 to 3 Yards.

Target: ZF-2 (Undead)

Rounds Fired Per Distance: 5 Rounds.

Total Rounds Fired: 15 Rounds.

Point Penalty: As per target score.

Repetitions: 3 Reps.

Starting Position & Condition: Standing – Any pistol ready position you choose. Condition 1.

Description: At your personal go, from the 10 yard line, begin walking forward firing 5 rounds while in constant motion to the 5 yard line.

Goals: Meat Bag: 100 Points.   Survivor: 120 Points.   Z Fighter: 135 Point with all rounds in the black circle.

Variations:

- Infected Humans: Check behind you for obstructions and trip hazards. At your personal go, from the 3 yard line, carefully begin walking backwards firing 5 rounds while in constant motion to the 10 yard line.

- Mutants: Check around you for obstructions and trip hazards. At your personal go, from the 7 yard line, carefully begin walking 90* of the target left or right firing 5 rounds while in constant motion.

Date:	B.Z.	Battle Ground:	Weapon:	Undead / Infected / Mutant
# of 6's		# of 7's	# of 8's:	Notes:
# of 9's:		# of 10's:	SCORE: # X's	

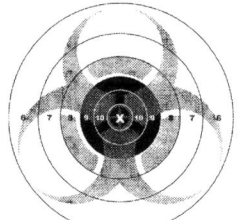

Date:	B.Z.	Battle Ground:	Weapon:	Undead / Infected / Mutant
# of 6's		# of 7's	# of 8's:	Notes:
# of 9's:		# of 10's:	SCORE: # X's	

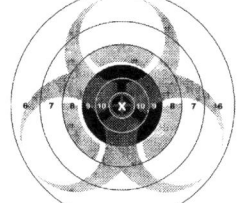

Date:	B.Z.	Battle Ground:	Weapon:	Undead / Infected / Mutant
# of 6's		# of 7's	# of 8's:	Notes:
# of 9's:		# of 10's:	SCORE: # X's	

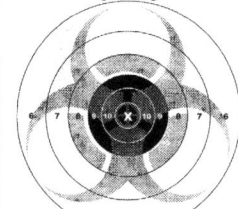

Date:	B.Z.	Battle Ground:	Weapon:	Undead / Infected / Mutant
# of 6's		# of 7's	# of 8's:	Notes:
# of 9's:		# of 10's:	SCORE: # X's	

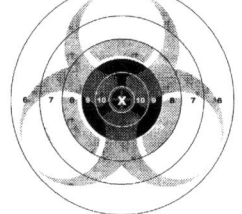

Z Fighter ©

www.GUNFIGHTERSERIES.com ©

Date:	B.Z.	Battle Ground:	Weapon:	Undead / Infected / Mutant
# of 6's		# of 7's	# of 8's:	Notes:
# of 9's:		# of 10's:	**SCORE:** # X's	

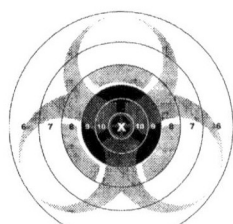

Date:	B.Z.	Battle Ground:	Weapon:	Undead / Infected / Mutant
# of 6's		# of 7's	# of 8's:	Notes:
# of 9's:		# of 10's:	**SCORE:** # X's	

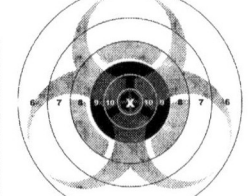

Date:	B.Z.	Battle Ground:	Weapon:	Undead / Infected / Mutant
# of 6's		# of 7's	# of 8's:	Notes:
# of 9's:		# of 10's:	**SCORE:** # X's	

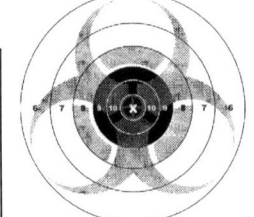

Date:	B.Z.	Battle Ground:	Weapon:	Undead / Infected / Mutant
# of 6's		# of 7's	# of 8's:	Notes:
# of 9's:		# of 10's:	**SCORE:** # X's	

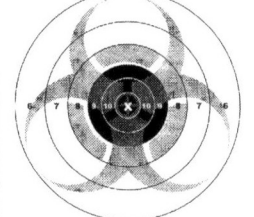

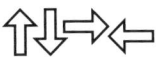

Date:	B.Z.	Battle Ground:	Weapon:	Undead / Infected / Mutant
# of 6's		# of 7's	# of 8's:	Notes:
# of 9's:		# of 10's:	**SCORE:** # X's	

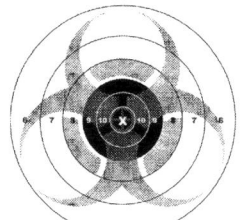

Date:	B.Z.	Battle Ground:	Weapon:	Undead / Infected / Mutant
# of 6's		# of 7's	# of 8's:	Notes:
# of 9's:		# of 10's:	**SCORE:** # X's	

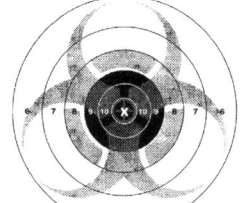

Date:	B.Z.	Battle Ground:	Weapon:	Undead / Infected / Mutant
# of 6's		# of 7's	# of 8's:	Notes:
# of 9's:		# of 10's:	**SCORE:** # X's	

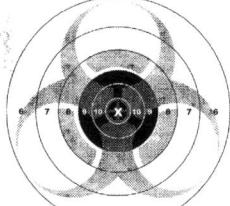

Date:	B.Z.	Battle Ground:	Weapon:	Undead / Infected / Mutant
# of 6's		# of 7's	# of 8's:	Notes:
# of 9's:		# of 10's:	**SCORE:** # X's	

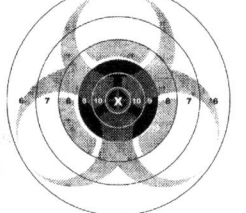

Z Fighter ©

Pistol Drills - 15

www.GUNFIGHTERSERIES.com ©

Date:	B.Z.	Battle Ground:	Weapon:	Undead / Infected / Mutant
# of 6's:		# of 7's:	# of 8's:	Notes:
# of 9's:		# of 10's:	SCORE: # X's	

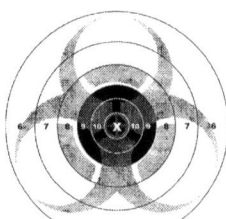

Date:	B.Z.	Battle Ground:	Weapon:	Undead / Infected / Mutant
# of 6's:		# of 7's:	# of 8's:	Notes:
# of 9's:		# of 10's:	SCORE: # X's	

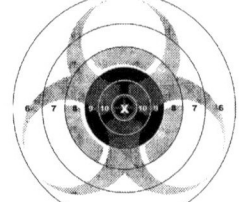

Date:	B.Z.	Battle Ground:	Weapon:	Undead / Infected / Mutant
# of 6's:		# of 7's:	# of 8's:	Notes:
# of 9's:		# of 10's:	SCORE: # X's	

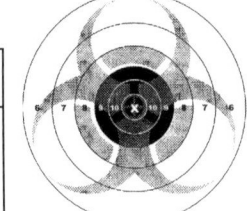

Date:	B.Z.	Battle Ground:	Weapon:	Undead / Infected / Mutant
# of 6's:		# of 7's:	# of 8's:	Notes:
# of 9's:		# of 10's:	SCORE: # X's	

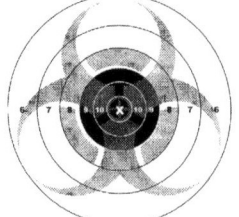

Date:	B.Z.	Battle Ground:	Weapon:	Undead / Infected / Mutant
# of 6's		# of 7's	# of 8's:	Notes:
# of 9's:		# of 10's:	SCORE: # X's	

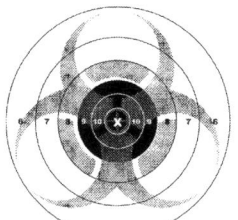

Date:	B.Z.	Battle Ground:	Weapon:	Undead / Infected / Mutant
# of 6's		# of 7's	# of 8's:	Notes:
# of 9's:		# of 10's:	SCORE: # X's	

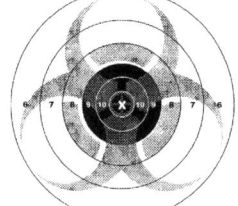

Date:	B.Z.	Battle Ground:	Weapon:	Undead / Infected / Mutant
# of 6's		# of 7's	# of 8's:	Notes:
# of 9's:		# of 10's:	SCORE: # X's	

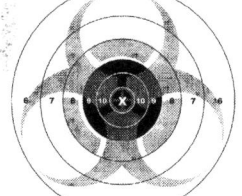

Date:	B.Z.	Battle Ground:	Weapon:	Undead / Infected / Mutant
# of 6's		# of 7's	# of 8's:	Notes:
# of 9's:		# of 10's:	SCORE: # X's	

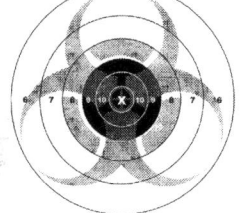

Z Fighter ©   Pistol Drills - 15

CARBINE DRILL: I'M GOOD

Purpose: Develop consistent marksmanship follow through and trigger reset.

Distance: 5 Yards.

Target: Z Dot size per goal standard. (Recommend using the KYL target.)

Rounds Fired Per Rep: 1 Round.

Total Rounds Fired: 10 Rounds.

Point Penalty: Live or Die.

Repetitions: 10 Reps.

Starting Position & Condition: Standing - Carbine aimed at target. Condition 1.

Description: At a personal go, aim at target, fire a shot, while focusing on not moving the sights. Keep the trigger pressed back after the shot and keep your aim on the target after you have pressed the trigger to break the shot. While keeping your finger on the trigger, slowly release the trigger until you hear a click.

Note: You will need to know your close range hold over.

Goals: Meat Bag: All in or touching a 1.5 inch Z dot.   Survivor: All in or touching a 1.25 inch Z dot.   Z Fighter: All in or touching a 1 inch Z dot.

Variations:

⊕ Infected Humans: Engage from 10 yards.

⊕ Mutants: Use 1.25 inch Z dot from 10 yards. Take a side step left or right before each shot.

I'M GOOD

Date:	B.Z.	Weapon:	Sling: Y / N	Undead / Infected / Mutant
Range:	Z Dot Size:	# Outside Circle:	Live / Die	Notes:

Date:	B.Z.	Weapon:	Sling: Y / N	Undead / Infected / Mutant
Range:	Z Dot Size:	# Outside Circle:	Live / Die	Notes:

Date:	B.Z.	Weapon:	Sling: Y / N	Undead / Infected / Mutant
Range:	Z Dot Size:	# Outside Circle:	Live / Die	Notes:

Date:	B.Z.	Weapon:	Sling: Y / N	Undead / Infected / Mutant
Range:	Z Dot Size:	# Outside Circle:	Live / Die	Notes:

Carbine Drills - 1

I'M GOOD

Date:	B.Z.	Weapon:	Sling: Y / N	Undead / Infected / Mutant
Range: Z Dot Size:		# Outside Circle:	Live / Die	Notes:

Date:	B.Z.	Weapon:	Sling: Y / N	Undead / Infected / Mutant
Range: Z Dot Size:		# Outside Circle:	Live / Die	Notes:

Date:	B.Z.	Weapon:	Sling: Y / N	Undead / Infected / Mutant
Range: Z Dot Size:		# Outside Circle:	Live / Die	Notes:

Date:	B.Z.	Weapon:	Sling: Y / N	Undead / Infected / Mutant
Range: Z Dot Size:		# Outside Circle:	Live / Die	Notes:

I'M GOOD

Date:	B.Z.	Weapon:	Sling: Y / N	Undead / Infected / Mutant
Range:	Z Dot Size:	# Outside Circle:	Live / Die	Notes:

Date:	B.Z.	Weapon:	Sling: Y / N	Undead / Infected / Mutant
Range:	Z Dot Size:	# Outside Circle:	Live / Die	Notes:

Date:	B.Z.	Weapon:	Sling: Y / N	Undead / Infected / Mutant
Range:	Z Dot Size:	# Outside Circle:	Live / Die	Notes:

Date:	B.Z.	Weapon:	Sling: Y / N	Undead / Infected / Mutant
Range:	Z Dot Size:	# Outside Circle:	Live / Die	Notes:

Z Fighter ©

Carbine Drills - 1

I'M GOOD

Date:	B.Z.	Weapon:	Sling: Y / N	Undead / Infected / Mutant
Range:	Z Dot Size:	# Outside Circle:	Live / Die	Notes:

Date:	B.Z.	Weapon:	Sling: Y / N	Undead / Infected / Mutant
Range:	Z Dot Size:	# Outside Circle:	Live / Die	Notes:

Date:	B.Z.	Weapon:	Sling: Y / N	Undead / Infected / Mutant
Range:	Z Dot Size:	# Outside Circle:	Live / Die	Notes:

Date:	B.Z.	Weapon:	Sling: Y / N	Undead / Infected / Mutant
Range:	Z Dot Size:	# Outside Circle:	Live / Die	Notes:

I'M GOOD

Date:	B.Z.	Weapon:	Sling: Y / N	Undead / Infected / Mutant
Range:	Z Dot Size:	# Outside Circle:	Live / Die	Notes:

Date:	B.Z.	Weapon:	Sling: Y / N	Undead / Infected / Mutant
Range:	Z Dot Size:	# Outside Circle:	Live / Die	Notes:

Date:	B.Z.	Weapon:	Sling: Y / N	Undead / Infected / Mutant
Range:	Z Dot Size:	# Outside Circle:	Live / Die	Notes:

Date:	B.Z.	Weapon:	Sling: Y / N	Undead / Infected / Mutant
Range:	Z Dot Size:	# Outside Circle:	Live / Die	Notes:

Carbine Drills - 1

CARBINE DRILL: I'M SOLID

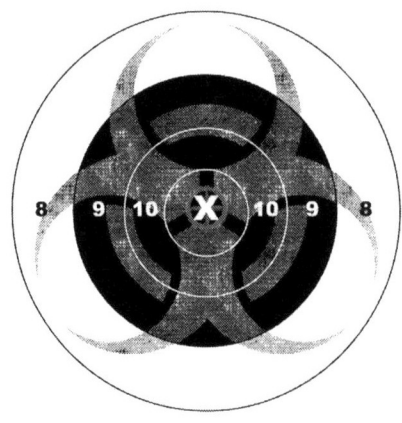

Purpose: Accuracy with long distance hold over.

Distance: 10, 15, 25, 35, and 50 yards.

Target: ZF-1 (Undead)

Rounds Fired Per Distance: 3 Rounds.

Total Rounds Fired: 15 Rounds.

Point Penalty: As per target score.

Repetitions: 1 Rep.

Starting Position & Condition: Standing – Any carbine ready position you choose. Condition 1.

Description: At your personal go, raise your carbine, take good aim and fire 3 rounds into the target from each distance of 10, 15, 25, 35 and 50 yards. The goal is to keep all rounds in the black. Take your time and make every shot count. There is no time limit and if you feel you are going to break a bad shot, stop and start that shot over.

Note: You will need to know your close range hold over.

Goals: Meat Bag: 135 points with all rounds in black. Survivor: 150 Points. Z Fighter: 150 Points with 10 X's.

Variations:

⊕ Infected Humans: 5 Second par time per yard line.

⊕ Mutants: Start the drill at the timer beep. Record entire drill time. Run from yard line to yard line.

I'M SOLID

Date:	B.Z.	Battle Ground:	Weapon:	Undead / Infected / Mutant
# of Misses:		# of 8's:	# of 9's:	Notes:
# of 10's:		Drill Time:	**SCORE:** # X's	

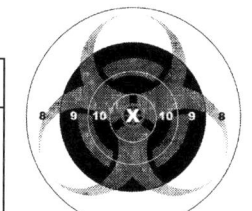

Date:	B.Z.	Battle Ground:	Weapon:	Undead / Infected / Mutant
# of Misses:		# of 8's:	# of 9's:	Notes:
# of 10's:		Drill Time:	**SCORE:** # X's	

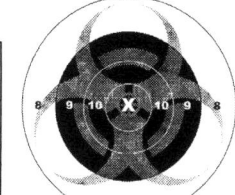

Date:	B.Z.	Battle Ground:	Weapon:	Undead / Infected / Mutant
# of Misses:		# of 8's:	# of 9's:	Notes:
# of 10's:		Drill Time:	**SCORE:** # X's	

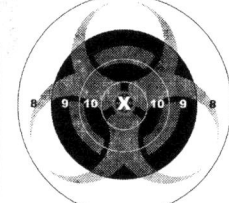

Date:	B.Z.	Battle Ground:	Weapon:	Undead / Infected / Mutant
# of Misses:		# of 8's:	# of 9's:	Notes:
# of 10's:		Drill Time:	**SCORE:** # X's	

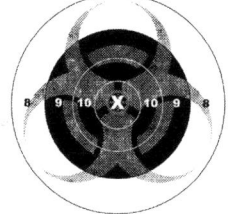

I'M SOLID

Date:	B.Z.	Battle Ground:	Weapon:	Undead / Infected / Mutant
# of Misses:		# of 8's:	# of 9's:	Notes:
# of 10's:		Drill Time:	SCORE: # X's	

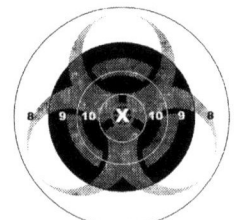

Date:	B.Z.	Battle Ground:	Weapon:	Undead / Infected / Mutant
# of Misses:		# of 8's:	# of 9's:	Notes:
# of 10's:		Drill Time:	SCORE: # X's	

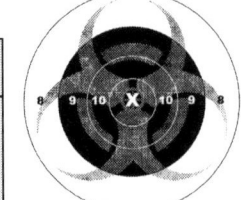

Date:	B.Z.	Battle Ground:	Weapon:	Undead / Infected / Mutant
# of Misses:		# of 8's:	# of 9's:	Notes:
# of 10's:		Drill Time:	SCORE: # X's	

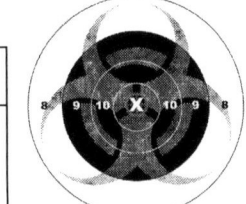

Date:	B.Z.	Battle Ground:	Weapon:	Undead / Infected / Mutant
# of Misses:		# of 8's:	# of 9's:	Notes:
# of 10's:		Drill Time:	SCORE: # X's	

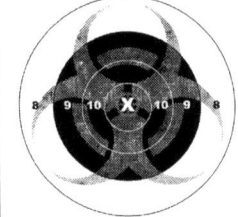

I'M SOLID

Date:	B.Z.	Battle Ground:	Weapon:	Undead / Infected / Mutant
# of Misses:		# of 8's:	# of 9's:	Notes:
# of 10's:		Drill Time:	**SCORE:** # X's	

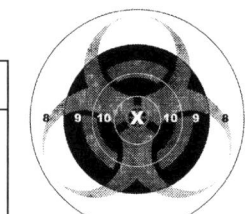

Date:	B.Z.	Battle Ground:	Weapon:	Undead / Infected / Mutant
# of Misses:		# of 8's:	# of 9's:	Notes:
# of 10's:		Drill Time:	**SCORE:** # X's	

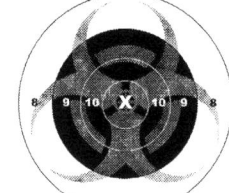

Date:	B.Z.	Battle Ground:	Weapon:	Undead / Infected / Mutant
# of Misses:		# of 8's:	# of 9's:	Notes:
# of 10's:		Drill Time:	**SCORE:** # X's	

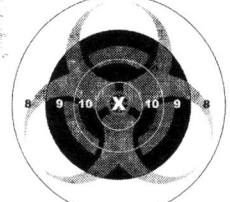

Date:	B.Z.	Battle Ground:	Weapon:	Undead / Infected / Mutant
# of Misses:		# of 8's:	# of 9's:	Notes:
# of 10's:		Drill Time:	**SCORE:** # X's	

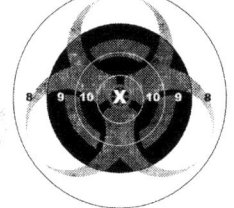

Z Fighter ©

I'M SOLID

Date:	B.Z.	Battle Ground:	Weapon:	Undead / Infected / Mutant
# of Misses:		# of 8's:	# of 9's:	Notes:
# of 10's:		Drill Time:	SCORE: # X's	

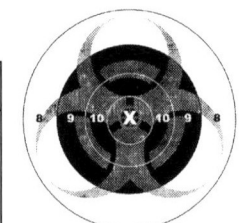

Date:	B.Z.	Battle Ground:	Weapon:	Undead / Infected / Mutant
# of Misses:		# of 8's:	# of 9's:	Notes:
# of 10's:		Drill Time:	SCORE: # X's	

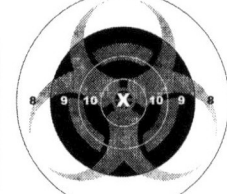

Date:	B.Z.	Battle Ground:	Weapon:	Undead / Infected / Mutant
# of Misses:		# of 8's:	# of 9's:	Notes:
# of 10's:		Drill Time:	SCORE: # X's	

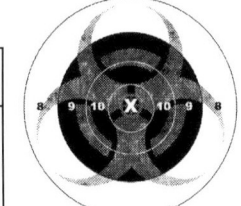

Date:	B.Z.	Battle Ground:	Weapon:	Undead / Infected / Mutant
# of Misses:		# of 8's:	# of 9's:	Notes:
# of 10's:		Drill Time:	SCORE: # X's	

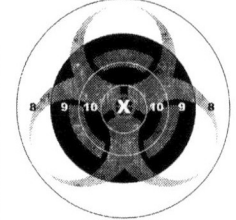

www.GUNFIGHTERSERIES.com ©

I'M SOLID

Date:	B.Z.	Battle Ground:	Weapon:	Undead / Infected / Mutant
# of Misses:		# of 8's:	# of 9's:	Notes:
# of 10's:		Drill Time:	**SCORE:** # X's	

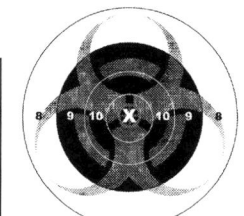

Date:	B.Z.	Battle Ground:	Weapon:	Undead / Infected / Mutant
# of Misses:		# of 8's:	# of 9's:	Notes:
# of 10's:		Drill Time:	**SCORE:** # X's	

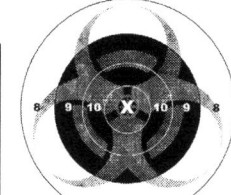

Date:	B.Z.	Battle Ground:	Weapon:	Undead / Infected / Mutant
# of Misses:		# of 8's:	# of 9's:	Notes:
# of 10's:		Drill Time:	**SCORE:** # X's	

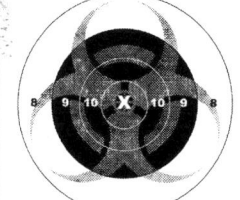

Date:	B.Z.	Battle Ground:	Weapon:	Undead / Infected / Mutant
# of Misses:		# of 8's:	# of 9's:	Notes:
# of 10's:		Drill Time:	**SCORE:** # X's	

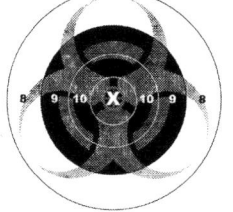

CARBINE DRILL: NOSE JOB

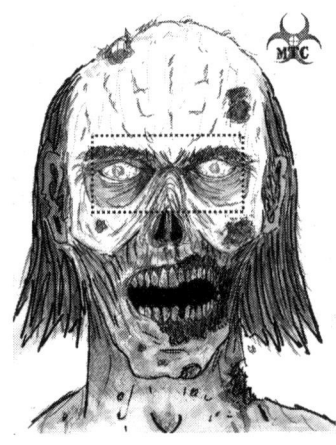

Purpose: Increase competency of the use of the low ready position.

Distance: 7 Yards.

Target: MTC Z-1 (Undead)

Par Time: 1.25 Second.

Extra Equipment Needed: Shot timer.

Rounds Fired Per Rep: 1 Round.

Total Rounds Fired: 10 Rounds.

Point Penalty: 1 Point per perfect rep.

Repetitions: 10 Reps.

Starting Position & Condition: Standing - Low ready. Condition 1.

Description: Low ready position is the butt stock is on your shoulder with the muzzle pointed into the dirt 6 to 8 feet in front of you while you are looking at the target. From the low ready position, at the timer beep, raise the carbine and take aim at the target with a flash sight picture and fire a round within 1 second into the ocular Z box. Count number of shots inside ocular Z box, subtract number of shots over par to equal your final score.

Goals: Meat Bag: 6 Points.   Survivor: 8 Points.   Z Fighter: 10 Points.

Variations:

⊕ Infected Humans: Start at 7 yards, with your back facing the target.

⊕ Mutants: 10 Yards with a side step left or right. Par time of 1.5 second.

NOSE JOB

Date:	B.Z.	Weapon:	Sights:	Undead / Infected / Mutant
# In Z Box:		# Over Par:	**Score:**	Notes:
Date:	B.Z.	Weapon:	Sights:	Undead / Infected / Mutant
# In Z Box:		# Over Par:	**Score:**	Notes:
Date:	B.Z.	Weapon:	Sights:	Undead / Infected / Mutant
# In Z Box:		# Over Par:	**Score:**	Notes:
Date:	B.Z.	Weapon:	Sights:	Undead / Infected / Mutant
# In Z Box:		# Over Par:	**Score:**	Notes:

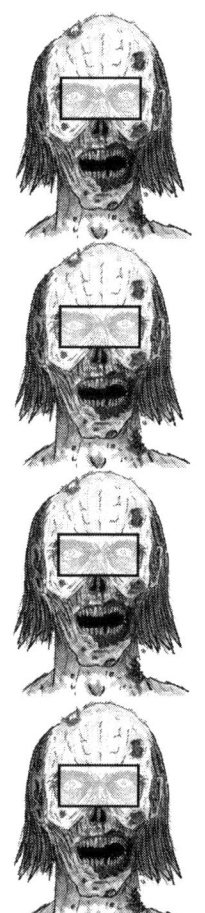

Z Fighter ©

NOSE JOB

Date: B.Z	Weapon:	Sights:	Undead / Infected / Mutant
# In Z Box:	# Over Par:	**Score:**	Notes:
Date: B.Z.	Weapon:	Sights:	Undead / Infected / Mutant
# In Z Box:	# Over Par:	**Score:**	Notes:
Date: B.Z.	Weapon:	Sights:	Undead / Infected / Mutant
# In Z Box:	# Over Par:	**Score:**	Notes:
Date: B.Z.	Weapon:	Sights:	Undead / Infected / Mutant
# In Z Box:	# Over Par:	**Score:**	Notes:

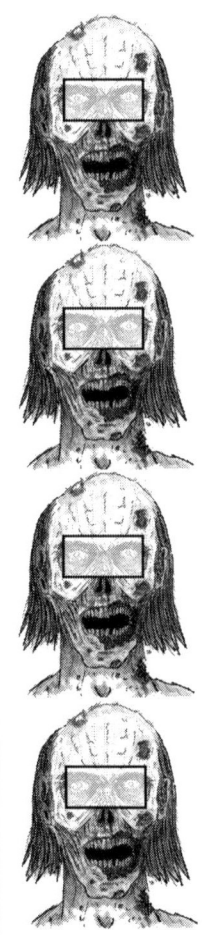

NOSE JOB

Date:	B.Z.	Weapon:	Sights:	Undead / Infected / Mutant
# In Z Box:		# Over Par:	**Score:**	Notes:
Date:	B.Z.	Weapon:	Sights:	Undead / Infected / Mutant
# In Z Box:		# Over Par:	**Score:**	Notes:
Date:	B.Z.	Weapon:	Sights:	Undead / Infected / Mutant
# In Z Box:		# Over Par:	**Score:**	Notes:
Date:	B.Z.	Weapon:	Sights:	Undead / Infected / Mutant
# In Z Box:		# Over Par:	**Score:**	Notes:

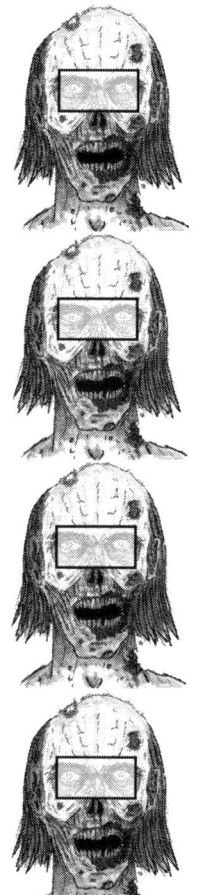

Z Fighter ©

NOSE JOB

Date: B.Z.	Weapon:	Sights:	Undead / Infected / Mutant
# In Z Box:	# Over Par:	**Score:**	Notes:

Date: B.Z.	Weapon:	Sights:	Undead / Infected / Mutant
# In Z Box:	# Over Par:	**Score:**	Notes:

Date: B.Z.	Weapon:	Sights:	Undead / Infected / Mutant
# In Z Box:	# Over Par:	**Score:**	Notes:

Date: B.Z.	Weapon:	Sights:	Undead / Infected / Mutant
# In Z Box:	# Over Par:	**Score:**	Notes:

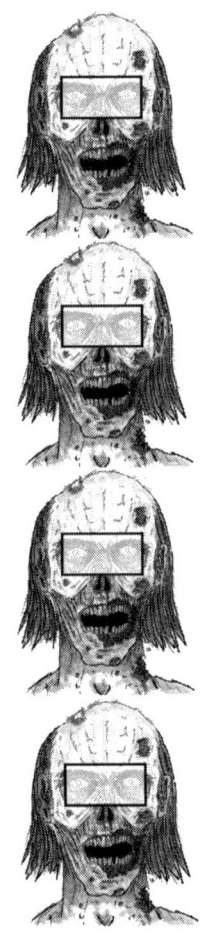

NOSE JOB

Date:	B.Z.	Weapon:	Sights:	Undead / Infected / Mutant
# In Z Box:		# Over Par:	**Score:**	Notes:
Date:	B.Z.	Weapon:	Sights:	Undead / Infected / Mutant
# In Z Box:		# Over Par:	**Score:**	Notes:
Date:	B.Z.	Weapon:	Sights:	Undead / Infected / Mutant
# In Z Box:		# Over Par:	**Score:**	Notes:
Date:	B.Z.	Weapon:	Sights:	Undead / Infected / Mutant
# In Z Box:		# Over Par:	**Score:**	Notes:

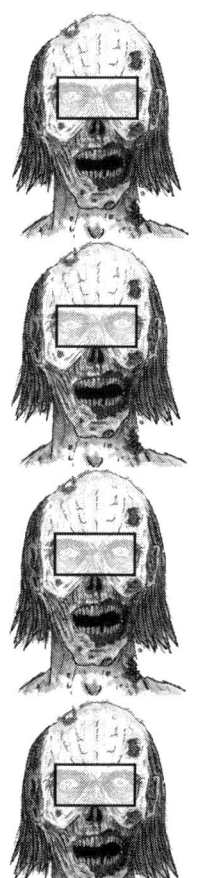

Z Fighter ©

CARBINE DRILL: 10K

Purpose: Increase accuracy and efficiency using a flash sight picture.

Distance: 15 Yards.

Target: ZF-1 x 2 (Undead).

Par Time: 1.25 Seconds.

Extra Equipment Needed: Shot timer.

Rounds Fired Per Rep: 1 Round.   **Total Rounds Fired:** 10 Rounds.

Point Penalty: As per target score.

Repetitions: 10 Reps.

Starting Position & Condition: Standing – Ready. Weapon condition 1.

Description: At the timer beep, bring sights up on target while selecting fire on fire control, press trigger firing shot as soon as sights are at desired point to put accurate fire on target.

Goals: Meat Bag: All hits inside black target area with all shots under par time.   Survivor: 100 points with all shots under par time.
Z Fighter: 100 points with all shots under 1.0 par time

Variations:

⊕   Infected Humans: Start each repetition by running to the target and back before starting the timer.

⊕   Mutants: Same as Infected Humans, using a ZF-2 target.

10K

Date:		B.Z.	Location:	Weapon:			Sights:	
	Undead / Infected / Mutant			Side:	Dominant / Support		Notes:	
# Outside The Black:			# Over Par:	**Total Score:**				
Date:		B.Z.	Location:	Weapon:			Sights:	
Undead / Infected /			Undead / Infected / Mutant	Side:	Dominant / Support		Notes:	
# Outside The Black:			# Over Par:	**Total Score:**				
Date:		B.Z.	Location:	Weapon:			Sights:	
	Undead / Infected / Mutant			Side:	Dominant / Support		Notes:	
# Outside The Black:			# Over Par:	**Total Score:**				
Date:		B.Z.	Location:	Weapon:			Sights:	
	Undead / Infected / Mutant			Side:	Dominant / Support		Notes:	
# Outside The Black:			# Over Par:	**Total Score:**				
Date:		B.Z.	Location:	Weapon:			Sights:	
	Undead / Infected / Mutant			Side:	Dominant / Support		Notes:	
# Outside The Black:			# Over Par:	**Total Score:**				

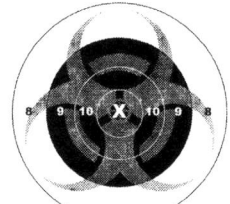
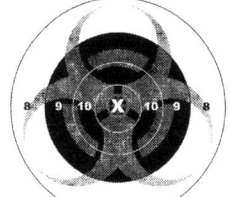
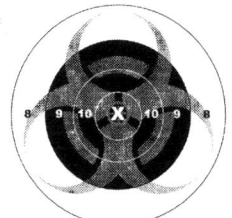
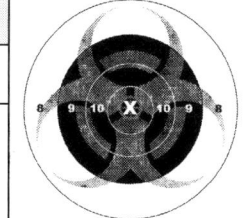

Z Fighter ©

Carbine Drills - 4

10K

Date:	B.Z.	Location:	Weapon:	Sights:	
	Undead / Infected / Mutant		Side: Dominant / Support	Notes:	
# Outside The Black:		# Over Par:	**Total Score:**		
Date:	B.Z.	Location:	Weapon:	Sights:	
	Undead / Infected / Mutant		Side: Dominant / Support	Notes:	
# Outside The Black:		# Over Par:	**Total Score:**		
Date:	B.Z.	Location:	Weapon:	Sights:	
	Undead / Infected / Mutant		Side: Dominant / Support	Notes:	
# Outside The Black:		# Over Par:	**Total Score:**		
Date:	B.Z.	Location:	Weapon:	Sights:	
	Undead / Infected / Mutant		Side: Dominant / Support	Notes:	
# Outside The Black:		# Over Par:	**Total Score:**		
Date:	B.Z.	Location:	Weapon:	Sights:	
	Undead / Infected / Mutant		Side: Dominant / Support	Notes:	
# Outside The Black:		# Over Par:	**Total Score:**		

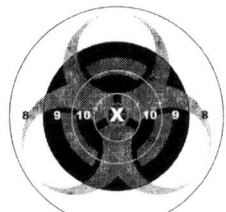
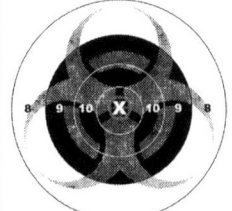
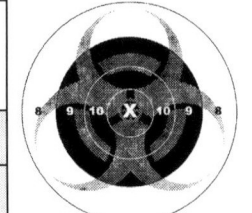

10K

Date:		B.Z.	Location:			Weapon:			Sights:	
	Undead /	Infected /	Mutant			Side: Dominant / Support			Notes:	
# Outside The Black:			# Over Par:			**Total Score:**				
Date:		B.Z.	Location:			Weapon:			Sights:	
Undead /	Infected /		Undead /	Infected /	Mutant	Side: Dominant / Support			Notes:	
# Outside The Black:			# Over Par:			**Total Score:**				
Date:		B.Z.	Location:			Weapon:			Sights:	
	Undead /	Infected /	Mutant			Side: Dominant / Support			Notes:	
# Outside The Black:			# Over Par:			**Total Score:**				
Date:		B.Z.	Location:			Weapon:			Sights:	
	Undead /	Infected /	Mutant			Side: Dominant / Support			Notes:	
# Outside The Black:			# Over Par:			**Total Score:**				
Date:		B.Z.	Location:			Weapon:			Sights:	
	Undead /	Infected /	Mutant			Side: Dominant / Support			Notes:	
# Outside The Black:			# Over Par:			**Total Score:**				

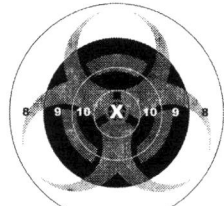
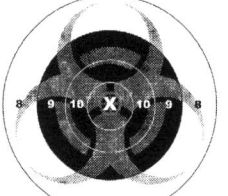
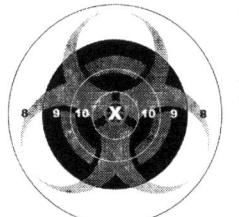
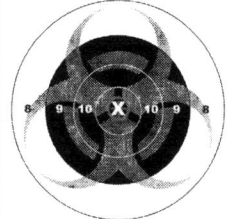

10K

Date:		B.Z.	Location:	Weapon:			Sights:	
	Undead / Infected / Mutant			Side:	Dominant / Support		Notes:	
# Outside The Black:			# Over Par:	Total Score:				
Date:		B.Z.	Location:	Weapon:			Sights:	
Undead / Infected /			Undead / Infected / Mutant	Side:	Dominant / Support		Notes:	
# Outside The Black:			# Over Par:	Total Score:				
Date:		B.Z.	Location:	Weapon:			Sights:	
	Undead / Infected / Mutant			Side:	Dominant / Support		Notes:	
# Outside The Black:			# Over Par:	Total Score:				
Date:		B.Z.	Location:	Weapon:			Sights:	
	Undead / Infected / Mutant			Side:	Dominant / Support		Notes:	
# Outside The Black:			# Over Par:	Total Score:				
Date:		B.Z.	Location:	Weapon:			Sights:	
	Undead / Infected / Mutant			Side:	Dominant / Support		Notes:	
# Outside The Black:			# Over Par:	Total Score:				

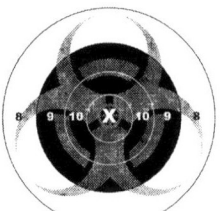
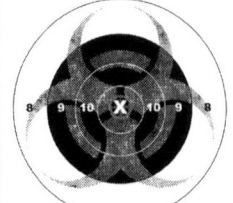
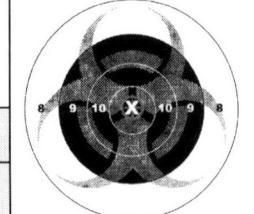
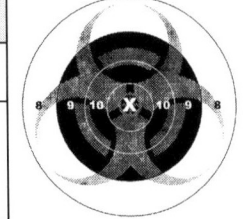

10K

Date:	B.Z.	Location:	Weapon:	Sights:	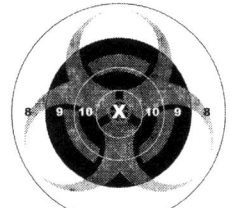
	Undead / Infected / Mutant		Side: Dominant / Support	Notes:	
# Outside The Black:		# Over Par:	**Total Score:**		
Date:	B.Z.	Location:	Weapon:	Sights:	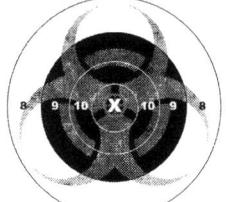
Undead / Infected /		Undead / Infected / Mutant	Side: Dominant / Support	Notes:	
# Outside The Black:		# Over Par:	**Total Score:**		
Date:	B.Z.	Location:	Weapon:	Sights:	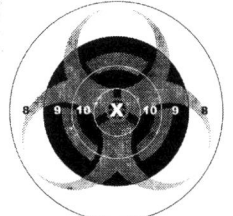
	Undead / Infected / Mutant		Side: Dominant / Support	Notes:	
# Outside The Black:		# Over Par:	**Total Score:**		
Date:	B.Z.	Location:	Weapon:	Sights:	
	Undead / Infected / Mutant		Side: Dominant / Support	Notes:	
# Outside The Black:		# Over Par:	**Total Score:**		
Date:	B.Z.	Location:	Weapon:	Sights:	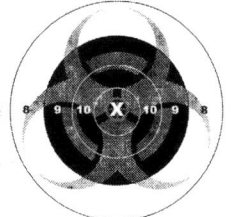
	Undead / Infected / Mutant		Side: Dominant / Support	Notes:	
# Outside The Black:		# Over Par:	**Total Score:**		

CARBINE DRILL: **LEFTY, RIGHTY, LAY-O**

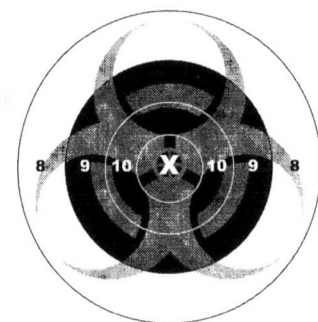 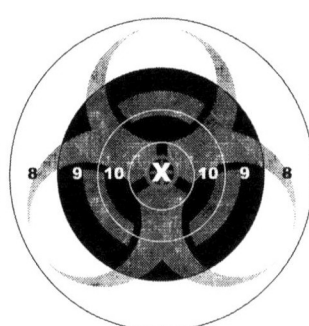

Purpose: Increase competency and accuracy transitioning between dominant and support side.

Distance: 25 Yards.

Target: ZF-1 x 2 (Undead).

Total Rounds Fired: 20 Rounds.

Point Penalty: Per target score.

Repetitions: 1 Rep.

Starting Position & Condition: Standing - Low ready. Condition 1.

Description: On your personal go with carbine in you right shoulder, raise the rifle and fire one round into the right target. While keeping your rifle pointed at the targets, put rifle on safe, place the butt stock in your opposite shoulder, move your firing hand forward to the handguard, then move your support hand back to the firing position. Engage the left target with one round from your left shoulder. Repeating the same sequence going back to right shoulder then left again. Continue this sequence for all 20 rounds. Right target for right shoulder x 10 shots / Left target for left shoulder x 10 shots.

Goals: Meat Bag: 160 points.   Survivor: 180 points.   Z Fighter: 200 points.

Variations:

⊕ Infected Humans: 120 Second par time.

⊕ Mutants: 50 Yards with 130 second par time.

LEFTY, RIGHTY, LAY-O

Date:	B.Z.	Battle Ground:	Rep Time:	Undead / Infected / Mutant
Weapon:		Sights:	Sling Used: Y / N	Notes:
Left Score:		**Right Score:**	**TOTAL SCORE:**	

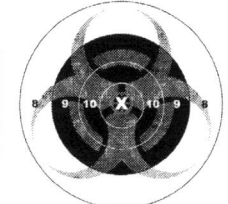 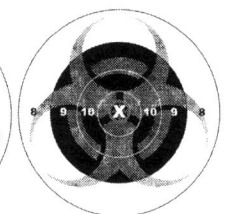

Date:	B.Z.	Battle Ground:	Rep Time:	Undead / Infected / Mutant
Weapon:		Sights:	Sling Used: Y / N	Notes:
Left Score:		**Right Score:**	**TOTAL SCORE:**	

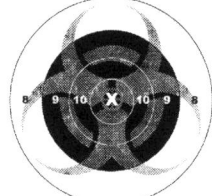 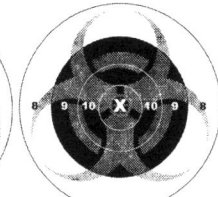

Date:	B.Z.	Battle Ground:	Rep Time:	Undead / Infected / Mutant
Weapon:		Sights:	Sling Used: Y / N	Notes:
Left Score:		**Right Score:**	**TOTAL SCORE:**	

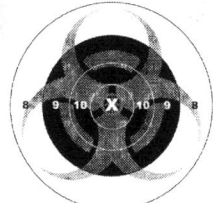 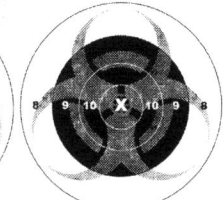

Date:	B.Z.	Battle Ground:	Rep Time:	Undead / Infected / Mutant
Weapon:		Sights:	Sling Used: Y / N	Notes:
Left Score:		**Right Score:**	**TOTAL SCORE:**	

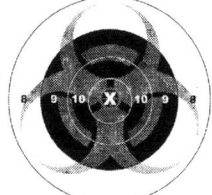 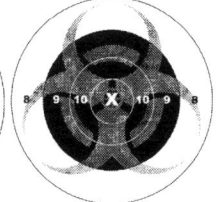

Z Fighter ©   Carbine Drills - 5

LEFTY, RIGHTY, LAY-O

Date:	B.Z.	Battle Ground:	Rep Time:	Undead / Infected / Mutant
Weapon:		Sights:	Sling Used: Y / N	Notes:
Left Score:		**Right Score:**	**TOTAL SCORE:**	

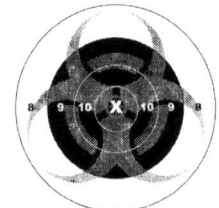 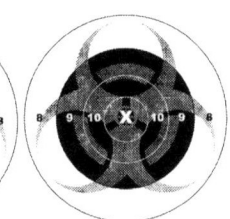

Date:	B.Z.	Battle Ground:	Rep Time:	Undead / Infected / Mutant
Weapon:		Sights:	Sling Used: Y / N	Notes:
Left Score:		**Right Score:**	**TOTAL SCORE:**	

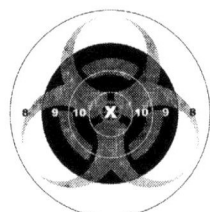 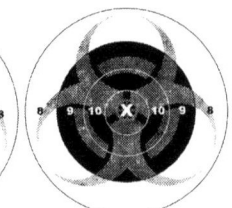

Date:	B.Z.	Battle Ground:	Rep Time:	Undead / Infected / Mutant
Weapon:		Sights:	Sling Used: Y / N	Notes:
Left Score:		**Right Score:**	**TOTAL SCORE:**	

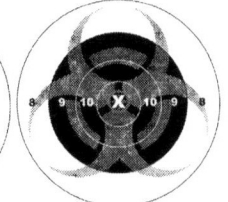

Date:	B.Z.	Battle Ground:	Rep Time:	Undead / Infected / Mutant
Weapon:		Sights:	Sling Used: Y / N	Notes:
Left Score:		**Right Score:**	**TOTAL SCORE:**	

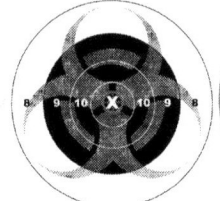 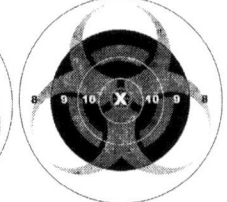

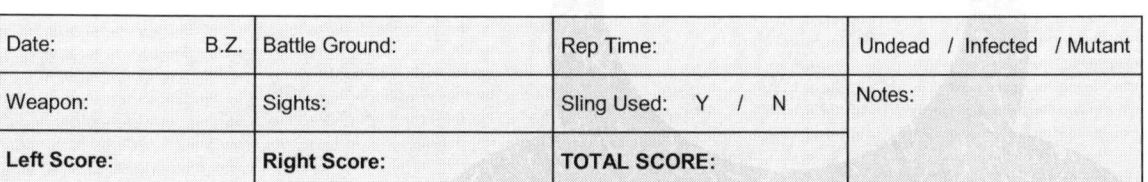

LEFTY, RIGHTY, LAY-O

Date:	B.Z.	Battle Ground:	Rep Time:	Undead / Infected / Mutant
Weapon:		Sights:	Sling Used: Y / N	Notes:
Left Score:		**Right Score:**	**TOTAL SCORE:**	

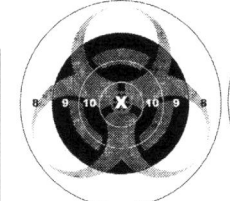 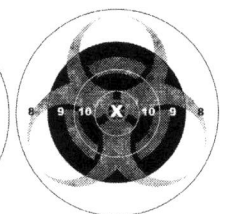

Date:	B.Z.	Battle Ground:	Rep Time:	Undead / Infected / Mutant
Weapon:		Sights:	Sling Used: Y / N	Notes:
Left Score:		**Right Score:**	**TOTAL SCORE:**	

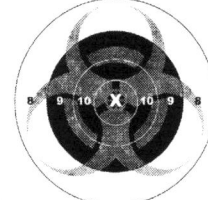 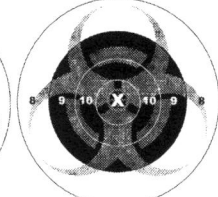

Date:	B.Z.	Battle Ground:	Rep Time:	Undead / Infected / Mutant
Weapon:		Sights:	Sling Used: Y / N	Notes:
Left Score:		**Right Score:**	**TOTAL SCORE:**	

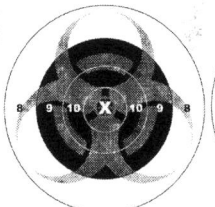 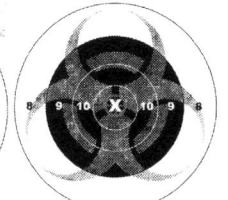

Date:	B.Z.	Battle Ground:	Rep Time:	Undead / Infected / Mutant
Weapon:		Sights:	Sling Used: Y / N	Notes:
Left Score:		**Right Score:**	**TOTAL SCORE:**	

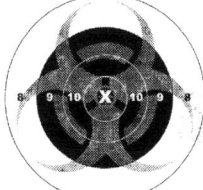 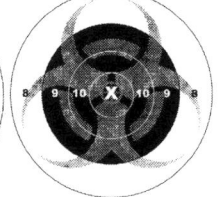

LEFTY, RIGHTY, LAY-O

Date:	B.Z.	Battle Ground:	Rep Time:	Undead / Infected / Mutant
Weapon:		Sights:	Sling Used: Y / N	Notes:
Left Score:		**Right Score:**	**TOTAL SCORE:**	

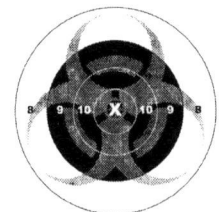 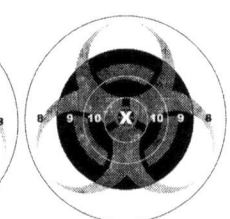

Date:	B.Z.	Battle Ground:	Rep Time:	Undead / Infected / Mutant
Weapon:		Sights:	Sling Used: Y / N	Notes:
Left Score:		**Right Score:**	**TOTAL SCORE:**	

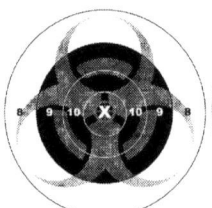 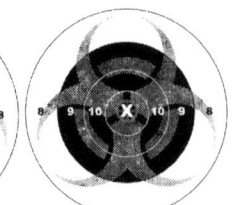

Date:	B.Z.	Battle Ground:	Rep Time:	Undead / Infected / Mutant
Weapon:		Sights:	Sling Used: Y / N	Notes:
Left Score:		**Right Score:**	**TOTAL SCORE:**	

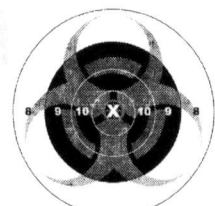 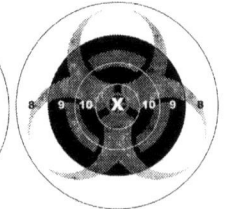

Date:	B.Z.	Battle Ground:	Rep Time:	Undead / Infected / Mutant
Weapon:		Sights:	Sling Used: Y / N	Notes:
Left Score:		**Right Score:**	**TOTAL SCORE:**	

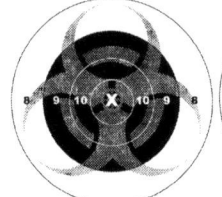 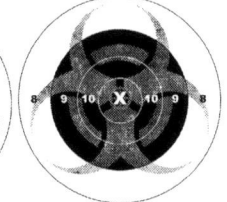

LEFTY, RIGHTY, LAY-O

Date:	B.Z.	Battle Ground:	Rep Time:	Undead / Infected / Mutant
Weapon:		Sights:	Sling Used: Y / N	Notes:
Left Score:		**Right Score:**	**TOTAL SCORE:**	

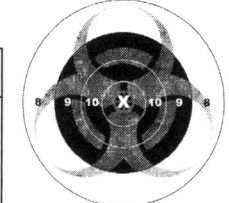 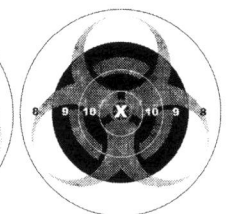

Date:	B.Z.	Battle Ground:	Rep Time:	Undead / Infected / Mutant
Weapon:		Sights:	Sling Used: Y / N	Notes:
Left Score:		**Right Score:**	**TOTAL SCORE:**	

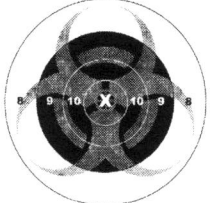 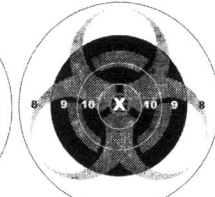

Date:	B.Z.	Battle Ground:	Rep Time:	Undead / Infected / Mutant
Weapon:		Sights:	Sling Used: Y / N	Notes:
Left Score:		**Right Score:**	**TOTAL SCORE:**	

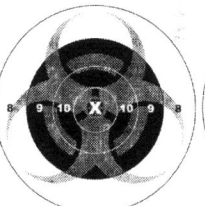 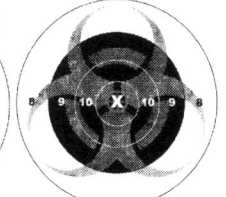

Date:	B.Z.	Battle Ground:	Rep Time:	Undead / Infected / Mutant
Weapon:		Sights:	Sling Used: Y / N	Notes:
Left Score:		**Right Score:**	**TOTAL SCORE:**	

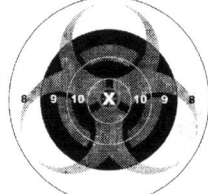 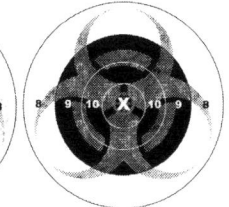

Z Fighter ©

CARBINE DRILL: **LEPRECHAUN**

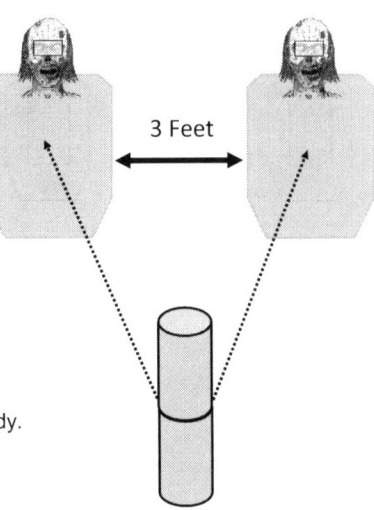

Purpose: Increase competency and accuracy transitioning between dominant and support side.

Distance: 15 Yards.

Target: ZIPSC x2 targets. Position the targets 3 feet apart.

Extra Equipment Needed: Shot timer, double stacked barrels or other vertical barrier.

Total Rounds Fired: 10 Rounds.

Point Penalty: Time plus penalty. Add 3 seconds for rounds outside the Z/A box. Add 5 seconds for rounds outside the head / body.

Starting Position & Condition: Standing - Low Ready behind a vertical barrier. Condition 1.

Description: At the timer beep, keeping your torso behind cover, lean to the right with carbine in you right shoulder, engage the right target in the ocular Z box. Lean back behind cover, transition the carbine to your left shoulder, lean left far enough to engage the left target with 1 round to the ocular Z box. Return to cover, returning the carbine to the right shoulder and repeating the same sequence until you have fire 10 rounds total, 5 into each targets ocular Z box.

Goals: Meat Bag: 60 Seconds.   Survivor: 50 Seconds.   Z Fighter: 40 Seconds.

Variations:

⊕ Infected Humans: 2 Shots to the body A Box and 1 to the ocular Z box of each target. Total of 30 rounds.

Goals: Meat Bag: 120 Seconds.   Survivor: 90 Seconds.   Z Fighter: 60 Seconds.

⊕ Mutants: 2 Shots to the body A Box and 1 to the ocular Z box of each target from a distance of 25 yards. Goal: Beat your personal best time.

LEPRECHAUN

Date:	B.Z.	Battle Ground:	Undead / Infected / Mutant	Notes:
Weapon:		Sights:	Sling Used: Y / N	
Rep Time:		Left Penalties:	Right Penalties:	**TOTAL TIME:**

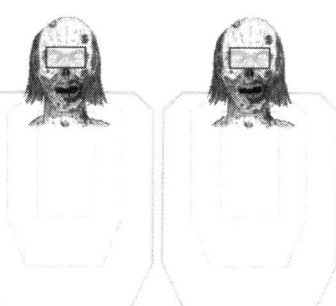

Date:	B.Z.	Battle Ground:	Undead / Infected / Mutant	Notes:
Weapon:		Sights:	Sling Used: Y / N	
Rep Time:		Left Penalties:	Right Penalties:	**TOTAL TIME:**

Date:	B.Z.	Battle Ground:	Undead / Infected / Mutant	Notes:
Weapon:		Sights:	Sling Used: Y / N	
Rep Time:		Left Penalties:	Right Penalties:	**TOTAL TIME:**

LEPRECHAUN

Date: B.Z.	Battle Ground:	Undead / Infected / Mutant	Notes:
Weapon:	Sights:	Sling Used: Y / N	
Rep Time:	Left Penalties:	Right Penalties:	**TOTAL TIME:**

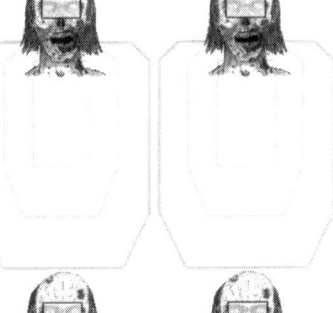

Date: B.Z.	Battle Ground:	Undead / Infected / Mutant	Notes:
Weapon:	Sights:	Sling Used: Y / N	
Rep Time:	Left Penalties:	Right Penalties:	**TOTAL TIME:**

Date: B.Z.	Battle Ground:	Undead / Infected / Mutant	Notes:
Weapon:	Sights:	Sling Used: Y / N	
Rep Time:	Left Penalties:	Right Penalties:	**TOTAL TIME:**

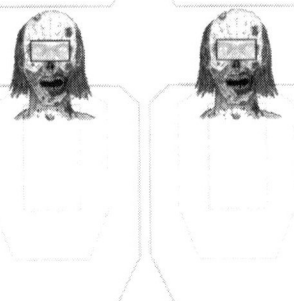

LEPRECHAUN

Date:	B.Z.	Battle Ground:	Undead / Infected / Mutant	Notes:
Weapon:		Sights:	Sling Used: Y / N	
Rep Time:		Left Penalties:	Right Penalties:	**TOTAL TIME:**

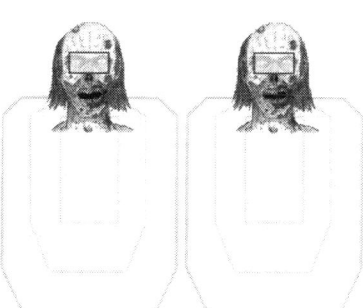

Date:	B.Z.	Battle Ground:	Undead / Infected / Mutant	Notes:
Weapon:		Sights:	Sling Used: Y / N	
Rep Time:		Left Penalties:	Right Penalties:	**TOTAL TIME:**

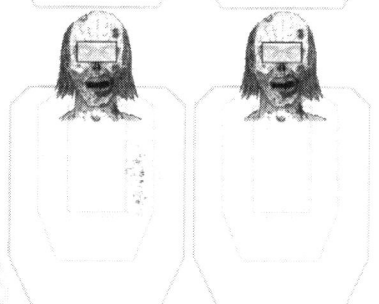

Date:	B.Z.	Battle Ground:	Undead / Infected / Mutant	Notes:
Weapon:		Sights:	Sling Used: Y / N	
Rep Time:		Left Penalties:	Right Penalties:	**TOTAL TIME:**

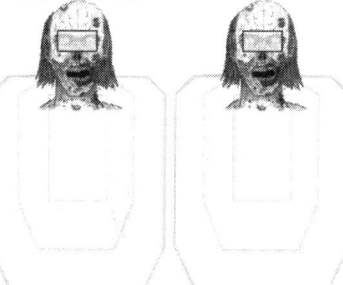

LEPRECHAUN

Date:	B.Z.	Battle Ground:	Undead / Infected / Mutant	Notes:
Weapon:		Sights:	Sling Used: Y / N	
Rep Time:		Left Penalties:	Right Penalties:	**TOTAL TIME:**

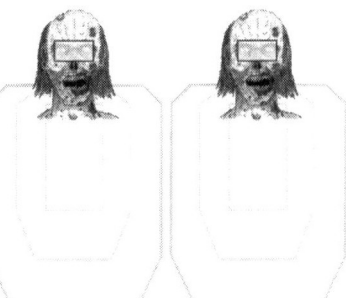

Date:	B.Z.	Battle Ground:	Undead / Infected / Mutant	Notes:
Weapon:		Sights:	Sling Used: Y / N	
Rep Time:		Left Penalties:	Right Penalties:	**TOTAL TIME:**

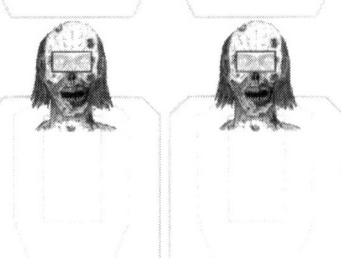

Date:	B.Z.	Battle Ground:	Undead / Infected / Mutant	Notes:
Weapon:		Sights:	Sling Used: Y / N	
Rep Time:		Left Penalties:	Right Penalties:	**TOTAL TIME:**

LEPRECHAUN

Date:	B.Z.	Battle Ground:	Undead / Infected / Mutant	Notes:
Weapon:		Sights:	Sling Used: Y / N	
Rep Time:		Left Penalties:	Right Penalties:	**TOTAL TIME:**

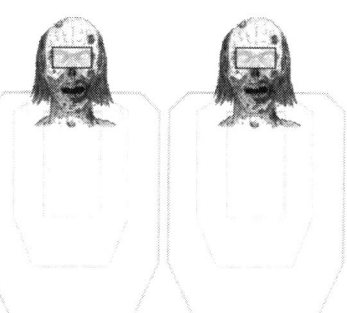

Date:	B.Z.	Battle Ground:	Undead / Infected / Mutant	Notes:
Weapon:		Sights:	Sling Used: Y / N	
Rep Time:		Left Penalties:	Right Penalties:	**TOTAL TIME:**

Date:	B.Z.	Battle Ground:	Undead / Infected / Mutant	Notes:
Weapon:		Sights:	Sling Used: Y / N	
Rep Time:		Left Penalties:	Right Penalties:	**TOTAL TIME:**

Z Fighter ©

CARBINE DRILL: **SEGEN**

Purpose: Develop consistent one hand accuracy under pressure.

Distance: 10 Yards.

Target: Z Qual-1 (Undead)

Extra Equipment Needed: Shot timer.

Par Time: 30 Seconds.

Total Rounds Fired: 10 Rounds.

Point Penalty: As per target score.

Repetitions: 1 Rep.

Starting Position & Condition: Standing – Port ready. Condition 1.

Description: At the timer beep, shoulder the carbine <u>one handed</u>, aim at target, put fire control selector on fire and fire 10 one handed rounds into the target within 30 seconds.

Goals: Meat Bag: All rounds in or touching the black. Survivor: 25 points Z Fighter: 50 Points.

Variations:

⊕ Infected Humans: Use support side from 10 yards.

⊕ Mutants: 15 yards taking a step left or right before each shot.

SEGEN

Date:	B.Z.	Location:	Weapon:	Sights:
Undead / Infected / Mutant		Side: Dominant / Support	Distance:	Notes:
# Over Par:		# Off Target:	**Total Score:**	

Date:	B.Z.	Location:	Weapon:	Sights:
Undead / Infected / Mutant		Side: Dominant / Support	Distance:	Notes:
# Over Par:		# Off Target:	**Total Score:**	

Date:	B.Z.	Location:	Weapon:	Sights:
Undead / Infected / Mutant		Side: Dominant / Support	Distance:	Notes:
# Over Par:		# Off Target:	**Total Score:**	

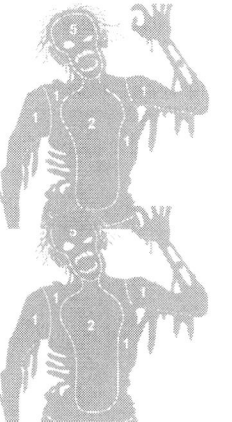

Date:	B.Z.	Location:	Weapon:	Sights:
Undead / Infected / Mutant		Side: Dominant / Support	Distance:	Notes:
# Over Par:		# Off Target:	**Total Score:**	

SEGEN

Date:	B.Z.	Location:	Weapon:	Sights:
Undead / Infected / Mutant		Side: Dominant / Support	Distance:	Notes:
# Over Par:		# Off Target:	**Total Score:**	

Date:	B.Z.	Location:	Weapon:	Sights:
Undead / Infected / Mutant		Side: Dominant / Support	Distance:	Notes:
# Over Par:		# Off Target:	**Total Score:**	

Date:	B.Z.	Location:	Weapon:	Sights:
Undead / Infected / Mutant		Side: Dominant / Support	Distance:	Notes:
# Over Par:		# Off Target:	**Total Score:**	

Date:	B.Z.	Location:	Weapon:	Sights:
Undead / Infected / Mutant		Side: Dominant / Support	Distance:	Notes:
# Over Par:		# Off Target:	**Total Score:**	

SEGEN

Date:	B.Z.	Location:	Weapon:	Sights:
Undead / Infected / Mutant		Side: Dominant / Support	Distance:	Notes:
# Over Par:		# Off Target:	**Total Score:**	

Date:	B.Z.	Location:	Weapon:	Sights:
Undead / Infected / Mutant		Side: Dominant / Support	Distance:	Notes:
# Over Par:		# Off Target:	**Total Score:**	

Date:	B.Z.	Location:	Weapon:	Sights:
Undead / Infected / Mutant		Side: Dominant / Support	Distance:	Notes:
# Over Par:		# Off Target:	**Total Score:**	

Date:	B.Z.	Location:	Weapon:	Sights:
Undead / Infected / Mutant		Side: Dominant / Support	Distance:	Notes:
# Over Par:		# Off Target:	**Total Score:**	

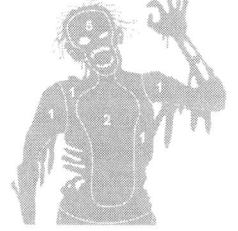

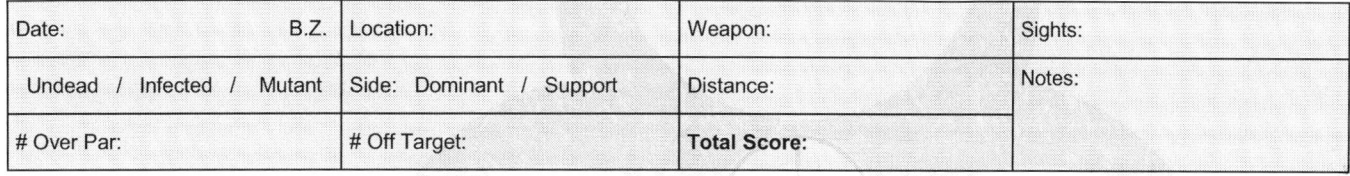

www.GUNFIGHTERSERIES.com ©

SEGEN

Date:	B.Z.	Location:	Weapon:	Sights:
Undead / Infected / Mutant		Side: Dominant / Support	Distance:	Notes:
# Over Par:		# Off Target:	**Total Score:**	

Date:	B.Z.	Location:	Weapon:	Sights:
Undead / Infected / Mutant		Side: Dominant / Support	Distance:	Notes:
# Over Par:		# Off Target:	**Total Score:**	

Date:	B.Z.	Location:	Weapon:	Sights:
Undead / Infected / Mutant		Side: Dominant / Support	Distance:	Notes:
# Over Par:		# Off Target:	**Total Score:**	

Date:	B.Z.	Location:	Weapon:	Sights:
Undead / Infected / Mutant		Side: Dominant / Support	Distance:	Notes:
# Over Par:		# Off Target:	**Total Score:**	

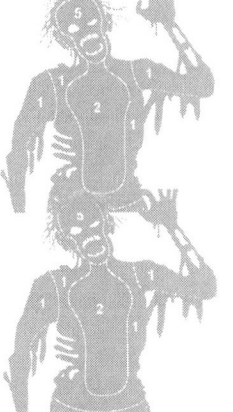

SEGEN

Date:	B.Z.	Location:	Weapon:	Sights:
Undead / Infected / Mutant		Side: Dominant / Support	Distance:	Notes:
# Over Par:		# Off Target:	**Total Score:**	

Date:	B.Z.	Location:	Weapon:	Sights:
Undead / Infected / Mutant		Side: Dominant / Support	Distance:	Notes:
# Over Par:		# Off Target:	**Total Score:**	

Date:	B.Z.	Location:	Weapon:	Sights:
Undead / Infected / Mutant		Side: Dominant / Support	Distance:	Notes:
# Over Par:		# Off Target:	**Total Score:**	

Date:	B.Z.	Location:	Weapon:	Sights:
Undead / Infected / Mutant		Side: Dominant / Support	Distance:	Notes:
# Over Par:		# Off Target:	**Total Score:**	

Carbine Drills - 7

CARBINE DRILL: **BOOMSTICK**

Purpose: Develop upper body strength and consistent one handed marksmanship.

Distance: 10 Yards.

Target: Z-QUAL1 x2 (Undead)

Total Rounds Fired: 10 Rounds.

Starting Position & Condition: Standing, low ready. Condition 1.

Description: Raise the carbine so you are shouldering one handed, aim at target, put fire control selector on fire and fire 5 one handed shots from each shoulder. (Left target for left shoulder / right target for right shoulder) When switching the carbine from one shoulder to the other, make sure you put the fire control selector set on safe and you can use both hands to switch the carbine from one shoulder to the other. You must fire all 5 shots from each shoulder without taking the carbine off of that shoulder during that part of the drill or the drill is a failure. The longer you take to fire, the more unstable your shoulder will become, however your accuracy will suffer if you fire too fast and don't have good fundamentals. Make your shots count. Don't just blast away. Upper body strength is necessary for this drill.

Goals: Meat Bag: All rounds in or touching the black.   Survivor: 25 Points.   Z Fighter: 50 Points.

Variations:

⊕   Infected Humans: 15 Yards.

⊕   Mutants: 15 yards with double the round count. 100 Points max.

BOOMSTICK

Date:	B.Z.	Battle Ground:	Weapon:	Undead / Infected / Mutant
Left Side Score:			Right Side Score:	Total Score:

Date:	B.Z.	Battle Ground:	Weapon:	Undead / Infected / Mutant
Left Side Score:			Right Side Score:	Total Score:

Date:	B.Z.	Battle Ground:	Weapon:	Undead / Infected / Mutant
Left Side Score:			Right Side Score:	Total Score:

Date:	B.Z.	Battle Ground:	Weapon:	Undead / Infected / Mutant
Left Side Score:			Right Side Score:	Total Score:

Date:	B.Z.	Battle Ground:	Weapon:	Undead / Infected / Mutant
Left Side Score:			Right Side Score:	Total Score:

Z Fighter ©

www.GUNFIGHTERSERIES.com ©

BOOMSTICK

Date:	B.Z.	Battle Ground:	Weapon:	Undead / Infected / Mutant
Left Side Score:			Right Side Score:	**Total Score:**

Date:	B.Z.	Battle Ground:	Weapon:	Undead / Infected / Mutant
Left Side Score:			Right Side Score:	**Total Score:**

Date:	B.Z.	Battle Ground:	Weapon:	Undead / Infected / Mutant
Left Side Score:			Right Side Score:	**Total Score:**

Date:	B.Z.	Battle Ground:	Weapon:	Undead / Infected / Mutant
Left Side Score:			Right Side Score:	**Total Score:**

Date:	B.Z.	Battle Ground:	Weapon:	Undead / Infected / Mutant
Left Side Score:			Right Side Score:	**Total Score:**

BOOMSTICK

Date:	B.Z.	Battle Ground:	Weapon:	Undead / Infected / Mutant
Left Side Score:			Right Side Score:	Total Score:

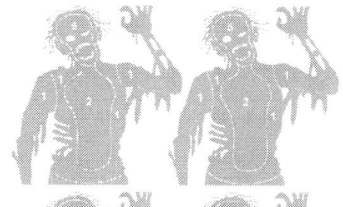

Date:	B.Z.	Battle Ground:	Weapon:	Undead / Infected / Mutant
Left Side Score:			Right Side Score:	Total Score:

Date:	B.Z.	Battle Ground:	Weapon:	Undead / Infected / Mutant
Left Side Score:			Right Side Score:	Total Score:

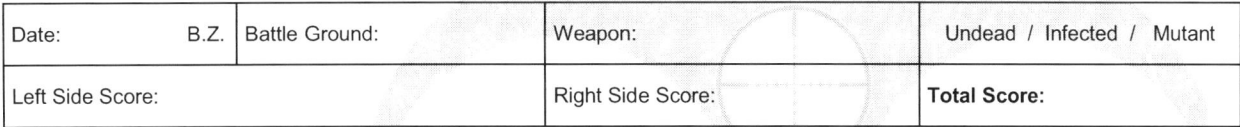

Date:	B.Z.	Battle Ground:	Weapon:	Undead / Infected / Mutant
Left Side Score:			Right Side Score:	Total Score:

Date:	B.Z.	Battle Ground:	Weapon:	Undead / Infected / Mutant
Left Side Score:			Right Side Score:	Total Score:

BOOMSTICK

Date:	B.Z.	Battle Ground:	Weapon:	Undead / Infected / Mutant
Left Side Score:			Right Side Score:	**Total Score:**

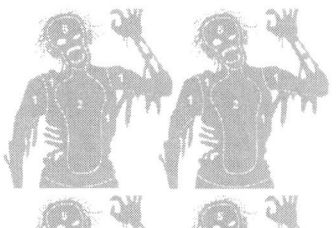

Date:	B.Z.	Battle Ground:	Weapon:	Undead / Infected / Mutant
Left Side Score:			Right Side Score:	**Total Score:**

Date:	B.Z.	Battle Ground:	Weapon:	Undead / Infected / Mutant
Left Side Score:			Right Side Score:	**Total Score:**

Date:	B.Z.	Battle Ground:	Weapon:	Undead / Infected / Mutant
Left Side Score:			Right Side Score:	**Total Score:**

Date:	B.Z.	Battle Ground:	Weapon:	Undead / Infected / Mutant
Left Side Score:			Right Side Score:	**Total Score:**

BOOMSTICK

Date:	B.Z.	Battle Ground:	Weapon:	Undead / Infected / Mutant
Left Side Score:			Right Side Score:	Total Score:

Date:	B.Z.	Battle Ground:	Weapon:	Undead / Infected / Mutant
Left Side Score:			Right Side Score:	Total Score:

Date:	B.Z.	Battle Ground:	Weapon:	Undead / Infected / Mutant
Left Side Score:			Right Side Score:	Total Score:

Date:	B.Z.	Battle Ground:	Weapon:	Undead / Infected / Mutant
Left Side Score:			Right Side Score:	Total Score:

Date:	B.Z.	Battle Ground:	Weapon:	Undead / Infected / Mutant
Left Side Score:			Right Side Score:	Total Score:

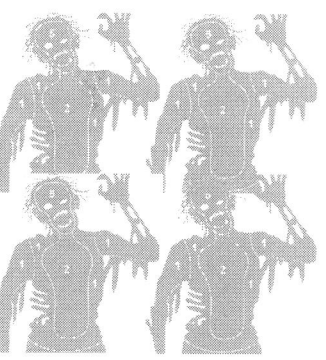

Z Fighter ©   Carbine Drills - 8

CARBINE DRILL: FEED

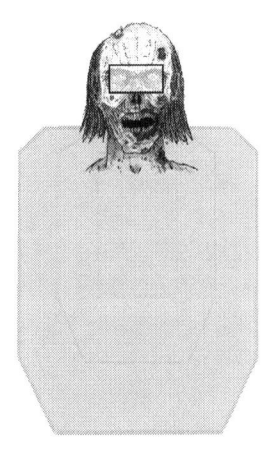

Purpose: Increase reloading speed, nervous system memory of an emergency reload and recoil management.

Distance: 10 Yards.   **Target:** ZIPSC (Undead).

Extra Equipment Needed: Timer, 2 magazines and 1 magazine pouch.

Par Time: Per goal standard.

Rounds Fired Per Rep: 3 Rounds.   **Total Rounds Fired:** 15 Rounds.

Point Penalty: Live or Die.

Repetitions: 5 Reps.

Starting Position & Condition: Standing – Carbine pointed at target. Condition 1 with a magazine with 1 round inserted in the carbine.

Description: At the timer beep, fire 2 rounds into the A Zone body, reload the carbine, aim and fire 1 round into the ocular Z box. Record the time. Repeat 4 more times. Left handed shooters add .5 seconds. You must get all 3 shots into the A & Z box to live.

Note: Be sure to know your close range hold over.

Goals: Meat Bag: 6.5 Second par time.   Survivor: 5.5 Second par time.   Z Fighter: 4.5 Second par time.

Variations:

⊕   Infected Humans: Engage from 25 yards.

⊕   Mutants: Engage from 25 yards, fire 3 - 5 rounds into the body A box and 1 round into the head Z box. Sidestep left / right while reloading.

FEED

Date:	B.Z.	Battle Ground:	Weapon:	Sights:	Undead / Infected / Mutant
Rep 1 Time:		Rep 2 Time:	Rep 3 Time:	Rep 4 Time:	Rep 5 Time:
Reload Time:		Reload Time:	Reload Time:	Reload Time:	Reload Time:
Live / Die		Live / Die	Live / Die	Live / Die	Live / Die
Ave Reload Time:		**Ave Total Rep Time:**			Notes:

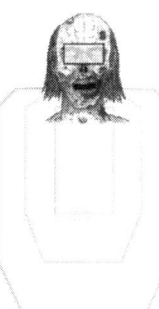

Date:	B.Z.	Battle Ground:	Weapon:	Sights:	Undead / Infected / Mutant
Rep 1 Time:		Rep 2 Time:	Rep 3 Time:	Rep 4 Time:	Rep 5 Time:
Reload Time:		Reload Time:	Reload Time:	Reload Time:	Reload Time:
Live / Die		Live / Die	Live / Die	Live / Die	Live / Die
Ave Reload Time:		**Ave Total Rep Time:**			Notes:

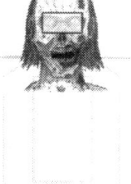

Date:	B.Z.	Battle Ground:	Weapon:	Sights:	Undead / Infected / Mutant
Rep 1 Time:		Rep 2 Time:	Rep 3 Time:	Rep 4 Time:	Rep 5 Time:
Reload Time:		Reload Time:	Reload Time:	Reload Time:	Reload Time:
Live / Die		Live / Die	Live / Die	Live / Die	Live / Die
Ave Reload Time:		**Ave Total Rep Time:**			Notes:

Z Fighter ©

www.GUNFIGHTERSERIES.com ©

FEED

Date: B.Z.	Battle Ground:	Weapon:	Sights:	Undead / Infected / Mutant
Rep 1 Time:	Rep 2 Time:	Rep 3 Time:	Rep 4 Time:	Rep 5 Time:
Reload Time:	Reload Time:	Reload Time:	Reload Time:	Reload Time:
Live / Die	Live / Die	Live / Die	Live / Die	Live / Die
Ave Reload Time:		Ave Total Rep Time:		Notes:

Date: B.Z.	Battle Ground:	Weapon:	Sights:	Undead / Infected / Mutant
Rep 1 Time:	Rep 2 Time:	Rep 3 Time:	Rep 4 Time:	Rep 5 Time:
Reload Time:	Reload Time:	Reload Time:	Reload Time:	Reload Time:
Live / Die	Live / Die	Live / Die	Live / Die	Live / Die
Ave Reload Time:		Ave Total Rep Time:		Notes:

Date: B.Z.	Battle Ground:	Weapon:	Sights:	Undead / Infected / Mutant
Rep 1 Time:	Rep 2 Time:	Rep 3 Time:	Rep 4 Time:	Rep 5 Time:
Reload Time:	Reload Time:	Reload Time:	Reload Time:	Reload Time:
Live / Die	Live / Die	Live / Die	Live / Die	Live / Die
Ave Reload Time:		Ave Total Rep Time:		Notes:

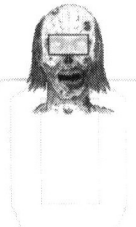

FEED

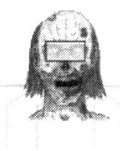

Date:	B.Z.	Battle Ground:	Weapon:	Sights:	Undead / Infected / Mutant
Rep 1 Time:		Rep 2 Time:	Rep 3 Time:	Rep 4 Time:	Rep 5 Time:
Reload Time:		Reload Time:	Reload Time:	Reload Time:	Reload Time:
Live / Die		Live / Die	Live / Die	Live / Die	Live / Die
Ave Reload Time:			Ave Total Rep Time:		Notes:

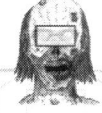

Date:	B.Z.	Battle Ground:	Weapon:	Sights:	Undead / Infected / Mutant
Rep 1 Time:		Rep 2 Time:	Rep 3 Time:	Rep 4 Time:	Rep 5 Time:
Reload Time:		Reload Time:	Reload Time:	Reload Time:	Reload Time:
Live / Die		Live / Die	Live / Die	Live / Die	Live / Die
Ave Reload Time:			Ave Total Rep Time:		Notes:

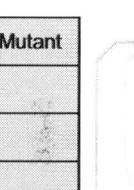

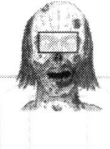

Date:	B.Z.	Battle Ground:	Weapon:	Sights:	Undead / Infected / Mutant
Rep 1 Time:		Rep 2 Time:	Rep 3 Time:	Rep 4 Time:	Rep 5 Time:
Reload Time:		Reload Time:	Reload Time:	Reload Time:	Reload Time:
Live / Die		Live / Die	Live / Die	Live / Die	Live / Die
Ave Reload Time:			Ave Total Rep Time:		Notes:

Z Fighter ©   Carbine Drills - 9

FEED

Date: B.Z.	Battle Ground:	Weapon:	Sights:	Undead / Infected / Mutant
Rep 1 Time:	Rep 2 Time:	Rep 3 Time:	Rep 4 Time:	Rep 5 Time:
Reload Time:	Reload Time:	Reload Time:	Reload Time:	Reload Time:
Live / Die	Live / Die	Live / Die	Live / Die	Live / Die
Ave Reload Time:	Ave Total Rep Time:		Notes:	

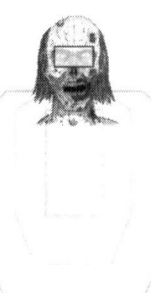

Date: B.Z.	Battle Ground:	Weapon:	Sights:	Undead / Infected / Mutant
Rep 1 Time:	Rep 2 Time:	Rep 3 Time:	Rep 4 Time:	Rep 5 Time:
Reload Time:	Reload Time:	Reload Time:	Reload Time:	Reload Time:
Live / Die	Live / Die	Live / Die	Live / Die	Live / Die
Ave Reload Time:	Ave Total Rep Time:		Notes:	

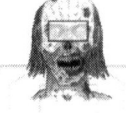

Date: B.Z.	Battle Ground:	Weapon:	Sights:	Undead / Infected / Mutant
Rep 1 Time:	Rep 2 Time:	Rep 3 Time:	Rep 4 Time:	Rep 5 Time:
Reload Time:	Reload Time:	Reload Time:	Reload Time:	Reload Time:
Live / Die	Live / Die	Live / Die	Live / Die	Live / Die
Ave Reload Time:	Ave Total Rep Time:		Notes:	

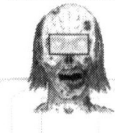

www.GUNFIGHTERSERIES.com ©

FEED

Date:	B.Z.	Battle Ground:	Weapon:	Sights:	Undead / Infected / Mutant
Rep 1 Time:		Rep 2 Time:	Rep 3 Time:	Rep 4 Time:	Rep 5 Time:
Reload Time:		Reload Time:	Reload Time:	Reload Time:	Reload Time:
Live / Die		Live / Die	Live / Die	Live / Die	Live / Die
Ave Reload Time:			Ave Total Rep Time:		Notes:

Date:	B.Z.	Battle Ground:	Weapon:	Sights:	Undead / Infected / Mutant
Rep 1 Time:		Rep 2 Time:	Rep 3 Time:	Rep 4 Time:	Rep 5 Time:
Reload Time:		Reload Time:	Reload Time:	Reload Time:	Reload Time:
Live / Die		Live / Die	Live / Die	Live / Die	Live / Die
Ave Reload Time:			Ave Total Rep Time:		Notes:

Date:	B.Z.	Battle Ground:	Weapon:	Sights:	Undead / Infected / Mutant
Rep 1 Time:		Rep 2 Time:	Rep 3 Time:	Rep 4 Time:	Rep 5 Time:
Reload Time:		Reload Time:	Reload Time:	Reload Time:	Reload Time:
Live / Die		Live / Die	Live / Die	Live / Die	Live / Die
Ave Reload Time:			Ave Total Rep Time:		Notes:

CARBINE DRILL: **THROES**

Purpose: Increase consistent shot cadence under movement pressure.

Distance: 25, 20, 15, 10, 5 yards.

Target: ZIPSC

Extra Equipment Needed: Shot timer.

Total Rounds Fired: 15 Rounds.

Point Penalty: Time plus penalty. Add 3 seconds for rounds outside the Z/A box. Add 5 seconds for rounds outside the head / body.

Repetitions: 1 Rep.

Starting Position & Condition: Standing – Ready position of choice. Weapon in condition 1.

Description: At the 25 yard line, at the timer beep, fire 1 round into the body box. Place carbine on safe, move quickly to the 20 yard line, fire 2 rounds into the body box. Place carbine on safe, move quickly to the 15 yard line, fire 3 rounds into the body box. Place carbine on safe, move quickly to the 10 yard line, fire 4 rounds into the body box. Place carbine on safe, move quickly to the 5 yard line, fire 5 rounds into the body box. Record time, point penalty and score.

Goals: Meat Bag: All in body box under 25 Seconds   Survivor: All in body box under 22.5 Seconds   Z Fighter: All in under 20 Seconds

Variations:

⊕   Infected Humans: All rounds fired to the ocular Z box. Add +5 seconds to the goal par times.

⊕   Mutants: Double the distance (50, 40. 30, 20, 10 yards) Double the shots fired at each yard line = 30 total.

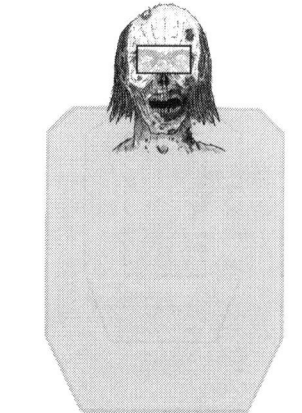

Target		
5 Yard	X5
10 Yard	X4
15 yard	X3
20 yard	x2
25 Yard	x1

THROES

Date:	B.Z.	Battle Ground:	Weapon:	Sights:
Side: Dominant / Support		Undead / Infected / Mutant	Rep Time:	Point Penalty:
Notes:				**Total Score:**

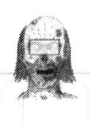

Date:	B.Z.	Battle Ground:	Weapon:	Sights:
Side: Dominant / Support		Undead / Infected / Mutant	Rep Time:	Point Penalty:
Notes:				**Total Score:**

Date:	B.Z.	Battle Ground:	Weapon:	Sights:
Side: Dominant / Support		Undead / Infected / Mutant	Rep Time:	Point Penalty:
Notes:				**Total Score:**

Date:	B.Z.	Battle Ground:	Weapon:	Sights:
Side: Dominant / Support		Undead / Infected / Mutant	Rep Time:	Point Penalty:
Notes:				**Total Score:**

Date:	B.Z.	Battle Ground:	Weapon:	Sights:
Side: Dominant / Support		Undead / Infected / Mutant	Rep Time:	Point Penalty:
Notes:				**Total Score:**

Z Fighter ©

THROES

Date:	B.Z.	Battle Ground:	Weapon:	Sights:
Side: Dominant / Support		Undead / Infected / Mutant	Rep Time:	Point Penalty:
Notes:				**Total Score:**

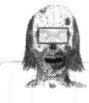

Date:	B.Z.	Battle Ground:	Weapon:	Sights:
Side: Dominant / Support		Undead / Infected / Mutant	Rep Time:	Point Penalty:
Notes:				**Total Score:**

Date:	B.Z.	Battle Ground:	Weapon:	Sights:
Side: Dominant / Support		Undead / Infected / Mutant	Rep Time:	Point Penalty:
Notes:				**Total Score:**

Date:	B.Z.	Battle Ground:	Weapon:	Sights:
Side: Dominant / Support		Undead / Infected / Mutant	Rep Time:	Point Penalty:
Notes:				**Total Score:**

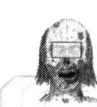

Date:	B.Z.	Battle Ground:	Weapon:	Sights:
Side: Dominant / Support		Undead / Infected / Mutant	Rep Time:	Point Penalty:
Notes:				**Total Score:**

www.GUNFIGHTERSERIES.com ©

THROES

Date:	B.Z.	Battle Ground:	Weapon:	Sights:
Side: Dominant / Support		Undead / Infected / Mutant	Rep Time:	Point Penalty:
Notes:				**Total Score:**

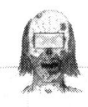

Date:	B.Z.	Battle Ground:	Weapon:	Sights:
Side: Dominant / Support		Undead / Infected / Mutant	Rep Time:	Point Penalty:
Notes:				**Total Score:**

Date:	B.Z.	Battle Ground:	Weapon:	Sights:
Side: Dominant / Support		Undead / Infected / Mutant	Rep Time:	Point Penalty:
Notes:				**Total Score:**

Date:	B.Z.	Battle Ground:	Weapon:	Sights:
Side: Dominant / Support		Undead / Infected / Mutant	Rep Time:	Point Penalty:
Notes:				**Total Score:**

Date:	B.Z.	Battle Ground:	Weapon:	Sights:
Side: Dominant / Support		Undead / Infected / Mutant	Rep Time:	Point Penalty:
Notes:				**Total Score:**

THROES

Date:	B.Z.	Battle Ground:	Weapon:	Sights:
Side: Dominant / Support		Undead / Infected / Mutant	Rep Time:	Point Penalty:
Notes:				**Total Score:**

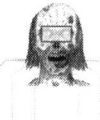

Date:	B.Z.	Battle Ground:	Weapon:	Sights:
Side: Dominant / Support		Undead / Infected / Mutant	Rep Time:	Point Penalty:
Notes:				**Total Score:**

Date:	B.Z.	Battle Ground:	Weapon:	Sights:
Side: Dominant / Support		Undead / Infected / Mutant	Rep Time:	Point Penalty:
Notes:				**Total Score:**

Date:	B.Z.	Battle Ground:	Weapon:	Sights:
Side: Dominant / Support		Undead / Infected / Mutant	Rep Time:	Point Penalty:
Notes:				**Total Score:**

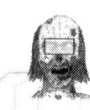

Date:	B.Z.	Battle Ground:	Weapon:	Sights:
Side: Dominant / Support		Undead / Infected / Mutant	Rep Time:	Point Penalty:
Notes:				**Total Score:**

THROES

Date:	B.Z.	Battle Ground:	Weapon:	Sights:
Side: Dominant / Support		Undead / Infected / Mutant	Rep Time:	Point Penalty:
Notes:				**Total Score:**

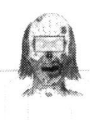

Date:	B.Z.	Battle Ground:	Weapon:	Sights:
Side: Dominant / Support		Undead / Infected / Mutant	Rep Time:	Point Penalty:
Notes:				**Total Score:**

Date:	B.Z.	Battle Ground:	Weapon:	Sights:
Side: Dominant / Support		Undead / Infected / Mutant	Rep Time:	Point Penalty:
Notes:				**Total Score:**

Date:	B.Z.	Battle Ground:	Weapon:	Sights:
Side: Dominant / Support		Undead / Infected / Mutant	Rep Time:	Point Penalty:
Notes:				**Total Score:**

Date:	B.Z.	Battle Ground:	Weapon:	Sights:
Side: Dominant / Support		Undead / Infected / Mutant	Rep Time:	Point Penalty:
Notes:				**Total Score:**

Z Fighter ©   Carbine Drills - 10

CARBINE DRILL: **SWARM**

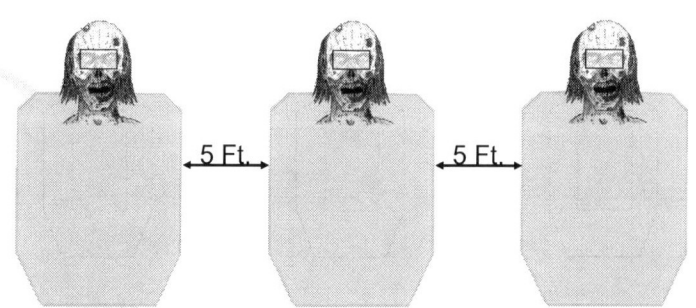

Purpose: Increase accuracy, speed and recoil management with multiple targets.

Distance: 15 Yards.

Target: ZIPSC X 3 spaced 5 feet apart.

Extra Equipment Needed: Shot timer.

Rounds Fired per Rep: 9 Rounds.

Total Rounds Fired: 27 Rounds.

Point Penalty: Live or Die.

Repetitions: 3 Reps.

Starting Position & Condition: Standing - Low ready. Condition 1.

Description: At the timer beep, fire 2 rounds into the A Zone body box, then 1 round to the ocular Z box, transition to next target with the same shot pattern and then transition to the last target with the same shot pattern. Goal is all rounds with goal par time and within A and Z zone boxes. If you fail goal par time or have rounds out of designated zone boxes during a repetition, you die!

Goals: Meat Bag: 10 Seconds.   Survivor: 8 Seconds.   Z Fighter: 6 Seconds.

Variations:

⊕ Infected Humans: 20 Yards.

⊕ Mutants: 20 yards with 4 shots to the body A box and 1 shot to the ocular Z box of each target. 15 Rounds per rep.

SWARM

Date: B.Z.	Battle Ground:	Weapon:	Undead / Infected / Mutant
Rep 1 Time:	**Rep 2 Time:**	**Rep 3 Time:**	Notes:
# Outside Box:	# Outside Box:	# Outside Box:	
Rep 1: Live / Die	Rep 2: Live / Die	Rep 3: Live / Die	Left to Right / Right to Left

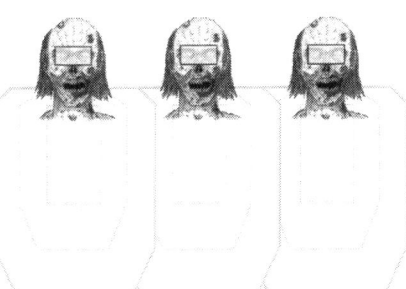

Date: B.Z.	Battle Ground:	Weapon:	Undead / Infected / Mutant
Rep 1 Time:	**Rep 2 Time:**	**Rep 3 Time:**	Notes:
# Outside Box:	# Outside Box:	# Outside Box:	
Rep 1: Live / Die	Rep 2: Live / Die	Rep 3: Live / Die	Left to Right / Right to Left

Date: B.Z.	Battle Ground:	Weapon:	Undead / Infected / Mutant
Rep 1 Time:	**Rep 2 Time:**	**Rep 3 Time:**	Notes:
# Outside Box:	# Outside Box:	# Outside Box:	
Rep 1: Live / Die	Rep 2: Live / Die	Rep 3: Live / Die	Left to Right / Right to Left

www.GUNFIGHTERSERIES.com ©

SWARM

Date: B.Z.	Battle Ground:	Weapon:	Undead / Infected / Mutant
Rep 1 Time:	**Rep 2 Time:**	**Rep 3 Time:**	Notes:
# Outside Box:	# Outside Box:	# Outside Box:	
Rep 1: Live / Die	Rep 2: Live / Die	Rep 3: Live / Die	Left to Right / Right to Left

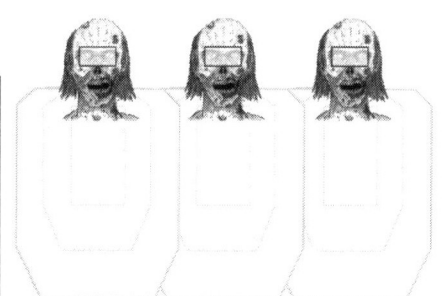

Date: B.Z.	Battle Ground:	Weapon:	Undead / Infected / Mutant
Rep 1 Time:	**Rep 2 Time:**	**Rep 3 Time:**	Notes:
# Outside Box:	# Outside Box:	# Outside Box:	
Rep 1: Live / Die	Rep 2: Live / Die	Rep 3: Live / Die	Left to Right / Right to Left

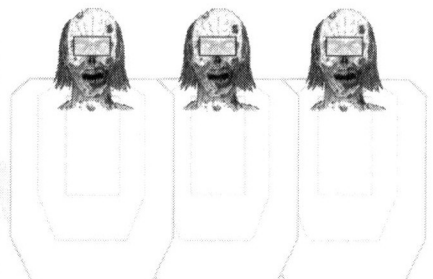

Date: B.Z.	Battle Ground:	Weapon:	Undead / Infected / Mutant
Rep 1 Time:	**Rep 2 Time:**	**Rep 3 Time:**	Notes:
# Outside Box:	# Outside Box:	# Outside Box:	
Rep 1: Live / Die	Rep 2: Live / Die	Rep 3: Live / Die	Left to Right / Right to Left

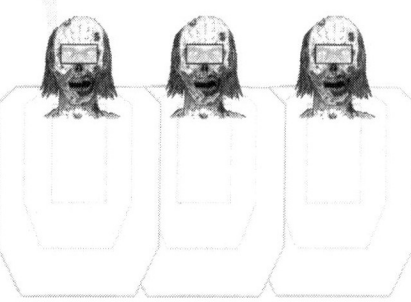

SWARM

Date:	B.Z.	Battle Ground:	Weapon:	Undead / Infected / Mutant
Rep 1 Time:		Rep 2 Time:	Rep 3 Time:	Notes:
# Outside Box:		# Outside Box:	# Outside Box:	
Rep 1: Live / Die		Rep 2: Live / Die	Rep 3: Live / Die	Left to Right / Right to Left

Date:	B.Z.	Battle Ground:	Weapon:	Undead / Infected / Mutant
Rep 1 Time:		Rep 2 Time:	Rep 3 Time:	Notes:
# Outside Box:		# Outside Box:	# Outside Box:	
Rep 1: Live / Die		Rep 2: Live / Die	Rep 3: Live / Die	Left to Right / Right to Left

Date:	B.Z.	Battle Ground:	Weapon:	Undead / Infected / Mutant
Rep 1 Time:		Rep 2 Time:	Rep 3 Time:	Notes:
# Outside Box:		# Outside Box:	# Outside Box:	
Rep 1: Live / Die		Rep 2: Live / Die	Rep 3: Live / Die	Left to Right / Right to Left

Z Fighter ©

SWARM

Date:	B.Z.	Battle Ground:	Weapon:	Undead / Infected / Mutant
Rep 1 Time:		**Rep 2 Time:**	**Rep 3 Time:**	Notes:
# Outside Box:		# Outside Box:	# Outside Box:	
Rep 1: Live / Die		Rep 2: Live / Die	Rep 3: Live / Die	Left to Right / Right to Left

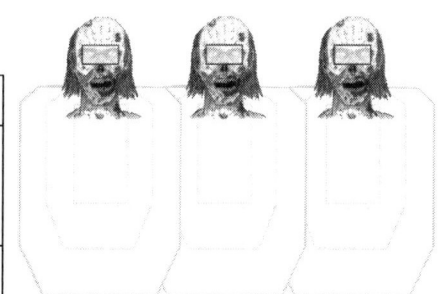

Date:	B.Z.	Battle Ground:	Weapon:	Undead / Infected / Mutant
Rep 1 Time:		**Rep 2 Time:**	**Rep 3 Time:**	Notes:
# Outside Box:		# Outside Box:	# Outside Box:	
Rep 1: Live / Die		Rep 2: Live / Die	Rep 3: Live / Die	Left to Right / Right to Left

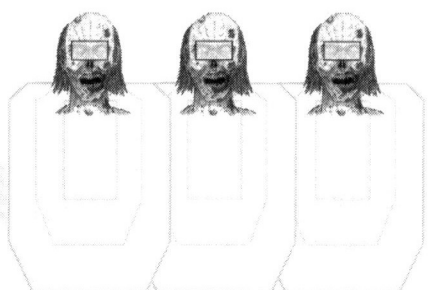

Date:	B.Z.	Battle Ground:	Weapon:	Undead / Infected / Mutant
Rep 1 Time:		**Rep 2 Time:**	**Rep 3 Time:**	Notes:
# Outside Box:		# Outside Box:	# Outside Box:	
Rep 1: Live / Die		Rep 2: Live / Die	Rep 3: Live / Die	Left to Right / Right to Left

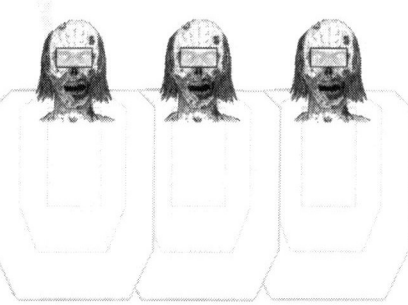

SWARM

Date: B.Z.	Battle Ground:	Weapon:	Undead / Infected / Mutant
Rep 1 Time:	**Rep 2 Time:**	**Rep 3 Time:**	Notes:
# Outside Box:	# Outside Box:	# Outside Box:	
Rep 1: Live / Die	Rep 2: Live / Die	Rep 3: Live / Die	Left to Right / Right to Left

Date: B.Z.	Battle Ground:	Weapon:	Undead / Infected / Mutant
Rep 1 Time:	**Rep 2 Time:**	**Rep 3 Time:**	Notes:
# Outside Box:	# Outside Box:	# Outside Box:	
Rep 1: Live / Die	Rep 2: Live / Die	Rep 3: Live / Die	Left to Right / Right to Left

Date: B.Z.	Battle Ground:	Weapon:	Undead / Infected / Mutant
Rep 1 Time:	**Rep 2 Time:**	**Rep 3 Time:**	Notes:
# Outside Box:	# Outside Box:	# Outside Box:	
Rep 1: Live / Die	Rep 2: Live / Die	Rep 3: Live / Die	Left to Right / Right to Left

CARBINE DRILL: **DEAD PREZIDENTS**

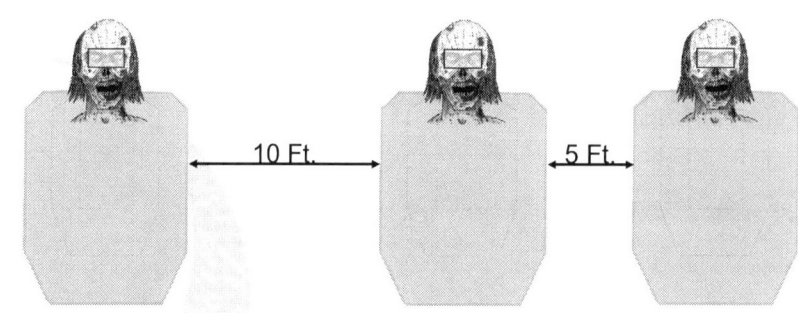

Purpose: Increase accuracy, speed and recoil management with multiple targets.

Distance: 10 Yards.

Target: ZIPSC X 3 spaced 5 and 10 feet apart.

Extra Equipment Needed: Shot timer. 1 Extra magazine with mag pouch.

Rounds Fired per Rep: 6 Rounds. (2 Mags of 3 rounds each.)   **Total Rounds Fired:** 18 Rounds.

Point Penalty: Live or Die.

Repetitions: 3 Reps.

Starting Position & Condition: Standing with your back facing the targets. - Low ready. Condition 1.

Description: At the timer beep, turn to face the targets and fire 1 round into the A Zone body box of each target. Reload. Then fire 1 round into the ocular Z box of each target.   If you fail goal par time or have rounds out of designated zone boxes during a repetition, you die!

Goals: Meat Bag: 12 Seconds.   Survivor: 9 Seconds.   Z Fighter: 8 Seconds.

Variations:

- ⊕ Infected Humans: From 15 yards with 1 magazines of 6 rounds, second magazine of 3 rounds. Start with 2 shots to the A zone body box of each target. Reload. Then 1 shot to the ocular Z box of each target.   Add 2 seconds to each goal par time.

- ⊕ Mutants: From 15 yards with 2 magazines of 15 rounds each. Shoot 4 rounds into the A zone body box plus one round into the ocular Z box of each target. Reload. Then repeat with 4 rounds into the A zone body box plus one round into the ocular Z box of each target.

DEAD PREZIDENTS

Date:	B.Z.	Battle Ground:	Weapon:	Undead / Infected / Mutant
Rep 1 Time:		**Rep 2 Time:**	**Rep 3 Time:**	Notes:
Reload Split Time:		Reload Split Time:	Reload Split Time:	
# Outside Box:		# Outside Box:	# Outside Box:	
Rep 1: Live / Die		Rep 2: Live / Die	Rep 3: Live / Die	

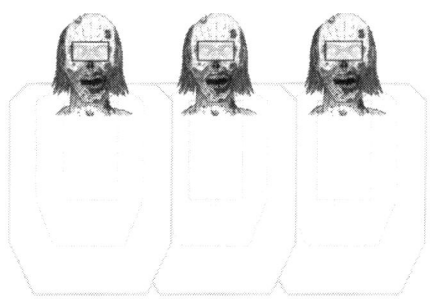

Date:	B.Z.	Battle Ground:	Weapon:	Undead / Infected / Mutant
Rep 1 Time:		**Rep 2 Time:**	**Rep 3 Time:**	Notes:
Reload Split Time:		Reload Split Time:	Reload Split Time:	
# Outside Box:		# Outside Box:	# Outside Box:	
Rep 1: Live / Die		Rep 2: Live / Die	Rep 3: Live / Die	

Date:	B.Z.	Battle Ground:	Weapon:	Undead / Infected / Mutant
Rep 1 Time:		**Rep 2 Time:**	**Rep 3 Time:**	Notes:
Reload Split Time:		Reload Split Time:	Reload Split Time:	
# Outside Box:		# Outside Box:	# Outside Box:	
Rep 1: Live / Die		Rep 2: Live / Die	Rep 3: Live / Die	

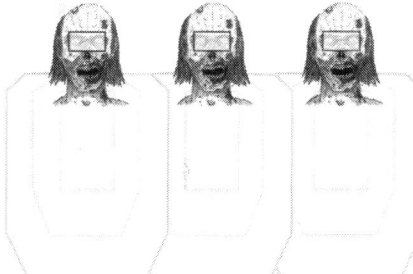

Z Fighter ©

Carbine Drills - 12

DEAD PREZIDENTS

Date: B.Z.	Battle Ground:	Weapon:	Undead / Infected / Mutant
Rep 1 Time:	**Rep 2 Time:**	**Rep 3 Time:**	Notes:
Reload Split Time:	Reload Split Time:	Reload Split Time:	
# Outside Box:	# Outside Box:	# Outside Box:	
Rep 1: Live / Die	Rep 2: Live / Die	Rep 3: Live / Die	

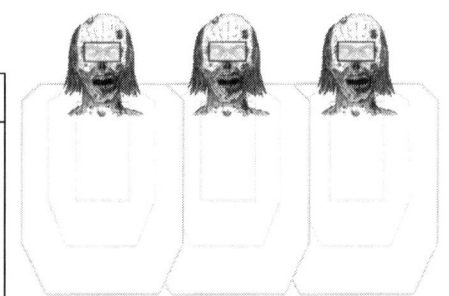

Date: B.Z.	Battle Ground:	Weapon:	Undead / Infected / Mutant
Rep 1 Time:	**Rep 2 Time:**	**Rep 3 Time:**	Notes:
Reload Split Time:	Reload Split Time:	Reload Split Time:	
# Outside Box:	# Outside Box:	# Outside Box:	
Rep 1: Live / Die	Rep 2: Live / Die	Rep 3: Live / Die	

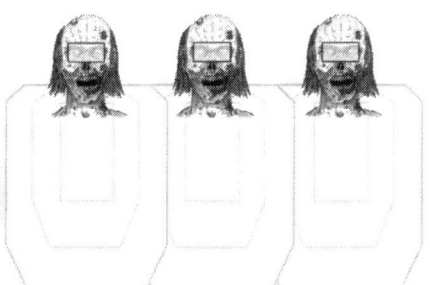

Date: B.Z.	Battle Ground:	Weapon:	Undead / Infected / Mutant
Rep 1 Time:	**Rep 2 Time:**	**Rep 3 Time:**	Notes:
Reload Split Time:	Reload Split Time:	Reload Split Time:	
# Outside Box:	# Outside Box:	# Outside Box:	
Rep 1: Live / Die	Rep 2: Live / Die	Rep 3: Live / Die	

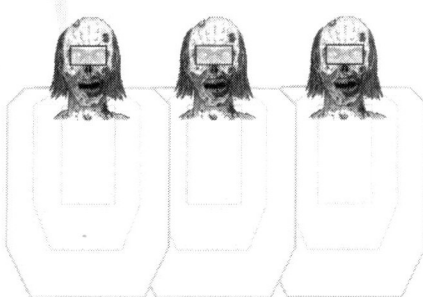

DEAD PREZIDENTS

Date:	B.Z.	Battle Ground:	Weapon:	Undead / Infected / Mutant
Rep 1 Time:		**Rep 2 Time:**	**Rep 3 Time:**	Notes:
Reload Split Time:		Reload Split Time:	Reload Split Time:	
# Outside Box:		# Outside Box:	# Outside Box:	
Rep 1: Live / Die		Rep 2: Live / Die	Rep 3: Live / Die	

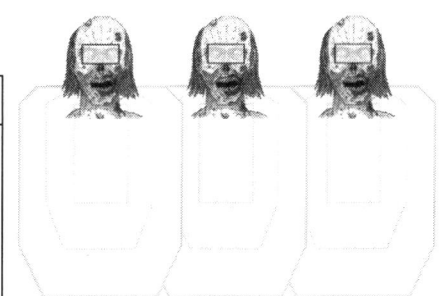

Date:	B.Z.	Battle Ground:	Weapon:	Undead / Infected / Mutant
Rep 1 Time:		**Rep 2 Time:**	**Rep 3 Time:**	Notes:
Reload Split Time:		Reload Split Time:	Reload Split Time:	
# Outside Box:		# Outside Box:	# Outside Box:	
Rep 1: Live / Die		Rep 2: Live / Die	Rep 3: Live / Die	

Date:	B.Z.	Battle Ground:	Weapon:	Undead / Infected / Mutant
Rep 1 Time:		**Rep 2 Time:**	**Rep 3 Time:**	Notes:
Reload Split Time:		Reload Split Time:	Reload Split Time:	
# Outside Box:		# Outside Box:	# Outside Box:	
Rep 1: Live / Die		Rep 2: Live / Die	Rep 3: Live / Die	

Z Fighter ©

Carbine Drills - 12

DEAD PREZIDENTS

Date: B.Z.	Battle Ground:	Weapon:	Undead / Infected / Mutant
Rep 1 Time:	**Rep 2 Time:**	**Rep 3 Time:**	Notes:
Reload Split Time:	Reload Split Time:	Reload Split Time:	
# Outside Box:	# Outside Box:	# Outside Box:	
Rep 1: Live / Die	Rep 2: Live / Die	Rep 3: Live / Die	

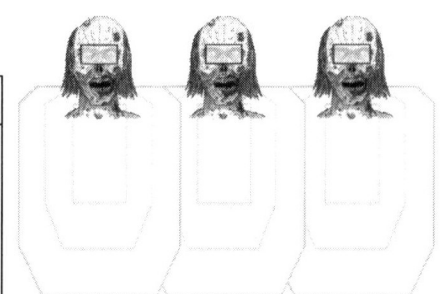

Date: B.Z.	Battle Ground:	Weapon:	Undead / Infected / Mutant
Rep 1 Time:	**Rep 2 Time:**	**Rep 3 Time:**	Notes:
Reload Split Time:	Reload Split Time:	Reload Split Time:	
# Outside Box:	# Outside Box:	# Outside Box:	
Rep 1: Live / Die	Rep 2: Live / Die	Rep 3: Live / Die	

Date: B.Z.	Battle Ground:	Weapon:	Undead / Infected / Mutant
Rep 1 Time:	**Rep 2 Time:**	**Rep 3 Time:**	Notes:
Reload Split Time:	Reload Split Time:	Reload Split Time:	
# Outside Box:	# Outside Box:	# Outside Box:	
Rep 1: Live / Die	Rep 2: Live / Die	Rep 3: Live / Die	

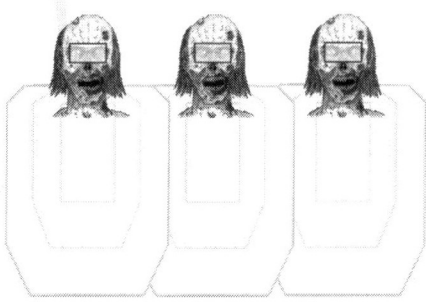

DEAD PREZIDENTS

Date: B.Z.	Battle Ground:	Weapon:	Undead / Infected / Mutant
Rep 1 Time:	**Rep 2 Time:**	**Rep 3 Time:**	Notes:
Reload Split Time:	Reload Split Time:	Reload Split Time:	
# Outside Box:	# Outside Box:	# Outside Box:	
Rep 1: Live / Die	Rep 2: Live / Die	Rep 3: Live / Die	

Date: B.Z.	Battle Ground:	Weapon:	Undead / Infected / Mutant
Rep 1 Time:	**Rep 2 Time:**	**Rep 3 Time:**	Notes:
Reload Split Time:	Reload Split Time:	Reload Split Time:	
# Outside Box:	# Outside Box:	# Outside Box:	
Rep 1: Live / Die	Rep 2: Live / Die	Rep 3: Live / Die	

Date: B.Z.	Battle Ground:	Weapon:	Undead / Infected / Mutant
Rep 1 Time:	**Rep 2 Time:**	**Rep 3 Time:**	Notes:
Reload Split Time:	Reload Split Time:	Reload Split Time:	
# Outside Box:	# Outside Box:	# Outside Box:	
Rep 1: Live / Die	Rep 2: Live / Die	Rep 3: Live / Die	

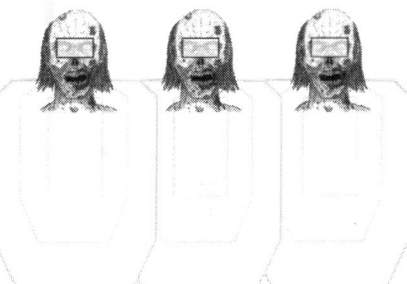

Z Fighter ©

Carbine Drills - 12

CARBINE DRILL: MEAT GRINDER

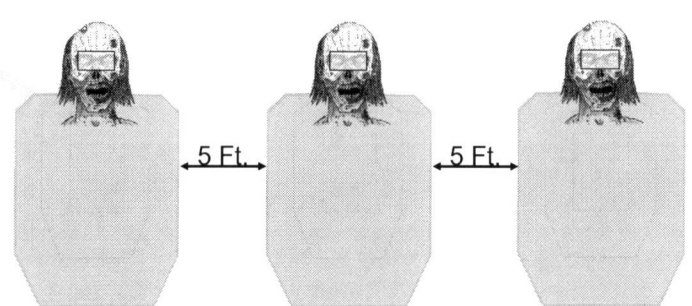

Purpose: Develop upper body strength and consistent one handed multiple target accuracy.

Distance: 10 Yards.

Target: ZIPSC X 3 spaced 5 feet apart.

Par Time: 15 Seconds.

Total Rounds Fired: 15 Rounds.

Point Penalty: Live or Die.

Repetitions: 1 Rep.

Starting Position & Condition: Standing – Port ready. Condition 1.

Description: At the timer beep, shoulder the carbine <u>one handed</u>, aim at target, put fire control selector on fire and fire 5 rounds into the (5 point) A Zone body box of each target. Record your time and goal score.

Goals: Meat Bag: All shots in body.   Survivor: All shots in the A Zone body box.   Z Fighter: 4 shots in body box and 1 shot in ocular box of each target.

Variations:

⊕ Infected Humans: 15 Yards. Taking a step backwards before each target.

⊕ Mutants: 15 Yards. Taking a sidestep before each target.

MEAT GRINDER

Date:	B.Z.	Battle Ground:	Weapon:	Sights:
Undead / Infected / Mutant			Side: Dominant / Support	Distance:
Drill Time:	All In: Live / Die		Notes:	

Date:	B.Z.	Battle Ground:	Weapon:	Sights:
Undead / Infected / Mutant			Side: Dominant / Support	Distance:
Drill Time:	All In: Live / Die		Notes:	

Date:	B.Z.	Battle Ground:	Weapon:	Sights:
Undead / Infected / Mutant			Side: Dominant / Support	Distance:
Drill Time:	All In: Live / Die		Notes:	

Z Fighter © Carbine Drills - 13

MEAT GRINDER

www.GUNFIGHTERSERIES.com ©

Date:	B.Z.	Battle Ground:	Weapon:	Sights:
Undead / Infected / Mutant			Side: Dominant / Support	Distance:
Drill Time:	All In: Live / Die		Notes:	

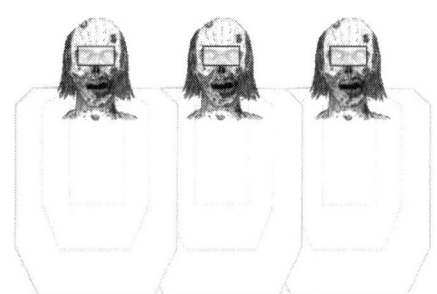

Date:	B.Z.	Battle Ground:	Weapon:	Sights:
Undead / Infected / Mutant			Side: Dominant / Support	Distance:
Drill Time:	All In: Live / Die		Notes:	

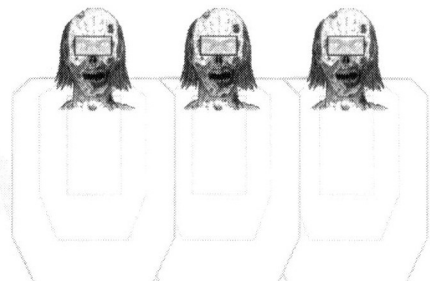

Date:	B.Z.	Battle Ground:	Weapon:	Sights:
Undead / Infected / Mutant			Side: Dominant / Support	Distance:
Drill Time:	All In: Live / Die		Notes:	

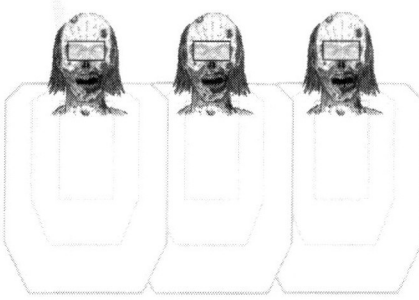

MEAT GRINDER

Date:	B.Z.	Battle Ground:	Weapon:	Sights:
Undead / Infected / Mutant			Side: Dominant / Support	Distance:
Drill Time:		**All In: Live / Die**	Notes:	

Date:	B.Z.	Battle Ground:	Weapon:	Sights:
Undead / Infected / Mutant			Side: Dominant / Support	Distance:
Drill Time:		**All In: Live / Die**	Notes:	

Date:	B.Z.	Battle Ground:	Weapon:	Sights:
Undead / Infected / Mutant			Side: Dominant / Support	Distance:
Drill Time:		**All In: Live / Die**	Notes:	

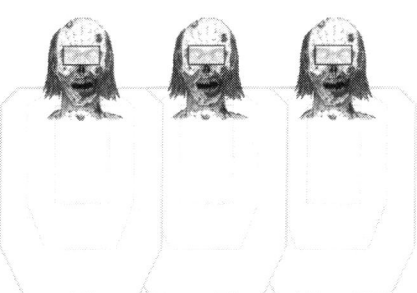

Z Fighter ©

Carbine Drills - 13

MEAT GRINDER

Date:	B.Z.	Battle Ground:	Weapon:	Sights:
Undead / Infected / Mutant			Side: Dominant / Support	Distance:
Drill Time:	**All In: Live / Die**		Notes:	

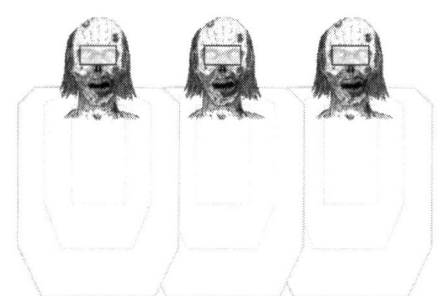

Date:	B.Z.	Battle Ground:	Weapon:	Sights:
Undead / Infected / Mutant			Side: Dominant / Support	Distance:
Drill Time:	**All In: Live / Die**		Notes:	

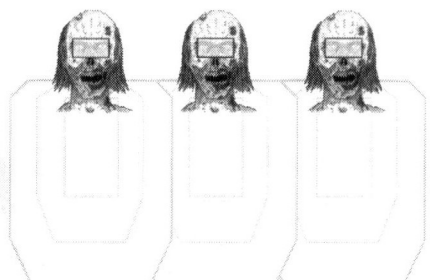

Date:	B.Z.	Battle Ground:	Weapon:	Sights:
Undead / Infected / Mutant			Side: Dominant / Support	Distance:
Drill Time:	**All In: Live / Die**		Notes:	

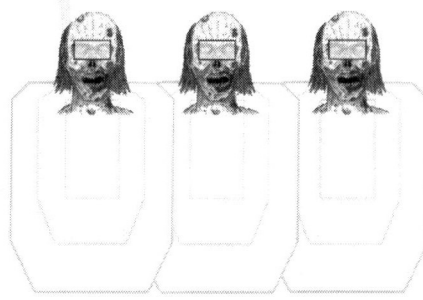

MEAT GRINDER

Date:	B.Z.	Battle Ground:	Weapon:	Sights:
Undead / Infected / Mutant			Side: Dominant / Support	Distance:
Drill Time:	**All In: Live / Die**		Notes:	

Date:	B.Z.	Battle Ground:	Weapon:	Sights:
Undead / Infected / Mutant			Side: Dominant / Support	Distance:
Drill Time:	**All In: Live / Die**		Notes:	

Date:	B.Z.	Battle Ground:	Weapon:	Sights:
Undead / Infected / Mutant			Side: Dominant / Support	Distance:
Drill Time:	**All In: Live / Die**		Notes:	

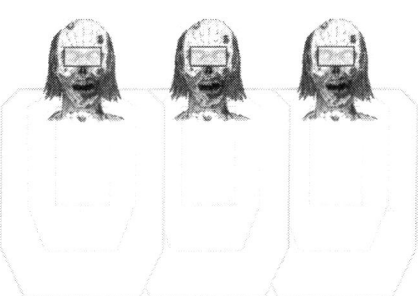

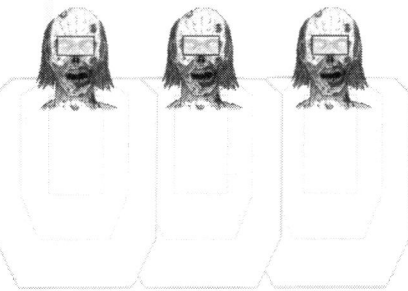

Carbine Drills - 13

CARBINE DRILL: **CARDIO**

Purpose: Determining best shooting positions with carbine to balance speed and accuracy.

Distance: 100, 90, 80, 70, 60, 50, 40, 30, 20, 10 Yards.

Target: ZIPSC Hostage (Place a photo of a loved one on the hostage).

Extra Equipment Needed: Shot timer.

Rounds Fired Per Rep: 10 Rounds.   **Total Rounds Fired:** 30 Rounds.

Point Penalty: Time plus penalty.   **Repetitions:** 3 Reps.

Starting Position & Condition: Standing carbine low ready, back facing target. Condition 1.

Description: At the timer beep, at the 100 yard line, turn and face the target. Using any shooting position, aim and fire 1 round into the ocular Z box. Make safe, low ready carry, move quickly to 90 yard line. Using any shooting position, aim and fire 1 round into the ocular Z Box. Make safe, low ready carry, move quickly to 80 yard line. Continue until you fire your last shot at 10 yards. Record time and score.

For every hit in the Z head outside the ocular Z box, add 3 seconds to your time. For every miss, add 10 seconds to your time. Hit the hostage, add 30 seconds. Add the penalty time onto your recorded time for that repetition. Average all of the repetitions for your time score.

Goals: Meat Bag: 180 Seconds.   Survivor: 150 Seconds.   Z Fighter: 120 Seconds.

Variations:

⊕   Infected Humans: Double the round count.

⊕   Mutants: Reverse direction of movement, starting at 10 yards.

CARDIO

Date:	B.Z.	Battle Ground:	Carbine:	Undead / Infected / Mutant
Rep 1 Time:		Rep 2 Time:	Rep 3 Time:	Notes:
+ Penalties:		+ Penalties:	+ Penalties:	
= Rep 1 Score:		= Rep 2 Score:	= Rep 3 Score:	Ave Rep Score:

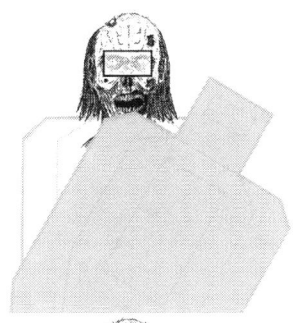

Date:	B.Z.	Battle Ground:	Carbine:	Undead / Infected / Mutant
Rep 1 Time:		Rep 2 Time:	Rep 3 Time:	Notes:
+ Penalties:		+ Penalties:	+ Penalties:	
= Rep 1 Score:		= Rep 2 Score:	= Rep 3 Score:	Ave Rep Score:

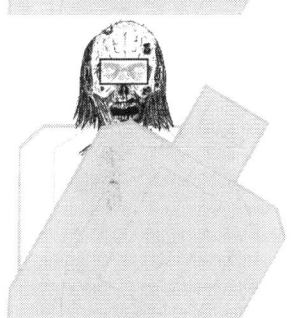

Date:	B.Z.	Battle Ground:	Carbine:	Undead / Infected / Mutant
Rep 1 Time:		Rep 2 Time:	Rep 3 Time:	Notes:
+ Penalties:		+ Penalties:	+ Penalties:	
= Rep 1 Score:		= Rep 2 Score:	= Rep 3 Score:	Ave Rep Score:

Z Fighter ©

CARDIO

Date:	B.Z.	Battle Ground:	Carbine:	Undead / Infected / Mutant
Rep 1 Time:		Rep 2 Time:	Rep 3 Time:	Notes:
+ Penalties:		+ Penalties:	+ Penalties:	
= Rep 1 Score:		= Rep 2 Score:	= Rep 3 Score:	Ave Rep Score:

Date:	B.Z.	Battle Ground:	Carbine:	Undead / Infected / Mutant
Rep 1 Time:		Rep 2 Time:	Rep 3 Time:	Notes:
+ Penalties:		+ Penalties:	+ Penalties:	
= Rep 1 Score:		= Rep 2 Score:	= Rep 3 Score:	Ave Rep Score:

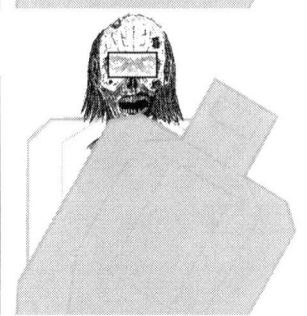

Date:	B.Z.	Battle Ground:	Carbine:	Undead / Infected / Mutant
Rep 1 Time:		Rep 2 Time:	Rep 3 Time:	Notes:
+ Penalties:		+ Penalties:	+ Penalties:	
= Rep 1 Score:		= Rep 2 Score:	= Rep 3 Score:	Ave Rep Score:

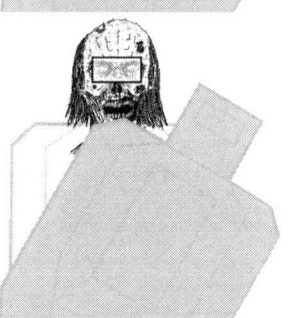

CARDIO

Date:	B.Z.	Battle Ground:	Carbine:	Undead / Infected / Mutant
Rep 1 Time:		Rep 2 Time:	Rep 3 Time:	Notes:
+ Penalties:		+ Penalties:	+ Penalties:	
= Rep 1 Score:		**= Rep 2 Score:**	**= Rep 3 Score:**	**Ave Rep Score:**

Date:	B.Z.	Battle Ground:	Carbine:	Undead / Infected / Mutant
Rep 1 Time:		Rep 2 Time:	Rep 3 Time:	Notes:
+ Penalties:		+ Penalties:	+ Penalties:	
= Rep 1 Score:		**= Rep 2 Score:**	**= Rep 3 Score:**	**Ave Rep Score:**

Date:	B.Z.	Battle Ground:	Carbine:	Undead / Infected / Mutant
Rep 1 Time:		Rep 2 Time:	Rep 3 Time:	Notes:
+ Penalties:		+ Penalties:	+ Penalties:	
= Rep 1 Score:		**= Rep 2 Score:**	**= Rep 3 Score:**	**Ave Rep Score:**

www.GUNFIGHTERSERIES.com ©

CARDIO

Date:	B.Z.	Battle Ground:	Carbine:	Undead / Infected / Mutant
Rep 1 Time:		Rep 2 Time:	Rep 3 Time:	Notes:
+ Penalties:		+ Penalties:	+ Penalties:	
= Rep 1 Score:		**= Rep 2 Score:**	**= Rep 3 Score:**	**Ave Rep Score:**

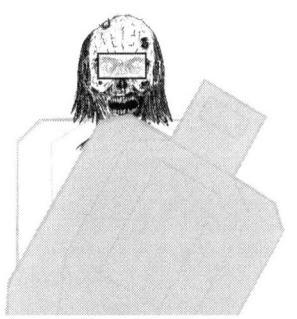

Date:	B.Z.	Battle Ground:	Carbine:	Undead / Infected / Mutant
Rep 1 Time:		Rep 2 Time:	Rep 3 Time:	Notes:
+ Penalties:		+ Penalties:	+ Penalties:	
= Rep 1 Score:		**= Rep 2 Score:**	**= Rep 3 Score:**	**Ave Rep Score:**

Date:	B.Z.	Battle Ground:	Carbine:	Undead / Infected / Mutant
Rep 1 Time:		Rep 2 Time:	Rep 3 Time:	Notes:
+ Penalties:		+ Penalties:	+ Penalties:	
= Rep 1 Score:		**= Rep 2 Score:**	**= Rep 3 Score:**	**Ave Rep Score:**

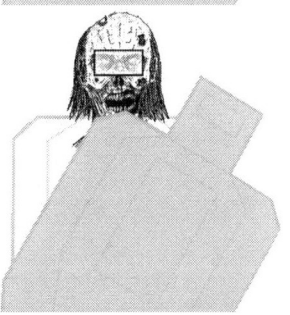

CARDIO

Date: B.Z.	Battle Ground:	Carbine:	Undead / Infected / Mutant
Rep 1 Time:	Rep 2 Time:	Rep 3 Time:	Notes:
+ Penalties:	+ Penalties:	+ Penalties:	
= Rep 1 Score:	**= Rep 2 Score:**	**= Rep 3 Score:**	**Ave Rep Score:**

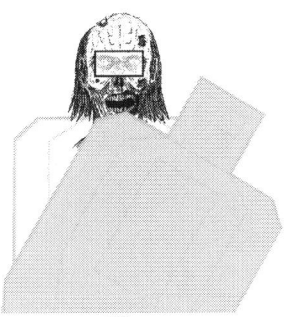

Date: B.Z.	Battle Ground:	Carbine:	Undead / Infected / Mutant
Rep 1 Time:	Rep 2 Time:	Rep 3 Time:	Notes:
+ Penalties:	+ Penalties:	+ Penalties:	
= Rep 1 Score:	**= Rep 2 Score:**	**= Rep 3 Score:**	**Ave Rep Score:**

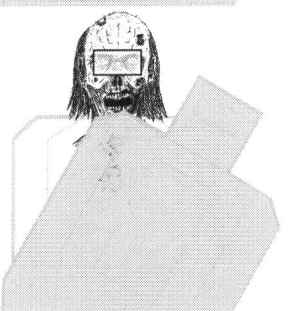

Date: B.Z.	Battle Ground:	Carbine:	Undead / Infected / Mutant
Rep 1 Time:	Rep 2 Time:	Rep 3 Time:	Notes:
+ Penalties:	+ Penalties:	+ Penalties:	
= Rep 1 Score:	**= Rep 2 Score:**	**= Rep 3 Score:**	**Ave Rep Score:**

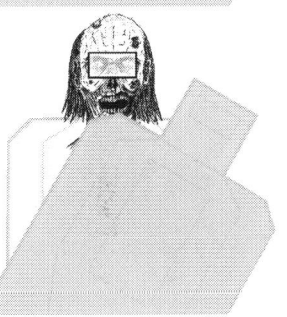

Z Fighter ©   Carbine Drills - 14

CARBINE DRILL: Z FORMATION

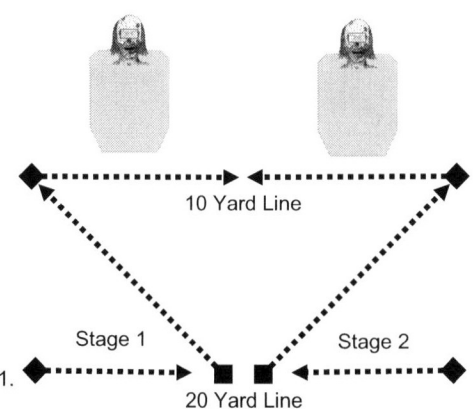

Purpose: Accuracy while moving.

Distance: 20 - 10 Yards.   **Target:** ZIPSC (Undead)

Rounds Fired Per Stage: 15 Rounds.   **Total Rounds Fired:** 60 Rounds.

Point Penalty: 5 Points A/Z box. 3 Points outside A/Z Box. 0 Points off target.

Repetitions: 2 Reps of each stage.

Starting Position & Condition: From 20 yard line. Standing – Low ready with carbine pointed down range. Condition 1.

Description: With the rifle pointed down range, keeping your eyes on the target, perform the prescribed stage repetition.

Stage 1: At your own personal go, with rifle in your right shoulder, fire 5 rounds into the A zone body box while moving left to right (laterally). Switch rifle to your left shoulder, fire 5 rounds into the A zone body box while advancing right to left (diagonally) to the 10 yard line. Switch rifle to your right shoulder, fire 5 rounds into the A zone body box while moving right to left (laterally) from the 10 yard line.

Stage 2: Starting from the 20 yard line. At your own personal go, with rifle in your left shoulder, conduct the same drill traveling in opposite directions switching shoulders as needed.

Goals: Meat Bag: 240 Points   Survivor: 270 Points   Z Fighter: 300 Points

Variations:

⊕   Infected Human: Fire 4 rounds into the A zone body box and 1 round into the ocular Z box on each leg.

⊕   Mutants: Fire 4 rounds into the A zone body box and 1 round into the ocular Z box on each leg. 30 Second par time per rep. No more than 10 rounds per magazine, forcing reloads.

Z FORMATION

Date:	B.Z	Battle Ground:	Undead / Infected / Mutants	Notes:
Weapon:		Sights:	Sling Used: Y / N	
Rep 1 Time:		Rep 2 Time:	Foot Wear:	
Rep 1 Score:		**Rep 2 Score**:	**Total Score**:	

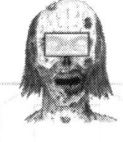

Date:	B.Z	Battle Ground:	Undead / Infected / Mutants	Notes:
Weapon:		Sights:	Sling Used: Y / N	
Rep 1 Time:		Rep 2 Time:	Foot Wear:	
Rep 1 Score:		**Rep 2 Score**:	**Total Score**:	

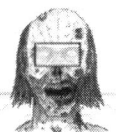

Date:	B.Z	Battle Ground:	Undead / Infected / Mutants	Notes:
Weapon:		Sights:	Sling Used: Y / N	
Rep 1 Time:		Rep 2 Time:	Foot Wear:	
Rep 1 Score:		**Rep 2 Score**:	**Total Score**:	

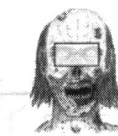

Date:	B.Z	Battle Ground:	Undead / Infected / Mutants	Notes:
Weapon:		Sights:	Sling Used: Y / N	
Rep 1 Time:		Rep 2 Time:	Foot Wear:	
Rep 1 Score:		**Rep 2 Score**:	**Total Score**:	

Z Fighter ©

Carbine Drills - 15

Z FORMATION

Date:	B.Z	Battle Ground:	Undead / Infected / Mutants	
Weapon:		Sights:	Sling Used: Y / N	Notes:
Rep 1 Time:		Rep 2 Time:	Foot Wear:	
Rep 1 Score:		**Rep 2 Score**:	**Total Score**:	

Date:	B.Z	Battle Ground:	Undead / Infected / Mutants	
Weapon:		Sights:	Sling Used: Y / N	Notes:
Rep 1 Time:		Rep 2 Time:	Foot Wear:	
Rep 1 Score:		**Rep 2 Score**:	**Total Score**:	

Date:	B.Z	Battle Ground:	Undead / Infected / Mutants	
Weapon:		Sights:	Sling Used: Y / N	Notes:
Rep 1 Time:		Rep 2 Time:	Foot Wear:	
Rep 1 Score:		**Rep 2 Score**:	**Total Score**:	

Date:	B.Z	Battle Ground:	Undead / Infected / Mutants	
Weapon:		Sights:	Sling Used: Y / N	Notes:
Rep 1 Time:		Rep 2 Time:	Foot Wear:	
Rep 1 Score:		**Rep 2 Score**:	**Total Score**:	

www.GUNFIGHTERSERIES.com ©

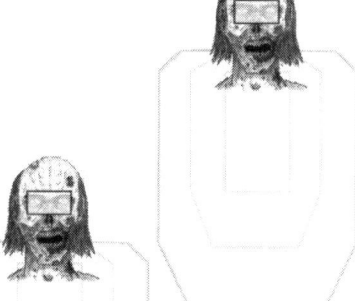

Z FORMATION

Date:	B.Z	Battle Ground:	Undead / Infected / Mutants	Notes:
Weapon:		Sights:	Sling Used: Y / N	
Rep 1 Time:		Rep 2 Time:	Foot Wear:	
Rep 1 Score:		**Rep 2 Score**:	**Total Score**:	

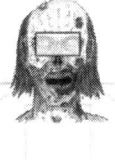

Date:	B.Z	Battle Ground:	Undead / Infected / Mutants	Notes:
Weapon:		Sights:	Sling Used: Y / N	
Rep 1 Time:		Rep 2 Time:	Foot Wear:	
Rep 1 Score:		**Rep 2 Score**:	**Total Score**:	

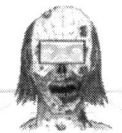

Date:	B.Z	Battle Ground:	Undead / Infected / Mutants	Notes:
Weapon:		Sights:	Sling Used: Y / N	
Rep 1 Time:		Rep 2 Time:	Foot Wear:	
Rep 1 Score:		**Rep 2 Score**:	**Total Score**:	

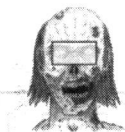

Date:	B.Z	Battle Ground:	Undead / Infected / Mutants	Notes:
Weapon:		Sights:	Sling Used: Y / N	
Rep 1 Time:		Rep 2 Time:	Foot Wear:	
Rep 1 Score:		**Rep 2 Score**:	**Total Score**:	

Z FORMATION

Date:	B.Z	Battle Ground:	Undead / Infected / Mutants	Notes:
Weapon:		Sights:	Sling Used: Y / N	
Rep 1 Time:		Rep 2 Time:	Foot Wear:	
Rep 1 Score:		**Rep 2 Score**:	**Total Score**:	

Date:	B.Z	Battle Ground:	Undead / Infected / Mutants	Notes:
Weapon:		Sights:	Sling Used: Y / N	
Rep 1 Time:		Rep 2 Time:	Foot Wear:	
Rep 1 Score:		**Rep 2 Score**:	**Total Score**:	

Date:	B.Z	Battle Ground:	Undead / Infected / Mutants	Notes:
Weapon:		Sights:	Sling Used: Y / N	
Rep 1 Time:		Rep 2 Time:	Foot Wear:	
Rep 1 Score:		**Rep 2 Score**:	**Total Score**:	

Date:	B.Z	Battle Ground:	Undead / Infected / Mutants	Notes:
Weapon:		Sights:	Sling Used: Y / N	
Rep 1 Time:		Rep 2 Time:	Foot Wear:	
Rep 1 Score:		**Rep 2 Score**:	**Total Score**:	

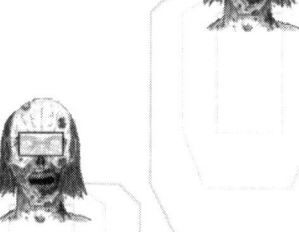
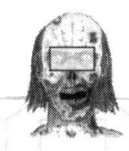
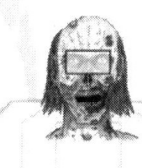

www.GUNFIGHTERSERIES.com ©

Z FORMATION

Date:	B.Z	Battle Ground:	Undead / Infected / Mutants	
Weapon:		Sights:	Sling Used: Y / N	Notes:
Rep 1 Time:		Rep 2 Time:	Foot Wear:	
Rep 1 Score:		**Rep 2 Score**:	**Total Score:**	

Date:	B.Z	Battle Ground:	Undead / Infected / Mutants	
Weapon:		Sights:	Sling Used: Y / N	Notes:
Rep 1 Time:		Rep 2 Time:	Foot Wear:	
Rep 1 Score:		**Rep 2 Score**:	**Total Score:**	

Date:	B.Z	Battle Ground:	Undead / Infected / Mutants	
Weapon:		Sights:	Sling Used: Y / N	Notes:
Rep 1 Time:		Rep 2 Time:	Foot Wear:	
Rep 1 Score:		**Rep 2 Score**:	**Total Score:**	

Date:	B.Z	Battle Ground:	Undead / Infected / Mutants	
Weapon:		Sights:	Sling Used: Y / N	Notes:
Rep 1 Time:		Rep 2 Time:	Foot Wear:	
Rep 1 Score:		**Rep 2 Score**:	**Total Score:**	

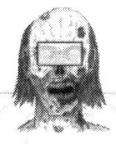
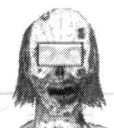
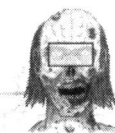

TRANSITION DRILL: **TRANS**

Purpose: Increase weapon transition speed, nervous system memory of a transition to pistol and recoil management.

Distance: 5 Yards.

Target: ZIPSC (Undead)

Par Time: Per goal standard.

Extra Equipment Needed: Shot timer, pistol in condition 1, pistol holster and carbine sling.

Rounds Fired Per Rep: 3 Rounds. (2 Carbine & 1 Pistol)

Total Rounds Fired: 15 Rounds. (10 Carbine & 5 Pistol)

Point Penalty: Live or Die.

Repetitions: 5 Reps.

Starting Position & Condition: Standing - Carbine pointed at target. Pistol holstered. Condition 1 both weapons.

Description: At the timer beep, with carbine, fire 2 rounds into the body A zone, let carbine hang by your sling and transition to pistol, aim and fire 1 rounds into the ocular Z box after transitioning. Record the time. Repeat 4 more times. Record your results for reference.

Goals: Meat Bag: 5 Seconds.   Survivor: 4 Seconds.   Z Fighter: 2.75 Seconds.

Variations:

⊕   Infected Human: From 7 yards, firing 5 rounds into body A box, take a step back while transitioning the fire1 pistol round into ocular Z box. Add 1 second to par time.

⊕   Mutants: From 10 yards, moving laterally left or right, firing 5 rounds into body A box and 1 pistol round into ocular Z box.

TRANS

Date:	B.Z.	Battle Ground:	Weapon:	Sights:	A Box: Head / Body
Rep 1 Time:		Rep 2 Time:	Rep 3 Time:	Rep 4 Time:	Rep 5 Time:
Transition Time:		Reload Time:	Reload Time:	Reload Time:	Reload Time:
A Box: Live / Die		A Box: Live / Die	A Box: Live / Die	A Box: Live / Die	A Box: Live / Die
Average Rep Time:		Notes:			

Date:	B.Z.	Battle Ground:	Weapon:	Sights:	A Box: Head / Body
Rep 1 Time:		Rep 2 Time:	Rep 3 Time:	Rep 4 Time:	Rep 5 Time:
Transition Time:		Reload Time:	Reload Time:	Reload Time:	Reload Time:
A Box: Live / Die		A Box: Live / Die	A Box: Live / Die	A Box: Live / Die	A Box: Live / Die
Average Rep Time:		Notes:			

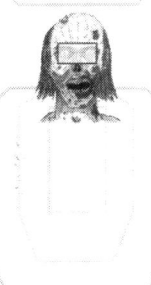

Date:	B.Z.	Battle Ground:	Weapon:	Sights:	A Box: Head / Body
Rep 1 Time:		Rep 2 Time:	Rep 3 Time:	Rep 4 Time:	Rep 5 Time:
Transition Time:		Reload Time:	Reload Time:	Reload Time:	Reload Time:
A Box: Live / Die		A Box: Live / Die	A Box: Live / Die	A Box: Live / Die	A Box: Live / Die
Average Rep Time:		Notes:			

Z Fighter ©

Transition Drills - 1

TRANS

www.GUNFIGHTERSERIES.com ©

Date: B.Z.	Battle Ground:	Weapon:	Sights:	A Box: Head / Body
Rep 1 Time:	Rep 2 Time:	Rep 3 Time:	Rep 4 Time:	Rep 5 Time:
Transition Time:	Reload Time:	Reload Time:	Reload Time:	Reload Time:
A Box: Live / Die	A Box: Live / Die	A Box: Live / Die	A Box: Live / Die	A Box: Live / Die
Average Rep Time:		Notes:		

Date: B.Z.	Battle Ground:	Weapon:	Sights:	A Box: Head / Body
Rep 1 Time:	Rep 2 Time:	Rep 3 Time:	Rep 4 Time:	Rep 5 Time:
Transition Time:	Reload Time:	Reload Time:	Reload Time:	Reload Time:
A Box: Live / Die	A Box: Live / Die	A Box: Live / Die	A Box: Live / Die	A Box: Live / Die
Average Rep Time:		Notes:		

Date: B.Z.	Battle Ground:	Weapon:	Sights:	A Box: Head / Body
Rep 1 Time:	Rep 2 Time:	Rep 3 Time:	Rep 4 Time:	Rep 5 Time:
Transition Time:	Reload Time:	Reload Time:	Reload Time:	Reload Time:
A Box: Live / Die	A Box: Live / Die	A Box: Live / Die	A Box: Live / Die	A Box: Live / Die
Average Rep Time:		Notes:		

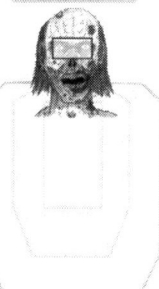

TRANS

Date:	B.Z.	Battle Ground:	Weapon:	Sights:	A Box: Head / Body
Rep 1 Time:		Rep 2 Time:	Rep 3 Time:	Rep 4 Time:	Rep 5 Time:
Transition Time:		Reload Time:	Reload Time:	Reload Time:	Reload Time:
A Box: Live / Die		A Box: Live / Die	A Box: Live / Die	A Box: Live / Die	A Box: Live / Die
Average Rep Time:		Notes:			

Date:	B.Z.	Battle Ground:	Weapon:	Sights:	A Box: Head / Body
Rep 1 Time:		Rep 2 Time:	Rep 3 Time:	Rep 4 Time:	Rep 5 Time:
Transition Time:		Reload Time:	Reload Time:	Reload Time:	Reload Time:
A Box: Live / Die		A Box: Live / Die	A Box: Live / Die	A Box: Live / Die	A Box: Live / Die
Average Rep Time:		Notes:			

Date:	B.Z.	Battle Ground:	Weapon:	Sights:	A Box: Head / Body
Rep 1 Time:		Rep 2 Time:	Rep 3 Time:	Rep 4 Time:	Rep 5 Time:
Transition Time:		Reload Time:	Reload Time:	Reload Time:	Reload Time:
A Box: Live / Die		A Box: Live / Die	A Box: Live / Die	A Box: Live / Die	A Box: Live / Die
Average Rep Time:		Notes:			

Z Fighter ©

Transition Drills - 1

TRANS

Date: B.Z.	Battle Ground:	Weapon:	Sights:	A Box: Head / Body
Rep 1 Time:	Rep 2 Time:	Rep 3 Time:	Rep 4 Time:	Rep 5 Time:
Transition Time:	Reload Time:	Reload Time:	Reload Time:	Reload Time:
A Box: Live / Die	A Box: Live / Die	A Box: Live / Die	A Box: Live / Die	A Box: Live / Die
Average Rep Time:		Notes:		

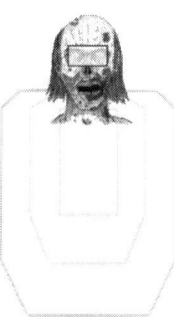

Date: B.Z.	Battle Ground:	Weapon:	Sights:	A Box: Head / Body
Rep 1 Time:	Rep 2 Time:	Rep 3 Time:	Rep 4 Time:	Rep 5 Time:
Transition Time:	Reload Time:	Reload Time:	Reload Time:	Reload Time:
A Box: Live / Die	A Box: Live / Die	A Box: Live / Die	A Box: Live / Die	A Box: Live / Die
Average Rep Time:		Notes:		

Date: B.Z.	Battle Ground:	Weapon:	Sights:	A Box: Head / Body
Rep 1 Time:	Rep 2 Time:	Rep 3 Time:	Rep 4 Time:	Rep 5 Time:
Transition Time:	Reload Time:	Reload Time:	Reload Time:	Reload Time:
A Box: Live / Die	A Box: Live / Die	A Box: Live / Die	A Box: Live / Die	A Box: Live / Die
Average Rep Time:		Notes:		

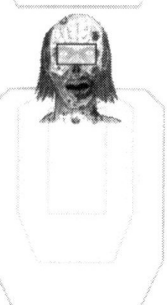

TRANS

Date: B.Z.	Battle Ground:	Weapon:	Sights:	A Box: Head / Body
Rep 1 Time:	Rep 2 Time:	Rep 3 Time:	Rep 4 Time:	Rep 5 Time:
Transition Time:	Reload Time:	Reload Time:	Reload Time:	Reload Time:
A Box: Live / Die	A Box: Live / Die	A Box: Live / Die	A Box: Live / Die	A Box: Live / Die
Average Rep Time:		Notes:		

Date: B.Z.	Battle Ground:	Weapon:	Sights:	A Box: Head / Body
Rep 1 Time:	Rep 2 Time:	Rep 3 Time:	Rep 4 Time:	Rep 5 Time:
Transition Time:	Reload Time:	Reload Time:	Reload Time:	Reload Time:
A Box: Live / Die	A Box: Live / Die	A Box: Live / Die	A Box: Live / Die	A Box: Live / Die
Average Rep Time:		Notes:		

Date: B.Z.	Battle Ground:	Weapon:	Sights:	A Box: Head / Body
Rep 1 Time:	Rep 2 Time:	Rep 3 Time:	Rep 4 Time:	Rep 5 Time:
Transition Time:	Reload Time:	Reload Time:	Reload Time:	Reload Time:
A Box: Live / Die	A Box: Live / Die	A Box: Live / Die	A Box: Live / Die	A Box: Live / Die
Average Rep Time:		Notes.		

Transition Drills - 1

TRANSITION DRILL: **FINISH HIM!!**

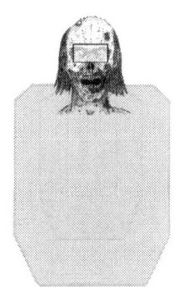

Purpose: Close range weapon transitions.

Distance: 7 Yards.

Target: ZIPSC X1 (Undead) and MTC Z-1 X1 (Undead) at ground level.

Extra Equipment Needed: Shot timer. Carbine with sling. Pistol with holster.

Rounds Fired Per Rep: 3 Rounds. 1 Carbine mag of 2 rounds. 1 Pistol mag of 1 round.

Total Rounds Fired: 9 Round.

Repetitions: 3 Reps.

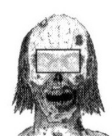

Point Penalty: Time plus penalty.

Starting Position & Condition: Standing, tactical carbine ready. Condition 1 both weapons. Pistol holstered.

Description: Starting at 7 yards, at the timer beep, with carbine aim and fire 2 rounds into the body A box of the ZIPSC target while advancing to the 5 yard line. The undead falls to the ground but is still crawling (Simulated). Carbine goes dry. Transitioning to pistol. From the 5 yard fire 1 round into the head ocular Z box of the ground level MTC Z-1 target to neutralize the threat.

For every hit outside the body A or head ocular Z box, add 3 seconds to your time. For every miss, add 5 seconds to your time. Add the penalty time onto your recorded time for that repetition.

Goals: Meat Bag: 5 Seconds.   Survivor: 4.5 Seconds.   Z Fighter: 3.75 Seconds.

Variations:

⊕   Infected Humans: Stationary from 7 yards with carbine, then take 1 large step backwards to gain standoff distance while transitioning to pistol. (Add 1 second to par)

⊕   Mutants: From 10 yards, sidestep left or right while firing 5 rounds into body A box and 1 pistol round into head Z box. (Add 2 seconds to par)

FINISH HIM!!

Date: B.Z.	Battle Ground:	Weapons:	Undead / Infected / Mutant
Rep 1 Time:	Rep 2 Time:	Rep 3 Time:	Notes:
Rep 1 Trans Split Time:	Rep 2 Trans Split Time:	Rep 3 Trans Split Time:	
All in A / Z Box: Y / N	All in A / Z Box: Y / N	All in A / Z Box: Y / N	
Rep 1 + Penalties:	Rep 2 + Penalties:	Rep 3 + Penalties:	
Rep 1 Time Score:	**Rep 2 Time Score:**	**Rep 3 Time Score:**	**Best Time Score:**
Date: B.Z.	Battle Ground:	Weapons:	Undead / Infected / Mutant
Rep 1 Time:	Rep 2 Time:	Rep 3 Time:	Notes:
Rep 1 Trans Split Time:	Rep 2 Trans Split Time:	Rep 3 Trans Split Time:	
All in A / Z Box: Y / N	All in A / Z Box: Y / N	All in A / Z Box: Y / N	
Rep 1 + Penalties:	Rep 2 + Penalties:	Rep 3 + Penalties:	
Rep 1 Time Score:	**Rep 2 Time Score:**	**Rep 3 Time Score:**	**Best Time Score:**
Date: B.Z.	Battle Ground:	Weapons:	Undead / Infected / Mutant
Rep 1 Time:	Rep 2 Time:	Rep 3 Time:	Notes:
Rep 1 Trans Split Time:	Rep 2 Trans Split Time:	Rep 3 Trans Split Time:	
All in A / Z Box: Y / N	All in A / Z Box: Y / N	All in A / Z Box: Y / N	
Rep 1 + Penalties:	Rep 2 + Penalties:	Rep 3 + Penalties:	
Rep 1 Time Score:	**Rep 2 Time Score:**	**Rep 3 Time Score:**	**Best Time Score:**

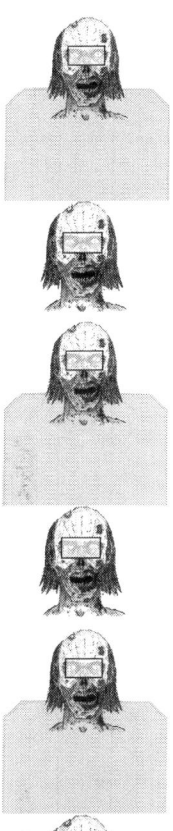

Transition Drills - 2

www.GUNFIGHTERSERIES.com ©

FINISH HIM!!

Date: B.Z.	Battle Ground:	Weapons:	Undead / Infected / Mutant
Rep 1 Time:	Rep 2 Time:	Rep 3 Time:	Notes:
Rep 1 Trans Split Time:	Rep 2 Trans Split Time:	Rep 3 Trans Split Time:	
All in A / Z Box: Y / N	All in A / Z Box: Y / N	All in A / Z Box: Y / N	
Rep 1 + Penalties:	Rep 2 + Penalties:	Rep 3 + Penalties:	
Rep 1 Time Score:	**Rep 2 Time Score:**	**Rep 3 Time Score:**	**Best Time Score:**
Date: B.Z.	Battle Ground:	Weapons:	Undead / Infected / Mutant
Rep 1 Time:	Rep 2 Time:	Rep 3 Time:	Notes:
Rep 1 Trans Split Time:	Rep 2 Trans Split Time:	Rep 3 Trans Split Time:	
All in A / Z Box: Y / N	All in A / Z Box: Y / N	All in A / Z Box: Y / N	
Rep 1 + Penalties:	Rep 2 + Penalties:	Rep 3 + Penalties:	
Rep 1 Time Score:	**Rep 2 Time Score:**	**Rep 3 Time Score:**	**Best Time Score:**
Date: B.Z.	Battle Ground:	Weapons:	Undead / Infected / Mutant
Rep 1 Time:	Rep 2 Time:	Rep 3 Time:	Notes:
Rep 1 Trans Split Time:	Rep 2 Trans Split Time:	Rep 3 Trans Split Time:	
All in A / Z Box: Y / N	All in A / Z Box: Y / N	All in A / Z Box: Y / N	
Rep 1 + Penalties:	Rep 2 + Penalties:	Rep 3 + Penalties:	
Rep 1 Time Score:	**Rep 2 Time Score:**	**Rep 3 Time Score:**	**Best Time Score:**

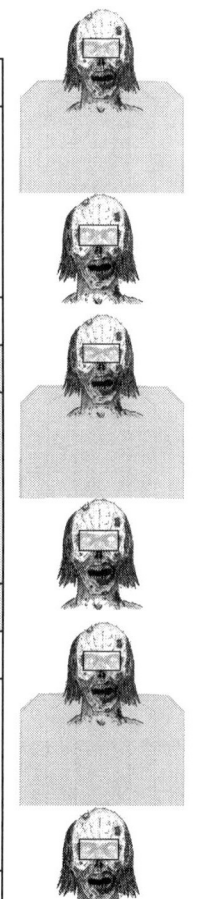

FINISH HIM!!

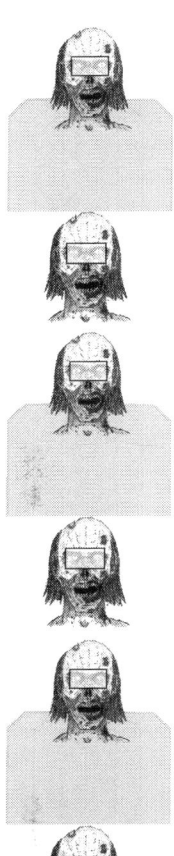

Date: B.Z.	Battle Ground:	Weapons:	Undead / Infected / Mutant
Rep 1 Time:	Rep 2 Time:	Rep 3 Time:	Notes:
Rep 1 Trans Split Time:	Rep 2 Trans Split Time:	Rep 3 Trans Split Time:	
All in A / Z Box: Y / N	All in A / Z Box: Y / N	All in A / Z Box: Y / N	
Rep 1 + Penalties:	Rep 2 + Penalties:	Rep 3 + Penalties:	
Rep 1 Time Score:	**Rep 2 Time Score:**	**Rep 3 Time Score:**	**Best Time Score:**
Date: B.Z.	Battle Ground:	Weapons:	Undead / Infected / Mutant
Rep 1 Time:	Rep 2 Time:	Rep 3 Time:	Notes:
Rep 1 Trans Split Time:	Rep 2 Trans Split Time:	Rep 3 Trans Split Time:	
All in A / Z Box: Y / N	All in A / Z Box: Y / N	All in A / Z Box: Y / N	
Rep 1 + Penalties:	Rep 2 + Penalties:	Rep 3 + Penalties:	
Rep 1 Time Score:	**Rep 2 Time Score:**	**Rep 3 Time Score:**	**Best Time Score:**
Date: B.Z.	Battle Ground:	Weapons:	Undead / Infected / Mutant
Rep 1 Time:	Rep 2 Time:	Rep 3 Time:	Notes:
Rep 1 Trans Split Time:	Rep 2 Trans Split Time:	Rep 3 Trans Split Time:	
All in A / Z Box: Y / N	All in A / Z Box: Y / N	All in A / Z Box: Y / N	
Rep 1 + Penalties:	Rep 2 + Penalties:	Rep 3 + Penalties:	
Rep 1 Time Score:	**Rep 2 Time Score:**	**Rep 3 Time Score:**	**Best Time Score:**

Z Fighter ©

Transition Drills - 2

FINISH HIM!!

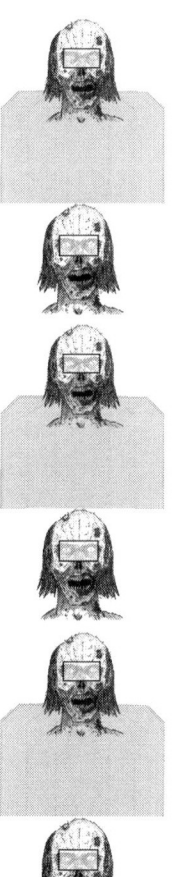

Date: B.Z.	Battle Ground:	Weapons:	Undead / Infected / Mutant
Rep 1 Time:	Rep 2 Time:	Rep 3 Time:	Notes:
Rep 1 Trans Split Time:	Rep 2 Trans Split Time:	Rep 3 Trans Split Time:	
All in A / Z Box: Y / N	All in A / Z Box: Y / N	All in A / Z Box: Y / N	
Rep 1 + Penalties:	Rep 2 + Penalties:	Rep 3 + Penalties:	
Rep 1 Time Score:	**Rep 2 Time Score:**	**Rep 3 Time Score:**	**Best Time Score:**
Date: B.Z.	Battle Ground:	Weapons:	Undead / Infected / Mutant
Rep 1 Time:	Rep 2 Time:	Rep 3 Time:	Notes:
Rep 1 Trans Split Time:	Rep 2 Trans Split Time:	Rep 3 Trans Split Time:	
All in A / Z Box: Y / N	All in A / Z Box: Y / N	All in A / Z Box: Y / N	
Rep 1 + Penalties:	Rep 2 + Penalties:	Rep 3 + Penalties:	
Rep 1 Time Score:	**Rep 2 Time Score:**	**Rep 3 Time Score:**	**Best Time Score:**
Date: B.Z.	Battle Ground:	Weapons:	Undead / Infected / Mutant
Rep 1 Time:	Rep 2 Time:	Rep 3 Time:	Notes:
Rep 1 Trans Split Time:	Rep 2 Trans Split Time:	Rep 3 Trans Split Time:	
All in A / Z Box: Y / N	All in A / Z Box: Y / N	All in A / Z Box: Y / N	
Rep 1 + Penalties:	Rep 2 + Penalties:	Rep 3 + Penalties:	
Rep 1 Time Score:	**Rep 2 Time Score:**	**Rep 3 Time Score:**	**Best Time Score:**

FINISH HIM!!

Date: B.Z.	Battle Ground:	Weapons:	Undead / Infected / Mutant
Rep 1 Time:	Rep 2 Time:	Rep 3 Time:	Notes:
Rep 1 Trans Split Time:	Rep 2 Trans Split Time:	Rep 3 Trans Split Time:	
All in A / Z Box: Y / N	All in A / Z Box: Y / N	All in A / Z Box: Y / N	
Rep 1 + Penalties:	Rep 2 + Penalties:	Rep 3 + Penalties:	
Rep 1 Time Score:	**Rep 2 Time Score:**	**Rep 3 Time Score:**	**Best Time Score:**
Date: B.Z.	Battle Ground:	Weapons:	Undead / Infected / Mutant
Rep 1 Time:	Rep 2 Time:	Rep 3 Time:	Notes:
Rep 1 Trans Split Time:	Rep 2 Trans Split Time:	Rep 3 Trans Split Time:	
All in A / Z Box: Y / N	All in A / Z Box: Y / N	All in A / Z Box: Y / N	
Rep 1 + Penalties:	Rep 2 + Penalties:	Rep 3 + Penalties:	
Rep 1 Time Score:	**Rep 2 Time Score:**	**Rep 3 Time Score:**	**Best Time Score:**
Date: B.Z.	Battle Ground:	Weapons:	Undead / Infected / Mutant
Rep 1 Time:	Rep 2 Time:	Rep 3 Time:	Notes:
Rep 1 Trans Split Time:	Rep 2 Trans Split Time:	Rep 3 Trans Split Time:	
All in A / Z Box: Y / N	All in A / Z Box: Y / N	All in A / Z Box: Y / N	
Rep 1 + Penalties:	Rep 2 + Penalties:	Rep 3 + Penalties:	
Rep 1 Time Score:	**Rep 2 Time Score:**	**Rep 3 Time Score:**	**Best Time Score:**

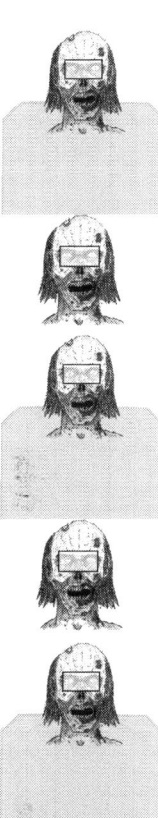

Z Fighter ©

Transition Drills - 2

TRANSITION DRILL: **CREEPY CRAWLERS**

Purpose: Equipment placement strategies, urban prone familiarization and weapon transitions.

Distance: 7 Yards.

Target: Upper half of a ZIPSC (Undead) placed at ground level.

Extra Equipment Needed: Shot timer. 1 Barrier. Carbine with sling. Pistol with holster.

Rounds Fired Per Rep: 6 Rounds. 1 Carbine mag of 3 rounds. 1 Pistol mag of 3 rounds.

Total Rounds Fired: 18 Round.

Repetitions: 3 Reps. **Point Penalty:** Time plus penalty.

Starting Position & Condition: Kneeling behind barrier, tactical carbine ready. Condition 1 both weapons. Pistol holstered.

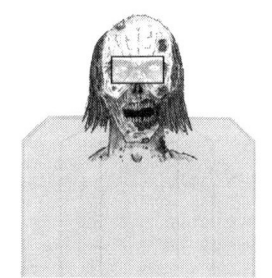

3' Tall Barrier

Description: At the timer beep, roll onto the ground to your right into an urban prone position exposing only your head and your carbine. With carbine, aim and fire 1 round into the ocular Z box. Put carbine on safe, keeping positive control of your weapon then return to the kneeling position. Aim and fire 1 round into the ocular Z box. Put carbine on safe, keeping positive control of your weapon then roll to the left into a urban prone position. Aim and fire 1 round. Carbine will go dry. Staying in urban prone, transition to pistol, aim then fire 1 round into the ocular Z box. Maintaining positive control of both weapons, return to the kneeling position, aim then fire 1 round. Roll back right into an urban prone position and fire last round into the ocular Z box. *Left handed shooters begin the drill by rolling left.

For every hit outside the head ocular Z box, add 2 seconds to your time. For every miss, add 5 seconds to your time. Add the penalty time onto your recorded time for that repetition.

Goals: Meat Bag: All in A and Z box. Survivor: 60 Seconds all in A and Z box. Z Fighter: 45 Seconds all in A and Z box.

Variations:

⊕ Infected Humans: Multiple round count by 3 and fire 2 rounds into body A box and 1 round into head Z box for each engagement.

⊕ Mutants: Same as Infected Humans from 15 yards.

CREEPY CRAWLERS

Date:	B.Z.	Battle Ground:	Weapons:	Undead / Infected
Rep 1 Time:		Rep 2 Time:	Rep 3 Time:	Notes:
All in A / Z Box: Y / N		All in A / Z Box: Y / N	All in A / Z Box: Y / N	
Rep 1 + Penalties:		Rep 2 + Penalties:	Rep 3 + Penalties:	
Rep 1 Time Score:		**Rep 2 Time Score:**	**Rep 3 Time Score:**	**Best Time Score:**

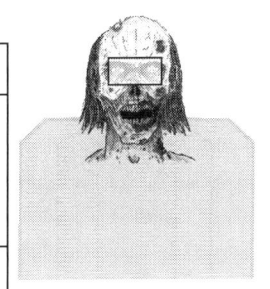

Date:	B.Z.	Battle Ground:	Weapons:	Undead / Infected
Rep 1 Time:		Rep 2 Time:	Rep 3 Time:	Notes:
All in A / Z Box: Y / N		All in A / Z Box: Y / N	All in A / Z Box: Y / N	
Rep 1 + Penalties:		Rep 2 + Penalties:	Rep 3 + Penalties:	
Rep 1 Time Score:		**Rep 2 Time Score:**	**Rep 3 Time Score:**	**Best Time Score:**

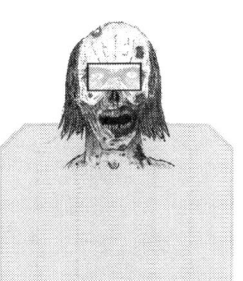

Date:	B.Z.	Battle Ground:	Weapons:	Undead / Infected
Rep 1 Time:		Rep 2 Time:	Rep 3 Time:	Notes:
All in A / Z Box: Y / N		All in A / Z Box: Y / N	All in A / Z Box: Y / N	
Rep 1 + Penalties:		Rep 2 + Penalties:	Rep 3 + Penalties:	
Rep 1 Time Score:		**Rep 2 Time Score:**	**Rep 3 Time Score:**	**Best Time Score:**

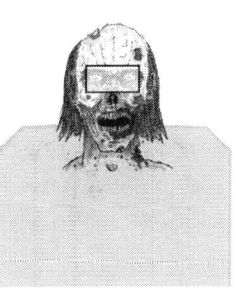

Z Fighter ©

Transition Drills - 3

CREEPY CRAWLERS

Date: B.Z.	Battle Ground:	Weapons:	Undead / Infected	
Rep 1 Time:	Rep 2 Time:	Rep 3 Time:	Notes:	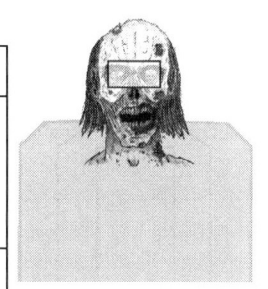
All in A / Z Box: Y / N	All in A / Z Box: Y / N	All in A / Z Box: Y / N		
Rep 1 + Penalties:	Rep 2 + Penalties:	Rep 3 + Penalties:		
Rep 1 Time Score:	**Rep 2 Time Score:**	**Rep 3 Time Score:**	**Best Time Score:**	

Date: B.Z.	Battle Ground:	Weapons:	Undead / Infected	
Rep 1 Time:	Rep 2 Time:	Rep 3 Time:	Notes:	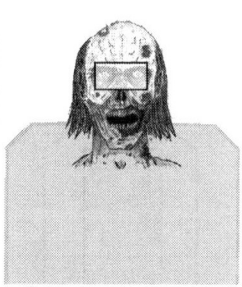
All in A / Z Box: Y / N	All in A / Z Box: Y / N	All in A / Z Box: Y / N		
Rep 1 + Penalties:	Rep 2 + Penalties:	Rep 3 + Penalties:		
Rep 1 Time Score:	**Rep 2 Time Score:**	**Rep 3 Time Score:**	**Best Time Score:**	

Date: B.Z.	Battle Ground:	Weapons:	Undead / Infected	
Rep 1 Time:	Rep 2 Time:	Rep 3 Time:	Notes:	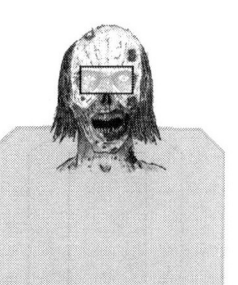
All in A / Z Box: Y / N	All in A / Z Box: Y / N	All in A / Z Box: Y / N		
Rep 1 + Penalties:	Rep 2 + Penalties:	Rep 3 + Penalties:		
Rep 1 Time Score:	**Rep 2 Time Score:**	**Rep 3 Time Score:**	**Best Time Score:**	

CREEPY CRAWLERS

Date: B.Z.	Battle Ground:	Weapons:	Undead / Infected
Rep 1 Time:	Rep 2 Time:	Rep 3 Time:	Notes:
All in A / Z Box: Y / N	All in A / Z Box: Y / N	All in A / Z Box: Y / N	
Rep 1 + Penalties:	Rep 2 + Penalties:	Rep 3 + Penalties:	
Rep 1 Time Score:	**Rep 2 Time Score:**	**Rep 3 Time Score:**	**Best Time Score:**

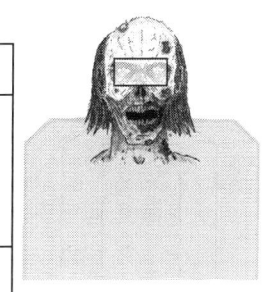

Date: B.Z.	Battle Ground:	Weapons:	Undead / Infected
Rep 1 Time:	Rep 2 Time:	Rep 3 Time:	Notes:
All in A / Z Box: Y / N	All in A / Z Box: Y / N	All in A / Z Box: Y / N	
Rep 1 + Penalties:	Rep 2 + Penalties:	Rep 3 + Penalties:	
Rep 1 Time Score:	**Rep 2 Time Score:**	**Rep 3 Time Score:**	**Best Time Score:**

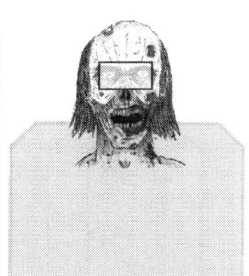

Date: B.Z.	Battle Ground:	Weapons:	Undead / Infected
Rep 1 Time:	Rep 2 Time:	Rep 3 Time:	Notes:
All in A / Z Box: Y / N	All in A / Z Box: Y / N	All in A / Z Box: Y / N	
Rep 1 + Penalties:	Rep 2 + Penalties:	Rep 3 + Penalties:	
Rep 1 Time Score:	**Rep 2 Time Score:**	**Rep 3 Time Score:**	**Best Time Score:**

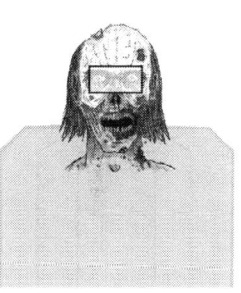

Z Fighter ©

Transition Drills - 3

CREEPY CRAWLERS

Date:	B.Z.	Battle Ground:	Weapons:	Undead / Infected
Rep 1 Time:		Rep 2 Time:	Rep 3 Time:	Notes:
All in A / Z Box: Y / N		All in A / Z Box: Y / N	All in A / Z Box: Y / N	
Rep 1 + Penalties:		Rep 2 + Penalties:	Rep 3 + Penalties:	
Rep 1 Time Score:		**Rep 2 Time Score:**	**Rep 3 Time Score:**	**Best Time Score:**

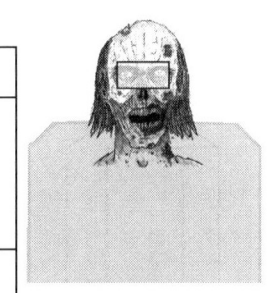

Date:	B.Z.	Battle Ground:	Weapons:	Undead / Infected
Rep 1 Time:		Rep 2 Time:	Rep 3 Time:	Notes:
All in A / Z Box: Y / N		All in A / Z Box: Y / N	All in A / Z Box: Y / N	
Rep 1 + Penalties:		Rep 2 + Penalties:	Rep 3 + Penalties:	
Rep 1 Time Score:		**Rep 2 Time Score:**	**Rep 3 Time Score:**	**Best Time Score:**

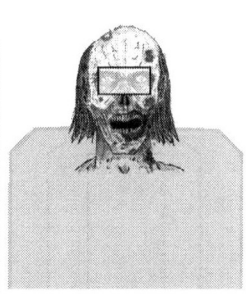

Date:	B.Z.	Battle Ground:	Weapons:	Undead / Infected
Rep 1 Time:		Rep 2 Time:	Rep 3 Time:	Notes:
All in A / Z Box: Y / N		All in A / Z Box: Y / N	All in A / Z Box: Y / N	
Rep 1 + Penalties:		Rep 2 + Penalties:	Rep 3 + Penalties:	
Rep 1 Time Score:		**Rep 2 Time Score:**	**Rep 3 Time Score:**	**Best Time Score:**

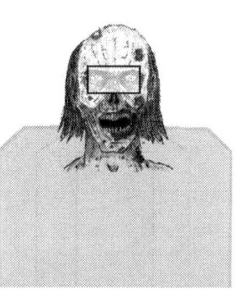

CREEPY CRAWLERS

Date: B.Z.	Battle Ground:	Weapons:	Undead / Infected
Rep 1 Time:	Rep 2 Time:	Rep 3 Time:	Notes:
All in A / Z Box: Y / N	All in A / Z Box: Y / N	All in A / Z Box: Y / N	
Rep 1 + Penalties:	Rep 2 + Penalties:	Rep 3 + Penalties:	
Rep 1 Time Score:	**Rep 2 Time Score:**	**Rep 3 Time Score:**	**Best Time Score:**

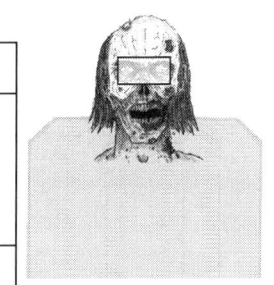

Date: B.Z.	Battle Ground:	Weapons:	Undead / Infected
Rep 1 Time:	Rep 2 Time:	Rep 3 Time:	Notes:
All in A / Z Box: Y / N	All in A / Z Box: Y / N	All in A / Z Box: Y / N	
Rep 1 + Penalties:	Rep 2 + Penalties:	Rep 3 + Penalties:	
Rep 1 Time Score:	**Rep 2 Time Score:**	**Rep 3 Time Score:**	**Best Time Score:**

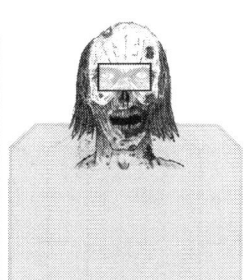

Date: B.Z.	Battle Ground:	Weapons:	Undead / Infected
Rep 1 Time:	Rep 2 Time:	Rep 3 Time:	Notes:
All in A / Z Box: Y / N	All in A / Z Box: Y / N	All in A / Z Box: Y / N	
Rep 1 + Penalties:	Rep 2 + Penalties:	Rep 3 + Penalties:	
Rep 1 Time Score:	**Rep 2 Time Score:**	**Rep 3 Time Score:**	**Best Time Score:**

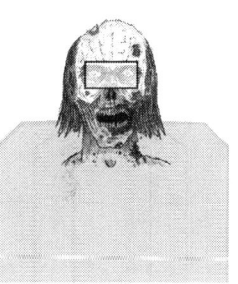

Z Fighter ©

Transition Drills - 3

TRANSITION DRILL: GET OFF THE X

Purpose: Increase accuracy while moving.

Distance: 15 to 5 Yards.

Target: ZIPSC (Undead)

Extra Equipment Needed: Pistol, holster, yard line markers.

Rounds Fired Per Rep: 5 Carbine & 2 pistol rounds.

Total Rounds Fired: 20 Carbine & 8 pistol rounds.

Point Penalty: 5 Points A / Z boxes. 3 points for in body / head outside the A / Z box.

Repetitions: 4 Reps. (2 of each stage)

Starting Position & Condition: Standing – Low ready with carbine pointed down range. Condition 1.

Description: With the rifle pointed down range, keeping your eyes on the target, perform the prescribed stage repetition.

Stage 1: From 20 yards. At your own personal go, with rifle in your right shoulder, fire 5 rounds into the targets A Zone body box then transition to pistol firing 2 more rounds into the ocular Z box while moving forward left to right (diagonally).

Stage 2: From 20 yards. At your own personal go, with rifle in your left shoulder, fire 5 rounds into the targets A Zone body box then transition to pistol firing 2 more rounds into the ocular Z box while moving right to left (diagonally).

Goals: Meat Bag: 70 Points.   Survivor: 120 Points.   Z Fighter: 140 Points.

Variations:

⊕ Infected Humans: All shorts are to the head.

⊕ Mutants: All shorts are to the head with a 15 second stage par time.

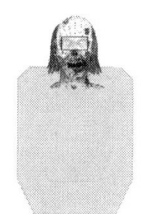
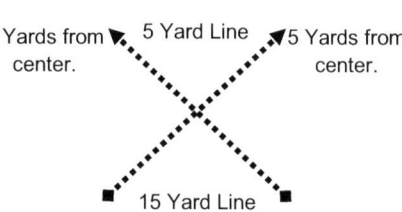

GET OFF THE X

Date:	B.Z	Carbine:	Pistol:	Notes
Undead / Infected / Mutant		Left to Right Score:	Right to Left Score:	
Body / Head		Left to Right Score:	Right to Left Score:	**Total Score:**
Date:	B.Z	Carbine:	Pistol:	Notes
Undead / Infected / Mutant		Left to Right Score:	Right to Left Score:	
Body / Head		Left to Right Score:	Right to Left Score:	**Total Score:**
Date:	B.Z	Carbine:	Pistol:	Notes
Undead / Infected / Mutant		Left to Right Score:	Right to Left Score:	
Body / Head		Left to Right Score:	Right to Left Score:	**Total Score:**
Date:	B.Z	Carbine:	Pistol:	Notes
Undead / Infected / Mutant		Left to Right Score:	Right to Left Score:	
Body / Head		Left to Right Score:	Right to Left Score:	**Total Score:**
Date:	B.Z	Carbine:	Pistol:	Notes
Undead / Infected / Mutant		Left to Right Score:	Right to Left Score:	
Body / Head		Left to Right Score:	Right to Left Score:	**Total Score:**

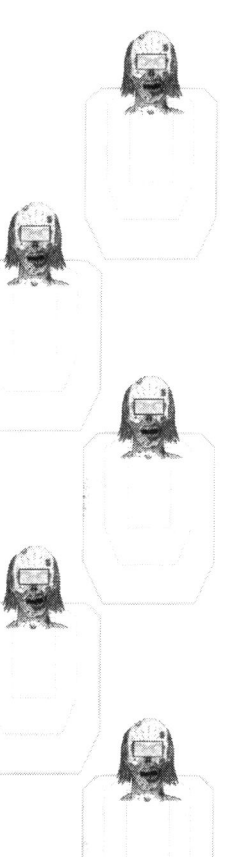

Z Fighter ©

GET OFF THE X

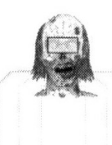

Date: B.Z	Carbine:	Pistol:	Notes
Undead / Infected / Mutant	Left to Right Score:	Right to Left Score:	
Body / Head	Left to Right Score:	Right to Left Score:	**Total Score:**
Date: B.Z	Carbine:	Pistol:	Notes
Undead / Infected / Mutant	Left to Right Score:	Right to Left Score:	
Body / Head	Left to Right Score:	Right to Left Score:	**Total Score:**
Date: B.Z	Carbine:	Pistol:	Notes
Undead / Infected / Mutant	Left to Right Score:	Right to Left Score:	
Body / Head	Left to Right Score:	Right to Left Score:	**Total Score:**
Date: B.Z	Carbine:	Pistol:	Notes
Undead / Infected / Mutant	Left to Right Score:	Right to Left Score:	
Body / Head	Left to Right Score:	Right to Left Score:	**Total Score:**
Date: B.Z	Carbine:	Pistol:	Notes
Undead / Infected / Mutant	Left to Right Score:	Right to Left Score:	
Body / Head	Left to Right Score:	Right to Left Score:	**Total Score:**

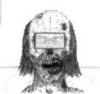
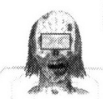

GET OFF THE X

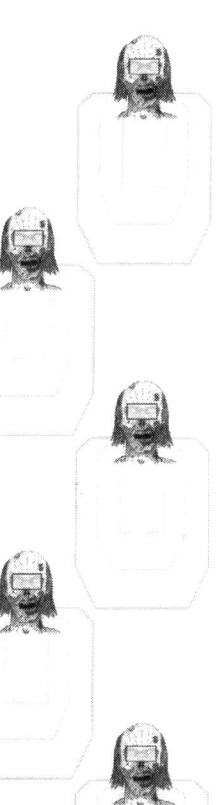

Date: B.Z	Carbine:	Pistol:	Notes
Undead / Infected / Mutant	Left to Right Score:	Right to Left Score:	
Body / Head	Left to Right Score:	Right to Left Score:	**Total Score:**
Date: B.Z	Carbine:	Pistol:	Notes
Undead / Infected / Mutant	Left to Right Score:	Right to Left Score:	
Body / Head	Left to Right Score:	Right to Left Score:	**Total Score:**
Date: B.Z	Carbine:	Pistol:	Notes
Undead / Infected / Mutant	Left to Right Score:	Right to Left Score:	
Body / Head	Left to Right Score:	Right to Left Score:	**Total Score:**
Date: B.Z	Carbine:	Pistol:	Notes
Undead / Infected / Mutant	Left to Right Score:	Right to Left Score:	
Body / Head	Left to Right Score:	Right to Left Score:	**Total Score:**
Date: B.Z	Carbine:	Pistol:	Notes
Undead / Infected / Mutant	Left to Right Score:	Right to Left Score:	
Body / Head	Left to Right Score:	Right to Left Score:	**Total Score:**

Z Fighter ©

Transition Drills - 4

GET OFF THE X

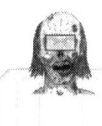

Date: B.Z	Carbine:	Pistol:	Notes
Undead / Infected / Mutant	Left to Right Score:	Right to Left Score:	
Body / Head	Left to Right Score:	Right to Left Score:	**Total Score:**
Date: B.Z	Carbine:	Pistol:	Notes
Undead / Infected / Mutant	Left to Right Score:	Right to Left Score:	
Body / Head	Left to Right Score:	Right to Left Score:	**Total Score:**
Date: B.Z	Carbine:	Pistol:	Notes
Undead / Infected / Mutant	Left to Right Score:	Right to Left Score:	
Body / Head	Left to Right Score:	Right to Left Score:	**Total Score:**
Date: B.Z	Carbine:	Pistol:	Notes
Undead / Infected / Mutant	Left to Right Score:	Right to Left Score:	
Body / Head	Left to Right Score:	Right to Left Score:	**Total Score:**
Date: B.Z	Carbine:	Pistol:	Notes
Undead / Infected / Mutant	Left to Right Score:	Right to Left Score:	
Body / Head	Left to Right Score:	Right to Left Score:	**Total Score:**

GET OFF THE X

Date:	B.Z	Carbine:	Pistol:	Notes
Undead / Infected / Mutant		Left to Right Score:	Right to Left Score:	
Body / Head		Left to Right Score:	Right to Left Score:	**Total Score:**
Date:	B.Z	Carbine:	Pistol:	Notes
Undead / Infected / Mutant		Left to Right Score:	Right to Left Score:	
Body / Head		Left to Right Score:	Right to Left Score:	**Total Score:**
Date:	B.Z	Carbine:	Pistol:	Notes
Undead / Infected / Mutant		Left to Right Score:	Right to Left Score:	
Body / Head		Left to Right Score:	Right to Left Score:	**Total Score:**
Date:	B.Z	Carbine:	Pistol:	Notes
Undead / Infected / Mutant		Left to Right Score:	Right to Left Score:	
Body / Head		Left to Right Score:	Right to Left Score:	**Total Score:**
Date:	B.Z	Carbine:	Pistol:	Notes
Undead / Infected / Mutant		Left to Right Score:	Right to Left Score:	
Body / Head		Left to Right Score:	Right to Left Score:	**Total Score:**

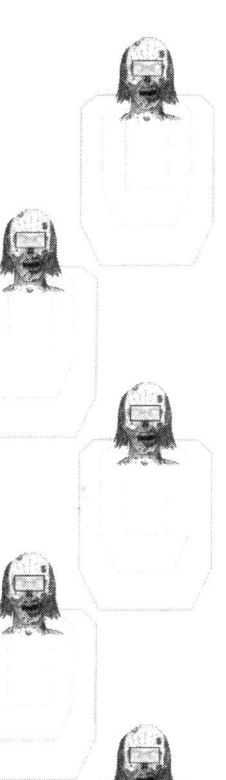

Transition Drills - 4

Z Fighter ©

TRANSITION DRILL: **SERPENTINE**

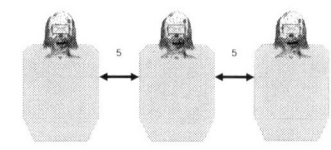

Target: ZIPSC X 3 targets (5 feet apart)   **Distance:** 20 to 5 Yards.

Extra equipment required: Shot timer, yard line markers, pistol, holster.

Total Rounds Fired: 24 Carbine rounds and 6 pistol rounds.   **Per Course:** 12 Carbine rounds and 3 pistol rounds.

Scoring: Point Penalty: 5 Points A / Z boxes. 3 points for in body / head outside the A / Z box. (Minus 5 points for any shot over par)

Starting Position & Condition: Standing – Any ready position of choice. Weapon condition 1.

Description: At the 20 yard line, pick either the A or B course. At the timer beep, fire 2 rounds into the (5 point) A Zone body box of each ZIPSC QUAL1 target while advancing diagonally to the 15 yard maker. Fire 2 rounds into the (5 point) A Zone body box of each ZIPSC target while advancing diagonally to the 10 yard maker. Your carbine will go dry, transition to your pistol. Fire 1 pistol round into the (5 point) ocular Z box of each ZIPSC target while advancing diagonally to the 5 yard maker. Repeat on opposite (A or B) course. Record score and time at the end of each course.

Shooter must remain moving during entire course (no pausing); 6 rounds must be fired while moving from marker to marker (*can not save all rounds for the 5 yard line*) and shooter must complete before par. Hint: Switching shoulders during this course of fire is recommended, but not mandatory.

Goal: Meat Bag: 114 points under 25 second par time.   Survivor: 132 points under 20 second par time.
        Z Fighter: 150 points under 18 second par time.

Variations:

⊕ Infected Humans: Add 6 more carbine rounds per rep. Engage each ZIPSC with 2 shots to the body box and 1 shot to the ocular Z box.

⊕ Mutants: Add 18 more carbine rounds per rep. Engage each ZIPSC with 4 shots to the body box and 1 shot to the ocular Z box.

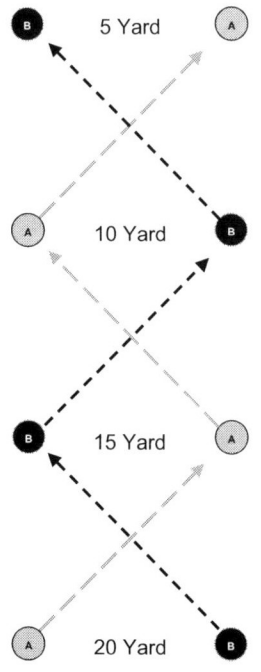

SERPENTINE

Date:	B.Z	Carbine:	Pistol:
Undead / Infected / Mutant			Special Equipment:
Rep 1: Time		Shots Over Par:	Rep 1 Score:
Rep 2: Time		Shots Over Par:	Rep 2 Score:
Notes:			**Total Score:**
Date:	B.Z	Carbine:	Pistol:
Undead / Infected / Mutant			Special Equipment:
Rep 1: Time		Shots Over Par:	Rep 1 Score:
Rep 2: Time		Shots Over Par:	Rep 2 Score:
Notes:			**Total Score:**
Date:	B.Z	Carbine:	Pistol:
Undead / Infected / Mutant			Special Equipment:
Rep 1: Time		Shots Over Par:	Rep 1 Score:
Rep 2: Time		Shots Over Par:	Rep 2 Score:
Notes:			**Total Score:**

Transition Drills - 5

SERPENTINE

Date:		B.Z	Carbine:	Pistol:
	Undead / Infected / Mutant			Special Equipment:
Rep 1: Time			Shots Over Par:	Rep 1 Score:
Rep 2: Time			Shots Over Par:	Rep 2 Score:
Notes:				**Total Score:**
Date:		B.Z	Carbine:	Pistol:
	Undead / Infected / Mutant			Special Equipment:
Rep 1: Time			Shots Over Par:	Rep 1 Score:
Rep 2: Time			Shots Over Par:	Rep 2 Score:
Notes:				**Total Score:**
Date:		B.Z	Carbine:	Pistol:
	Undead / Infected / Mutant			Special Equipment:
Rep 1: Time			Shots Over Par:	Rep 1 Score:
Rep 2: Time			Shots Over Par:	Rep 2 Score:
Notes:				**Total Score:**

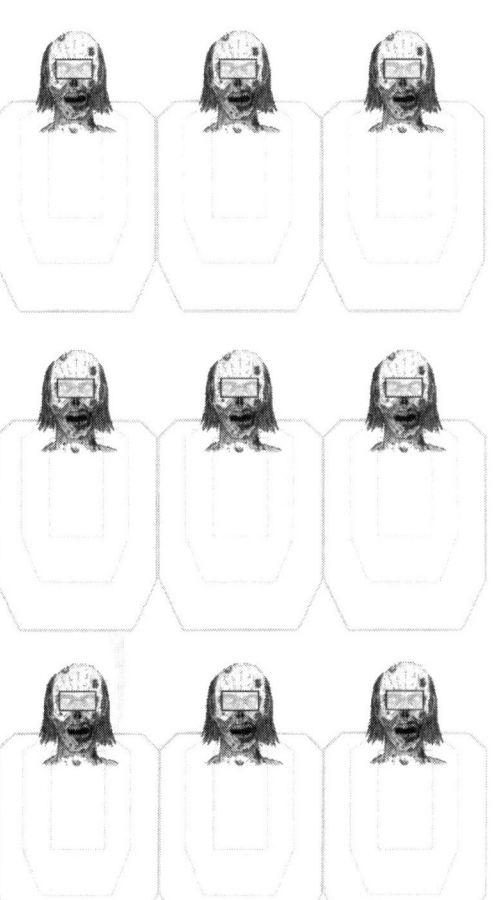

www.GUNFIGHTERSERIES.com ©

SERPENTINE

Date:		B.Z	Carbine:		Pistol:	
	Undead / Infected / Mutant				Special Equipment:	
Rep 1: Time			Shots Over Par:		Rep 1 Score:	
Rep 2: Time			Shots Over Par:		Rep 2 Score:	
Notes:					**Total Score:**	
Date:		B.Z	Carbine:		Pistol:	
	Undead / Infected / Mutant				Special Equipment:	
Rep 1: Time			Shots Over Par:		Rep 1 Score:	
Rep 2: Time			Shots Over Par:		Rep 2 Score:	
Notes:					**Total Score:**	
Date:		B.Z	Carbine:		Pistol:	
	Undead / Infected / Mutant				Special Equipment:	
Rep 1: Time			Shots Over Par:		Rep 1 Score:	
Rep 2: Time			Shots Over Par:		Rep 2 Score:	
Notes:					**Total Score:**	

Z Fighter ©

Transition Drills - 5

SERPENTINE

Date:		B.Z	Carbine:		Pistol:	
	Undead / Infected / Mutant				Special Equipment:	
Rep 1: Time			Shots Over Par:		Rep 1 Score:	
Rep 2: Time			Shots Over Par:		Rep 2 Score:	
Notes:					**Total Score:**	
Date:		B.Z	Carbine:		Pistol:	
	Undead / Infected / Mutant				Special Equipment:	
Rep 1: Time			Shots Over Par:		Rep 1 Score:	
Rep 2: Time			Shots Over Par:		Rep 2 Score:	
Notes:					**Total Score:**	
Date:		B.Z	Carbine:		Pistol:	
	Undead / Infected / Mutant				Special Equipment:	
Rep 1: Time			Shots Over Par:		Rep 1 Score:	
Rep 2: Time			Shots Over Par:		Rep 2 Score:	
Notes:					**Total Score:**	

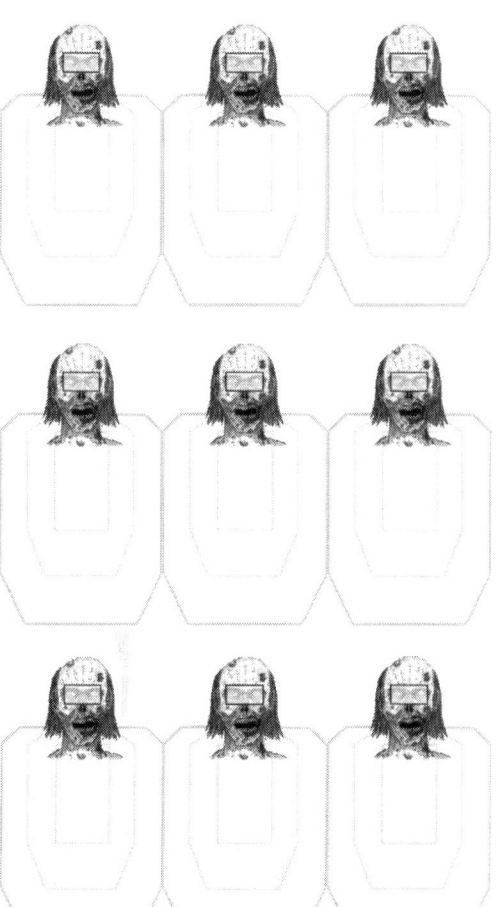

www.GUNFIGHTERSERIES.com ©

SERPENTINE

Date:		B.Z	Carbine:	Pistol:	
	Undead / Infected / Mutant			Special Equipment:	
Rep 1: Time			Shots Over Par:	Rep 1 Score:	
Rep 2: Time			Shots Over Par:	Rep 2 Score:	
Notes:				Total Score:	
Date:		B.Z	Carbine:	Pistol:	
	Undead / Infected / Mutant			Special Equipment:	
Rep 1: Time			Shots Over Par:	Rep 1 Score:	
Rep 2: Time			Shots Over Par:	Rep 2 Score:	
Notes:				Total Score:	
Date:		B.Z	Carbine:	Pistol:	
	Undead / Infected / Mutant			Special Equipment:	
Rep 1: Time			Shots Over Par:	Rep 1 Score:	
Rep 2: Time			Shots Over Par:	Rep 2 Score:	
Notes:				Total Score:	

Transition Drills - 5

Z Fighter ©

ZF-3 Precision Rifle Diagnostics Instructions

Purpose: Test different precision rifle skills to determine which Z Fighter Gunfighter drills to work on.

Distance: 100 Yards   **Target:** ZF-3

Par Time: 120 Seconds.

Extra Equipment: Shot timer, 2 rifle magazines, 1 magazine pouch.

Load Out: 1 Rifle magazine with 4 rounds and 1 rifle magazine with 6 rounds.

Starting Position and Condition: Standing - Rifle in low ready. Condition 1.

Description: At the timer beep:

- Assume a good prone shooting position, aim and fire 1 round into the rectangular block (A1), then immediately

- From a prone shooting position, rapid fire 3 rounds into the diamond target (B6), then immediately

- Reload from prone or kneeling. Shooters choice.

- From a kneeling shooting position, rapid fire 3 rounds into the diamond target (B6), then immediately

- Assume a good prone shooting position, slow fire 1 round in each of the remaining head targets (C1,D1,E1) starting with largest and finishing with the smallest.

Record your name, date and the time it took you to complete the course of fire. If you don't hit the goals on a given skill, practice on the listed drills for that goal.

Goals and Performance Diagnostics

If all rounds are not in:	**1st Shot Goal:** Hit within or touching rectangle under 30 seconds. If not, practice:	**Ave Split Time of Shots 2-7 Goal:** Hit within or touching diamond with shot to shot intervals at 0.5 seconds or less. If not, practice:	**Shots 8-10 Goal:** Big, medium, and small Z heads: hit within or touching the boxes. If not, practice:
FUNDAMENTALLY AWESOME	COLD BODY	FUNDAMENTALLY AWESOME	COLD BODY
TYRANT VIRUS	THAT WAS CLOSE	BOUNDARIES	THAT WAS CLOSE
BOUNDARIES	TYRANT VIRUS	SIT, KNEEL, STAND	TYRANT VIRUS
SIT, KNEEL, STAND	BOUNDARIES	CLEAR THE WAY	BOUNDARIES
ZNIPER	CLEAR THE WAY		CLEAR THE WAY
HEAD HUNTER			ZNIPER
PRZ SKILLZ 1			HEAD HUNTER
Overall Completion Time:		**Goal:** Under 120 second par time.	

Z Fighter ©

Precision Rifle Diagnostic

www.GUNFIGHTERSERIES.com ©

Precision Rifle Performance Diagnostics

Date:	B.Z.	Battle Ground:	Rifle:	Scope:
1st Shot Time:		Ave Split Time of Shots 2 - 4	Ave Split Time of Shots 5 - 7:	Overall Completion Time:
1st Shot In: Y / N		Shots 2 - 7 In: Y / N	Kneeling: Supported / Unsupported	Shots 8-10 In: Y / N
Notes:				

Date:	B.Z.	Battle Ground:	Rifle:	Scope:
1st Shot Time:		Ave Split Time of Shots 2 - 4	Ave Split Time of Shots 5 - 7:	Overall Completion Time:
1st Shot In: Y / N		Shots 2 - 7 In: Y / N	Kneeling: Supported / Unsupported	Shots 8-10 In: Y / N
Notes:				

Date:	B.Z.	Battle Ground:	Rifle:	Scope:
1st Shot Time:		Ave Split Time of Shots 2 - 4	Ave Split Time of Shots 5 - 7:	Overall Completion Time:
1st Shot In: Y / N		Shots 2 - 7 In: Y / N	Kneeling: Supported / Unsupported	Shots 8-10 In: Y / N
Notes:				

Date:	B.Z.	Battle Ground:	Rifle:	Scope:
1st Shot Time:		Ave Split Time of Shots 2 - 4	Ave Split Time of Shots 5 - 7:	Overall Completion Time:
1st Shot In: Y / N		Shots 2 - 7 In: Y / N	Kneeling: Supported / Unsupported	Shots 8-10 In: Y / N
Notes:				

Precision Rifle Performance Diagnostics

Date:	B.Z.	Battle Ground:	Rifle:	Scope:
1st Shot Time:		Ave Split Time of Shots 2 - 4	Ave Split Time of Shots 5 - 7:	Overall Completion Time:
1st Shot In: Y / N		Shots 2 - 7 In: Y / N	Kneeling: Supported / Unsupported	Shots 8-10 In: Y / N
Notes:				

Date:	B.Z.	Battle Ground:	Rifle:	Scope:
1st Shot Time:		Ave Split Time of Shots 2 - 4	Ave Split Time of Shots 5 - 7:	Overall Completion Time:
1st Shot In: Y / N		Shots 2 - 7 In: Y / N	Kneeling: Supported / Unsupported	Shots 8-10 In: Y / N
Notes:				

Date:	B.Z.	Battle Ground:	Rifle:	Scope:
1st Shot Time:		Ave Split Time of Shots 2 - 4	Ave Split Time of Shots 5 - 7:	Overall Completion Time:
1st Shot In: Y / N		Shots 2 - 7 In: Y / N	Kneeling: Supported / Unsupported	Shots 8-10 In: Y / N
Notes:				

Date:	B.Z.	Battle Ground:	Rifle:	Scope:
1st Shot Time:		Ave Split Time of Shots 2 - 4	Ave Split Time of Shots 5 - 7:	Overall Completion Time:
1st Shot In: Y / N		Shots 2 - 7 In: Y / N	Kneeling: Supported / Unsupported	Shots 8-10 In: Y / N
Notes:				

Z Fighter ©

Precision Rifle Diagnostic

www.GUNFIGHTERSERIES.com ©

Precision Rifle Performance Diagnostics

Date:	B.Z.	Battle Ground:	Rifle:	Scope:
1st Shot Time:		Ave Split Time of Shots 2 - 4	Ave Split Time of Shots 5 - 7:	Overall Completion Time:
1st Shot In: Y / N		Shots 2 - 7 In: Y / N	Kneeling: Supported / Unsupported	Shots 8-10 In: Y / N
Notes:				

Date:	B.Z.	Battle Ground:	Rifle:	Scope:
1st Shot Time:		Ave Split Time of Shots 2 - 4	Ave Split Time of Shots 5 - 7:	Overall Completion Time:
1st Shot In: Y / N		Shots 2 - 7 In: Y / N	Kneeling: Supported / Unsupported	Shots 8-10 In: Y / N
Notes:				

Date:	B.Z.	Battle Ground:	Rifle:	Scope:
1st Shot Time:		Ave Split Time of Shots 2 - 4	Ave Split Time of Shots 5 - 7:	Overall Completion Time:
1st Shot In: Y / N		Shots 2 - 7 In: Y / N	Kneeling: Supported / Unsupported	Shots 8-10 In: Y / N
Notes:				

Date:	B.Z.	Battle Ground:	Rifle:	Scope:
1st Shot Time:		Ave Split Time of Shots 2 - 4	Ave Split Time of Shots 5 - 7:	Overall Completion Time:
1st Shot In: Y / N		Shots 2 - 7 In: Y / N	Kneeling: Supported / Unsupported	Shots 8-10 In: Y / N
Notes:				

Precision Rifle Performance Diagnostics

Date:	B.Z.	Battle Ground:	Rifle:	Scope:
1st Shot Time:		Ave Split Time of Shots 2 - 4	Ave Split Time of Shots 5 - 7:	Overall Completion Time:
1st Shot In: Y / N		Shots 2 - 7 In: Y / N	Kneeling: Supported / Unsupported	Shots 8-10 In: Y / N
Notes:				

Date:	B.Z.	Battle Ground:	Rifle:	Scope:
1st Shot Time:		Ave Split Time of Shots 2 - 4	Ave Split Time of Shots 5 - 7:	Overall Completion Time:
1st Shot In: Y / N		Shots 2 - 7 In: Y / N	Kneeling: Supported / Unsupported	Shots 8-10 In: Y / N
Notes:				

Date:	B.Z.	Battle Ground:	Rifle:	Scope:
1st Shot Time:		Ave Split Time of Shots 2 - 4	Ave Split Time of Shots 5 - 7:	Overall Completion Time:
1st Shot In: Y / N		Shots 2 - 7 In: Y / N	Kneeling: Supported / Unsupported	Shots 8-10 In: Y / N
Notes:				

Date:	B.Z.	Battle Ground:	Rifle:	Scope:
1st Shot Time:		Ave Split Time of Shots 2 - 4	Ave Split Time of Shots 5 - 7:	Overall Completion Time:
1st Shot In: Y / N		Shots 2 - 7 In: Y / N	Kneeling: Supported / Unsupported	Shots 8-10 In: Y / N
Notes:				

Z. Fighter ©

Precision Rifle Diagnostic

PRECISION RIFLE DRILL: **COLD BODY**

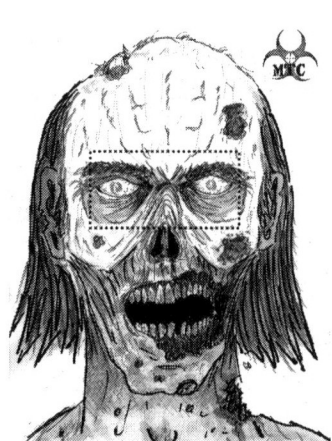

Purpose: Test shooters ability to adjust for cold bore offset in apocalyptic conditions.

Distance: Unknown distance between 50 - 200 Yards.

Target: MTC Z-1 (Undead)

Extra Equipment Needed: Shot timer. 1 Barricade. Standard equipment loadout.

Total Rounds Fired: 1 Round.

Point Penalty: I Win / I Suck

Starting Position & Condition: Standing. Condition 4.

Description: Stage rifle in a safe manner in condition 4 at the firing line next to the prescribed barricade. Begin drill by jogging for no less than 5 minutes. Upon returning, immediately start the 60 second countdown. At the timer beep, quickly estimate range to target, make elevation scope turret adjustment as needed, create any stable firing position (other than prone) using provided support, load rifle with 1 round then fire 1 round into the ocular Z box. Record time, score, atmospherics and turret settings if on ZERO or adjusted for CB (Cold Bore) / CCB (Clean Cold Bore).

Goals: Meat Bag: Z box hit under 60 seconds.   Survivor: Z box hit under 45 seconds.   Z Fighter: Z box hit under 30 seconds.

Variations:

⊕   Infected Humans: Double tap the ocular Z box. Just in case...

⊕   Mutants: Also include 10-15 push ups after the 5 min jog. Shooting position must be in the standing.

COLD BODY

Date: B.Z.	Battle Ground:	Scope:	Barricade:
Temp:	Baro:	CB / CCB	Notes:
Range To Target:	Angle: Cosign:	Elev: Wind:	
Undead / Infected / Mutant	Sitting / Kneeling / Standing	**I Win / I Suck**	Time:

Date: B.Z.	Battle Ground:	Scope:	Barricade:
Temp:	Baro:	CB / CCB	Notes:
Range To Target:	Angle: Cosign:	Elev: Wind:	
Undead / Infected / Mutant	Sitting / Kneeling / Standing	**I Win / I Suck**	Time:

Date: B.Z.	Battle Ground:	Scope:	Barricade:
Temp:	Baro:	CB / CCB	Notes:
Range To Target:	Angle: Cosign:	Elev: Wind:	
Undead / Infected / Mutant	Sitting / Kneeling / Standing	**I Win / I Suck**	Time:

Date: B.Z.	Battle Ground:	Scope:	Barricade:
Temp:	Baro:	CB / CCB	Notes:
Range To Target:	Angle: Cosign:	Elev: Wind:	
Undead / Infected / Mutant	Sitting / Kneeling / Standing	**I Win / I Suck**	Time:

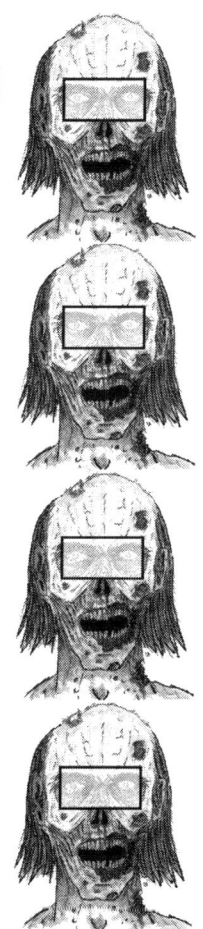

COLD BODY

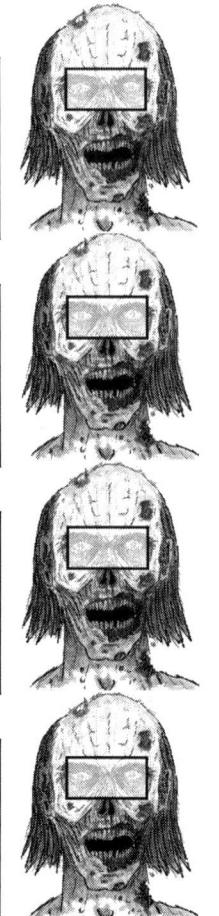

Date:	B.Z.	Battle Ground:	Scope:	Barricade:
Temp:		Baro:	CB / CCB	Notes:
Range To Target:		Angle: Cosign:	Elev: Wind:	
Undead / Infected / Mutant		Sitting / Kneeling / Standing	**I Win / I Suck**	**Time:**

Date:	B.Z.	Battle Ground:	Scope:	Barricade:
Temp:		Baro:	CB / CCB	Notes:
Range To Target:		Angle: Cosign:	Elev: Wind:	
Undead / Infected / Mutant		Sitting / Kneeling / Standing	**I Win / I Suck**	**Time:**

Date:	B.Z.	Battle Ground:	Scope:	Barricade:
Temp:		Baro:	CB / CCB	Notes:
Range To Target:		Angle: Cosign:	Elev: Wind:	
Undead / Infected / Mutant		Sitting / Kneeling / Standing	**I Win / I Suck**	**Time:**

Date:	B.Z.	Battle Ground:	Scope:	Barricade:
Temp:		Baro:	CB / CCB	Notes:
Range To Target:		Angle: Cosign:	Elev: Wind:	
Undead / Infected / Mutant		Sitting / Kneeling / Standing	**I Win / I Suck**	**Time:**

COLD BODY

Date:	B.Z.	Battle Ground:	Scope:	Barricade:
Temp:		Baro:	CB / CCB	Notes:
Range To Target:		Angle: Cosign:	Elev: Wind:	
Undead / Infected / Mutant		Sitting / Kneeling / Standing	**I Win / I Suck**	**Time:**

Date:	B.Z.	Battle Ground:	Scope:	Barricade:
Temp:		Baro:	CB / CCB	Notes:
Range To Target:		Angle: Cosign:	Elev: Wind:	
Undead / Infected / Mutant		Sitting / Kneeling / Standing	**I Win / I Suck**	**Time:**

Date:	B.Z.	Battle Ground:	Scope:	Barricade:
Temp:		Baro:	CB / CCB	Notes:
Range To Target:		Angle: Cosign:	Elev: Wind:	
Undead / Infected / Mutant		Sitting / Kneeling / Standing	**I Win / I Suck**	**Time:**

Date:	B.Z.	Battle Ground:	Scope:	Barricade:
Temp:		Baro:	CB / CCB	Notes:
Range To Target:		Angle: Cosign:	Elev: Wind:	
Undead / Infected / Mutant		Sitting / Kneeling / Standing	**I Win / I Suck**	**Time:**

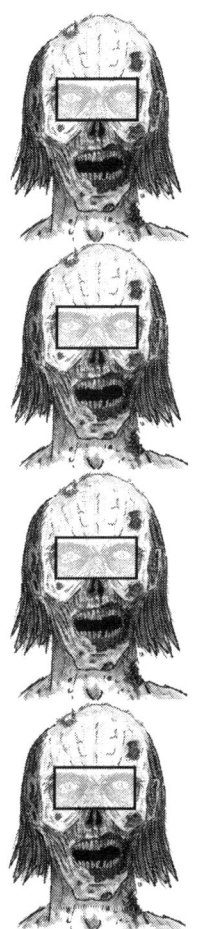

Precision Rifle Drills - 1

COLD BODY

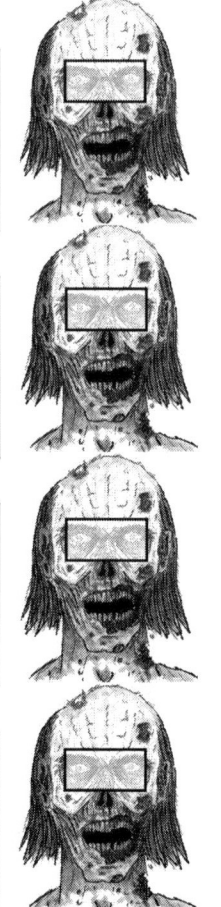

Date:	B.Z.	Battle Ground:	Scope:	Barricade:
Temp:		Baro:	CB / CCB	Notes:
Range To Target:		Angle: Cosign:	Elev: Wind:	
Undead / Infected / Mutant		Sitting / Kneeling / Standing	**I Win / I Suck**	**Time:**

Date:	B.Z.	Battle Ground:	Scope:	Barricade:
Temp:		Baro:	CB / CCB	Notes:
Range To Target:		Angle: Cosign:	Elev: Wind:	
Undead / Infected / Mutant		Sitting / Kneeling / Standing	**I Win / I Suck**	**Time:**

Date:	B.Z.	Battle Ground:	Scope:	Barricade:
Temp:		Baro:	CB / CCB	Notes:
Range To Target:		Angle: Cosign:	Elev: Wind:	
Undead / Infected / Mutant		Sitting / Kneeling / Standing	**I Win / I Suck**	**Time:**

Date:	B.Z.	Battle Ground:	Scope:	Barricade:
Temp:		Baro:	CB / CCB	Notes:
Range To Target:		Angle: Cosign:	Elev: Wind:	
Undead / Infected / Mutant		Sitting / Kneeling / Standing	**I Win / I Suck**	**Time:**

COLD BODY

Date:	B.Z.	Battle Ground:	Scope:	Barricade:
Temp:		Baro:	CB / CCB	Notes:
Range To Target:		Angle: Cosign:	Elev: Wind:	
Undead / Infected / Mutant		Sitting / Kneeling / Standing	**I Win** / **I Suck**	Time:

Date:	B.Z.	Battle Ground:	Scope:	Barricade:
Temp:		Baro:	CB / CCB	Notes:
Range To Target:		Angle: Cosign:	Elev: Wind:	
Undead / Infected / Mutant		Sitting / Kneeling / Standing	**I Win** / **I Suck**	Time:

Date:	B.Z.	Battle Ground:	Scope:	Barricade:
Temp:		Baro:	CB / CCB	Notes:
Range To Target:		Angle: Cosign:	Elev: Wind:	
Undead / Infected / Mutant		Sitting / Kneeling / Standing	**I Win** / **I Suck**	Time:

Date:	B.Z.	Battle Ground:	Scope:	Barricade:
Temp:		Baro:	CB / CCB	Notes:
Range To Target:		Angle: Cosign:	Elev: Wind:	
Undead / Infected / Mutant		Sitting / Kneeling / Standing	**I Win** / **I Suck**	Time:

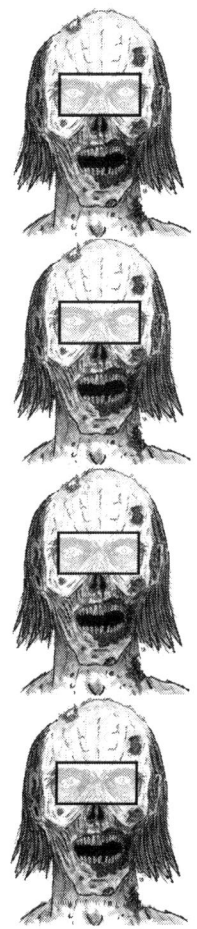

Z Fighter ©

Precision Rifle Drills - 1

PRECISION RIFLE DRILL: **FUNDAMENTALLY AWESOME**

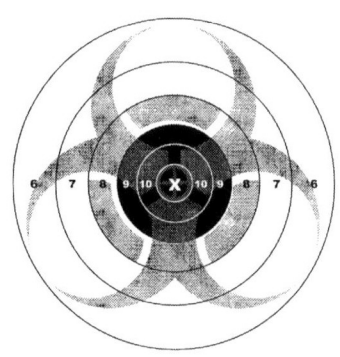

ZF-2

Purpose: To reinforce solid shooting position, Natural Point of Aim and follow through.

Distance: 100 Yards.

Target: ZF-2 (Undead)

Par Time: 25 Seconds.

Extra Equipment Needed: Shot timer.

Total Rounds Fired: 5 Rounds.

Point Penalty: Per target score.

Starting Position & Condition: See description.

Description (DRY): Assume a good prone position with a condition 4 rifle. Conduct a set of 10 dry fires as fast as possible while maintaining perfect sight alignment and sight picture.

Description (LIVE): Assume a good prone position with a condition 4 rifle. At the timer beep, fire 5 rounds at the target. For tightest groups; take a little extra time to ensure your body position and NPA are correct.

Goals: Novice: 45 points under par.   Expert: 50 points under par.   Gunfighter: 50 points with 5 X's under par.

Variations:

- Infected Humans: Start standing behind your rifle. Immediately before the start of the drill, run 50 yards and do 10 push-ups or jumping jacks to get your heart hate up.

- Mutants: From 200 yards. Start standing behind your rifle. Immediately before the start of the drill, run 50 yards and do 10 push-ups or jumping jacks to get your heart hate up.

FUNDAMENTALLY AWESOME

Date:	B.Z.	Battle Ground:	Scope:	Elev:	Wind:	Notes:
100 yards / 200 yards		Dry Fire X 10: Y / N	Undead / Infected / Mutant	**Score:**	**# of X's:**	

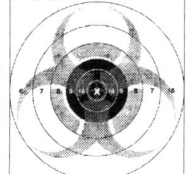

Date:	B.Z.	Battle Ground:	Scope:	Elev:	Wind:	Notes:
100 yards / 200 yards		Dry Fire X 10: Y / N	Undead / Infected / Mutant	**Score:**	**# of X's:**	

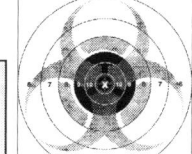

Date:	B.Z.	Battle Ground:	Scope:	Elev:	Wind:	Notes:
100 yards / 200 yards		Dry Fire X 10: Y / N	Undead / Infected / Mutant	**Score:**	**# of X's:**	

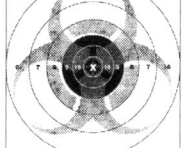

Date:	B.Z.	Battle Ground:	Scope:	Elev:	Wind:	Notes:
100 yards / 200 yards		Dry Fire X 10: Y / N	Undead / Infected / Mutant	**Score:**	**# of X's:**	

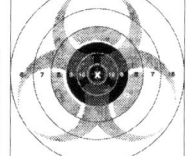

Date:	B.Z.	Battle Ground:	Scope:	Elev:	Wind:	Notes:
100 yards / 200 yards		Dry Fire X 10: Y / N	Undead / Infected / Mutant	**Score:**	**# of X's:**	

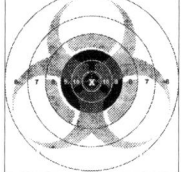

Z Fighter © Precision Rifle Drills - 2

FUNDAMENTALLY AWESOME

Date: B.Z.	Battle Ground:	Scope:	Elev: Wind:	Notes:
100 yards / 200 yards	Dry Fire X 10: Y / N	Undead / Infected / Mutant	**Score:** **# of X's:**	

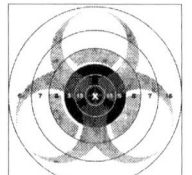

Date: B.Z.	Battle Ground:	Scope:	Elev: Wind:	Notes:
100 yards / 200 yards	Dry Fire X 10: Y / N	Undead / Infected / Mutant	**Score:** **# of X's:**	

Date: B.Z.	Battle Ground:	Scope:	Elev: Wind:	Notes:
100 yards / 200 yards	Dry Fire X 10: Y / N	Undead / Infected / Mutant	**Score:** **# of X's:**	

Date: B.Z.	Battle Ground:	Scope:	Elev: Wind:	Notes:
100 yards / 200 yards	Dry Fire X 10: Y / N	Undead / Infected / Mutant	**Score:** **# of X's:**	

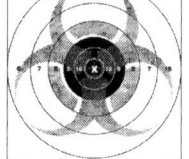

Date: B.Z.	Battle Ground:	Scope:	Elev: Wind:	Notes:
100 yards / 200 yards	Dry Fire X 10: Y / N	Undead / Infected / Mutant	**Score:** **# of X's:**	

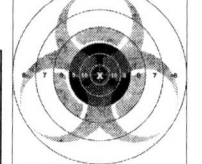

FUNDAMENTALLY AWESOME

Date:	B.Z.	Battle Ground:	Scope:	Elev:	Wind:	Notes:
100 yards / 200 yards		Dry Fire X 10: Y / N	Undead / Infected / Mutant	**Score:**	**# of X's:**	

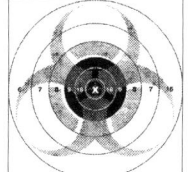

Date:	B.Z.	Battle Ground:	Scope:	Elev:	Wind:	Notes:
100 yards / 200 yards		Dry Fire X 10: Y / N	Undead / Infected / Mutant	**Score:**	**# of X's:**	

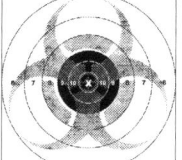

Date:	B.Z.	Battle Ground:	Scope:	Elev:	Wind:	Notes:
100 yards / 200 yards		Dry Fire X 10: Y / N	Undead / Infected / Mutant	**Score:**	**# of X's:**	

Date:	B.Z.	Battle Ground:	Scope:	Elev:	Wind:	Notes:
100 yards / 200 yards		Dry Fire X 10: Y / N	Undead / Infected / Mutant	**Score:**	**# of X's:**	

Date:	B.Z.	Battle Ground:	Scope:	Elev:	Wind:	Notes:
100 yards / 200 yards		Dry Fire X 10: Y / N	Undead / Infected / Mutant	**Score:**	**# of X's:**	

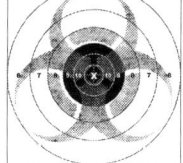

Z Fighter ©   Precision Rifle Drills - 2

FUNDAMENTALLY AWESOME

Date:	B.Z.	Battle Ground:	Scope:	Elev:	Wind:	Notes:
100 yards / 200 yards		Dry Fire X 10: Y / N	Undead / Infected / Mutant	**Score:**	# of X's:	

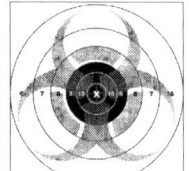

Date:	B.Z.	Battle Ground:	Scope:	Elev:	Wind:	Notes:
100 yards / 200 yards		Dry Fire X 10: Y / N	Undead / Infected / Mutant	**Score:**	# of X's:	

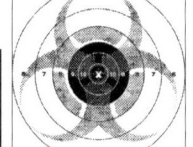

Date:	B.Z.	Battle Ground:	Scope:	Elev:	Wind:	Notes:
100 yards / 200 yards		Dry Fire X 10: Y / N	Undead / Infected / Mutant	**Score:**	# of X's:	

Date:	B.Z.	Battle Ground:	Scope:	Elev:	Wind:	Notes:
100 yards / 200 yards		Dry Fire X 10: Y / N	Undead / Infected / Mutant	**Score:**	# of X's:	

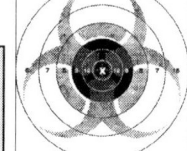

Date:	B.Z.	Battle Ground:	Scope:	Elev:	Wind:	Notes:
100 yards / 200 yards		Dry Fire X 10: Y / N	Undead / Infected / Mutant	**Score:**	# of X's:	

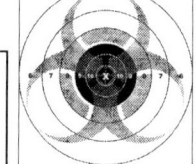

FUNDAMENTALLY AWESOME

Date:	B.Z.	Battle Ground:	Scope:	Elev:	Wind:	Notes:
100 yards / 200 yards		Dry Fire X 10: Y / N	Undead / Infected / Mutant	**Score:**	# of X's:	

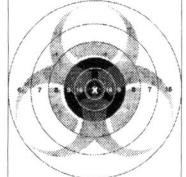

Date:	B.Z.	Battle Ground:	Scope:	Elev:	Wind:	Notes:
100 yards / 200 yards		Dry Fire X 10: Y / N	Undead / Infected / Mutant	**Score:**	# of X's:	

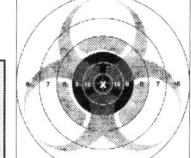

Date:	B.Z.	Battle Ground:	Scope:	Elev:	Wind:	Notes:
100 yards / 200 yards		Dry Fire X 10: Y / N	Undead / Infected / Mutant	**Score:**	# of X's:	

Date:	B.Z.	Battle Ground:	Scope:	Elev:	Wind:	Notes:
100 yards / 200 yards		Dry Fire X 10: Y / N	Undead / Infected / Mutant	**Score:**	# of X's:	

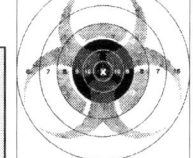

Date:	B.Z.	Battle Ground:	Scope:	Elev:	Wind:	Notes:
100 yards / 200 yards		Dry Fire X 10: Y / N	Undead / Infected / Mutant	**Score:**	# of X's:	

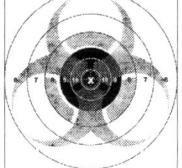

Z Fighter ©   Precision Rifle Drills - 2

PRECISION RIFLE DRILL: **TYRANT VIRUS**

Purpose: To reinforce solid shooting position, Natural Point of Aim and follow through.

Distance: 100 Yards.

Target: Helix

Rounds Fired Per String: 4 Round.

Total Rounds Fired: 16 Rounds.

Point Penalty: Per target score.

Repetitions: 1 Rep of 4 strings.

Starting Position & Condition: See description.

Description:

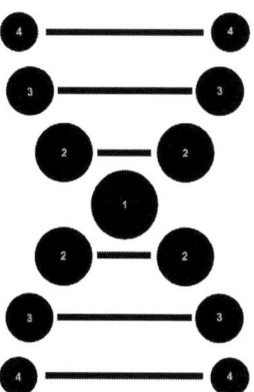

String 1: On your personal go from a good prone supported shooting position, with rifle in your right shoulder, fire 1 round into the top right helix strand starting with the largest circle #1, #2, #3 and finishing with #4.

String 2: On your personal go from a good prone supported shooting position, with rifle in your left shoulder, fire 1 round into the top left helix strand starting with the largest circle #1, #2, #3 and finishing with #4.

String 3: On your personal go from a good prone supported shooting position, with rifle in your right shoulder, fire 1 round into the bottom right helix strand starting with the largest circle #1, #2, #3 and finishing with #4.

String 4: On your personal go from a good prone supported shooting position, with rifle in your left shoulder, fire 1 round into the bottom left helix strand starting with the largest circle #1, #2, #3 and finishing with #4.

Goals: Meat Bag: 18 Points.   Survivor: 30 Points.   Z Fighter: 40 Points

Variations:

⊕ Infected Humans: Par time of 45 seconds per string.

⊕ Mutants: Start 10 yards behind firing position. Par time of 30 seconds per string.

TYRANT VIRUS

Date:	B.Z.	Battle Ground:	Rifle:	Undead / Infected / Mutant	Notes:
String 1 # Out:		String 2 # Out:	String 3 # Out:	String 4 # Out:	
String 1 Score:		String 2 Score:	String 3 Score:	String 4 Score:	**Total Score:**

Date:	B.Z.	Battle Ground:	Rifle:	Undead / Infected / Mutant	Notes:
String 1 # Out:		String 2 # Out:	String 3 # Out:	String 4 # Out:	
String 1 Score:		String 2 Score:	String 3 Score:	String 4 Score:	**Total Score:**

Date:	B.Z.	Battle Ground:	Rifle:	Undead / Infected / Mutant	Notes:
String 1 # Out:		String 2 # Out:	String 3 # Out:	String 4 # Out:	
String 1 Score:		String 2 Score:	String 3 Score:	String 4 Score:	**Total Score:**

Z Fighter ©

Precision Rifle Drills - 3

www.GUNFIGHTERSERIES.com ©

TYRANT VIRUS

Date: B.Z.	Battle Ground:	Rifle:	Undead / Infected / Mutant	Notes:
String 1 # Out:	String 2 # Out:	String 3 # Out:	String 4 # Out:	
String 1 Score:	String 2 Score:	String 3 Score:	String 4 Score:	**Total Score:**

Date: B.Z.	Battle Ground:	Rifle:	Undead / Infected / Mutant	Notes:
String 1 # Out:	String 2 # Out:	String 3 # Out:	String 4 # Out:	
String 1 Score:	String 2 Score:	String 3 Score:	String 4 Score:	**Total Score:**

Date: B.Z.	Battle Ground:	Rifle:	Undead / Infected / Mutant	Notes:
String 1 # Out:	String 2 # Out:	String 3 # Out:	String 4 # Out:	
String 1 Score:	String 2 Score:	String 3 Score:	String 4 Score:	**Total Score:**

TYRANT VIRUS

Date: B.Z.	Battle Ground:	Rifle:	Undead / Infected / Mutant	Notes:
String 1 # Out:	String 2 # Out:	String 3 # Out:	String 4 # Out:	
String 1 Score:	String 2 Score:	String 3 Score:	String 4 Score:	**Total Score:**

Date: B.Z.	Battle Ground:	Rifle:	Undead / Infected / Mutant	Notes:
String 1 # Out:	String 2 # Out:	String 3 # Out:	String 4 # Out:	
String 1 Score:	String 2 Score:	String 3 Score:	String 4 Score:	**Total Score:**

Date: B.Z.	Battle Ground:	Rifle:	Undead / Infected / Mutant	Notes:
String 1 # Out:	String 2 # Out:	String 3 # Out:	String 4 # Out:	
String 1 Score:	String 2 Score:	String 3 Score:	String 4 Score:	**Total Score:**

Z Fighter ©   Precision Rifle Drills - 3

www.GUNFIGHTERSERIES.com ©

TYRANT VIRUS

Date: B.Z.	Battle Ground:	Rifle:	Undead / Infected / Mutant	Notes:
String 1 # Out:	String 2 # Out:	String 3 # Out:	String 4 # Out:	
String 1 Score:	String 2 Score:	String 3 Score:	String 4 Score:	**Total Score:**

Date: B.Z.	Battle Ground:	Rifle:	Undead / Infected / Mutant	Notes:
String 1 # Out:	String 2 # Out:	String 3 # Out:	String 4 # Out:	
String 1 Score:	String 2 Score:	String 3 Score:	String 4 Score:	**Total Score:**

Date: B.Z.	Battle Ground:	Rifle:	Undead / Infected / Mutant	Notes:
String 1 # Out:	String 2 # Out:	String 3 # Out:	String 4 # Out:	
String 1 Score:	String 2 Score:	String 3 Score:	String 4 Score:	**Total Score:**

TYRANT VIRUS

Date:	B.Z.	Battle Ground:	Rifle:	Undead / Infected / Mutant	Notes:
String 1 # Out:		String 2 # Out:	String 3 # Out:	String 4 # Out:	
String 1 Score:		String 2 Score:	String 3 Score:	String 4 Score:	**Total Score:**

Date:	B.Z.	Battle Ground:	Rifle:	Undead / Infected / Mutant	Notes:
String 1 # Out:		String 2 # Out:	String 3 # Out:	String 4 # Out:	
String 1 Score:		String 2 Score:	String 3 Score:	String 4 Score:	**Total Score:**

Date:	B.Z.	Battle Ground:	Rifle:	Undead / Infected / Mutant	Notes:
String 1 # Out:		String 2 # Out:	String 3 # Out:	String 4 # Out:	
String 1 Score:		String 2 Score:	String 3 Score:	String 4 Score:	**Total Score:**

Z Fighter ©   Precision Rifle Drills - 3

PRECISION RIFLE DRILL: **BOUNDARIES**

Purpose: To learn and test your accuracy limits.

Distance: 100 Yards.

Target: KYL (Undead)

Rounds Fired Per String: 5 Rounds.

Total Rounds Fired: 15 Rounds.

Point Penalty: Per target score.

Repetitions: 1 Rep of 3 strings.

Starting Position & Condition: See string description. Condition 1.

Description:

String 1: On your personal go from a good prone shooting position, either supported or with sling, fire 1 round into each dot on the far left column starting from the biggest on top to the smallest on bottom.   Log your accuracy dot size limit.

String 2: On your personal go from a kneeling shooting position, either supported or with sling, fire 1 round into each dot in the middle column starting at the biggest on top to the smallest dot. Log your accuracy dot size limit.

String 3: On your personal go from a standing shooting position, either supported or with sling, fire 1 round into each dot in the far right column starting at the biggest on top to the smallest dot. Log your accuracy dot size limit.

Goals: Meat Bag: 18 Points   Survivor: 30 Points   Z Fighter: 45 Points

Variations:

⊕   Infected Humans: Par time of 45 seconds per string.

⊕   Mutants: Start 10 yards behind firing position. Par time of 30 seconds per string.

BOUNDARIES

Date:		B.Z.	Battle Ground:	Rifle:	Scope:	Undead / Infected / Mutant
Rep 1 Dots:	1" / 1.25" / 1.5" / 1.75" / 2"			Rep 1 Score:		Supported / Unsupported / Sling
Rep 2 Dots:	1" / 1.25" / 1.5" / 1.75" / 2"			Rep 2 Score:		Support Type:
Rep 3 Dots:	1" / 1.25" / 1.5" / 1.75" / 2"			Rep 3 Score:		**Total Score:**
Notes:						

Date:		B.Z.	Battle Ground:	Rifle:	Scope:	Undead / Infected / Mutant
Rep 1 Dots:	1" / 1.25" / 1.5" / 1.75" / 2"			Rep 1 Score:		Supported / Unsupported / Sling
Rep 2 Dots:	1" / 1.25" / 1.5" / 1.75" / 2"			Rep 2 Score:		Support Type:
Rep 3 Dots:	1" / 1.25" / 1.5" / 1.75" / 2"			Rep 3 Score:		**Total Score:**
Notes:						

Date:		B.Z.	Battle Ground:	Rifle:	Scope:	Undead / Infected / Mutant
Rep 1 Dots:	1" / 1.25" / 1.5" / 1.75" / 2"			Rep 1 Score:		Supported / Unsupported / Sling
Rep 2 Dots:	1" / 1.25" / 1.5" / 1.75" / 2"			Rep 2 Score:		Support Type:
Rep 3 Dots:	1" / 1.25" / 1.5" / 1.75" / 2"			Rep 3 Score:		**Total Score:**
Notes:						

Z Fighter ©

Precision Rifle Drills - 4

BOUNDARIES

Date:		B.Z.	Battle Ground:	Rifle:	Scope:	Undead / Infected / Mutant
Rep 1 Dots:	1" /	1.25" /	1.5" / 1.75" / 2"	Rep 1 Score:		Supported / Unsupported / Sling
Rep 2 Dots:	1" /	1.25" /	1.5" / 1.75" / 2"	Rep 2 Score:		Support Type:
Rep 3 Dots:	1" /	1.25" /	1.5" / 1.75" / 2"	Rep 3 Score:		**Total Score:**
Notes:						

Date:		B.Z.	Battle Ground:	Rifle:	Scope:	Undead / Infected / Mutant
Rep 1 Dots:	1" /	1.25" /	1.5" / 1.75" / 2"	Rep 1 Score:		Supported / Unsupported / Sling
Rep 2 Dots:	1" /	1.25" /	1.5" / 1.75" / 2"	Rep 2 Score:		Support Type:
Rep 3 Dots:	1" /	1.25" /	1.5" / 1.75" / 2"	Rep 3 Score:		**Total Score:**
Notes:						

Date:		B.Z.	Battle Ground:	Rifle:	Scope:	Undead / Infected / Mutant
Rep 1 Dots:	1" /	1.25" /	1.5" / 1.75" / 2"	Rep 1 Score:		Supported / Unsupported / Sling
Rep 2 Dots:	1" /	1.25" /	1.5" / 1.75" / 2"	Rep 2 Score:		Support Type:
Rep 3 Dots:	1" /	1.25" /	1.5" / 1.75" / 2"	Rep 3 Score:		**Total Score:**
Notes:						

BOUNDARIES

Date:		B.Z.	Battle Ground:	Rifle:	Scope:	Undead / Infected / Mutant
Rep 1 Dots:	1" / 1.25" / 1.5" / 1.75" / 2"			Rep 1 Score:		Supported / Unsupported / Sling
Rep 2 Dots:	1" / 1.25" / 1.5" / 1.75" / 2"			Rep 2 Score:		Support Type:
Rep 3 Dots:	1" / 1.25" / 1.5" / 1.75" / 2"			Rep 3 Score:		**Total Score:**
Notes:						

Date:		B.Z.	Battle Ground:	Rifle:	Scope:	Undead / Infected / Mutant
Rep 1 Dots:	1" / 1.25" / 1.5" / 1.75" / 2"			Rep 1 Score:		Supported / Unsupported / Sling
Rep 2 Dots:	1" / 1.25" / 1.5" / 1.75" / 2"			Rep 2 Score:		Support Type:
Rep 3 Dots:	1" / 1.25" / 1.5" / 1.75" / 2"			Rep 3 Score:		**Total Score:**
Notes:						

Date:		B.Z.	Battle Ground:	Rifle:	Scope:	Undead / Infected / Mutant
Rep 1 Dots:	1" / 1.25" / 1.5" / 1.75" / 2"			Rep 1 Score:		Supported / Unsupported / Sling
Rep 2 Dots:	1" / 1.25" / 1.5" / 1.75" / 2"			Rep 2 Score:		Support Type:
Rep 3 Dots:	1" / 1.25" / 1.5" / 1.75" / 2"			Rep 3 Score:		**Total Score:**
Notes:						

Z Fighter ©

Precision Rifle Drills - 4

www.GUNFIGHTERSERIES.com ©

BOUNDARIES

Date:		B.Z.	Battle Ground:				Rifle:	Scope:	Undead / Infected / Mutant
Rep 1 Dots:	1" /	1.25" /	1.5"	/	1.75" /	2"	Rep 1 Score:		Supported / Unsupported / Sling
Rep 2 Dots:	1" /	1.25" /	1.5"	/	1.75" /	2"	Rep 2 Score:		Support Type:
Rep 3 Dots:	1" /	1.25" /	1.5"	/	1.75" /	2"	Rep 3 Score:		**Total Score:**
Notes:									

Date:		B.Z.	Battle Ground:				Rifle:	Scope:	Undead / Infected / Mutant
Rep 1 Dots:	1" /	1.25" /	1.5"	/	1.75" /	2"	Rep 1 Score:		Supported / Unsupported / Sling
Rep 2 Dots:	1" /	1.25" /	1.5"	/	1.75" /	2"	Rep 2 Score:		Support Type:
Rep 3 Dots:	1" /	1.25" /	1.5"	/	1.75" /	2"	Rep 3 Score:		**Total Score:**
Notes:									

Date:		B.Z.	Battle Ground:				Rifle:	Scope:	Undead / Infected / Mutant
Rep 1 Dots:	1" /	1.25" /	1.5"	/	1.75" /	2"	Rep 1 Score:		Supported / Unsupported / Sling
Rep 2 Dots:	1" /	1.25" /	1.5"	/	1.75" /	2"	Rep 2 Score:		Support Type:
Rep 3 Dots:	1" /	1.25" /	1.5"	/	1.75" /	2"	Rep 3 Score:		**Total Score:**
Notes:									

BOUNDARIES

Date:		B.Z.	Battle Ground:				Rifle:	Scope:	Undead / Infected / Mutant
Rep 1 Dots:	1" /	1.25" /	1.5"	/	1.75" /	2"	Rep 1 Score:		Supported / Unsupported / Sling
Rep 2 Dots:	1" /	1.25" /	1.5"	/	1.75" /	2"	Rep 2 Score:		Support Type:
Rep 3 Dots:	1" /	1.25" /	1.5"	/	1.75" /	2"	Rep 3 Score:		**Total Score:**
Notes:									

Date:		B.Z.	Battle Ground:				Rifle:	Scope:	Undead / Infected / Mutant
Rep 1 Dots:	1" /	1.25" /	1.5"	/	1.75" /	2"	Rep 1 Score:		Supported / Unsupported / Sling
Rep 2 Dots:	1" /	1.25" /	1.5"	/	1.75" /	2"	Rep 2 Score:		Support Type:
Rep 3 Dots:	1" /	1.25" /	1.5"	/	1.75" /	2"	Rep 3 Score:		**Total Score:**
Notes:									

Date:		B.Z.	Battle Ground:				Rifle:	Scope:	Undead / Infected / Mutant
Rep 1 Dots:	1" /	1.25" /	1.5"	/	1.75" /	2"	Rep 1 Score:		Supported / Unsupported / Sling
Rep 2 Dots:	1" /	1.25" /	1.5"	/	1.75" /	2"	Rep 2 Score:		Support Type:
Rep 3 Dots:	1" /	1.25" /	1.5"	/	1.75" /	2"	Rep 3 Score:		**Total Score:**
Notes:									

Z Fighter ©

PRECISION RIFLE DRILL: **SIT, KNEEL, STAND**

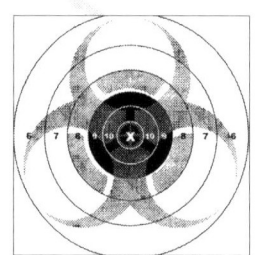 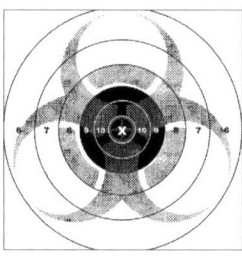 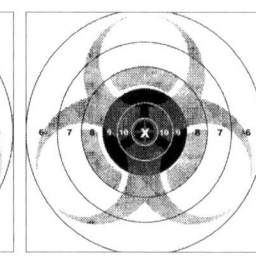

Purpose: Increase tripod proficiency and accuracy in multiple shooting positions.

Distance: 100 Yards.

Target: ZF-2 X 3

Par Time: 2 Minutes per rep.

Extra Equipment Needed: Shot timer. Barricade or tripod shooting support.

Rounds Fired Per Rep: 3 Rounds.

Total Rounds Fired: 9 Rounds.

Point Penalty: Per target score.

Repetitions: 3 Reps.

Starting Position & Condition: See description for position. Condition 1.

Description Sitting: Assume a good sitting position utilizing a barricade or tripod support. At the timer beep, slow fire 3 rounds into the first target. Reload.

Description Kneeling: Assume a good kneeling position utilizing a barricade or tripod support. At the timer beep, slow fire 3 rounds into the second target. Reload.

Description Standing: Assume a good standing position utilizing a barricade or tripod support. At the timer beep, slow fire 3 rounds into the third target. Score targets.

Goals: Meat Bag: 80 Points   Survivor: 90 Points   Z Fighter: 90 Points with 9 X's under par.

Variations:

⊕ Infected Humans: Start from a standing low ready position and give yourself a 45 second par time per 3 shot repetition.

⊕ Mutants: Start from a standing low ready position and give yourself a 30 second par time per 3 shot repetition.

SIT, KNEEL, STAND

Date:	B.Z.	Rifle:	Scope:	Barricade:	Notes:
Sitting Score:		Kneeling Score:	Standing Score:	**Total Score:**	

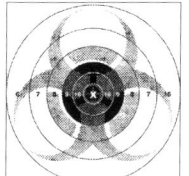

Date:	B.Z.	Rifle:	Scope:	Barricade:	Notes:
Sitting Score:		Kneeling Score:	Standing Score:	**Total Score:**	

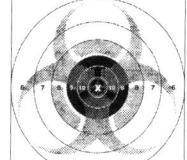

Date:	B.Z.	Rifle:	Scope:	Barricade:	Notes:
Sitting Score:		Kneeling Score:	Standing Score:	**Total Score:**	

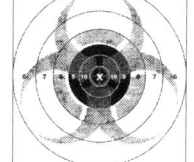

Date:	B.Z.	Rifle:	Scope:	Barricade:	Notes:
Sitting Score:		Kneeling Score:	Standing Score:	**Total Score:**	

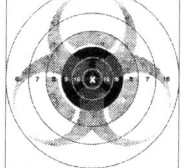

Date:	B.Z.	Rifle:	Scope:	Barricade:	Notes:
Sitting Score:		Kneeling Score:	Standing Score:	**Total Score:**	

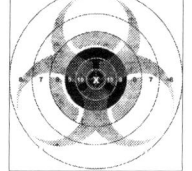

Z Fighter ©

Precision Rifle Drills - 5

SIT, KNEEL, STAND

Date:	B.Z.	Rifle:	Scope:	Barricade:	Notes:
Sitting Score:		Kneeling Score:	Standing Score:	**Total Score:**	

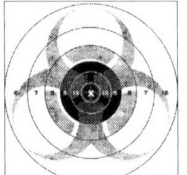

Date:	B.Z.	Rifle:	Scope:	Barricade:	Notes:
Sitting Score:		Kneeling Score:	Standing Score:	**Total Score:**	

Date:	B.Z.	Rifle:	Scope:	Barricade:	Notes:
Sitting Score:		Kneeling Score:	Standing Score:	**Total Score:**	

Date:	B.Z.	Rifle:	Scope:	Barricade:	Notes:
Sitting Score:		Kneeling Score:	Standing Score:	**Total Score:**	

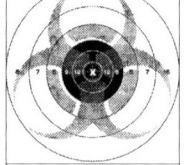

Date:	B.Z.	Rifle:	Scope:	Barricade:	Notes:
Sitting Score:		Kneeling Score:	Standing Score:	**Total Score:**	

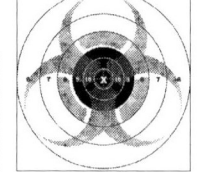

SIT, KNEEL, STAND

Date:	B.Z.	Rifle:	Scope:	Barricade:	Notes:
Sitting Score:		Kneeling Score:	Standing Score:	**Total Score:**	

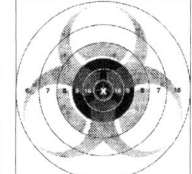

Date:	B.Z.	Rifle:	Scope:	Barricade:	Notes:
Sitting Score:		Kneeling Score:	Standing Score:	**Total Score:**	

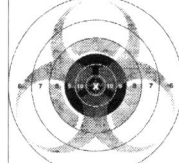

Date:	B.Z.	Rifle:	Scope:	Barricade:	Notes:
Sitting Score:		Kneeling Score:	Standing Score:	**Total Score:**	

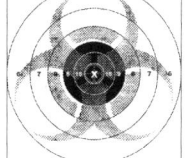

Date:	B.Z.	Rifle:	Scope:	Barricade:	Notes:
Sitting Score:		Kneeling Score:	Standing Score:	**Total Score:**	

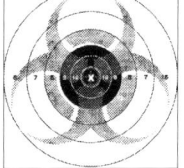

Date:	B.Z.	Rifle:	Scope:	Barricade:	Notes:
Sitting Score:		Kneeling Score:	Standing Score:	**Total Score:**	

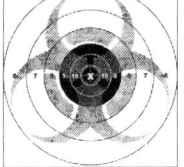

SIT, KNEEL, STAND

Date:	B.Z.	Rifle:	Scope:	Barricade:	Notes:
Sitting Score:		Kneeling Score:	Standing Score:	**Total Score:**	

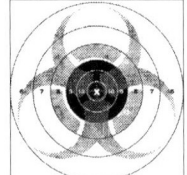

Date:	B.Z.	Rifle:	Scope:	Barricade:	Notes:
Sitting Score:		Kneeling Score:	Standing Score:	**Total Score:**	

Date:	B.Z.	Rifle:	Scope:	Barricade:	Notes:
Sitting Score:		Kneeling Score:	Standing Score:	**Total Score:**	

Date:	B.Z.	Rifle:	Scope:	Barricade:	Notes:
Sitting Score:		Kneeling Score:	Standing Score:	**Total Score:**	

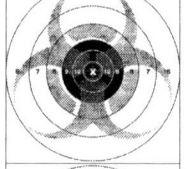

Date:	B.Z.	Rifle:	Scope:	Barricade:	Notes:
Sitting Score:		Kneeling Score:	Standing Score:	**Total Score:**	

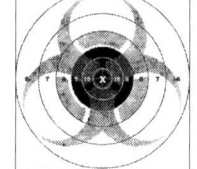

SIT, KNEEL, STAND

Date:	B.Z.	Rifle:	Scope:	Barricade:	Notes:
Sitting Score:		Kneeling Score:	Standing Score:	**Total Score:**	

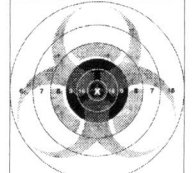

Date:	B.Z.	Rifle:	Scope:	Barricade:	Notes:
Sitting Score:		Kneeling Score:	Standing Score:	**Total Score:**	

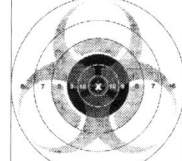

Date:	B.Z.	Rifle:	Scope:	Barricade:	Notes:
Sitting Score:		Kneeling Score:	Standing Score:	**Total Score:**	

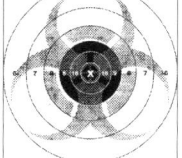

Date:	B.Z.	Rifle:	Scope:	Barricade:	Notes:
Sitting Score:		Kneeling Score:	Standing Score:	**Total Score:**	

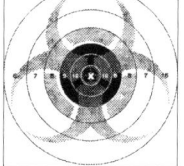

Date:	B.Z.	Rifle:	Scope:	Barricade:	Notes:
Sitting Score:		Kneeling Score:	Standing Score:	**Total Score:**	

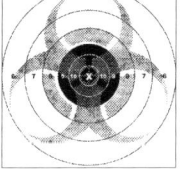

PRECISION RIFLE DRILL: **THAT WAS CLOSE**

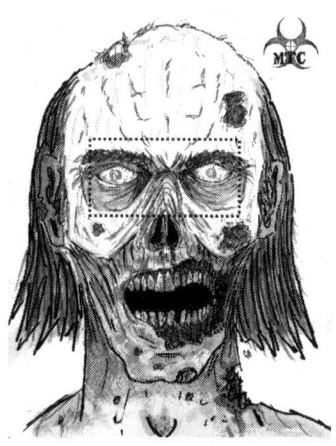

Purpose: Close range defensive shooting with a precision rifle.

Distance: 15 Yards.

Target: MTC Z-1 (Undead).

Par Time: 1.75 Seconds.

Extra Equipment Needed: Shot timer.

Rounds Fired Per Rep: 1 Round.

Total Rounds Fired: 5 Rounds.

Point Penalty: Live or Die.

Repetitions: 5 Reps.

Starting Position & Condition: Standing low ready. Precision rifle condition 1.

Description: At the timer beep, present your rifle to the threat and fire as soon as you acquire a flash sight picture of the head ocular Z box.

NOTE: It's best to patrol with your rifle scope on it's lowest power setting.

Goals: Meat Bag: All in the head.   Survivor: 3 in the ocular Z box.   Z Fighter: All 5 in the ocular Z box.

Variations:

⊕ Infected Humans: From 20 yards with a 2 second par time.

⊕ Mutants: Start with your back facing the target. From 20 yards with a 2.5 second par time.

THAT WAS CLOSE

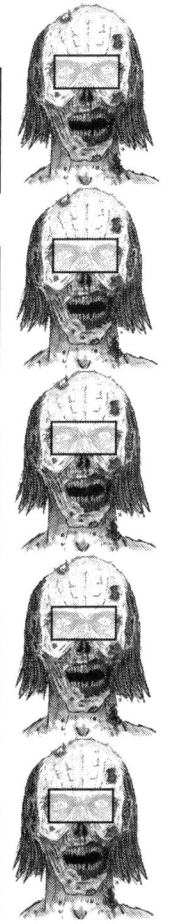

Date:	B.Z.	Battle Ground:	Rifle:	Scope / Micro Dot	Power Setting:
Undead / Infected / Mutant			# In Z Box:	# Over Par:	**Total Score:**

Date:	B.Z.	Battle Ground:	Rifle:	Scope / Micro Dot	Power Setting:
Undead / Infected / Mutant			# In Z Box:	# Over Par:	**Total Score:**

Date:	B.Z.	Battle Ground:	Rifle:	Scope / Micro Dot	Power Setting:
Undead / Infected / Mutant			# In Z Box:	# Over Par:	**Total Score:**

Date:	B.Z.	Battle Ground:	Rifle:	Scope / Micro Dot	Power Setting:
Undead / Infected / Mutant			# In Z Box:	# Over Par:	**Total Score:**

Date:	B.Z.	Battle Ground:	Rifle:	Scope / Micro Dot	Power Setting:
Undead / Infected / Mutant			# In Z Box:	# Over Par:	**Total Score:**

Z Fighter ©

THAT WAS CLOSE

Date:	B.Z.	Battle Ground:	Rifle:	Scope / Micro Dot	Power Setting:
Undead / Infected / Mutant			# In Z Box:	# Over Par:	**Total Score:**

Date:	B.Z.	Battle Ground:	Rifle:	Scope / Micro Dot	Power Setting:
Undead / Infected / Mutant			# In Z Box:	# Over Par:	**Total Score:**

Date:	B.Z.	Battle Ground:	Rifle:	Scope / Micro Dot	Power Setting:
Undead / Infected / Mutant			# In Z Box:	# Over Par:	**Total Score:**

Date:	B.Z.	Battle Ground:	Rifle:	Scope / Micro Dot	Power Setting:
Undead / Infected / Mutant			# In Z Box:	# Over Par:	**Total Score:**

Date:	B.Z.	Battle Ground:	Rifle:	Scope / Micro Dot	Power Setting:
Undead / Infected / Mutant			# In Z Box:	# Over Par:	**Total Score:**

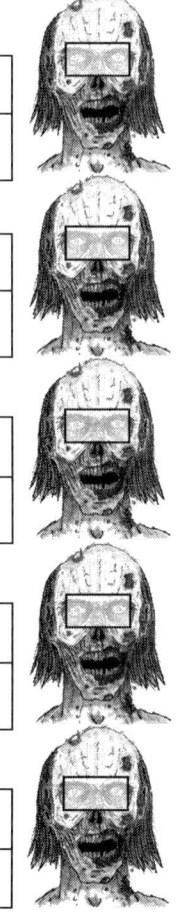

THAT WAS CLOSE

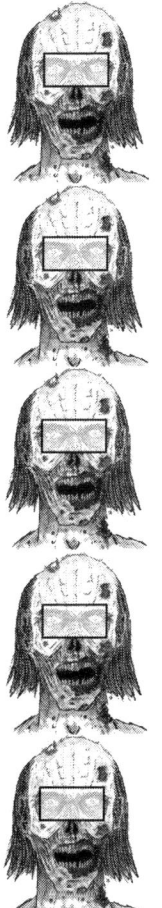

Date:	B.Z.	Battle Ground:	Rifle:	Scope / Micro Dot	Power Setting:
Undead / Infected / Mutant			# In Z Box:	# Over Par:	**Total Score:**

Date:	B.Z.	Battle Ground:	Rifle:	Scope / Micro Dot	Power Setting:
Undead / Infected / Mutant			# In Z Box:	# Over Par:	**Total Score:**

Date:	B.Z.	Battle Ground:	Rifle:	Scope / Micro Dot	Power Setting:
Undead / Infected / Mutant			# In Z Box:	# Over Par:	**Total Score:**

Date:	B.Z.	Battle Ground:	Rifle:	Scope / Micro Dot	Power Setting:
Undead / Infected / Mutant			# In Z Box:	# Over Par:	**Total Score:**

Date:	B.Z.	Battle Ground:	Rifle:	Scope / Micro Dot	Power Setting:
Undead / Infected / Mutant			# In Z Box:	# Over Par:	**Total Score:**

Z Fighter ©   Precision Rifle Drills - 6

THAT WAS CLOSE

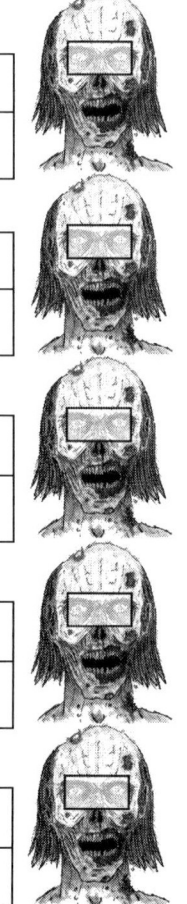

Date:		B.Z.	Battle Ground:	Rifle:	Scope / Micro Dot	Power Setting:
	Undead / Infected / Mutant			# In Z Box:	# Over Par:	**Total Score:**

Date:		B.Z.	Battle Ground:	Rifle:	Scope / Micro Dot	Power Setting:
	Undead / Infected / Mutant			# In Z Box:	# Over Par:	**Total Score:**

Date:		B.Z.	Battle Ground:	Rifle:	Scope / Micro Dot	Power Setting:
	Undead / Infected / Mutant			# In Z Box:	# Over Par:	**Total Score:**

Date:		B.Z.	Battle Ground:	Rifle:	Scope / Micro Dot	Power Setting:
	Undead / Infected / Mutant			# In Z Box:	# Over Par:	**Total Score:**

Date:		B.Z.	Battle Ground:	Rifle:	Scope / Micro Dot	Power Setting:
	Undead / Infected / Mutant			# In Z Box:	# Over Par:	**Total Score:**

THAT WAS CLOSE

Date:	B.Z.	Battle Ground:	Rifle:	Scope / Micro Dot	Power Setting:
Undead / Infected / Mutant			# In Z Box:	# Over Par:	**Total Score:**

Date:	B.Z.	Battle Ground:	Rifle:	Scope / Micro Dot	Power Setting:
Undead / Infected / Mutant			# In Z Box:	# Over Par:	**Total Score:**

Date:	B.Z.	Battle Ground:	Rifle:	Scope / Micro Dot	Power Setting:
Undead / Infected / Mutant			# In Z Box:	# Over Par:	**Total Score:**

Date:	B.Z.	Battle Ground:	Rifle:	Scope / Micro Dot	Power Setting:
Undead / Infected / Mutant			# In Z Box:	# Over Par:	**Total Score:**

Date:	B.Z.	Battle Ground:	Rifle:	Scope / Micro Dot	Power Setting:
Undead / Infected / Mutant			# In Z Box:	# Over Par:	**Total Score:**

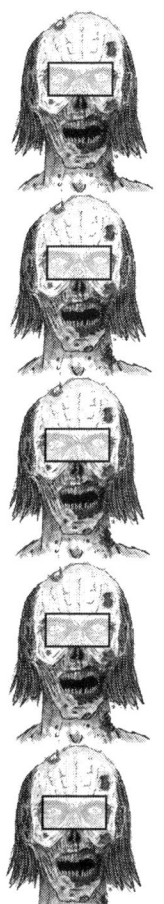

Z Fighter ©

PRECISION RIFLE DRILL: **RUN AWAY!!!**

Purpose: Close range defensive shooting.

Distance: 5, 15, 25, 50, 75,100 and Yards.

Target: ZIPSC (Undead)

Extra Equipment Needed: Shot timer. Pistol, 1 mag with 6 rounds and holster. 1 Rifle mag with 5 rounds. 6 barricades positions.

Total Rounds Fired: 6 pistol & 5 rifle rounds.

Point Penalty: Time plus penalty. (7 shot in ocular Z box. 4 shots in body A box.)

Starting Position & Condition: Standing - Surrender / Interview. Pistol holstered in condition 1. Rifle slung across back. Condition 3.

Description: From the 5 yard line - At the timer beep, draw pistol and fire 2 rounds to the body A box and 1 round into ocular Z box. Weapon on safe, in the low ready or port carry, turn around up range safely and move to the 15 yard line. Turn down range then engage 2 rounds to the body A box and 1 into the ocular Z box. Holster empty pistol and safely unsling rifle.

Rifle on safe, in the low ready or port carry, turn around and safely move up range to the 25 yard line. Turn down range from any position engage 1 rounds to the ocular Z box. Continue the drill using any position and aiming at ocular Z box until completed at 100 yards.

Record time, score targets. For every hit in the 3 scoring zone, add 10 seconds to your time. For every hit in the 0 scoring zone, add 30 seconds to your time. Add the penalty time onto your recorded time.

Goals: Meat Bag: 180 Seconds.   Survivor: 100 Seconds.   Z Fighter: 60 Seconds

Variations:

⊕   Infected Humans: Carry a fully stocked Go-Bag.

⊕   Mutants: Run entire drill in a protective mask and Go-Bag.

RUN AWAY!!!

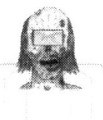

Date:	B.Z.	Battle Ground:	Rifle:	Scope:	Pistol:
Total Time:		# of Z Box:	# of Body A:	Penalties:	**Total Time Score:**

Date:	B.Z.	Battle Ground:	Rifle:	Scope:	Pistol:
Total Time:		# of Z Box:	# of Body A:	Penalties:	**Total Time Score:**

Date:	B.Z.	Battle Ground:	Rifle:	Scope:	Pistol:
Total Time:		# of Z Box:	# of Body A:	Penalties:	**Total Time Score:**

Date:	B.Z.	Battle Ground:	Rifle:	Scope:	Pistol:
Total Time:		# of Z Box:	# of Body A:	Penalties:	**Total Time Score:**

Date:	B.Z.	Battle Ground:	Rifle:	Scope:	Pistol:
Total Time:		# of Z Box:	# of Body A:	Penalties:	**Total Time Score:**

Z Fighter ©   Precision Rifle Drills - 7

www.GUNFIGHTERSERIES.com ©

RUN AWAY!!!

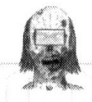

Date:	B.Z.	Battle Ground:	Rifle:	Scope:	Pistol:
Total Time:		# of Z Box:	# of Body A:	Penalties:	**Total Time Score:**

Date:	B.Z.	Battle Ground:	Rifle:	Scope:	Pistol:
Total Time:		# of Z Box:	# of Body A:	Penalties:	**Total Time Score:**

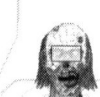

Date:	B.Z.	Battle Ground:	Rifle:	Scope:	Pistol:
Total Time:		# of Z Box:	# of Body A:	Penalties:	**Total Time Score:**

Date:	B.Z.	Battle Ground:	Rifle:	Scope:	Pistol:
Total Time:		# of Z Box:	# of Body A:	Penalties:	**Total Time Score:**

Date:	B.Z.	Battle Ground:	Rifle:	Scope:	Pistol:
Total Time:		# of Z Box:	# of Body A:	Penalties:	**Total Time Score:**

RUN AWAY!!!

Date:	B.Z.	Battle Ground:	Rifle:	Scope:	Pistol:
Total Time:		# of Z Box:	# of Body A:	Penalties:	**Total Time Score:**

Date:	B.Z.	Battle Ground:	Rifle:	Scope:	Pistol:
Total Time:		# of Z Box:	# of Body A:	Penalties:	**Total Time Score:**

Date:	B.Z.	Battle Ground:	Rifle:	Scope:	Pistol:
Total Time:		# of Z Box:	# of Body A:	Penalties:	Total Time Score:

Date:	B.Z.	Battle Ground:	Rifle:	Scope:	Pistol:
Total Time:		# of Z Box:	# of Body A:	Penalties:	**Total Time Score:**

Date:	B.Z.	Battle Ground:	Rifle:	Scope:	Pistol:
Total Time:		# of Z Box:	# of Body A:	Penalties:	Total Time Score:

RUN AWAY!!!

Date:	B.Z.	Battle Ground:	Rifle:	Scope:	Pistol:
Total Time:		# of Z Box:	# of Body A:	Penalties:	**Total Time Score:**

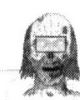

Date:	B.Z.	Battle Ground:	Rifle:	Scope:	Pistol:
Total Time:		# of Z Box:	# of Body A:	Penalties:	**Total Time Score:**

Date:	B.Z.	Battle Ground:	Rifle:	Scope:	Pistol:
Total Time:		# of Z Box:	# of Body A:	Penalties:	**Total Time Score:**

Date:	B.Z.	Battle Ground:	Rifle:	Scope:	Pistol:
Total Time:		# of Z Box:	# of Body A:	Penalties:	**Total Time Score:**

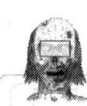

Date:	B.Z.	Battle Ground:	Rifle:	Scope:	Pistol:
Total Time:		# of Z Box:	# of Body A:	Penalties:	**Total Time Score:**

RUN AWAY!!!

Date:	B.Z.	Battle Ground:	Rifle:	Scope:	Pistol:
Total Time:		# of Z Box:	# of Body A:	Penalties:	**Total Time Score:**

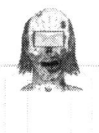

Date:	B.Z.	Battle Ground:	Rifle:	Scope:	Pistol:
Total Time:		# of Z Box:	# of Body A:	Penalties:	**Total Time Score:**

Date:	B.Z.	Battle Ground:	Rifle:	Scope:	Pistol:
Total Time:		# of Z Box:	# of Body A:	Penalties:	**Total Time Score:**

Date:	B.Z.	Battle Ground:	Rifle:	Scope:	Pistol:
Total Time:		# of Z Box:	# of Body A:	Penalties:	**Total Time Score:**

Date:	B.Z.	Battle Ground:	Rifle:	Scope:	Pistol:
Total Time:		# of Z Box:	# of Body A:	Penalties:	**Total Time Score:**

Z Fighter ©

Precision Rifle Drills - 7

PRECISION RIFLE DRILL: **CLEAR THE WAY**

Purpose: Rescue shooting with a precision rifle.

Distance: 100, 75 and 50 Yards.

Target: Hostage. MTC Z-1 (Undead) placed beside Hostage. Upper half of a ZIPSC placed at ground level.

Extra Equipment Needed: Shot timer.

Total Rounds Fired: 9 Rounds.

Point Penalty: Time plus penalty.

Repetitions: 1 Rep.

Starting Position & Condition: Standing behind your rifle. Precision rifle condition 1.

Description: From 100 yards, at the timer beep assume a good <u>prone position</u>. Fire 1 round into the head ocular Z box of zombie attacking the hostage, 1 round into the ocular Z box of the zombie beside the hostage and 1 round into the ocular Z box of the crawler below the hostage. Make a safe rifle, stand then move quickly to the 75 yard line. Repeat the same shot sequence from the <u>kneeling position</u>. Make a safe rifle, stand then move quickly to the 50 yard line. Repeat the same shot sequence from the <u>standing position.</u> Make safe rifle, record time, score and penalties. Add 3 seconds for every shot in the head, but outside the ocular Z box. Add 10 seconds for every miss off target. Add 30 seconds for every hostage hit.

NOTE: Beginners should focus more on accuracy than speed.

Goals: Meat Bag: 180 Seconds.   Survivor: 140 Seconds.   Z Fighter: 100 Seconds.

Variations:

⊕ Infected humans: Load 3 magazines with 6 rounds each. Double the round count fired at each target.

⊕ Mutants: Perform the drill starting at 200 yards, 150 yards then ending at 100 yards.

CLEAR THE WAY

Date: B.Z.	Battle Ground:	Rifle:	Scope / Micro Dot	Power Setting:
Undead / Infected / Mutant	Time:	# Out of Z Box:	Penalty #:	**Total Time Score:**

 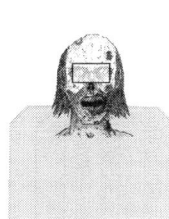

Date: B.Z.	Battle Ground:	Rifle:	Scope / Micro Dot	Power Setting:
Undead / Infected / Mutant	Time:	# Out of Z Box:	Penalty #:	**Total Time Score:**

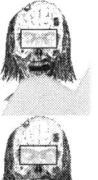 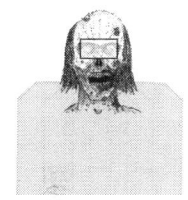

Date: B.Z.	Battle Ground:	Rifle:	Scope / Micro Dot	Power Setting:
Undead / Infected / Mutant	Time:	# Out of Z Box:	Penalty #:	**Total Time Score:**

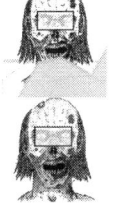 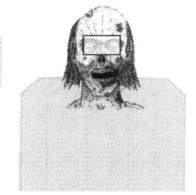

Date: B.Z.	Battle Ground:	Rifle:	Scope / Micro Dot	Power Setting:
Undead / Infected / Mutant	Time:	# Out of Z Box:	Penalty #:	**Total Time Score:**

 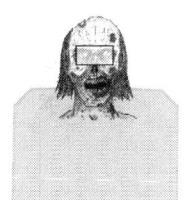

Z Fighter ©   Precision Rifle Drills - 8

CLEAR THE WAY

Date: B.Z.	Battle Ground:	Rifle:	Scope / Micro Dot	Power Setting:
Undead / Infected / Mutant	Time:	# Out of Z Box:	Penalty #:	**Total Time Score:**

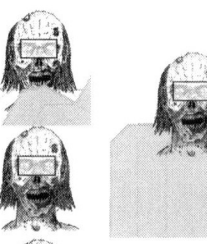

Date: B.Z.	Battle Ground:	Rifle:	Scope / Micro Dot	Power Setting:
Undead / Infected / Mutant	Time:	# Out of Z Box:	Penalty #:	**Total Time Score:**

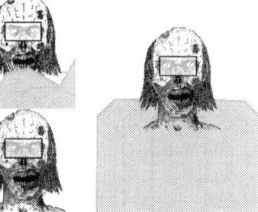

Date: B.Z.	Battle Ground:	Rifle:	Scope / Micro Dot	Power Setting:
Undead / Infected / Mutant	Time:	# Out of Z Box:	Penalty #:	**Total Time Score:**

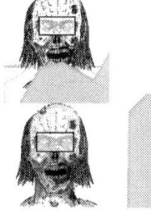
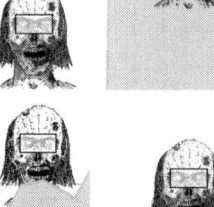

Date: B.Z.	Battle Ground:	Rifle:	Scope / Micro Dot	Power Setting:
Undead / Infected / Mutant	Time:	# Out of Z Box:	Penalty #:	**Total Time Score:**

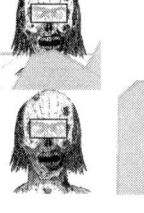

CLEAR THE WAY

Date: B.Z.	Battle Ground:	Rifle:	Scope / Micro Dot	Power Setting:
Undead / Infected / Mutant	Time:	# Out of Z Box:	Penalty #:	**Total Time Score:**

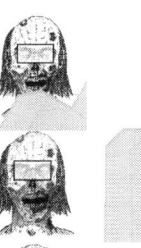
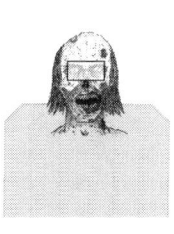

Date: B.Z.	Battle Ground:	Rifle:	Scope / Micro Dot	Power Setting:
Undead / Infected / Mutant	Time:	# Out of Z Box:	Penalty #:	**Total Time Score:**

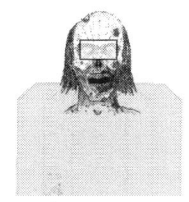

Date: B.Z.	Battle Ground:	Rifle:	Scope / Micro Dot	Power Setting:
Undead / Infected / Mutant	Time:	# Out of Z Box:	Penalty #:	**Total Time Score:**

Date: B.Z.	Battle Ground:	Rifle:	Scope / Micro Dot	Power Setting:
Undead / Infected / Mutant	Time:	# Out of Z Box:	Penalty #:	**Total Time Score:**

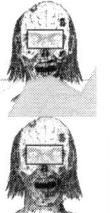
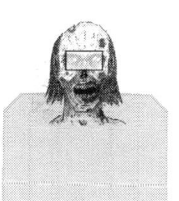

Z Fighter ©

Precision Rifle Drills - 8

CLEAR THE WAY

Date: B.Z.	Battle Ground:	Rifle:	Scope / Micro Dot	Power Setting:
Undead / Infected / Mutant	Time:	# Out of Z Box:	Penalty #:	**Total Time Score:**

Date: B.Z.	Battle Ground:	Rifle:	Scope / Micro Dot	Power Setting:
Undead / Infected / Mutant	Time:	# Out of Z Box:	Penalty #:	**Total Time Score:**

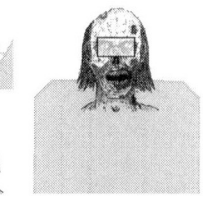

Date: B.Z.	Battle Ground:	Rifle:	Scope / Micro Dot	Power Setting:
Undead / Infected / Mutant	Time:	# Out of Z Box:	Penalty #:	**Total Time Score:**

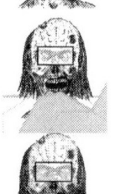
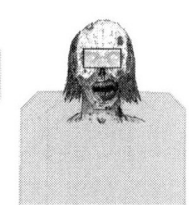

Date: B.Z.	Battle Ground:	Rifle:	Scope / Micro Dot	Power Setting:
Undead / Infected / Mutant	Time:	# Out of Z Box:	Penalty #:	**Total Time Score:**

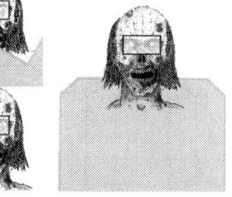

CLEAR THE WAY

Date:	B.Z.	Battle Ground:	Rifle:	Scope / Micro Dot	Power Setting:
Undead / Infected / Mutant		Time:	# Out of Z Box:	Penalty #:	**Total Time Score:**

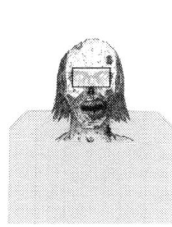

Date:	B.Z.	Battle Ground:	Rifle:	Scope / Micro Dot	Power Setting:
Undead / Infected / Mutant		Time:	# Out of Z Box:	Penalty #:	**Total Time Score:**

Date:	B.Z.	Battle Ground:	Rifle:	Scope / Micro Dot	Power Setting:
Undead / Infected / Mutant		Time:	# Out of Z Box:	Penalty #:	**Total Time Score:**

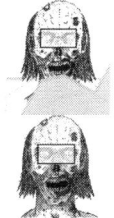
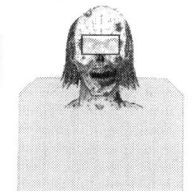

Date:	B.Z.	Battle Ground:	Rifle:	Scope / Micro Dot	Power Setting:
Undead / Infected / Mutant		Time:	# Out of Z Box:	Penalty #:	**Total Time Score:**

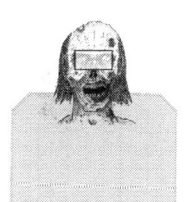

PRECISION RIFLE DRILL: **ZNIPER**

Purpose: Develop long range marksmanship fundamentals while establishing realistic capabilities.

Distance: 200 - 800 Yards.

Target: Steel head targets no wider than 8 inches or 8 inch steel circles.

Rounds Fired Per Rep: 1 Round.

Total Rounds Fired: ? Rounds.

Repetitions: 1 Rep.

Starting Position & Condition: Prone. Precision rifle condition 1.

Description: Record atmospherics and elevation/wind adjustments for range to target(s). On your personal go, fire one round at the closest target. If you hit, record your hit and move onto the next further target. If you miss any targets, you may reengage with only one shot. If you miss the second shot, the drill is over.

Goals: Meat Bag: 300 Yards.   Survivor: 550 Yards.   Z Fighter: 800 Yards.

Variations:

⊕ Infected Humans: Do 5 push ups before each shot.

⊕ Mutants: All elevation adjustments must come from memory, no references allowed. Do 5 push ups before each shot.

ZNIPER

Date: B.Z.	Rifle:	Dial Elev / Reticle Hold Over	Target Size:	Notes:
Undead / Infected / Mutant	Temp:	Humidity:	Baro:	
Target 1 Range:	Target 2 Range:	Target 3 Range:	Target 4 Range:	
Elev:	Elev:	Elev:	Elev:	
Wind:	Wind:	Wind:	Wind:	
Impact: 1st Rnd / 2nd Rnd	Impact: 1st Rnd / 2nd Rnd	Impact: 1st Rnd / 2nd Rnd	Impact: 1st Rnd / 2nd Rnd	
Target 5 Range:	Target 6 Range:	Target 7 Range:	Target 8 Range:	**Best Range:**
Elev:	Elev:	Elev:	Elev:	
Wind:	Wind:	Wind:	Wind:	
Impact: 1st Rnd / 2nd Rnd	Impact: 1st Rnd / 2nd Rnd	Impact: 1st Rnd / 2nd Rnd	Impact: 1st Rnd / 2nd Rnd	

Date: B.Z.	Rifle:	Dial Elev / Reticle Hold Over	Target Size:	Notes:
Undead / Infected / Mutant	Temp:	Humidity:	Baro:	
Target 1 Range:	Target 2 Range:	Target 3 Range:	Target 4 Range:	
Elev:	Elev:	Elev:	Elev:	
Wind:	Wind:	Wind:	Wind:	
Impact: 1st Rnd / 2nd Rnd	Impact: 1st Rnd / 2nd Rnd	Impact: 1st Rnd / 2nd Rnd	Impact: 1st Rnd / 2nd Rnd	
Target 5 Range:	Target 6 Range:	Target 7 Range:	Target 8 Range:	**Best Range:**
Elev:	Elev:	Elev:	Elev:	
Wind:	Wind:	Wind:	Wind:	
Impact: 1st Rnd / 2nd Rnd	Impact: 1st Rnd / 2nd Rnd	Impact: 1st Rnd / 2nd Rnd	Impact: 1st Rnd / 2nd Rnd	

ZNIPER

Date: B.Z.	Rifle:	Dial Elev / Reticle Hold Over	Target Size:	Notes:	
Undead / Infected / Mutant	Temp:	Humidity:	Baro:		
Target 1 Range:	Target 2 Range:	Target 3 Range:	Target 4 Range:		
Elev:	Elev:	Elev:	Elev:		
Wind:	Wind:	Wind:	Wind:		
Impact: 1st Rnd / 2nd Rnd	Impact: 1st Rnd / 2nd Rnd	Impact: 1st Rnd / 2nd Rnd	Impact: 1st Rnd / 2nd Rnd		
Target 5 Range:	Target 6 Range:	Target 7 Range:	Target 8 Range:	**Best Range:**	
Elev:	Elev:	Elev:	Elev:		
Wind:	Wind:	Wind:	Wind:		
Impact: 1st Rnd / 2nd Rnd	Impact: 1st Rnd / 2nd Rnd	Impact: 1st Rnd / 2nd Rnd	Impact: 1st Rnd / 2nd Rnd		

Date: B.Z.	Rifle:	Dial Elev / Reticle Hold Over	Target Size:	Notes:	
Undead / Infected / Mutant	Temp:	Humidity:	Baro:		
Target 1 Range:	Target 2 Range:	Target 3 Range:	Target 4 Range:		
Elev:	Elev:	Elev:	Elev:		
Wind:	Wind:	Wind:	Wind:		
Impact: 1st Rnd / 2nd Rnd	Impact: 1st Rnd / 2nd Rnd	Impact: 1st Rnd / 2nd Rnd	Impact: 1st Rnd / 2nd Rnd		
Target 5 Range:	Target 6 Range:	Target 7 Range:	Target 8 Range:	**Best Range:**	
Elev:	Elev:	Elev:	Elev:		
Wind:	Wind:	Wind:	Wind:		
Impact: 1st Rnd / 2nd Rnd	Impact: 1st Rnd / 2nd Rnd	Impact: 1st Rnd / 2nd Rnd	Impact: 1st Rnd / 2nd Rnd		

ZNIPER

Date:	B.Z.	Rifle:	Dial Elev / Reticle Hold Over	Target Size:	Notes:
Undead / Infected / Mutant		Temp:	Humidity:	Baro:	
Target 1 Range:		Target 2 Range:	Target 3 Range:	Target 4 Range:	
Elev:		Elev:	Elev:	Elev:	
Wind:		Wind:	Wind:	Wind:	
Impact: 1st Rnd / 2nd Rnd		Impact: 1st Rnd / 2nd Rnd	Impact: 1st Rnd / 2nd Rnd	Impact: 1st Rnd / 2nd Rnd	
Target 5 Range:		Target 6 Range:	Target 7 Range:	Target 8 Range:	**Best Range:**
Elev:		Elev:	Elev:	Elev:	
Wind:		Wind:	Wind:	Wind:	
Impact: 1st Rnd / 2nd Rnd		Impact: 1st Rnd / 2nd Rnd	Impact: 1st Rnd / 2nd Rnd	Impact: 1st Rnd / 2nd Rnd	

Date:	B.Z.	Rifle:	Dial Elev / Reticle Hold Over	Target Size:	Notes:
Undead / Infected / Mutant		Temp:	Humidity:	Baro:	
Target 1 Range:		Target 2 Range:	Target 3 Range:	Target 4 Range:	
Elev:		Elev:	Elev:	Elev:	
Wind:		Wind:	Wind:	Wind:	
Impact: 1st Rnd / 2nd Rnd		Impact: 1st Rnd / 2nd Rnd	Impact: 1st Rnd / 2nd Rnd	Impact: 1st Rnd / 2nd Rnd	
Target 5 Range:		Target 6 Range:	Target 7 Range:	Target 8 Range:	**Best Range:**
Elev:		Elev:	Elev:	Elev:	
Wind:		Wind:	Wind:	Wind:	
Impact: 1st Rnd / 2nd Rnd		Impact: 1st Rnd / 2nd Rnd	Impact: 1st Rnd / 2nd Rnd	Impact: 1st Rnd / 2nd Rnd	

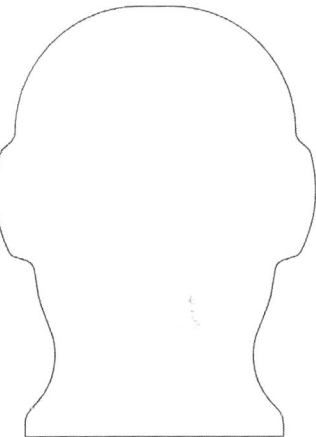

ZNIPER

Date:	B.Z.	Rifle:	Dial Elev / Reticle Hold Over	Target Size:	Notes:
Undead / Infected / Mutant		Temp:	Humidity:	Baro:	
Target 1 Range:		Target 2 Range:	Target 3 Range:	Target 4 Range:	
Elev:		Elev:	Elev:	Elev:	
Wind:		Wind:	Wind:	Wind:	
Impact: 1st Rnd / 2nd Rnd		Impact: 1st Rnd / 2nd Rnd	Impact: 1st Rnd / 2nd Rnd	Impact: 1st Rnd / 2nd Rnd	
Target 5 Range:		Target 6 Range:	Target 7 Range:	Target 8 Range:	**Best Range:**
Elev:		Elev:	Elev:	Elev:	
Wind:		Wind:	Wind:	Wind:	
Impact: 1st Rnd / 2nd Rnd		Impact: 1st Rnd / 2nd Rnd	Impact: 1st Rnd / 2nd Rnd	Impact: 1st Rnd / 2nd Rnd	

Date:	B.Z.	Rifle:	Dial Elev / Reticle Hold Over	Target Size:	Notes:
Undead / Infected / Mutant		Temp:	Humidity:	Baro:	
Target 1 Range:		Target 2 Range:	Target 3 Range:	Target 4 Range:	
Elev:		Elev:	Elev:	Elev:	
Wind:		Wind:	Wind:	Wind:	
Impact: 1st Rnd / 2nd Rnd		Impact: 1st Rnd / 2nd Rnd	Impact: 1st Rnd / 2nd Rnd	Impact: 1st Rnd / 2nd Rnd	
Target 5 Range:		Target 6 Range:	Target 7 Range:	Target 8 Range:	**Best Range:**
Elev:		Elev:	Elev:	Elev:	
Wind:		Wind:	Wind:	Wind:	
Impact: 1st Rnd / 2nd Rnd		Impact: 1st Rnd / 2nd Rnd	Impact: 1st Rnd / 2nd Rnd	Impact: 1st Rnd / 2nd Rnd	

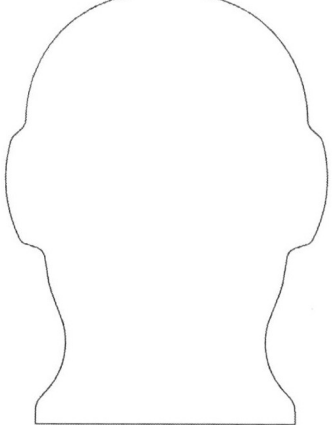

www.GUNFIGHTERSERIES.com ©

ZNIPER

Date: B.Z.	Rifle:	Dial Elev / Reticle Hold Over	Target Size:	Notes:
Undead / Infected / Mutant	Temp:	Humidity:	Baro:	
Target 1 Range:	Target 2 Range:	Target 3 Range:	Target 4 Range:	
Elev:	Elev:	Elev:	Elev:	
Wind:	Wind:	Wind:	Wind:	
Impact: 1st Rnd / 2nd Rnd	Impact: 1st Rnd / 2nd Rnd	Impact: 1st Rnd / 2nd Rnd	Impact: 1st Rnd / 2nd Rnd	
Target 5 Range:	Target 6 Range:	Target 7 Range:	Target 8 Range:	**Best Range:**
Elev:	Elev:	Elev:	Elev:	
Wind:	Wind:	Wind:	Wind:	
Impact: 1st Rnd / 2nd Rnd	Impact: 1st Rnd / 2nd Rnd	Impact: 1st Rnd / 2nd Rnd	Impact: 1st Rnd / 2nd Rnd	

Date: B.Z.	Rifle:	Dial Elev / Reticle Hold Over	Target Size:	Notes:
Undead / Infected / Mutant	Temp:	Humidity:	Baro:	
Target 1 Range:	Target 2 Range:	Target 3 Range:	Target 4 Range:	
Elev:	Elev:	Elev:	Elev:	
Wind:	Wind:	Wind:	Wind:	
Impact: 1st Rnd / 2nd Rnd	Impact: 1st Rnd / 2nd Rnd	Impact: 1st Rnd / 2nd Rnd	Impact: 1st Rnd / 2nd Rnd	
Target 5 Range:	Target 6 Range:	Target 7 Range:	Target 8 Range:	**Best Range:**
Elev:	Elev:	Elev:	Elev:	
Wind:	Wind:	Wind:	Wind:	
Impact: 1st Rnd / 2nd Rnd	Impact: 1st Rnd / 2nd Rnd	Impact: 1st Rnd / 2nd Rnd	Impact: 1st Rnd / 2nd Rnd	

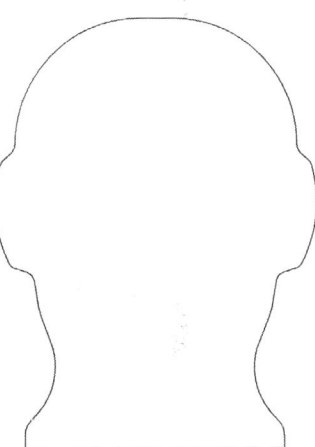

Z Fighter ©

Precision Rifle Drills - 9

PRECISION RIFLE DRILL: **HEAD HUNTER**

Purpose: Increase target transition speed.

Distance: Approx. 200, 225, 250, 275, 300 Yards.

Target: 5 Steel head targets no bigger than 8 inches wide or 8 inch steel circles.

Extra Equipment Needed: Shot timer.

Total Rounds Fired: 6 - 10 Rounds.

Repetitions: 1 Rep.

Starting Position & Condition: Standing - Low Ready. Precision rifle condition 1.

Description: Record atmospherics and elevation/wind adjustments for range to target(s). At the timer beep, assume a good prone supported position and engage the closest target. If you miss, reengage. If hit, move to the next furthest target. Continue until all 5 targets have been hit, you run out of ammo, or exceed par time. All 5 targets must be hit to pass this drill.

Goals: Meat Bag: 90 Seconds.   Survivor: 60 Seconds.   Z Fighter: 45 Seconds with no misses.

Variations:

⊕ Infected Humans: Double the target distance.

⊕ Mutants: Double the distance, and any shooting position other than prone.

HEAD HUNTER

Date:	B.Z.	Rifle:	Dial Elev / Reticle Hold Over	Target Size:
Undead / Infected / Mutant		Temp:	Humidity:	Baro:
Target 1 Range:		Elevation:	Windage:	Notes:
Target 2 Range:		Elevation:	Windage:	
Target 3 Range:		Elevation:	Windage:	
Target 4 Range:		Elevation:	Windage:	**Total Number of Shots:**
Target 5 Range:		Elevation:	Windage:	**Total Time:**
Date:	B.Z.	Rifle:	Dial Elev / Reticle Hold Over	Target Size:
Undead / Infected / Mutant		Temp:	Humidity:	Baro:
Target 1 Range:		Elevation:	Windage:	Notes:
Target 2 Range:		Elevation:	Windage:	
Target 3 Range:		Elevation:	Windage:	
Target 4 Range:		Elevation:	Windage:	**Total Number of Shots:**
Target 5 Range:		Elevation:	Windage:	**Total Time:**
Date:	B.Z.	Rifle:	Dial Elev / Reticle Hold Over	Target Size:
Undead / Infected / Mutant		Temp:	Humidity:	Baro:
Target 1 Range:		Elevation:	Windage:	Notes:
Target 2 Range:		Elevation:	Windage:	
Target 3 Range:		Elevation:	Windage:	
Target 4 Range:		Elevation:	Windage:	**Total Number of Shots:**
Target 5 Range:		Elevation:	Windage:	**Total Time:**

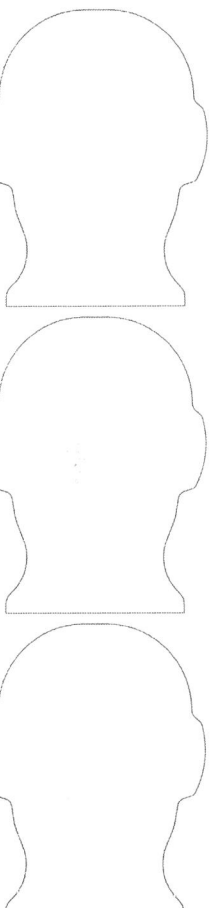

HEAD HUNTER

Date:	B.Z.	Rifle:	Dial Elev / Reticle Hold Over	Target Size:
Undead / Infected / Mutant		Temp:	Humidity:	Baro:
Target 1 Range:		Elevation:	Windage:	Notes:
Target 2 Range:		Elevation:	Windage:	
Target 3 Range:		Elevation:	Windage:	
Target 4 Range:		Elevation:	Windage:	**Total Number of Shots:**
Target 5 Range:		Elevation:	Windage:	**Total Time:**
Date:	B.Z.	Rifle:	Dial Elev / Reticle Hold Over	Target Size:
Undead / Infected / Mutant		Temp:	Humidity:	Baro:
Target 1 Range:		Elevation:	Windage:	Notes:
Target 2 Range:		Elevation:	Windage:	
Target 3 Range:		Elevation:	Windage:	
Target 4 Range:		Elevation:	Windage:	**Total Number of Shots:**
Target 5 Range:		Elevation:	Windage:	**Total Time:**
Date:	B.Z.	Rifle:	Dial Elev / Reticle Hold Over	Target Size:
Undead / Infected / Mutant		Temp:	Humidity:	Baro:
Target 1 Range:		Elevation:	Windage:	Notes:
Target 2 Range:		Elevation:	Windage:	
Target 3 Range:		Elevation:	Windage:	
Target 4 Range:		Elevation:	Windage:	**Total Number of Shots:**
Target 5 Range:		Elevation:	Windage:	**Total Time:**

HEAD HUNTER

Date:	B.Z.	Rifle:	Dial Elev / Reticle Hold Over	Target Size:
Undead / Infected / Mutant		Temp:	Humidity:	Baro:
Target 1 Range:		Elevation:	Windage:	Notes:
Target 2 Range:		Elevation:	Windage:	
Target 3 Range:		Elevation:	Windage:	
Target 4 Range:		Elevation:	Windage:	Total Number of Shots:
Target 5 Range:		Elevation:	Windage:	Total Time:
Date:	B.Z.	Rifle:	Dial Elev / Reticle Hold Over	Target Size:
Undead / Infected / Mutant		Temp:	Humidity:	Baro:
Target 1 Range:		Elevation:	Windage:	Notes:
Target 2 Range:		Elevation:	Windage:	
Target 3 Range:		Elevation:	Windage:	
Target 4 Range:		Elevation:	Windage:	Total Number of Shots:
Target 5 Range:		Elevation:	Windage:	Total Time:
Date:	B.Z.	Rifle:	Dial Elev / Reticle Hold Over	Target Size:
Undead / Infected / Mutant		Temp:	Humidity:	Baro:
Target 1 Range:		Elevation:	Windage:	Notes:
Target 2 Range:		Elevation:	Windage:	
Target 3 Range:		Elevation:	Windage:	
Target 4 Range:		Elevation:	Windage:	Total Number of Shots:
Target 5 Range:		Elevation:	Windage:	Total Time:

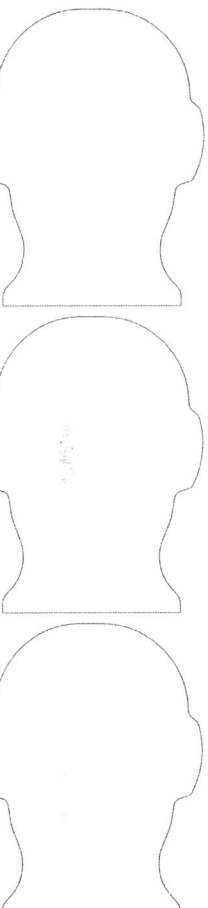

Z Fighter ©   Precision Rifle Drills - 10

HEAD HUNTER

Date:	B.Z.	Rifle:	Dial Elev / Reticle Hold Over	Target Size:
Undead / Infected / Mutant		Temp:	Humidity:	Baro:
Target 1 Range:		Elevation:	Windage:	Notes:
Target 2 Range:		Elevation:	Windage:	
Target 3 Range:		Elevation:	Windage:	
Target 4 Range:		Elevation:	Windage:	**Total Number of Shots:**
Target 5 Range:		Elevation:	Windage:	**Total Time:**
Date:	B.Z.	Rifle:	Dial Elev / Reticle Hold Over	Target Size:
Undead / Infected / Mutant		Temp:	Humidity:	Baro:
Target 1 Range:		Elevation:	Windage:	Notes:
Target 2 Range:		Elevation:	Windage:	
Target 3 Range:		Elevation:	Windage:	
Target 4 Range:		Elevation:	Windage:	**Total Number of Shots:**
Target 5 Range:		Elevation:	Windage:	**Total Time:**
Date:	B.Z.	Rifle:	Dial Elev / Reticle Hold Over	Target Size:
Undead / Infected / Mutant		Temp:	Humidity:	Baro:
Target 1 Range:		Elevation:	Windage:	Notes:
Target 2 Range:		Elevation:	Windage:	
Target 3 Range:		Elevation:	Windage:	
Target 4 Range:		Elevation:	Windage:	**Total Number of Shots:**
Target 5 Range:		Elevation:	Windage:	**Total Time:**

HEAD HUNTER

Date:	B.Z.	Rifle:	Dial Elev / Reticle Hold Over	Target Size:
Undead / Infected / Mutant		Temp:	Humidity:	Baro:
Target 1 Range:		Elevation:	Windage:	Notes:
Target 2 Range:		Elevation:	Windage:	
Target 3 Range:		Elevation:	Windage:	
Target 4 Range:		Elevation:	Windage:	**Total Number of Shots:**
Target 5 Range:		Elevation:	Windage:	**Total Time:**
Date:	B.Z.	Rifle:	Dial Elev / Reticle Hold Over	Target Size:
Undead / Infected / Mutant		Temp:	Humidity:	Baro:
Target 1 Range:		Elevation:	Windage:	Notes:
Target 2 Range:		Elevation:	Windage:	
Target 3 Range:		Elevation:	Windage:	
Target 4 Range:		Elevation:	Windage:	**Total Number of Shots:**
Target 5 Range:		Elevation:	Windage:	**Total Time:**
Date:	B.Z.	Rifle:	Dial Elev / Reticle Hold Over	Target Size:
Undead / Infected / Mutant		Temp:	Humidity:	Baro:
Target 1 Range:		Elevation:	Windage:	Notes:
Target 2 Range:		Elevation:	Windage:	
Target 3 Range:		Elevation:	Windage:	
Target 4 Range:		Elevation:	Windage:	**Total Number of Shots:**
Target 5 Range:		Elevation:	Windage:	**Total Time:**

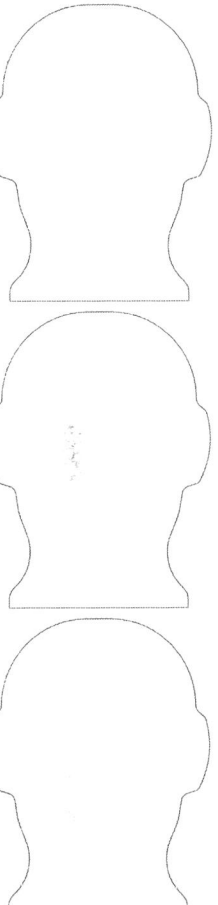

Z Fighter ©   Precision Rifle Drills - 10

PRECISION RIFLE DRILL: PRZ SKILLZ 1

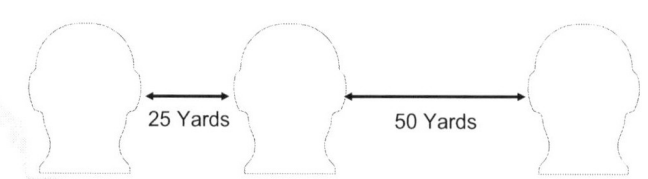

Purpose: Develop long range marksmanship fundamentals while establishing realistic capabilities.

Distance: 300 Yards

Target: 3 Steel head targets no bigger than 8 inches wide or 8 inch steel circles.

Place left target 25 yard from middle target. Place right target 50 yards from middle target.

Par Time: 90 Seconds   **Extra Equipment Needed:** Shot timer.

Total Rounds Fired: 6 - Unlimited rounds.

Repetitions: 1 Rep.

Starting Position & Condition: Standing 10 yards behind rifle on firing line. Precision rifle condition 1.

Description: Record atmospherics and elevation/wind adjustments for range to target(s). At the timer beep, move forward to the firing line, and assume a good prone supported position.

Engage the targets from left to right and may only advance to the next target once the previous target has been hit. Once you successfully engaged all three targets from left to right, then reengage in the same fashion from right to left starting with the far right target.

Continue until all targets have been hit, you run out of ammo, or exceed par time. All targets must be hit to pass this drill.

Goals: Meat Bag: 90 Seconds.   Survivor: 60 Seconds.   Z Fighter: 45 Seconds with no misses.

Variations:

⊕ Infected Humans: 2 Hits on each target before advancing to next. Just in case… (Mag change required)

⊕ Mutants: 2 Hits on each target before advancing to next. Using any shooting position other than prone. (Mag change required)

PRZ SKILLZ 1

Date:	B.Z.	Battle Ground:	Rifle:	Scope:
Undead / Infected / Mutant		Temp:	Humidity:	Baro:
Range:		Elevation:	Windage:	Notes:
Number of Misses:		**Total Number of Shots:**	**Total Time:**	
Date:	B.Z.	Battle Ground:	Rifle:	Scope:
Undead / Infected / Mutant		Temp:	Humidity:	Baro:
Range:		Elevation:	Windage:	Notes:
Number of Misses:		**Total Number of Shots:**	**Total Time:**	
Date:	B.Z.	Battle Ground:	Rifle:	Scope:
Undead / Infected / Mutant		Temp:	Humidity:	Baro:
Range:		Elevation:	Windage:	Notes:
Number of Misses:		**Total Number of Shots:**	**Total Time:**	
Date:	B.Z.	Battle Ground:	Rifle:	Scope:
Undead / Infected / Mutant		Temp:	Humidity:	Baro:
Range:		Elevation:	Windage:	Notes:
Number of Misses:		**Total Number of Shots:**	**Total Time:**	
Date:	B.Z.	Battle Ground:	Rifle:	Scope:
Undead / Infected / Mutant		Temp:	Humidity:	Baro:
Range:		Elevation:	Windage:	Notes:
Number of Misses:		**Total Number of Shots:**	**Total Time:**	

Z Fighter ©

Precision Rifle Drills - 11

PRZ SKILLZ 1

Date:	B.Z.	Battle Ground:	Rifle:	Scope:
Undead / Infected / Mutant		Temp:	Humidity:	Baro:
Range:		Elevation:	Windage:	Notes:
Number of Misses:		**Total Number of Shots:**	**Total Time:**	
Date:	B.Z.	Battle Ground:	Rifle:	Scope:
Undead / Infected / Mutant		Temp:	Humidity:	Baro:
Range:		Elevation:	Windage:	Notes:
Number of Misses:		**Total Number of Shots:**	**Total Time:**	
Date:	B.Z.	Battle Ground:	Rifle:	Scope:
Undead / Infected / Mutant		Temp:	Humidity:	Baro:
Range:		Elevation:	Windage:	Notes:
Number of Misses:		**Total Number of Shots:**	**Total Time:**	
Date:	B.Z.	Battle Ground:	Rifle:	Scope:
Undead / Infected / Mutant		Temp:	Humidity:	Baro:
Range:		Elevation:	Windage:	Notes:
Number of Misses:		**Total Number of Shots:**	**Total Time:**	
Date:	B.Z.	Battle Ground:	Rifle:	Scope:
Undead / Infected / Mutant		Temp:	Humidity:	Baro:
Range:		Elevation:	Windage:	Notes:
Number of Misses:		**Total Number of Shots:**	**Total Time:**	

www.GUNFIGHTERSERIES.com ©

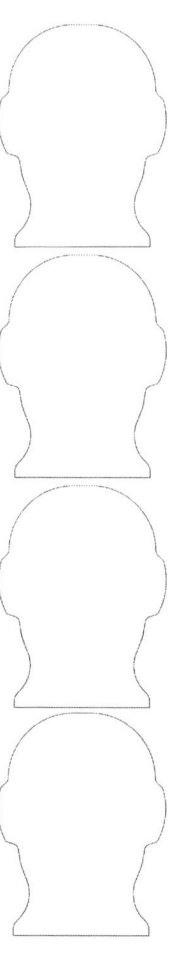

PRZ SKILLZ 1

Date:	B.Z.	Battle Ground:	Rifle:	Scope:
Undead / Infected / Mutant		Temp:	Humidity:	Baro:
Range:		Elevation:	Windage:	Notes:
Number of Misses:		**Total Number of Shots:**	**Total Time:**	
Date:	B.Z.	Battle Ground:	Rifle:	Scope:
Undead / Infected / Mutant		Temp:	Humidity:	Baro:
Range:		Elevation:	Windage:	Notes:
Number of Misses:		**Total Number of Shots:**	**Total Time:**	
Date:	B.Z.	Battle Ground:	Rifle:	Scope:
Undead / Infected / Mutant		Temp:	Humidity:	Baro:
Range:		Elevation:	Windage:	Notes:
Number of Misses:		**Total Number of Shots:**	**Total Time:**	
Date:	B.Z.	Battle Ground:	Rifle:	Scope:
Undead / Infected / Mutant		Temp:	Humidity:	Baro:
Range:		Elevation:	Windage:	Notes:
Number of Misses:		**Total Number of Shots:**	**Total Time:**	
Date:	B.Z.	Battle Ground:	Rifle:	Scope:
Undead / Infected / Mutant		Temp:	Humidity:	Baro:
Range:		Elevation:	Windage:	Notes:
Number of Misses:		**Total Number of Shots:**	**Total Time:**	

PRZ SKILLZ 1

Date:	B.Z.	Battle Ground:	Rifle:	Scope:
Undead / Infected / Mutant		Temp:	Humidity:	Baro:
Range:		Elevation:	Windage:	Notes:
Number of Misses:		**Total Number of Shots:**	**Total Time:**	
Date:	B.Z.	Battle Ground:	Rifle:	Scope:
Undead / Infected / Mutant		Temp:	Humidity:	Baro:
Range:		Elevation:	Windage:	Notes:
Number of Misses:		**Total Number of Shots:**	**Total Time:**	
Date:	B.Z.	Battle Ground:	Rifle:	Scope:
Undead / Infected / Mutant		Temp:	Humidity:	Baro:
Range:		Elevation:	Windage:	Notes:
Number of Misses:		**Total Number of Shots:**	**Total Time:**	
Date:	B.Z.	Battle Ground:	Rifle:	Scope:
Undead / Infected / Mutant		Temp:	Humidity:	Baro:
Range:		Elevation:	Windage:	Notes:
Number of Misses:		**Total Number of Shots:**	**Total Time:**	
Date:	B.Z.	Battle Ground:	Rifle:	Scope:
Undead / Infected / Mutant		Temp:	Humidity:	Baro:
Range:		Elevation:	Windage:	Notes:
Number of Misses:		**Total Number of Shots:**	**Total Time:**	

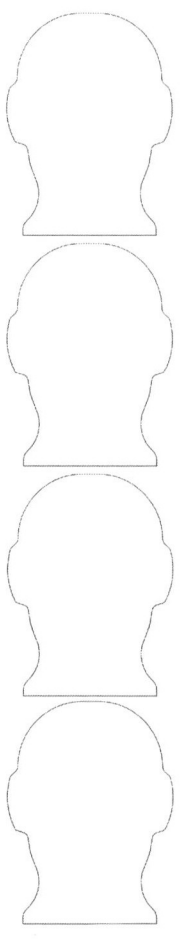

PRZ SKILLZ 1

Date:	B.Z.	Battle Ground:	Rifle:	Scope:
Undead / Infected / Mutant		Temp:	Humidity:	Baro:
Range:		Elevation:	Windage:	Notes:
Number of Misses:		**Total Number of Shots:**	**Total Time:**	
Date:	B.Z.	Battle Ground:	Rifle:	Scope:
Undead / Infected / Mutant		Temp:	Humidity:	Baro:
Range:		Elevation:	Windage:	Notes:
Number of Misses:		**Total Number of Shots:**	**Total Time:**	
Date:	B.Z.	Battle Ground:	Rifle:	Scope:
Undead / Infected / Mutant		Temp:	Humidity:	Baro:
Range:		Elevation:	Windage:	Notes:
Number of Misses:		**Total Number of Shots:**	**Total Time:**	
Date:	B.Z.	Battle Ground:	Rifle:	Scope:
Undead / Infected / Mutant		Temp:	Humidity:	Baro:
Range:		Elevation:	Windage:	Notes:
Number of Misses:		**Total Number of Shots:**	**Total Time:**	
Date:	B.Z.	Battle Ground:	Rifle:	Scope:
Undead / Infected / Mutant		Temp:	Humidity:	Baro:
Range:		Elevation:	Windage:	Notes:
Number of Misses:		**Total Number of Shots:**	**Total Time:**	

Z Fighter ©

Z FIGHTER STANDARD 1

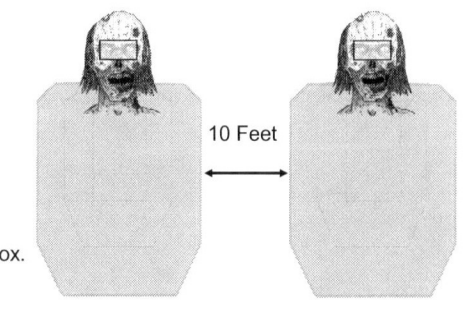

10 Feet

- **Ammo**: 12 Rounds (2 mags of 6) pistol. 18 Rounds (2 mags of 9) carbine. 2 Rounds precision rifle.
- **Target**: ZIPSC X2 (Infected Humans) 10 feet apart.
- **Par Time**: 120 seconds.
- **Scoring**: 5 Points ocular Z box (max 60 points). 3 Points for body A zone (Max 60 points). 0 Points outside A or Z box. Passing score is 100 Points of 120 total.
- **Starting Position & Condition**: Stage 1 start standing in the surrender / interview position. Pistol holstered in condition 1. Carbine staged at the 25 yard line in con-

Stage	Distance	#Rnds	Position/Description
1	7 Yards	6 P	Standing with <u>pistol</u> - 2 Shots to the body A box, 1 shot to the head Z box. (Each target)
			Run to 15 yard line.
	15 Yards	6 P	Standing to kneeling - 2 Shots to the body A box, 1 shot to the head Z box. (Each target)
			Run to 25 yard line.
	25 Yards	6 C	Standing with <u>carbine</u> - 2 Shots to the body A box, 1 shot to the head Z box. (Each target)
			Run to 50 yard line.
	50 Yards	3 + 3 C	Standing to kneeling - 2 Shots to the body A box, 1 shot to the head Z box. Reload. (Each target)
			Run to 75 yard line
	75 Yards	6 C	Standing to prone - 2 Shots to the body A box, 1 shot to the head Z box. (Each target)
			Run to 100 yard line
	100 Yards	2 PR	Standing to prone with <u>precision rifle</u> - 2 Shots to the head Z box. (Each target)

Z FIGHTER STANDARD 1

Date:	B.Z.	Battle Ground:	Infected / Mutant
Pistol:		Carbine:	Precision Rifle:
Completion Time:		Under Par: Yes / No	Shots Over Par:
# of Head Z Box (5 Points):		# of Body A Box (3 points):	# In Body (0 points):
Notes:			**Total Score:**

Date:	B.Z.	Battle Ground:	Infected / Mutant
Pistol:		Carbine:	Precision Rifle:
Completion Time:		Under Par: Yes / No	Shots Over Par:
# of Head Z Box (5 Points):		# of Body A Box (3 points):	# In Body (0 points):
Notes:			**Total Score:**

Date:	B.Z.	Battle Ground:	Infected / Mutant
Pistol:		Carbine:	Precision Rifle:
Completion Time:		Under Par: Yes / No	Shots Over Par:
# of Head Z Box (5 Points):		# of Body A Box (3 points):	# In Body (0 points):
Notes:			**Total Score:**

Z Qual Course of Fire - 1

Z Fighter ©

Z FIGHTER STANDARD 1

Date: B.Z.	Battle Ground:	Infected / Mutant
Pistol:	Carbine:	Precision Rifle:
Completion Time:	Under Par: Yes / No	Shots Over Par:
# of Head Z Box (5 Points):	# of Body A Box (3 points):	# In Body (0 points):
Notes:		**Total Score:**
Date: B.Z.	Battle Ground:	Infected / Mutant
Pistol:	Carbine:	Precision Rifle:
Completion Time:	Under Par: Yes / No	Shots Over Par:
# of Head Z Box (5 Points):	# of Body A Box (3 points):	# In Body (0 points):
Notes:		**Total Score:**
Date: B.Z.	Battle Ground:	Infected / Mutant
Pistol:	Carbine:	Precision Rifle:
Completion Time:	Under Par: Yes / No	Shots Over Par:
# of Head Z Box (5 Points):	# of Body A Box (3 points):	# In Body (0 points):
Notes:		**Total Score:**

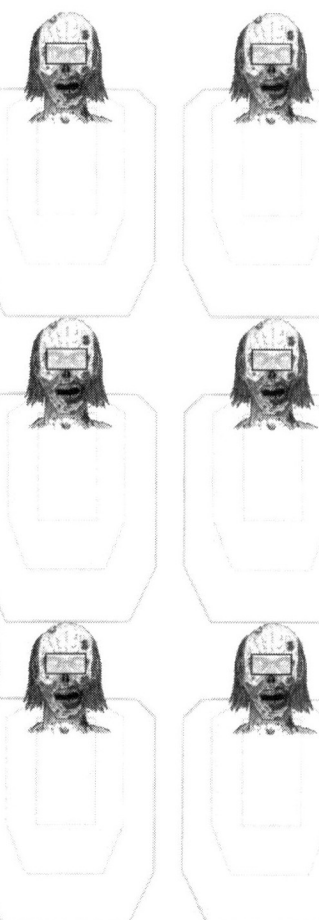

www.GUNFIGHTERSERIES.com ©

Z FIGHTER STANDARD 1

Date: B.Z.	Battle Ground:	Infected / Mutant
Pistol:	Carbine:	Precision Rifle:
Completion Time:	Under Par: Yes / No	Shots Over Par:
# of Head Z Box (5 Points):	# of Body A Box (3 points):	# In Body (0 points):
Notes:		**Total Score:**

Date: B.Z.	Battle Ground:	Infected / Mutant
Pistol:	Carbine:	Precision Rifle:
Completion Time:	Under Par: Yes / No	Shots Over Par:
# of Head Z Box (5 Points):	# of Body A Box (3 points):	# In Body (0 points):
Notes:		**Total Score:**

Date: B.Z.	Battle Ground:	Infected / Mutant
Pistol:	Carbine:	Precision Rifle:
Completion Time:	Under Par: Yes / No	Shots Over Par:
# of Head Z Box (5 Points):	# of Body A Box (3 points):	# In Body (0 points):
Notes:		**Total Score:**

Z Qual Course of Fire - 1

Z Fighter ©

Z FIGHTER STANDARD 1

Date:	B.Z.	Battle Ground:	Infected / Mutant
Pistol:		Carbine:	Precision Rifle:
Completion Time:		Under Par: Yes / No	Shots Over Par:
# of Head Z Box (5 Points):		# of Body A Box (3 points):	# In Body (0 points):
Notes:			**Total Score:**

Date:	B.Z.	Battle Ground:	Infected / Mutant
Pistol:		Carbine:	Precision Rifle:
Completion Time:		Under Par: Yes / No	Shots Over Par:
# of Head Z Box (5 Points):		# of Body A Box (3 points):	# In Body (0 points):
Notes:			**Total Score:**

Date:	B.Z.	Battle Ground:	Infected / Mutant
Pistol:		Carbine:	Precision Rifle:
Completion Time:		Under Par: Yes / No	Shots Over Par:
# of Head Z Box (5 Points):		# of Body A Box (3 points):	# In Body (0 points):
Notes:			**Total Score:**

Z FIGHTER STANDARD 1

Date:	B.Z.	Battle Ground:	Infected / Mutant
Pistol:		Carbine:	Precision Rifle:
Completion Time:		Under Par: Yes / No	Shots Over Par:
# of Head Z Box (5 Points):		# of Body A Box (3 points):	# In Body (0 points):
Notes:			**Total Score:**

Date:	B.Z.	Battle Ground:	Infected / Mutant
Pistol:		Carbine:	Precision Rifle:
Completion Time:		Under Par: Yes / No	Shots Over Par:
# of Head Z Box (5 Points):		# of Body A Box (3 points):	# In Body (0 points):
Notes:			**Total Score:**

Date:	B.Z.	Battle Ground:	Infected / Mutant
Pistol:		Carbine:	Precision Rifle:
Completion Time:		Under Par: Yes / No	Shots Over Par:
# of Head Z Box (5 Points):		# of Body A Box (3 points):	# In Body (0 points):
Notes:			**Total Score:**

Z Qual Course of Fire - 1

Z Fighter ©

NAME OF CUSTOM DRILL:

Purpose:

By:

Distance: Yards

Target:

Par Time: Seconds

Extra Equipment Needed:

Rounds per Repetition: Rounds

Total Rounds Fired: Rounds

Point Penalty:

Repetitions:

Starting Position & Condition: Start in the

Description:

Goals: Novice: Expert: Gunfighter:

Variations:

Custom Drill Name:

Date:	Location:	Weapon:	Sights:	Ammo
				Notes:
Date:	Location:	Weapon:	Sights:	Ammo
				Notes:
Date:	Location:	Weapon:	Sights:	Ammo
				Notes:
Date:	Location:	Weapon:	Sights:	Ammo
				Notes:
Date:	Location:	Weapon:	Sights:	Ammo
				Notes:

www.GUNFIGHTERSERIES.com ©

Custom Drill Name:

Date:	Location:	Weapon:	Sights:	Ammo
				Notes:
Date:	Location:	Weapon:	Sights:	Ammo
				Notes:
Date:	Location:	Weapon:	Sights:	Ammo
				Notes:
Date:	Location:	Weapon:	Sights:	Ammo
				Notes:
Date:	Location:	Weapon:	Sights:	Ammo
				Notes:

Custom Drill Name:

Date:	Location:	Weapon:	Sights:	Ammo
				Notes:
Date:	Location:	Weapon:	Sights:	Ammo
				Notes:
Date:	Location:	Weapon:	Sights:	Ammo
				Notes:
Date:	Location:	Weapon:	Sights:	Ammo
				Notes:
Date:	Location:	Weapon:	Sights:	Ammo
				Notes:

Z Fighter ©

NOTES:

NOTES:

Training Classes Taken

Date:	Institute:	Class Name:	Weapon:

Notes about subjects covered:
_____
_____
_____

Notes about equipment used:
_____
_____
_____

Instructors Name:	Contact Info:
Instructors Name:	Contact Info:
Students Name:	Contact Info:
Students Name:	Contact Info:
Students Name:	Contact Info:
Students Name:	Contact Info:
Students Name:	Contact Info:

Made in the USA
Middletown, DE
08 July 2022